The Prince's Darling

Book Three of The Stuart Monarch Series

Tonya Ulynn Brown

THE PRINCE'S DARLING
BY TONYA ULYNN BROWN

Published by Late November Literary
Winston Salem, NC 27107

ISBN: 979-8-9892723-8-9
Copyright 2024 by Tonya Ulynn Brown
Cover design by Sweet N' Spicy designs
Interior design by Late November Literary

Available in print or online. Visit latenovemberliterary.com

This is a work of fiction. The characters and events come from the author's imagination or are used for fictional purposes. Any brand names, places, or trademarks remain the property of their respective owners and are only used for fictional purposes.

Library of Congress Cataloging-in-Publication data
Brown, Toyna Ulynn.
The Prince's Darling / Tonya Ulynn Brown 1st ed.

Printed in the United States of America

The Stuart Monarch Series

~by Tonya Ulynn Brown

Book 1: The Queen's Almoner

Book 2: The King's Inquisitor

Book 3: The Prince's Darling

Author's Note

The events in this book would have taken place over the course of about five years. For the sake of plotting and length of story, I have consolidated some events into a more manageable timeline. For readers familiar with the history, you will find the murder trial of Thomas Overbury was pushed ahead to allow for my fictional characters to participate in the event. The execution of some of those involved in Overbury's death also happened sooner in the story than in reality. The death of Doctor Forman who died in 1611 was also adjusted. His involvement with Frances was not discovered until the murder trial in 1615.

In addition, the Hymenaei masque took place in celebration of the Earl and Countess of Essex's marriage in 1606. I have my characters doing a repeat performance of it, which actually did not happen. Otherwise, I have tried to maintain the accuracy of the events and the people involved (with the exception of my fictional characters) and hope those students of history can overlook the liberties I have taken.

One final note involves the age of Isobel Broune. If you read *The Queen's Almoner* or *The King's Inquisitor*, you might recognize Isobel as the inquisitive twelve-year-old in the first book's Epilogue, or as the crying toddler mentioned in the second book's Epilogue. This would have made her about 13 to 14 years old in this story. It wasn't unheard of for girls to be married off by that age during this time period, but I needed her to be a little older in order for her to get up to some of the shenanigans in which she participates. For this reason, I have waved my magic writer's wand and made her a few years older. Read on, and you'll understand exactly what I'm talking about.

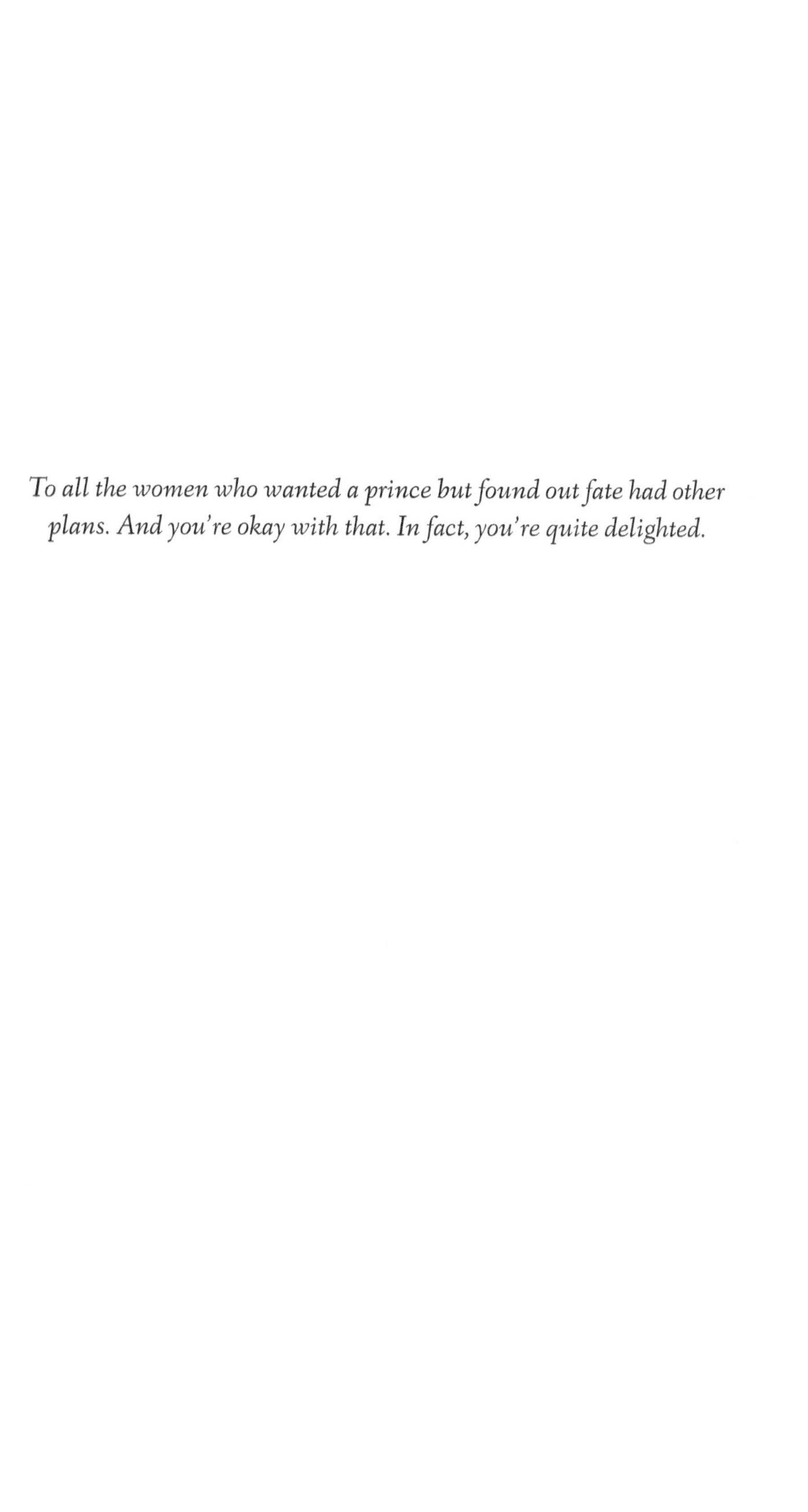

To all the women who wanted a prince but found out fate had other plans. And you're okay with that. In fact, you're quite delighted.

Prologue

Isobel

When I was a child, I discovered three things about myself: I had inherited my father's propensity for striking attire, I hated the color green, and I was in love with a prince. A prince who would never be king.

The first was a proclivity that would serve me well and endear me to one of the greatest courts in Europe.

The second, a singularity my mother lamented, was a hindrance. It served as a true thorn in my flesh and was the cause of much vexation throughout my life. And yet, I cannot deny the aversion quite possibly saved my life.

As for the third, I cannot measure the breadth or depth such a love has impressed upon me. To love a man whom the whole of England, and quite possibly the entirety of Protestant Europe adored, created a chasm in me that would never be filled. Linguistics, mathematics, sportsmanship, and military prowess; no earthly prince showed as much achievement. Music, dancing, art, and exploration; no other showed such appreciation of beauty. And most importantly, no goodlier a prince had ever shown such heart and love for Christ and the true faith! How could I do anything other than love him? How could I do anything other than lose my heart to such a man? And how could I do anything other than mourn the loss of such a prince until I take my dying breath? I could not. I should not.

But I did.

PART I

But the principal blessing that ye can get of good company will stand in your marrying of a godly and virtuous wife, for she must be nearer unto you than any other company, being flesh of your flesh, and bone of your bone, as Adam said of Hevah [Eve].
Book II Of a King's Duty in His Office
Basilikon Doron
A letter by King James
addressed to his oldest son,
Prince Henry

Chapter 1

Banqueting House, Palace of Whitehall, London
New Year's Day 1611
Isobel

I hated green, which was an unfortunate aversion given the fact my face and arms were currently covered with it.

In truth, that wasn't an entirely accurate statement. I didn't hate the color of the oak trees or the weeping willows that peppered the palace grounds. Nor did I dislike the bright greens of the meandering meadows that rolled across the expanse of our estate at Chadwyck House. As long as it wasn't touching any part of my skin, I could abide it. But the slimy, pea green water of stagnant ponds or the stinking rot of moss-slicked rocks and debris that lined the Thames turned my stomach and made my skin craw with a thousand wooly worms.

I never realized how completely repulsed by the color I was until I was covered with it. And since I had been chosen to portray one of the nymphs in Prince Henry's masque, my mother specified it absolutely could not be avoided. The lichen green used to dye my skin made me look as if I had been aboard a sea-faring vessel for too many days and was about to cast up my accounts.

Music drifted through the air as the musicians warmed up, preparing for tonight's performance. The flames of what seemed to be a thousand candles brightened the hall, throwing a lively yellow glow across the room and illuminating the colorful frocks and coats of the mass of courtiers who came to see the show.

And the bodies! The crush of people that poured into the hall once the doors opened was consuming. Laughter and conversation heated the air to a feverish level, making it difficult to breathe.

I scratched my arm and noticed tiny bumps had begun to emerge on the surface of my skin. I felt hot and prickly, and I could feel the beginnings of an ache in my head, just beneath my brow.

"Isobel, stop fidgeting." Mother adjusted the nymphal crown that had been woven into my hair. My silvery blonde locks had also been dyed the same lichen color and curly reeds of paper mâché made to mimic spiralis sprang from the thorny crown.

"Mother, I itch," I complained. "And I think I am going to throw up." I felt the floor tilting beneath my feet. A curtain portrayed a map of England, Scotland, and Ireland and veiled the opening scene of the masque. It had been hung above the dais, and the colorful hues of azure and gold blurred when I looked at it. I squeezed my eyes closed and took a deep breath. My mother, being the practical Scots wife that she was, led me to the dais to sit down and pushed my head between my knees.

"What is the matter?" I could hear Princess Elizabeth's voice of alarm floating somewhere above my head close by. She too had been allowed to play a nymph in her brother's masque and wore the same costume as I with leafy layers of greenery swathing her hips and falling to her knees. A cincture of pink roses accented with tiny white baby's breath was draped across her shoulder. Green hosiery and pointy green felt poulaines with bells hanging from the tips completed the outfit. She wore a spiralis crown on her head as well, a twin to the one I wore.

Mother wafted lukewarm air toward me with her feathered fan. "Isobel, stop that scratching," she instructed, frowning at me in disapproval. I did as I was told but felt the tears threatening to fall under the mounting feelings of frustration.

"Would you like something cool to drink, Issy? I can fetch something for you," Elizabeth offered.

My mother protested. "Nay, Your Highness, we don't want to bother ye. Henry can fetch something."

"Mother!" My brother Henry immediately launched his complaining. He had been occupied with twirling a top on the floor. "You told me to watch Mary. I can't do everything." His brow burrowed into his typical scowl, and he propped his hands on his hips. He looked like a grumpy old housewife scolding her children.

"Your face is going to stick that way, Harry," I teased. "Better lift your brow before that scowl is permanently imbedded on your countenance."

The nine-year-old stuck his tongue out at me.

"All right," my mother intervened, "Henry, take Mary to the refreshment table and get something to drink for Isobel. Ye and Mary can have a biscuit while ye are there. But hurry back, your sister is unwell."

Henry stamped his foot once to show his displeasure but dared not say anything more. He shoved the toy into his pocket then grabbed little Mary's hand and headed toward the other end of the hall. Mary was the most congenial four-year-old one could ever meet, and she went willingly, skipping along beside her big brother, chatting happily.

Mother continued to fan me while Elizabeth ran a hand up and down my back. Her curled fingers scratched gently along my back and the sensation calmed my irritated skin.

"Issy, perhaps you should not continue in this pursuit," Elizabeth suggested. "It's not worth the malaise."

This masque was sponsored by the prince. Horrified at the thought of failing him, I said, "Oberon, the Faery Prince must have six nymphs. I cannot disappoint His Highness. Besides, who will sing the aria? None of the other nymphs can reach the highest notes. Not even you."

The princess's mouth turned up in a wicked little grin. "It is not the end of the world if all does not go as planned. My brother can stand to face a little disappointment from time to time. No one else in all of England can fall into a dung pile and come out smelling like a rose."

That may be true, but the newly named Prince of Wales was the epitome of perfection. Tall and finely formed with a head of rose gold hair and pale, sky-blue eyes, he reminded me of the sun god called Apollo that I had seen in a picture book in my father's library. From his first breath, Prince Henry Frederick Stuart was groomed to be king, and it was a role he fulfilled with much alacrity.

I tucked my head down again but soon felt the hovering presence of someone else standing over me. I looked up to find my father, the Earl of Stratford, looking down on me. Concern crinkled his brow, but his attention was only partially on me. He searched the hall as if looking for someone before his eyes turned fully toward me.

"Be sure to find me after the masque, Isobel. The Duke of Penford is quite keen on introducing you to his son."

"William," Mother said with her cautious tone, "I thought we agreed the talk of marriage could wait."

"An introduction never hurt anyone," Father said, winking at me.

I smiled weakly at him. Father had recently gotten it into his head that it was time for me to think of marriage. I wholeheartedly agreed. But there was only one man I would consider marrying, and that was the Prince of Wales. All others paled in comparison, and I was certain they couldn't make me happy. Besides, I had seen the Duke of Penford's son. He was no prize. But I couldn't tell my father that.

Harry returned momentarily with a mug of small beer for me, and a biscuit covered in tiny pink sugar crystals. I took the refreshment without comment. Harry could be a thoughtful brother, as long as I didn't embarrass him by pointing out his thoughtfulness. I gulped the weak ale down instantly but only took a small bite of the biscuit. I was afraid the sweet would not stay down and I didn't want to take a chance on getting sick while performing. I then drank the rest of Mary's cider she had set on the floor beside me before lifting her arms to Father in a bid to be held.

"I'll eat it," the princess said of the biscuit I had set aside. "I'm so nervous. I'm afraid I am going to trip over my own feet in the nymph's reel and fall flat on my face." She took a small bite of the biscuit and chewed carefully.

"You won't fall," I assured her as I leaned over Mary's cider I still cupped in my lap. She was so graceful on her feet and had been instructed in the art of dancing practically since the time she could walk. "You're just nervous all eyes will be on you during this masque. And the baron will be watching."

Elizabeth made a face. The Earl of Suffolk's son had made it clear he was interested in naming himself a suitor for the princess. "Theophilus is twenty-seven years old. I don't want to marry an old man, even if I cannot marry for love."

The man was twelve years her senior. Yet, I thought Theophilus Howard, the Baron Howard de Walden, was a handsome man, no matter his age. He danced so gracefully and had the most attractive little mustache that he styled into a perfect point on each side of his lips. And as for marrying for love, well, a princess usually couldn't. They were used as pawns in some political game I didn't quite understand. But I did think it was possible to love another, even if he were older. Granted, Theophilus wasn't as attractive as the prince. But Prince Henry was young, and radiant, and oh so alive with vibrant energy. One couldn't help but love him.

A clap of hands interrupted my musing. Ben Jonson, the writer of the masque we would be performing, stood on the dais. Hair askew as if he had run his fingers through the curly strands and left them standing on end, he lifted his voice above the full roar of the performers. We were already in costume awaiting our director's instructions, so everyone turned their attention to him.

"The night has arrived, my friends. Remember, there are no insignificant characters. Every one of you has a message to render, a part to perform." I glanced at Princess Elizabeth. She and I were of a very small lot of performers who were not part of the King's Men, a group of players employed by Master Shakespeare and chosen to perform this masque. Prince Henry had insisted on a part for his sister to perform and she had requested that I, her maid of honor and closest friend, perform with her. That is how I came to be dressed as a green nymph and awaiting the prince's entrance to the masque. "The finishing touches were made to the frontispiece, and all is in place," Jonson continued. "I must say, Inigo, you have truly outdone yourself. This scenery is a magnificent piece of artistry, and we are but humble players on your glorious stage." Here Jonson motioned toward Inigo Jones, the designer of the stage upon which we were to perform. Shouts and whistles went up in recognition of Jones's theatrical masterpiece, although the players had yet to see it, and he waved the applause off with an embarrassed shrug. "Now, if my performers will take their places, all that is left to do is await the arrival of Their Majesties, and we shall begin."

The audience gave a collective sigh and another round of applause ensued. "Are you well enough to take your place, Issy?" Elizabeth looked toward me, concern coloring her expression. She had picked up my mask and the floral sash I had discarded and draped it over my shoulder.

"I wouldn't miss this for the world," I said, taking a deep breath and swallowing my queasiness. I stood and handed my mother the empty cup I had been holding, kissed Father on the cheek, then took the mask from Elizabeth's outstretched hand. Nothing would keep me from supporting our prince tonight. Not even the color green.

The lutenists took up their instruments. The violinists raised their bows and prepared for the opening notes. I climbed upon the rock on which I was to perch and positioned myself to await the entrance of the faery prince, Oberon. Through the mullioned windows stars twinkled, and the moon winked her celestial approval at the tableau below. On the other side of the stage, the princess had taken up her spot. I stared at her, feeling a mixture of nerves and excitement and the lingering nausea twirling circles in my belly. She grinned at me before her eyes lifted to something above my head.

Above us, in a box designed especially for their honor, King James and Queen Anne situated themselves. They were surrounded by their usual entourage of hangers-on, with the Viscount Rochester, Robert Carr, sitting to the right of the king, the honored spot of the king's favorite. James radiated majesty and awe, with a waist-length stole of red velvet lined with ermine wrapped around his shoulders. The queen donned a pink gown of Italian brocade trimmed in gold. Her deep, oval neckline was trimmed in carnation pink with a fine layer of linen masking her décolletage. The intricate needlework of her wide reticella collar encircled her lush, golden-frizzed hair. Queen Anne was stunning. But it was the viscount, in his doublet sewn of white cloth of silver and embroidered with black satin marigolds, that demanded admiration. His trunk hose was of black grosgrain, also embroidered with marigolds of contrasting gold thread. Even his shoes were embroidered with sun-colored marigolds and adorned with gold and black silk rosettes. Only the prince would have rivaled the viscount's elegance, but Henry would be portraying the faery prince, Oberon, this evening, and would be donned in a magnificent costume which I had not yet seen.

When the king's party was settled, four footmen were dispatched to snuff the candles that lined the hall, leaving only the ones around the stage burning. My heart thrummed wildly. Although the prince was not due to enter at the first, I anticipated his arrival on stage. The heat from the bodies gathered in the banqueting hall had reached a peak, and I felt lightheaded. I took three deep breaths, trying to calm my nerves and keep myself from passing out entirely.

With the sound of a cornet, the masque began. A satyr with legs and forearms covered with brown fur and a formidable set of stunted horns upon his brow flitted about the stage calling for his companions to come forth. A silvery globe equipped with six candles rose quietly above the backdrop of the stage. In the faint light of the artificial moon, I could see the pullies that were used to lift the moon, but the audience would not be able to detect the rigging. The moon would slowly be moved higher and higher throughout the masque to indicate the passage of time.

The satyr blew his cornet once more and called out. Immediately, another satyr joined him on stage and spoke his lines. The cornet was blown a third time summoning forth the remaining satyrs who were hidden behind the rock upon which I sat. The stage was flooded with fur-clad men who danced and chittered about until Silenus made his appearance and addressed his fellow satyrs.

The nausea, which had never truly dissipated, clawed at me once again. A thousand needles pricked at my skin. My legs, arms, neck, and face, all itching and burning. Suffocating. I squinted across the stage, trying to find Elizabeth, trying to focus my attention on our upcoming dance steps in order to calm my churning stomach and sooth my skin.

At last, Silenus spoke his words signaling our cue. The large canvas panels had been painted with pastoral scenes and pushed together to look like one large backdrop opened to reveal a large frontispiece hiding behind with a magnificent palace painted thereon. The crowd cooed their delight at the change of scenes, and I too found myself in awe of the ingenuity of Jones's creation. But there was no time to admire the view. The nymphs were moving now, and it was my turn to dance my way across the stage. I moved my body with the rhythm of the music, swaying with arms uplifted. The music swelled, and my heart pounded faster, a blend of nerves, nausea, and anticipation.

Silenus and his satyr companions continued their lines, taunting two sylvans that lay slumbering at the gates of the palace, where they were supposed to be on guard. The teasing continued, and the music built until finally the satyrs broke forth into a hypnotic verse.

The satyrs erupted into cackling and the sylvans awakened, surprised. There is more talking, more dancing and the pounding of the previous verse reverberated through my head. My head felt as if it were splitting in two. Nothing was as it should be. I saw two Silenuses, two moons, two Elizabeths. I fought to maintain my composure. The next two verses were quickly approaching, and the prince would enter, then two more verses before I must sing my part. But I was worried I would pitch over onto my face, unable to keep my footing.

At the end of the next two verses, the canvas panels split once more, revealing another scene and a host of faeries. Some dancing, some singing, some bearing lights. With them, a multitude of knights converge. And behind the menagerie of faery creatures, the prince, standing in his chariot drawn by two enormous white bears.

The audience gasped, but I knew not if it was the stunning bears or the magnificence of Prince Henry as Oberon that caught their fancy. He looked glorious, and I stumbled upon my feet when I caught sight of the prince in all his splendor.

He was dressed as an ancient warrior, more specifically, like a Roman Emperor. Candlelight flickered off his silver armor with sculpted leonine emblems adorning his breastplate, boots, and sleeves. He wore scarlet hose, and his feet were shod with white buskins decorated with silver spangles. Oberon, along with all the other knights in his entourage wore a high, white plume on his helmet and a band splayed across his chest. But whereas the other knights wore bands of bright blue, Henry's was scarlet, emphasizing his noble status. He stood erect, his jaw set and his eyes shining. Plates of colored glass encased the candles that lined the stage and were spun wildly, casting prisms of color to splash across the prince's face.

A swarm of butterflies burst in my belly, and warmth heated my cheeks. I could gaze upon him for days and never grow tired. Such was his beauty. But the music was moving forward, and my verse was quickly approaching. My mouth suddenly felt dry and the itching sensation that first burned on my skin now seemed to be constricting my throat. Panic seized me, and I forgot where I was instructed to stand when it came time for me to sing.

I stood frozen for a moment, caught in a trance by a mixture of adoration for the prince and fright for forgetting where I was. Just then, the princess was at my side, her hands on my arms, moving me into the place where I was to be. "Thank you," I mumbled numbly, then turned my face back toward the prince. At the appointed measure, I opened my mouth and without thought, began to sing the clear, high notes of the aria. Henry turned his eyes on me and listened.

When my part was finished, the masque continued, the sylvan said his lines, then Silenus. The satyrs moved about me, and the nymphs danced their reels. But I saw none of it, for Oberon had turned his face upon me and flashed his charming smile.

I lowered my eyes, embarrassed. He smiled at me. My heart was in my throat, which felt even tighter now. I suddenly realized how dry my mouth had become. I needed to move. I needed to keep up with the rest of the nymphs and do my part. But when I went to move my feet the floor tilted once more, and I couldn't seem to keep my balance. The last thing I remembered was the prince's crestfallen face as he watched me crumple to the floor.

Chapter 2

Border Region, Scotland
January 1612
Robert

She always came to me in my dreams. Long hair the color of flame caught on a summer's breeze, the fiery tendrils blowing across freckled cheeks and catching on fine lashes. Eyes the color of baked sugar, crinkled in laughter and lips as soft as crushed velvet whispering sweet sentiments into my ear.

But it wisnae Moira's sweet breath that brushed against my ear at the moment. I was jerked awake by the sudden realization someone was tugging on my ear. Hard.

"Get up, ye boil-brained codpiece."

The sentiments of Lord Scott of Buccleuch wurnae nearly as sweet, and his correction in the form of beatings was even less so. The smell of manure and damp earth penetrated my waking senses, and I was faintly aware of where I had been tossed the night before. Sticks of straw scratched at my cheek and poked my head, two sensations that might as well have been razors against my skin, and frigid air bit at my extremities. I shifted my weight, feeling the cold stiffness of frozen earth beneath me. Every cut and bruise on my body screamed at me not to move, to curl into a ball and go back to sleep. My muscles ached and even the hairs on my arms and the back of my neck seemed to be acutely aware of my body's condition. But I wisnae a clotpole. If I didnae get up in the next thirty seconds, I widnae be getting up at all. It was my bad luck that the constable had chosen to enlist the help of my half-brother instead of sending me to the tolbooth. Some punishments were worse than even death.

"Ye get up before our mother gets wind of yer antics. I have half a mind to tell her this time of the trouble ye have caused. She willnae be happy."

I opened one eye and looked up at my older brother. The Lord of Buccleuch was standing with one hand grasping his broad sword, the other clenched into a fist. His feet were posted in a wide stance and a scowl that has been part of his natural mien since I was a wee lad darkened his face. The son of my mother and her first husband, Lord Walter Scott took it upon himself to see to my education and training in the absence of my father. Never mind his training included reiving around the Scottish border and often down into nearby English towns.

"Get up," he said again, this time nudging me with the toe of his boot.

"I'm up! Stop haranguing me." I shoved his foot away, but that was a mistake. He moved so quickly I didnae see it coming. He kicked me over onto my back and slammed his foot down hard onto my chest. Pain shot through the back of my head as it cracked against the cold, hard floor of the stable.

"Ye have forgotten whose food has filled yer belly and under whose roof ye have kept warm. If ye dinnae be moving fast enough for my liking, then ye will be harrrrangued." He drew the last word out with his Lowland Scots brogue as his voice got louder.

Rubbing the back of my head, I went to stand but a sudden sharp pain in my side stole my breath. "I think my rib is broken," I heaved out. "Maybe even two." Perspiration beaded on my brow instantly as the pain shot through my body. I tenderly ran my fingers across my ribs in an effort to see if I could feel the break.

"Serves ye right," Buccleuch snarled. I didnae respond, only took the hand he extended to me. Taking a deep breath in anticipation of more pain, I hulled myself up off the stable floor.

I followed my brother out the door to his waiting steed. With one swift movement he swung his leg up over his horse and settled in, taking the reins.

It was still early, for the only people I saw moving about were the hostler and a stable boy who were mucking out the stalls. A milkmaid meandered slowly further down the road, carrying a large pitcher on each hip which swayed methodically with every step she took.

"Did ye bring a mount for me?" I said as I turned toward my brother. I scowled for I would get nay such consideration.

"Nay. I thought to have ye walk off the effects of the liquor ye consumed last night before ye went on yer wee raid."

"I wisnae drunk," I said, squinting up at him in the winter sunlight. "I kent full-well what I was doing."

"Aye. Which makes what ye did even worse. Lord Carruthers will have our heads at most or have us all in before the courts, at least, for that little stunt ye pulled. And it will be my name and my coin, once again, that will keep ye from swinging." He adjusted himself on his mount again before turning his eyes on me. His hard stare should have made me shift. It should have put the fear of the Almighty into me, spur me into making a last wish or want to kiss my bonny lass one final time. I pushed the last thought aside. There would be no more of that thinking, which is what spurred the fight last night in the first place. Those scoundrels paid for what they did to Moira. I personally saw to that.

"Get yerself cleaned up, ye smell of swine. Mother expects ye for dinner at noon and we need to talk first. Meet me in my study in half an hour." He snapped the reins, sending his horse into a trot. Broad shoulders straightened and head held aloft, he ambled away with the ease of a man who has never had to worry about his place a day in his life. His father, also of the same name, had been Lord Baron of Buccleuch, and our mother was the daughter of an earl. Walter's childhood would have been a happy one, at least until his father died. And even at that, he would have wanted for nothing. Our mother had married an earl after Walter's father died. My full-blooded siblings and I should have wanted for nothing as well, but Father had been accused of treason and exiled from Scotland a few months before I was born. With our family shamed, and all our property and titles confiscated, there was nothing left for us but humiliation. And as the youngest son of a disgraced and abased earl, I've never kent where I belonged.

A half hour later I walked into Branxholme Castle, scrubbed and clothed in a fresh tunic and doublet. It had been months since I had stepped foot into Branxholme and coming back almost felt like stepping into a tomb. The castle itself was a newer structure, my mother having completed the rebuilding of the old Branxholme in the name of her deceased first husband a mere thirty-five years earlier. It was Walter's inheritance, and he had graciously let my mother come and live here after my father had been exiled. She was destitute and shamed, the king having revoked her title and decreeing no one was to associate with her, the wife of a disgraced earl. She also had a brood of younger children including a sniveling bairn in tow, and my half-brother had taken us all in, providing for our needs and performing all the duties a father should have. Walter had been a friend to my father, when he was still an earl, siding with him during many of the schemes my father had conjured. The Lord of Buccleuch had even suffered exile himself at one point due to his association with my father. But he had returned. Returned to his title and his home, and his honor, and he never let me forget this home wisnae mine. My stay was only temporary. That was fine with me. For every time I walked into this place, I felt the weight of my insufficiencies and the reminder of what I might have been, had I remained the son of an earl.

"Did ye kill anyone?" Walter asked as I stepped into his study and closed the door behind me. The room was drafty, and the fire in the hearth flickered wildly upon my entrance. A piece of parchment laid out on his desk lifted and fell simultaneously. Old books lined the shelves in neat, colorful rows. A painting of Buccleuch's father with our mother hung on the north wall as a central focal point in the room. Other frames of dried, pressed flowers, sketches by some of Walter's children, and a letter from King James declaring Walter to be Lord Scott of Buccleuch were hung haphazardly at various heights upon the adjacent walls. He was a man at home in his element. A feeling I would probably never ken.

I didnae speak for a moment. I ran my thumb over the callous on my right middle finger, allowing the feel of it to calm my restlessness. The small, hardened patch of skin, from years of holding a pistol, was the only thing that kept me grounded. The knowledge that I could wield a pistol—as well as a sword—gave me something that was my own. Especially in this house, where Lord Buccleuch never let me forget I didnae belong.

My brother was a large man who commanded respect wherever he went. His presence in any room seemed to draw the air out of it. Like a vacuum in which every other person shrunk to a practically non-existent state, and every object so miniscule as to not even make an impression. He was seated in a chair behind his desk and stuffing the dried leaves of Spanish tobacco into a pipe. He lit it with a stick which he had ignited from the hearth then shook the flame away and tossed the stick into the fireplace. When he was situated, he leaned back in his seat and took a puff from his pipe, then pinned me with an appraising look.

Gray eyes that took on a green tinge in the late morning sunlight and set under a brooding brow stared at me. A scatter of freckles splashed across the ruddy complexion of his forehead. We looked a lot alike with these aspects, taking certain attributes from our mother. But that is where the similarities ended. A crooked nose that looked like it had been flattened with some sort of blunt instrument graced his round face. It wisnae necessarily an inheritance from his father but gifted him from a raid gone bad two decades earlier. Sandy hair pulled back into a neat, severe queue contradicted the wildness of the tasks with which my brother occupied himself. He was a reiver of some fame around the

Scottish border, and no one would mistake him for the gentleman he appeared to be.

He raised a brow at me, awaiting my answer.

"It was two against one," I said, deflecting the question.

"That isnae what I asked ye. Answer the question, Robbie. Ye ken I dinnae like evasion and have no patience for word games."

"Aye. Words are powerful. They can make or break a person, widnae ye say?"

He cocked his brow at me again. "What are ye getting at?"

"I'd like to be referred to as Robert from now on, sir. I'm of an age where Robbie just doesnae suit me. I want to be taken seriously, and a child's nickname doesnae solicit respect."

He barked a laugh and leaned forward, propping his arms on his desk. "Names dinnae solicit respect, my boy, actions do. And yer actions havnae demanded respect. In fact, they've done just the opposite. Yer lack of self-control, yer arrogance, and yer temper have worked together to prove ye arnae respectable. In fact, ye have brought shame on this family. Ye have trampled my benevolence under foot and shown me ye are incapable of being trusted."

Anger simmered through me. He would always see me as a child, treat me as a child. I was tired of the disrespect.

"How can I bring shame on this family? This isnae my family. Ye and I do not share a name. And if my family name had any respect attached to it, my father saw to eliminating that a long time ago." I hated that I was taking out my anger on my father. The man whom I had adored from my earliest memories. The man who had filled my every waking moment with a desire to please and a desire to avenge. I had never met him. A fact King James had guaranteed when he exiled him before my birth. But I was consumed with a yearning to ken him, to help him, and to bring him home. And other than Moira and my mother, he had been all I had ever cared about.

Walter sighed. "The Earl of Bothwell wreaks havoc still."

I stood abruptly. "Dinnae speak the name of my father with impudence on yer tongue! He was wronged, and I willnae rest until I have removed the stain from his name and seen him restored to his rightful titles."

"Are ye telling me that is what the raid on the Carruthers' land was all about? Or did it have something to do with a little red-headed chit that is no longer among us?"

I slammed my fist down on top of my brother's desk, snapping a pen that had been lying there. "Ye may only speak of my father with respect in yer tone, but ye may nay speak of Moira at all!"

Lord Buccleuch stood abruptly, shoving his chair back, and knocking it to the floor. Grabbing me by the collar of my tunic, he pulled me across his desk. The toe of my boots scraped across the floor as I tried to gain purchase. He seethed, "Ye willnae tell me who I can and cannae talk about in my own house!" I held my breath, unrepentant and waiting for his next move. The pale green of his eyes was gone, leaving orbs of black with a faint gray ring glaring back at me.

He held onto me a moment longer, a myriad of questions flitting across his face. When I didnae react, he released me and straightened my shirt. Setting his chair aright, he sat back down and folded his hands calmly as if he hid nae just experienced a sudden outburst, the likes of which he always accused me of having. I too sat down and waited for what would come next.

He took a calming breath and pulled the pipe from his mouth. "Carruthers said he has two dead men. Do ye ken anything about that?"

"Aye," I said simply.

He gazed at me for what seemed like an eternity. I presumed he was trying to decide what he was going to do with me. We had been through this before. Me causing some offense, and he doling out punishments.

"And do ye care to share yer knowledge with me?" he asked slowly this time as if his infinite patience was finally wearing thin.

"I willnae incriminate myself," I answered.

"Devil take ye, Robbie! I am trying to help ye here. Ye arnae on trial. Just tell me what ye ken about the two dead men. How did it happen?"

I still didnae answer. My brother had killed many a man during his border raids throughout the years. But he felt they were justified. I doubted he would think Moira was a good enough reason.

"What was it ye were trying to accomplish? The lass is dead," he said, as if reading my mind. "There is nothing ye can do to change that fact. Stirring up trouble with Clan Carruthers willnae bring her back."

I could feel anger stiffening my spine, the heat of it pooling in my chest. There was no need to remind me Moira was dead. I felt the emptiness she left in my gut every day since she was taken from me. Surely, he could comprehend retaliation, vengeance. He spoke that language well enough. But I refused to give him even a little rope with which to hang me. I glared at the mantle above the hearth for a long moment, considering my response. The head of a stag, mounted on a plaque of darkened oak above the fireplace, stared back at me. Its glassy eyes ogled me and shouted its condemnation.

"Was the bairn yers then?" he asked, shifting his questioning in a different direction.

My eyes shot to him. "How do ye ken about that?"

His eyes softened. "That kind of news gets around." The fire popped, sending sparks into the air. A tiny ember landed on the stones in front of the hearth, and I watched as it glowed a bright orange for a split second, then faded to black as the light died and the spark turned to ash. It reminded me of Moira and her short life, full of energy one day, and cold in her grave the next.

"'Tis nay what ye think," I said, feeling the need to protect her or at least the memory of her.

He let out a sigh. "Robbie—Robert," he corrected, "I ken the fire of youth. I ken how hard it can be to control yerself in the heat of the moment. Ye—"

"I nay need a lesson about the birds and the bees, Lord Buccleuch," I interrupted, annoyed. I wisnae sure if my annoyance was from his presumption of my ignorance with the way things were between a man and a woman or the kindness that had invaded his tone. It was uncharacteristic of him, and it unnerved me. Either way, he dinnae ken what he was talking about. He thought the bairn that grew in Moira's belly was mine. Although I assured Moira I would treat the child as my own, it wisnae me who planted the seed. But no one would ever ken that. Moira had taken that secret to the grave, and I would too.

"Well," he let out a breath as if thankful to be released from the task of educating me on matters of procreation, "What's done is done, and she's gone now, so it makes no matter. What does matter is how we proceed from henceforth." He picked up the parchment from his desk. "I have here a letter of introduction." He paused. "I am sending ye to England, to King James's court."

I sat up straighter. "What? Ye of all people ken that is the last place on earth I would want to find myself."

"All the same," he said. "I think it is high time ye make yerself kent to the king. See if ye can convince him to lift yer father's exile and let him return to Scotland."

My heart pounded in my ears. It's what I had always wanted. To have my father home would bring my mother great joy and give me a satisfaction I only dreamt of as a child. But London? And why me?

"Why not send Francis? He is the diplomat. He has a knack for politics and could plead Father's case better than I."

Walter shook his head. "Francis cannae involve himself at this time. He has too much going on at home."

"Then what about John? He could sell wine to a vintner. Surely, he could talk the king into anything." An edge of panic was rising in my chest. "Even Frederick or Harry would be a better choice."

"I have made my decision, Robert. Ye need to get away for a while. And no one else can plead yer father's case better than ye. Ye are the right man for the task."

"Ah. Ye are trying to rid yerself of me, is that it? Ye want me out of the way because ye fear Carruthers and his ilk?"

"I want ye out of the way because of the trouble ye are causing over this chit," he confirmed. "And ye've got too much pent-up anger over yer father to be of any use to me at this point." He folded the parchment then lit a candle above the fire to melt the stick of wax. Dripping wax onto the edges of the letter, he sealed it with his signet ring and handed it to me.

I stared at the letter in his hand for a moment. I may not have been staying here at Branxholme Castle for months now, but it was still the only home I had ever kent. My brother hid nae always been a loving brother, but he was security and familiarity. I slowly took the letter from his hand. The seal hid nae yet hardened, and my thumb brushed across the surface, smearing the soft, warm wax. It was one thing to leave on my own accord but to be forced to leave, without having a say in the matter, was just one more slight that cut at me like a knife to skin.

I took a deep breath to steady my voice. "Am I to be cast out then? What if the king doesnae want me at court? What if he sees me as just as much of a threat as my father was? Then what?"

"Then ye come home. I am not casting ye out, Robbie. Dinnae look so forlorn. Our mother would have my head if I did that. Ye go to London, see what King James says about releasing yer father from his exile, and return home with Lord Bothwell in tow. 'Tis really that simple."

"My father isnae in London. He his nae been there for several years. He is in Italy now." I ran my thumb across the letter I still held in my hand. The coarseness of the parchment, the tiny dips and grooves across the surface felt pleasant to the touch despite the contents of the message inside.

"Then go to Italy and get him. Or better yet, write to him and tell him the good news, then come home straightway. Ye still keep up correspondence with him, dinnae ye?"

I nodded. "Aye, but I have no coin. How am I to make such a journey?"

Lord Buccleuch slid his chair back and opened a drawer at the top of his desk. He withdrew a brown leather pouch that clinked when he tossed it onto the desk. "Here. This should hold ye over until ye can establish yerself at court. It might take a few months to work yer way into His Majesty's good graces. There is enough there to last six months, nine if ye are frugal."

I swallowed hard. Nine months? I hoped it widnae take that long. Living amongst the English wisnae the way I desired to spend my time. Especially not that long. "I can make a shilling last an interminable amount of time. Spending is Frederick and John's vice, not mine."

"All the more reason to send ye and not yer brothers," he said, baring his teeth in a grin, as if we had just concluded a lucrative business transaction. "Now, Mother is waiting for ye in her supper chamber. Please give her my apologies for not joining ye. I have some business to take care of in town." He stood to his feet and held out his hand to me as if to conclude a deal.

I ignored his gesture of good will. "Am I to leave today? Will ye not see me off?" I felt as if I were being thrown to the wolves. It was all so sudden, so final.

"I see no reason to delay. The sooner ye make the king's acquaintance, the sooner ye can seal the deal concerning yer father. Oh, dinnae look at me so sickly, Robert. Ye wanted to be treated as a man. Here is yer chance to do a manly thing. Ye were just boasting ye widnae rest until ye've seen yer father restored. Go do something of value for a change." He slapped me on the back as if we were old friends.

In one last swipe at his integrity, I said desperately, "I never thought ye to be a coward when it came to Clan Carruthers."

My words hit right where I intended. The color drained from his face, and his smile slipped.

"'Tis nay my concern," he said flatly before turning to go.

"They are responsible for Moira's death, and ye are just going to let them get away with it."

He stopped abruptly and turned back to me. Paying no heed to my slight, he said, "Ye should have never fallen in with the chit. Now that ye are a man, ye will do well to remember this one truth. Women are nothing but trouble. Keep yer wits about ye and whatever ye do, never ever let them get ye by the cullions." And with that, he quit the room.

Chapter 3

Branxholm Castle, Hawick, Scotland
January 1612
Robert

The Countess of Bothwell was a proud woman who had borne her humiliation well. She had retained the title of Bothwell even after my father had been stripped of his. "The king is far away in London and has no use for the appellation," she had once said, and no one ever questioned her about it again. Some of the servants at Branxholme Castle still called her Lady Buccleuch from time to time, out of an old habit, but Mother said she felt it slighted her living husband, in deference to her late one, and so commanded the use of that title in reference to her to be discontinued. A consideration my brother's wife, the current Lady Buccleuch, surely appreciated.

Mother sat in a large ornately carved chair that had been covered with red velvet demask. Her feet, which were occasionally inflicted with gout, were propped up on a cushion that sat atop a golden, silk-covered stool. A soft woolen plaid was spread across her lap. When I entered her supper chamber, her face lit up. "Oh, Robbie! Come." She motioned for me as she set her needlepoint aside.

The Prince's Darling

Heavy crimson curtains had been drawn back to let in the dreary winter sunlight, and a cheery fire burned ferociously in the hearth. When I was a child, this was my favorite room in the house, with its heavily tapestried walls and thick Turkish rugs. It felt safe and warm, and to a boy who was forever hiding from some older brother or sister, I found security within the tiny chamber. I loved the feel of the plush carpets beneath my feet, and on one occasion, had even rolled myself up in one of the rugs to hide. I was supposed to be playing hide and seek with my twin brothers, Frederick and Harry, and my two youngest sisters, Jean and Margaret. But whenever one of my brothers would catch me, they would pull my hair or twist my nose, so I didnae much like the game. I had hidden in the carpet and fallen asleep. Mother was sick with worry until she found me some hours later.

I went to her and bent my knee, kissing her hand.

She looked at me with her watery, unfocused eyes and laid a shaky hand atop my head. "When ye were a boy, ye used to lay yer head in my lap and fall asleep."

"I am a boy no longer, my Lady Mother." I moved to stand, but she pulled at my hands, forcing me to stay kneeling. She was quite strong for a woman of her age.

"Ye will always be my boy." She patted my hands. The smoothness of her palms felt soft and cool against my skin.

"Mother, ye are cold, let me grab a shawl for ye." I used the excuse to stand and move away from her. My heart wanted nothing more than to lay my head in her lap and let her caress my ear as she had done when I was a wee lad. The gesture of running a light fingertip around the coiling folds of my ear, pushing her fingers through the coppery strands of my hair was soothing and would often put me to sleep. I ached for those simple days when I was just a boy who loved his mother and longed to rescue his father.

But she would indulge my boyish daydreams if I let her, and it was time to cast off those childish whims. I grabbed a folded earasaid and brought it to her shoulders. She wiggled into its warmth.

I took a seat across from her as she rang for a servant to bring our dinner. Two footmen entered bearing trays laden with food.

"I hope ye dinnae mind, but I've ordered a light dinner for this afternoon. I've been feeling a little under the weather, and nothing has sat right on my stomach of late."

I dragged my eyes away from the soup the servant had placed before me. "Ye havenae been well? Why wisnae I informed?"

"Oh, it's just a little cold, I think. Nothing serious. And soup always makes a nice meal when the weather is frigid." She picked up her spoon and rubbed it with the corner of her earasaid. I watched her momentarily as she dipped her spoon into the cloudy broth of chicken and leeks. The soup was thickened with oatmeal stock and smelled peppery and comforting. Mother tipped her spoon into her mouth then lifted her eyes to mine. "Eat dear, before it gets cold."

I tore into a small roll of wheat bread and spread a pat of golden butter on it. The creamy substance melted on my tongue, and I wolfed down both halves before tearing another open and dipping it into my soup.

We ate in silence for a while until Mother laid her spoon aside and looked at me with her rheumy eyes.

"I have something for ye," she said, fumbling in her skirts in search of an object she pulled from a pocket. It appeared to be a jewel of some sort, a pendant possibly, and it too she polished with the edge of her plaid before pushing on a clasp and popping it open. She gazed silently at the jewel, running her thumbs over the surface of whatever was hidden inside. Then she shook her head lightly and snapped the locket closed. "I want ye to have this," she said softly, her voice warbling slightly as she handed the object to me.

I took the jewel and studied the outer surface. It was gold, beaten into the shape of an oval with tiny seed pearls and rubies encased in it. I pushed on the clasp and the top sprung open revealing a tiny portraiture inside. Staring back at me was my own likeness, including the coppery brown of my own hair, the feline-shaped eyes, and slim nose.

The only indication this wisnae me was the cobalt shade of the man's eyes.

I considered the portrait then turned my attention to my mother once more. Something akin to a skein of wool felt stuck in my throat. I swallowed once, then twice, trying to force the knot down.

"I have never seen this before. Where did ye get it?"

Mother resumed eating her soup. She picked up a roll and began to slather it with butter before dipping a portion of it into her soup. I was beginning to think she widnae answer when she finally said, "Yer father gave it to me. As ye can see it was quite long ago, when we were first married."

I kent from stories that my mother was a little older than my father, for she had already been married and widowed by the time they met. Father had been about ten and five when they married. I felt I was staring into a looking glass when I first laid eyes upon him. He was only a couple of years younger than I in the portrait.

"Why have ye never shown me this?" The injury in my voice was apparent, and I swallowed once more to regain composure. She kent how much I loved this man I had never met. My childhood was filled with memories of me questioning my mother about my father and her telling me story upon story about the man I longed so much to ken.

She sighed and laid her spoon aside once more. "Robbie, yer father —" she paused, and I wondered at her hesitation. Her voice didnae shake as mine had. It didnae sound as if it were affection that hindered her from talking of him. "He wisnae always a good man."

I stiffened, bracing myself for what my mother might say about my father. I hid nae heard her speak ill of him, but the truth was she rarely spoke of him at all, unless I asked her to.

"What do ye mean? He was accused of plots to kidnap the king, and he was involved in some border raids back when he was younger. But what do ye mean, he wisnae always a good man? Ye mean his integrity suffered for all the stories the king told of his treachery, correct?"

Mother looked at me then, her gray-green eyes penetrating my heart. "Nay, Robbie. I meant exactly what I said. He wisnae always a good man. There are many tales of his exploits. Some I can attest to, and some I can only speculate about. But what I do ken is the man he was when he was at home, and it is that man that I speak of now. He wisnae a man who had control of his anger. He would take his irritation out on the people around him. Many times, it was the servants. But at other times that person was me. Oh, he would always feel bad about it later. But in the moment, it was terrifying. And it was then I would find myself praying for his departure."

I gawked at her. She folded her napkin into a tiny square, then unfolded it, turning it over to set the folds all over again in the opposite direction.

"And then there was the darkness that seemed to overtake him at times. It was more than just a passing anger. It was as if some dark shadow would engulf him, plunging him into a depth of despair from which he couldnae recover. It made him a different man, and at times I felt as if I didnae ken him at all."

My mother's voice cracked, and she dabbed her eyes with the napkin with which she had been fiddling. This picture she painted of my father was unlike any she had shared before, and the likeness I found myself rejecting in its entirety. But it reminded me of an incident that occurred when I was about five years old.

I had come upon my eldest brother, Francis, who was my father's namesake, and my second oldest brother, John. We had had a good rain the day before and the earth was still soft and pliable under our fingers. Francis had fashioned a small figurine out of the soft mud, complete with perfectly proportioned limbs and an oval head. John was angry because he had tried to create a copy of my brother's image, but his mud doll looked deformed and grotesque, and Francis had laughed at it. Even so, they had set the dolls into the warm sun to bake into harden dirt. I had wanted to make a mud doll too, but Francis widnae let me. So, I found mother in the courtyard talking to one of the maids. I told her my brothers widnae let me play with them and she followed me to the place where they played to chastise them and see what they were about.

But when she came upon the mud figurines, our mother's face turned as red as a strawberry, and she screamed at my brothers for what they had done. She took the hardened dirt dolls and threw them onto the ground, smashing them under her shoe and crushing them into the earth. They were nothing but specks of dirt by the time Mother had finished her destruction.

"I willnae have my children bringing suspicions of witchcraft upon this house with yer ignorant play," she had yelled.

"'Tis nothing more than what we've seen Father making out of wax," Francis answered her haughtily.

Mother struck him, splitting his lip and bringing on blood. "Ye hold yer tongue, Francis Stewart, or ye will be finding yerself at the end of a noose. Or worse, upon the witch's pyre." Francis ran to his room crying, and John and I just stood there with mouths agape. I dinnae ken what a witch or a pyre was at that age. But the incident frightened me enough to never even play in the mud again.

It also explained another incident at a later age, which involved Francis once again. Some of the boys in town had accused our father of being a necromancer. Again, it was a word my young ears hid nae heard. Francis got into a row with the boys, and Walter had to come and break up the fight. It wisnae until I was much older that I found out what a necromancer was, but I never dared to ask Mother about such a thing, especially if it had to do with my father.

Now my mother's words of Father's dark shadows struck me anew and sent a jolt of anger through me. "Ye dinnae believe those old accusations, do ye?" I dropped my spoon into my bowl, my appetite suddenly gone.

"It doesnae matter if I believe the accusations. I ken what I saw with my own eyes. Yer father was a troubled man with many demons."

"Why are ye telling me all this? Why now?" I shoved myself away from the table and stood, fully prepared to flee the room if necessary.

"Robbie, please sit." She motioned once more to the chair I vacated, but I couldnae find it in me to placate her. She sighed once again, sounding as if her very will to live were being exhaled. I walked to the bookcase on the opposite side of the little chamber. When she saw I widnae sit, she set aside her earasaid and made as if to get up.

"Nay, Mother, dinnae fash yerself," I said as I sat back down across from her. The room suddenly felt hot, and I wiped a sleeve across my damp brow.

"I tell ye all this, not to make ye think ill of yer father. But ye have adored him over the years, and with the possibility of ye finally meeting him, I thought it best if ye ken the truth."

"So, Walter told ye of his scheme to send me to London?" I could feel my chest tightening just thinking of leaving my home, my family. Though my four oldest brothers and sisters no longer lived at Branxholme Castle, England felt a lifetime away from my siblings and my mother.

"He hopes ye will be able to talk His Majesty into lifting yer father's exile." She took another breath and opened her mouth, but nay words came.

"Are ye hoping I dinnae succeed? With all ye have told me of him today?" I feared what her answer would be, but I had to ken.

She smiled weakly. "Nay, my boy. He is my husband. How could I wish for anything less than his return home?" She reached out and patted my hand again, giving me the reassurance I needed. "I only tell ye these things to prepare ye. Ye have kept up correspondence with yer father these past few years. And ye have come to ken the broken man he has become. But if he were to be restored to his rightful title, and his property returned," here she paused once again, resuming the folding of her napkin, "he will be a different man entirely. I just want ye to be prepared."

My mouth was suddenly dry. I needed a strong drink. But I suspected this would be the last time I would see my mother in a verra long time. I kneeled before her once again and laid my head in her lap. I widnae cry. For I was beyond the age of childish tears. But I longed to smell the mint and anis that seemed to be permanently embedded in her skirts. She brushed the locks of my hair back, away from my face in her soothing way.

"Promise me ye will be careful," she said, her voice sounding frailer than it had only moments before.

"Ye ken I cannae do that," I said, straightening my spine. "I made a promise to Moira once that I wisnae able to keep. I willnae do it again."

"Even so," she said, taking up her needlework, "ye can consider yer poor mother and try to behave." Her eyes flashed with humor as she pulled her needle through the cloth and looped the thread into an intricate knot.

An innocent smile lifted my lips, and I stood, leaned into her, and kissed her wrinkled cheek. "Aye," I said, hoping to ease her mind.

She pulled a small pair of silver scissors from her pocket and snipped the thread free. I bowed to her, thinking our conversation was over when she spoke up once more in her motherly tone. "Oh, and Robbie," she said, pulling me up short, "dinnae do anything foolish and get yerself killed."

Chapter 4

London
February 1612
Robert

One thing I can say for English soil: it tastes the same as my own in Scotland. I observed this as I pulled my face off the ground after the tavern keeper at the Seven Stars had me tossed. A little misunderstanding over a lady had gotten out of hand, and the next thing I ken, I was being forcibly removed from the premises with compliments of a bloody nose, a torn doublet, and more bruised ribs.

It took a moment to regain my bearings. My hat was missing, but luckily my purse was still intact. I needed to be more careful of my surroundings and with whom I chose to associate. One of the men I had joined up with, a chap from Sheffield named Richard, had eyed my coin from the moment he joined our ragtag caravan. It only took one good kerfuffle to distract a man and cut his purse strings. I couldnae afford to lose my coin, so now was probably a good time to part ways with my travelling companions.

I dragged myself to the side of the road to avoid being trampled by the many carriages and horses on the thoroughfare. My nose was bleeding like a gutted pig, and I pulled the sleeve of my tunic down to sop up the flowing blood.

"Are you in need of some assistance?"

I looked up to see an older gentleman looking down at me. He was clothed in a black cloak with gold trimmings and knee-high boots that somehow appeared to be free from the London mud. On his head was the most illustrious cap, a type of puffy bonnet with a narrow brim adorned with a crimson ostrich feather.

"How do ye keep yer boots clean in this god-forsaken mud?" I pointed at his immaculate boots with one hand while I staunched my bleeding nose with the other.

He raised an amused brow. "Well, I start by not being tossed into the muddy streets." As if on cue, a carriage rolled swiftly past us, and the man moved quickly out of the way to avoid the mud spatter. With a clear shot, I got a face full of muddy snow, adding insult to my injury.

"I see quick reflexes are helpful as well," I said, wiping my face of the muck.

The man looked truly sorry. "Forgive me, when you have lived here as long as I have, you develop certain skills to keep your garments clean." He pulled a handkerchief from his pocket and handed me the clean cloth, indicating for me to wipe my face. "You are from the Scottish borders then?"

I wiped my face with his cloth. "How did ye ken?" I pulled the cloth from my face and was alarmed to see I had also gotten blood on this stranger's handkerchief, along with the mud.

"'Tis all right," the man said, pointing to the soiled handkerchief. I thought I detected a slight Scottish brogue in his speech, but it must have been softened by his apparent time away, if he had lived here long. "Your speech betrays you, my good man. From where exactly do you hail?"

"Hawick, sir. I just arrived this morning."

The man nodded in understanding. "Ah, Clan Scott land."

"Aye. Lord Buccleuch is my brother." I finished wiping my face and seeing the blood from my nose had slacked, I moved to stand. The man offered his hand in assistance and brought me to my feet.

"Forgive me. I have forgotten my manners. My name is Sir William Broune. Most people call me Lord Stratford, but my friends call me William."

"And what am I to call ye, sir? I asked, shaking his hand.

"Why don't you come to supper at Chadwyck House? Then you can call me William." He flashed a smile at me, and I couldnae help but be taken in by his kindness and hospitality.

"That is most generous of ye, sir. But I fear I am not fit to sit at table with someone of yer rank." I looked down at my torn and muddy clothes. I never gave clothing much thought unless I was taking them off a chit. But standing next to this lord made me all too aware of my tattered garb.

"Nonsense. I have three sons, two of which are at least your age if not older. I'm sure we could find something for you to wear to sup." His eyes roved over my form, as if he were calculating my measurements.

I didnae like the idea of taking charity from this man whom I had just met. But there was something disarming about him that made me like him. Perhaps it was our shared Scottish roots that made me feel more at ease in his company.

"I will pay for the clothing, Lord Stratford. I am not a penniless vagrant."

He pointed me in the direction of a carriage that sat across the street from us. "As you wish," he said. He stopped right at the door and hesitated before opening it. "I just realized; you never told me your name."

"My name is Robert," I answered as I climbed into his carriage.

Chapter 5

Chadwyck House, London
February 1612
Isobel

My childhood home was situated between two grassy knolls with the surrounding land cultivated into a deer park and a well-manicured topiary garden set within the courtyard. The house, a two-story manor built at the end of Henry VII's reign, was constructed of rose-colored bricks with tall, narrow, lead-lined windows painted with stylized Tudor motifs. There were twenty-two rooms which made it large enough to accommodate our sizable family. Yet it was small enough for my mother to manage, since at times she still considered herself a simple Scottish housewife, much to my father's chagrin. I loved our home, and when I was away at court, I missed it and its inhabitants dreadfully. But when I was at home, I always longed to be back at the Palace of Whitehall amongst my friends and the glamour of court life.

At present, I found myself installed in my old bedchamber, waiting for the snow to melt so I could return to Whitehall. I had come home for the Christmas celebrations with plans to return to Whitehall after the Twelfth Night celebrations were over. But dark clouds hung low over Chadwyck House, and the smell of snow clung heavily to the frosty air. If it snowed again, I would be stuck here at home for an indeterminate amount of time before Father would allow me to return to the Princess Elizabeth, and my duties as her lady-in-waiting.

A light scuffling at the door led me to know that Edith, our chambermaid, had come to clean my room. I was curled up on a crane-colored chaise longue with a soft woolen blanket tucked around me. I looked up from my book to see her flushed and eager face. Her excitement piqued my interest, and I was immediately curious of her news.

"Lady Isobel, your father has brought a young man home with him." She floated into the room as if walking on a cloud. Edith was as love-crazed as Juliet awaiting her Romeo when it came to young men.

My interest immediately waned. "Whatever for? Who is he?" I sank back into my chair and returned to my book.

"I know not, but he is young, perhaps your brother, Lord Tom's age, and has a roguish look about him. He is quite battered. I think he has been in a scuffle. His clothes are torn and soiled with blood and mud, and he has scrapes all over his face."

I wrinkled my nose at this description. "Blood," I said disdainfully. "Did Father rescue him then? Why did he bring him here? Why not set him up in a room at the Lion and Unicorn and pay for someone to assist him?"

She shrugged. "I know not that either, but he is so handsome." She fell into the chair opposite me, clasping her hands and holding them to her chest. I laughed at her impertinence.

"You better get up before Mistress Hunt sees you," I warned. The housekeeper was a castigator that held strict views about the place servants held in a noble household.

She looked at me then with much seriousness. "Aren't you the least bit curious as to what he looks like? Go down and meet him. He's in your father's study. Make an excuse to interrupt." She stood to her feet and motioned for me to move.

Edith came to Chadwyck House two years ago as an orphan with nowhere else to go. Mother had hired her against Mathilde Hunt's better judgement, promising the housekeeper that Edith was a cherub and would be the best little ladies' maid for me and my sister, Mary. Of course, Mary was only three years old at the time, and I would soon be leaving for court, so Edith had nothing else to do with her time once I left but to follow Mary around like a nursemaid. And since Mary was an angel herself, Edith was left to her own devices most of the time. That idleness led to an extremely vivid imagination.

"Why don't you just describe him to me?" I turned my attention once more to my book, hoping to put an end to the conversation. As an afterthought I said, "If Father wants me to meet him, he will call for me."

"Oh, my lady," she sighed again. "He's got auburn hair and the cutest little dimples in his cheeks."

I chuckled. "Is that all you can say about him? Auburn hair and dimples? Really Edith, what happened to that incredible imagination of yours? You just described half of the men in London."

She beamed at me. "Only, this man isn't from London. He speaks like Her Ladyship speaks when she is tired or agitated."

I peered at her. "With her Scottish brogue?"

The chambermaid nodded. "Yes. And I never fancied myself much for Scottish men, no offense meant toward your people, Lady Isobel, but this stranger is quite attractive."

I stared at her dumbfounded. "I was born in England, Edith. The English are my people."

"Yes, of course, my lady." The maid barely stopped for breath before continuing. "Did your father tell you the Prince of Wales would be dining with you all this evening?" She looked like a cat who had just stuffed a plump bird into its mouth. I dropped my book immediately.

"Prince Henry? Who told you this?" I sprang from my chaise longue and practically skipped to my wardrobe. Flinging open the doors, I immediately started sifting through the dresses that hung there. "I have nothing to wear!" I cried. "All my good dresses are at Whitehall."

Edith drew up behind me. "What about the peach chiffon, my lady? You do look beautiful in that color. The shade sets nicely against your pale skin, and your silvery blonde locks just gleam. You look divine when you wear it." Edith sighed, and I thought for a moment she would swoon.

I frowned. "The chiffon is a summer frock. I'll need something a little warmer for this old, drafty house." I slammed the wardrobe doors shut. "If only I could send word to Elizabeth and ask her to send something with Prince Henry." I tapped my finger against my chin in contemplation. It is quite unconventional, but he is an uncommon prince. I don't think he'd mind.

"He does seem to be taken with you, my lady. But the prince is not at Whitehall. He is coming from Richmond Palace, and he is already on his way."

I looked at Edith, confused. "How do you know all of this? Are you a spy, Edith?" She grinned and plopped down on my bed as if she had time to chat.

"I have ears, don't I? All one must do is loiter around the master's study for any length of time. You'll find out all kinds of important information."

"You naughty girl," I chastised, but there was no heat in my voice. It was so hard to be angry with Edith.

"Edith, remember your place!" The shrieking voice of Mistress Hunt pierced our ears from the doorway. The housekeeper had managed to sneak up on us while we were engaged in conversations about the prince. Edith jumped from the bed in a panic, but I stifled a giggle.

"It's all right, Mistress. She was just sharing some very important information with me."

"Forgive me, Lady Isobel, but there is never a reason for Edith to forget her place." The older woman stood with her hands folded on her rounded stomach, and her double chin resting on her large bosom. A pile of fluffy white hair stuck out from under her caul and matched the bushy brows that hung over faded blue eyes. Looking to the chambermaid, she said, "Edith, Her Ladyship has asked you attend to her at once. She has some tasks she needs you to see to before tonight's supper."

"Yes, mum." Edith curtsied to me, but her eyes did not meet mine. The housekeeper turned to go, but I slowed her departure. "Mistress Hunt, is it true the Prince of Wales will be dining with us this evening?"

"Yes, Lady Isobel. And His Lordship has invited another guest to join you all as well." Mistress Hunt offered no more information than what she deemed necessary. I was surprised she even mentioned Father's unknown guest. Perhaps she thought that would affect my manner of dress.

"Will you ask my mother to send Edith back to me when she is finished with her tasks? I want her to assist me with my dress."

"Perhaps Ann would serve you better this evening," Mistress Hunt suggested.

I shook my head. "Mother will be wanting her assistance."

"Yes, Lady Isobel," the woman said without further argument. She then departed my room, but not before she pulled the curtains open further to expose the bleak sunlight that was struggling to shine through the window. "The rate this snow is coming down, His Lordship will not allow you to return to Whitehall anytime soon." She strolled out of the room, as if she had not just crushed my hopes and ruined any happiness I might experience for the rest of the day. I scowled, but she didn't see me, thankfully. According to Mother, young ladies should not scowl, but that didn't stop the frown from creasing my brow.

Chapter 6

Chadwyck House, London
February 1612
Isobel

Edith had just finished pinning my last curl in place when a commotion on the lawn caught our attention. "It sounds like a carriage, my lady." Edith ran to the window. I followed her, but not as speedily, as my skirts were cumbersome and hindered quick movement. The chambermaid unlatched the window and swung it open, leaning out as far as she could in order to see.

"Come away, Edith, before you fall." I tugged on her skirt to convince her of the danger, but she ignored me in exchange for a glimpse of the visitors. I tried again, "It's freezing out there. Close the window."

"Oh, my lady! Look at that carriage! Have you ever seen such a beautiful coach?"

"I see them all the time, Edith. You forget that I live at court most of the time." I peered over her shoulder, however, more interested in the personages exiting the carriage than the vehicle itself.

A coachman alighted and swung the door open. The first to exit was the Prince of Wales.

"Oh my!" Edith gasped. "Is that the prince?"

"Indeed." Excitement pulled at the corners of my mouth, and a fluttering sensation of butterfly wings exploded in my chest.

"He is magnificent," Edith said in a breathy tone. It was always a delight to see Edith witness new things. She threw herself into her new experiences with gusto. But I could not think of a time since I had met her in which she had been so awed.

I didn't respond, only admired the Prince of Wales from my perch high above their heads. After the prince, another nobleman exited, and he turned to offer a hand to another rider. When a lady departed the carriage, I felt a twinge of jealousy at the beautiful woman whose crimson skirts unfurled against the backdrop of crystal white snow beneath her.

"Who's that?" Edith asked, her voice still hushed.

"That is Robert Carr, the Viscount Rochester," I said. "He is quite the peacock." The viscount was comely enough with light eyes and a long face. He wore the same facial hair most men found in fashion at court: a charming ginger mustache in the shape of bird's feathers that stuck straight out on both sides of his face and a narrow strip of red hair that extended from his bottom lip to well past the bottom of his chin.

Shifting her attention from the nobleman, Edith said, "The lady is exquisite." Edith's face had turned a rosy pink in the winter air, and her nose looked red. A pang of pity struck me for the chambermaid. I loved pretty frocks and the jewels and hair trinkets that accompanied them. But Edith would never know the feeling of putting on such a lovely dress and experiencing the thrill it gave nor the satisfaction of having all eyes admiring her. That was a despairing thought.

I didn't know who the woman was, but I was glad to see it was the viscount and not the prince who helped her out of the carriage. She was beautiful, and there was something alluring that seemed to draw the viscount's attention. After the Lady, another young man unfamiliar to me stepped from the carriage. He was not as handsome as the prince and viscount who both dwarfed the other man by at least a head. He had a head of brown, tightly curled hair that puffed out on both sides of his cap. Small, closely set eyes swept upward toward the house, giving it an appraising look. I instinctively stepped back, feeling myself and my maid unwilling participants in his appraisal.

"They just keep coming." Edith laughed. "How many nobles can fit into one carriage?"

"Come away, Edith, before you catch your death," I said, cutting our observations short. I pulled the window closed and drew the curtains over them, separating us from the visitors and their prying eyes. I walked back to my wardrobe. "Help me pick out my jewels so I can go greet the guests."

"Yes, my lady," Edith said in resignation. "It is a lucky stroke that you chose to wear the cream brocade. If you are to attract the prince's attention, you'll need to shine brighter than crimson to catch his eye tonight."

I was the last to arrive at the supper table, which, to my displeasure, relegated me to the only remaining seat. Dining at Chadwyck House was rarely a formal occasion, and our father and mother insisted all their children dine with them. When I was younger, it was always great fun to see who got to sit next to the parent or sibling they preferred, with our Grandpoppy Thomas, our father's father, being the prized dining partner. I was almost always the last at the table. My brothers teased me that, had I been a boy, I might have stood a chance at getting first pick of seats. As it was, I rarely got to sit next to our grandfather, for dressing always took me the longest. I didn't mind, however, for I would never appear without a fully placed costume or anything that did not make my eyes sparkle and my complexion fair.

A furtive glance around the table had me locating the prince, for he was all that mattered to me this evening. He stood along with all the other men when I entered, and I tamped down the giant smile that urgently pulled at my lips.

"Gentlemen, Lady Essex, may I present my oldest daughter, Lady Isobel." Father motioned toward me when I entered, and I curtsied to the onlookers before my second oldest brother, Will, pulled my chair out, allowing me to be seated between my younger brother Harry and a stranger. This had to be the man that Edith had spoken of.

The men bowed and I took my seat, careful not to brush against the stranger with my skirts. He was clean, at least, but his face still bore the traces of the cuts and scrapes Edith had mentioned, and a large, purple bruise was forming around his left eye. He wore my brother's borrowed clothes, for I recognized my oldest brother Tom's matching dark blue doublet and trunks from last season. I would have to give Edith a lesson on her descriptions though. The stranger's hair was not auburn, but more the color of very dark copper, and the contrast of his hair against his ruddy, sun-kissed skin was admirable, given it was the dead of winter.

The men seated themselves as my father continued. "We are delighted to have Prince Henry with us this evening and his companions, Lord Robert Carr, the Viscount Rochester, Lady Frances Devereux, the Countess of Essex, and Rochester's friend, Sir Thomas Overbury," he said, motioning to each in turn.

Although I had already seen the countess from my chamber window, the sight of her in such close proximity was mesmerizing. Her crimson gown of jacquard was trimmed in gold and cinched high above the waist with a golden velvet ribbon. A lace reticella collar wrapped around the back of her neck, but the front of her bodice was cut so low as to practically lay bare her creamy bosom. Though she was beautiful, with a slim nose and dark brow, one's eyes were drawn to the pale flesh exposed above her low neckline and I noticed Tom, too, was distracted by her long, white neck—amongst other things. A wicked little twinkle lit his eye as he tried to get Will's attention from across the table. Will, for his part, ignored Tom entirely, keeping his eyes downcast and a stain of red upon his cheeks. He was destined for the church, as our grandfather had been, and I was glad to see he wasn't so easily swayed by a slice of pale flesh and a pretty smile.

"And I would like everyone to meet our other guest, Robert Scott." Father held out a hand toward the stranger, indicating the young man that sat beside me.

The stranger cleared his throat and sat up straighter, as if he were going to speak. But Mother beat him to it. "The Scotts are infamous reivers around the Border Region, are they not, Robert?"

His eyes flicked to my mother's. "Aye," he confirmed, but did not elaborate.

"What's a reiver?" My little brother, Harry asked, perking up. Anything strange and new to him always sparked his interest.

"They are thieves," I said, allowing the disgust to soak my words. Harry's eyes widened with further interest.

"Lawful thieves," Tom crowed excitedly.

"Government sanctioned retribution, more like," Will corrected. "It's only legal if you are stealing back what has been stolen from you. Am I correct, Robert?"

The man beside me looked even more uncomfortable now. "Ye are correct," he responded hesitantly. "His Majesty has allowed such reckoning when the need arises." Turning back to my father, he said, "Forgive me, Lord Stratford, I didnae intend to accept yer invitation under false pretenses, but my family name is not Scott. That is my half-brother. My name is Robert Stewart."

An awkward silence ascended the supper table. The Almighty Himself could have spoken from Heaven and still not have stopped the conversation the way this stranger just did. The young man must have sensed the uneasiness for he shifted in his seat again. What wasn't as obvious, and I'm sure this man didn't even notice, was when my father glanced at my mother, conveying some secret message only the two of them understood. I caught it nonetheless, and I wondered at the significance.

"A Stewart!" cried the prince, breaking the tension. He dropped his cup onto the table with enthusiasm. "Are we related, sir? For I too share your Scottish roots."

Robert leaned forward, discomfort rolling off him in waves. He set his spoon down beside his plate but did not release it. Instead, he turned the utensil over again and again as if thinking about his response.

"Aye, Yer Highness," he said coolly. "We are cousins. My father is Francis Stewart."

"Cousins!" Henry stood to his feet. "Let us embrace, dear cousin! It is most unfortunate we have never met before."

Robert cursed under his breath, and I snuck a glance at him. He did not move but rather sat gripping the arms of his chair causing his knuckles to turn white. I looked to Father, hoping to understand what was transpiring before us. My father wore a look of concern, but it was the way my mother's brow furrowed and the deep grooves of a frown pressed upon her mouth that gave me pause.

Henry strode toward Robert with a splendid smile lighting up his face. Robert, on the other hand, did not smile. Instead, a muscle ticked in his jaw as if he were clenching his teeth. When he made no move to reciprocate the enthusiasm, I prodded him.

"'Tis rude to ignore your prince, Master Stewart," I said, sotto voce. A slight turn of his head toward me indicated he heard my words, but he did not look at me nor did he answer. For a moment I feared he truly would insult the prince with his refusal, but when Henry reached Robert's side, he slowly stood to his feet and reluctantly embraced his cousin.

Prince Henry hugged him warmly, a delighted smile lighting up his face. For Robert's part, however, the man looked as if he had just drowned a sack full of kittens.

"You must come stay with me at Richmond Palace," the prince offered, releasing the man, and holding him at arm's length. "That is unless you have somewhere else you need to be." Henry's brow lifted as he studied Robert's blank face. "I wouldn't want to keep you from whatever business you have here in London."

Robert took a step back. He hesitated momentarily, then finally murmured, "I am honored, Yer Highness." Surely, I wasn't the only one who heard the strain in his voice. He sounded anything but pleased.

"Please, you must call me Henry. We are cousins, after all." Henry released his cousin and turned back toward his seat.

Thomas Overbury spoke up. "Your Highness, have you forgotten the trip you are to take three days thence? Your father is counting on your assistance."

The prince looked disappointed. "Ah! It slipped my mind." Turning to Robert, he said, "My dear cousin, I have forgotten. I am for Leeds in a few days. But my business there will not take long. Will you join me when I return?"

Robert lifted a pitcher to fill his cup. "Aye, I can cast myself upon the good graces of the Seven Stars until yer return. I have some business of my own I must attend to."

"Nonsense," my father spoke up. "There is no need to spend unnecessary coin. We have plenty of room here at Chadwyck House. Why don't you stay here?"

I choked on the sip of small ale that I was swallowing. I didn't want this man lurking around our home, especially if I was going to be stuck here for a while longer. And especially if Mother and Father had some secret knowledge of him that troubled them. He was an ungrateful ruffian, reluctant to accept the prince's offer of friendship. What man of no consequence would refuse such generosity from the Prince of Wales? And more troubling, why would Father extend his hospitality to such a man?

"Are you all right, Issy?" Harry questioned as he pounded on my back. I gasped for another breath but nodded my head.

The stranger reached for my small ale and handed me my cup. "Here, drink this," he commanded.

"That's what I choked on," I gasped out, pushing the cup away. He withdrew his offer and set the cup back down in front of me.

"What exactly is your business in London, sir?" My mother was never one to mince words. I could tell by her previous reaction she was troubled by Robert's presence in London, though I knew not why.

Father coughed, then laughed shortly. "Come now, my lady wife, Robert's business is none of our concern." He smiled but pinned Robert with a look that suggested the man not take advantage of Father's kindness.

He was spared having to answer by the opening of the double wooden doors and the appearance of the servants bearing trays of food.

"Is Grandfather not joining us this evening, Father?" Tom asked. I could have kissed Tom for steering the conversation into safer waters. But he didn't do it for my benefit. He was our grandfather's namesake and was always looking out for our grandfather when he was at home.

"Your grandfather decided to take a walk around the courtyard this morning and took a bad fall," our mother explained as she arranged her napkin on her lap.

"A fall? Is he all right?" Tom pushed his chair back as if to stand.

"He is a little bruised and battered," our father interjected, motioning Tom to sit down, "but there are no broken bones, thankfully."

"He is taking his meal in his chamber, Tom. You can check on him after supper," Mother continued.

"How was your first year at St Andrews, Tom?" Prince Henry spoke up as a slice of roasted venison was laid on his charger. The servant moved on to Rochester, and another servant spooned boiled artichoke onto the prince's plate.

Tom pulled his eyes from the door, probably still considering our grandfather. "It went well enough, though my marks are not as astounding as Father had hoped." A flash of white teeth emphasized Tom's charm, and his blue eyes twinkled in amusement.

"That is because you actually have to study, Tom," Father said, unruffled. Tom was following in our father's footsteps, studying law at the same university our father had attended. But I knew from the letters he sent home he wasn't the stellar student Father had been.

"I imagine sitting in a classroom is enough to bore you brainless," the prince said, laughing. "My offer to come to court and study with me, still stands, Tom. I have the best tutors in the British Isles and the continent. The world is our classroom."

I accepted a small piece of venison from the dish that passed before me as I listened to the prince.

"Your Highness," my father began, "your offer is generous and one that Tom would gladly take you up on. But he needs specialized instruction from men trained in law if he wants to pursue the path he has chosen. St Andrews is the best place for that. He just needs to take it a little more seriously."

Harry pointed out the dish of artichokes to me. The viridescent bulbs were swimming in some kind of buttery herbal sauce. I swallowed hard before waving the dish away toward the stranger without taking any. I should stop thinking of him as the stranger, since I knew his name, but I preferred to pretend I had forgotten it.

"Ye do not like artichokes, Lady Isobel?" the stranger asked as the green leaves were dished onto his plate. Edith had been correct. He spoke with a heavy Scottish brogue.

"No," I said simply, feeling the heat of the attention burning on my cheeks.

"She doesn't eat anything green," Harry offered by way of explanation. "She hates green." He grinned at me, and I squinted my eyes at him, mentally willing him to stop talking about it.

"Why do ye hate green?" Robert asked, as he reached for a roll from the many baskets of bread that sat on the table. Another servant offered a dish of honeyed carrots to me, and I allowed some onto my plate before the carrots were passed on to Robert.

I did not answer the man's question. My dislike of all things green had drawn unwanted scrutiny on more than one occasion, and I did not wish to elaborate on it to this man I did not know.

"You don't like carrots? I asked in return, indicating the vegetable he had just passed on without putting any on his plate.

"Nay because they are orange," he said. "I dinnae care for the taste." He looked at me then and I noticed his eyes were a faint green, like the color of a misty autumn morning right before dawn. Green eyes. All the more reason not to like him.

"Answer Robert's question, Issy," Harry prodded. "Tell him why you don't like green."

I sat my spoon down and reached for a roll. "I do not wish to discuss it, Henry," I said, with great emphasis on his given name.

He snickered. "Come on, Issy. It's nothing to be embarrassed about." He turned his attention back to Robert. "My sister has never liked green. She says it makes her skin crawl. It makes her nauseous, and she breaks out into sweats. I even saw her throw up once when our nursemaid made her take a bite of her peas before leaving the table."

"Henry, we do not discuss such things at the supper table," Mother scolded, also using Harry's given name. How she even heard the conversation from her end of the table was a mystery. I sent her a pleading look, begging her to intervene in this whole conversation, but it was the prince who spoke up next.

"Speaking of sickness, remember when you fainted last year at the Oberon masque? My heart nearly stopped when you sunk to the floor in the middle of the nymph dance. I was quite concerned for your well-being." His eyes were warm, and I felt the already burning heat in my cheeks move to scalding temperatures.

"I appreciate your concern, Your Highness," I said softly, "but it was really nothing to be worried about."

"I think it was. You did hit the floor quite hard." He took a sip of his hippocras then dropped his cup to the table, motioning to a servant to fill it once more.

"I must admit," began the Countess of Essex, "when you fainted, my love, I thought that would be the end of Oberon the Faery Prince. But the King's Players moved so swiftly and carried on so effortlessly, I would have thought they had dealt with fainting nymphs all the time."

Her voice was husky and low, and the languorous way in which she spoke lent an air of seductiveness to her words. I blinked at her, not knowing what to say, mesmerized by her sultry voice. I was unaware the countess had been at the masque. I had been consumed with my role, and I was enthralled with seeing the prince. I had not noticed much of anything else that night except for Henry and my part in the masque.

"I would never have forgiven myself if any harm had come to our dear Isobel," the prince said. I lifted my eyes to see him watching me with his intent, sky blue gaze, and I felt the warmth of that blue sky all the way to my belly.

"Whatever caused you to faint straight away, my dear?" It was the countess again. She held her cup close to her lips and swirled the wine around the rim as she watched me. "Were you terribly nervous in front of all those people?"

I pushed my carrots around on my plate, wishing I could just slip under the table and forget this whole conversation. But the countess had such a commanding presence, I found it hard to resist her pull.

"Maybe a little," I admitted.

"We think she had some kind of reaction to the lichen dye used on her skin," my mother explained. "She had red welts all over her body by the time we got all of that green washed off."

"My apologies for appointing the green dye, my lady." The prince appeared deeply repentant, laying a hand over his heart in sincerity.

"An oatmeal bath seemed to sooth her itchy skin, but it wasn't until I administered the persimmon leaf tea that she truly started feeling better," Mother added, unable to help herself.

"Mother," I implored, "please."

The countess spoke up again. "I have heard of your knowledge of herbs and tinctures, Lady Stratford. How wonderful you knew what to do." Mother smiled, but secretly I knew she was beaming.

"And didn't you say you felt dizzy and a little nauseous, Issy?" It was Will that time. Will who usually took my side in everything and helped me out of scrapes when I needed him. Throwing his lot in with the rest of the supper party, to completely humiliate me. Though, I don't think he meant to.

"Yes," I mumbled, not liking all the attention on my embarrassing aversion.

"You brave, brave girl," the countess said, sending me a friendly smile down the table. "Well, you didn't cause yourself injury when you fell, that is what matters most. And the redness is gone." Turning her attention toward the prince she said, "Lady Isobel looks quite fetching this evening, doesn't she, Your Highness?"

"Lady Isobel always looks fetching," the prince confirmed. "It is for this reason that she must return to court immediately, for I fear what drab old traditions might sneak their way back into the Palace of Whitehall without her presence."

"I hear the French hood has made an appearance in her absence," teased Rochester.

"Oh pish!" cried the countess. "You are a terrible tease, my lord." She leaned into Rochester, who sat right next to her and squeezed his arm in playful banter.

The prince laughed, but insisted, "Princess Elizabeth has already begged me to bring her back with me. I do pray Lord Stratford will release her and allow me to take her back."

An excited warmth blossomed under my skin. But I couldn't tell if Henry pleaded for my return for his own benefit or for the princess. "I can be ready to go within the hour, Father. Please, I've grown restless within the confines of this old house."

Father held his cup, as if to give a toast. "As soon as the weather clears, you are free to return."

I felt my shoulders sag in disappointment, then snuck a glance out the tall, lead-lined windows of the dining hall, to where the snow was still coming down. *Dear God, let the sun come out,* I prayed silently. I was itching to return to Elizabeth and see what I was missing at court. But I would not question Father any further at the table. Once the guests had retired, I would corner him before he went to bed and needle him about it until he let me go. It has always worked in the past. If Mother wasn't around to be the voice of reason, Father usually gave in to my pleas.

Chapter 7

Chadwyck House, London
February 1612
Robert

What had I gotten myself into? I hid nae only agreed to accompany the prince back to Richmond Palace upon his return to London, but I accepted Sir William's generous offer to allow me to stay at Chadwyck House while I saw to my business. A business that verra well could put my life in danger, and the lives of anyone that might be found associating with me.

I assessed my new situation while I unbuttoned the blue doublet Tom had let me borrow and laid it over a wooden chair that stood in the corner of my chamber. The room was comfortable, with views of the deer park that stretched behind the expanse of the house. Two rolling hills lay at a little distance and a thick forest of bare, knotty trees rose up beyond the knolls. Even though everything was covered in a thick layer of snow, it was easy to imagine the beauty of the landscape. The vast expanse of land, the rolling hills, and thick forests, they wurnae much different from the home I grew up in at Branxholme Castle. But the similarities ended there. Inside this house, there was love and happiness. That was evident in the way the earl's children all dined with him and his wife and the jovial atmosphere in which we supped.

It had been a relaxed supper, at first. The earl's family were nice enough with the exception of his oldest daughter who treated me as if I had the plague. But the glance the earl and his wife had exchanged with each other when I announced my name didnae go unnoticed. Couple that with the prince's blind acceptance of me as a long-lost cousin, and the evening had quickly turned uncomfortable. If the prince kent the real reason I had come to London, he widnae be so quick to extend an invitation to me. His father and mine were enemies. And it was his father, King James, that had driven mine into exile all those years ago. It was his father that was the reason I grew up without a father. And if his father didnae agree to lift the Earl of Bothwell's exile, I would be forced to take matters into my own hands. And that widnae end well for King James.

A knock at my door drew me out of my thoughts. I opened to find Tom smiling at me.

"Oh, good! You are still dressed. We are meeting in the drawing room to play games. Please say you'll join us."

I could feel the pit of my stomach clench into a tight ball. I wisnae in a mood to pretend niceties. "My apologies, but I really dinnae want to put that doublet back on. I think I ate a stone's worth of food this evening. It was feeling a wee tight by the end of supper."

"No need! It is not a formal occasion. My father and mother will not be attending. Just us young people. You are fine the way you are." Tom smiled again, and I could see his father in his lopsided grin.

I sighed my resignation. "All right. For just a wee bit though. I am tired." I glanced behind me, feeling as if I were forgetting something. Determining I was leaving nothing of importance behind, I pulled the door closed behind us.

"I told the prince as much," Tom said. "But he insisted I invite you."

He led me down the long hallway that connected the Great Hall at Chadwyck House to the drawing room where the others had agreed to meet after supper. Frame after frame of oil portraits lined the hallway, the faces of long-gone Englishmen and women and their sour faces staring down their noses at us. I resisted the urge to reach out and touch the satiny-smooth paint and instead focused on keeping up with Tom and his long strides down the hall.

"He is a generous lord," I finally said half-heartedly.

Tom chuckled. "He is used to getting his way. Very few find it easy to refuse him." We were immediately before the drawing room, and I hid nae time to answer before Tom opened the door.

Upon entry, four sets of eyes lifted to us. The prince and Viscount Rochester were seated at a long table. The countess, Lady Frances, was of course, seated next to the viscount. She seemed quite attached to him during supper and hid nae strayed far from him since. Overbury stood at the hearth, leaning a hand on the mantle, and staring into the fire. He glanced at me momentarily before resuming his study of the fireplace, his interest in me miniscule.

The only eyes that didnae look in my direction were Lady Isobel's. She sat in a large chair on the other side of the hearth. She held a book in her hand and studied it most earnestly. She slid a pale, slender finger between the pages of her book and lifted a page, turning it gently. She was one of the most beautiful creatures I had ever laid eyes upon. Moon-kissed blonde strands of gently curling hair were piled atop an erect head that sat upon a long slender neck. Her pale flesh bore no blemishes, or at least, none I could see. Large, luminous blue eyes sat below those dark lashes that now fluttered every few seconds as she read her page. A blush of pale pink dusted her cheeks and her tiny bow-shaped mouth, the color of red wine, was pursed in concentration, hiding the adorable little gap between her two front teeth. Another thing I observed while sitting so close to her at supper.

I thought of Moira and her wild, Scottish appearance. Fiery, wind-blown locks blown over a set of amber eyes. Brown freckles spotting her sun-drenched skin. Hands chapped and cracked from years of doing laundry and a spine slightly curved prematurely from the labor. She would scoff at the comparison I made between her and Lady Isobel, probably deprecating herself while disparaging the likes of a lady who had never performed a day of hard labor in her life.

"Robert, come join us," the prince urged from his spot at the table, startling me out of my reverie. Tom seated himself next to the prince as Rochester shuffled a deck of cards in his hands. I sat down on the other side of him.

"Overbury, you must join us," Rochester commanded.

Overbury looked away from the hearth once more. "Forgive me, my lord, but I am tired from the journey. I would like to be excused to find rest in my chamber."

"Nonsense," the viscount retorted. "You rested all day in the carriage. You must play. It is more fun the more players there are."

"Let him be, dear. He does look a little peaked." It was Lady Frances this time. She shot a look at Overbury, who did not appear a bit pleased that the countess was speaking up for him. Perhaps it was the slight she dealt along with it.

"Where is Will?" Prince Henry questioned.

"You know my brother," Tom explained. "He has some Latin text to interpret or some such ecclesiastical efforts to perform. He could not be persuaded."

"When I last saw him, he was sitting with our grandfather and conversing about whether the church should use an elder-led structure or be governed entirely by bishops," Lady Isobel offered, without lifting her eyes from her page.

"Lady Isobel," the prince called next. "You will join us, won't you? Tom, scoot down, let Lady Isobel sit next to me." Prince Henry motioned for Tom to move, and a great shuffling ensued.

Lady Isobel looked up from her book finally, the pink on her cheeks burning a shade brighter. She looked pleased with the invitation, especially coming from the prince's lips. The earl's daughter closed her book and stood, studying the table setting.

"I am feeling a bit outnumbered, aren't you, Lady Isobel?" Lady Frances laughed softly.

"Why don't I call for Edith. She knows how to play lansquenet. That will balance the sexes a little more and give us another player."

"The servant? Issy, really," Tom interjected. "What would Mother and Father think? And the prince?"

"Prince Henry won't mind, will you, Your Highness? She is a good girl and won't cause any trouble. Besides Mother and Father aren't here. They never have to know."

I felt my brow lift at that. She seemed the obedient type. I widnae have taken her to have a rebellious streak.

"Call the chit, I care not," the prince confirmed. Lady Isobel excused herself momentarily as Rochester began to deal the cards.

"Tom, scoot over again. Let Edith sit next to me," Lady Isobel called over her shoulder as she exited the room.

Lady Isobel returned in the blink of an eye, with her chambermaid, Edith, in tow. The maid's brown eyes were as wide as goose eggs as she followed her lady into the drawing room and sat down next to Tom, where indicated. She looked like a rabbit caught in a snare, until the prince spoke up. "Welcome, Edith. So, you know how to play lansquenet?

"Yes, my lord, err, I mean, Your Highness." She bit her lip nervously. "Lady Isobel taught me this game a long time ago."

"Ah, good. Then let us begin. The cards have already been dealt." The prince motioned to the maid's cards, lying face down in front of her. With a shaky hand, she picked up her cards and sorted them into order.

"Rochester, I do believe you are cheating," the prince accused after several rounds were played.

The viscount's brows lifted in innocence. "Why, I would never, Your Grace."

I glanced at the viscount's figures. He had been recording the scores while he was the dealer. I dinnae ken this man nor his temperament. But I ken men like him. They were too proud to take corrections, especially from the likes of me. I wisnae about to humiliate this coxcomb by catching him miscalculating—or cheating.

"Cousin, take another look at his figures," Henry demanded. "Do you see where the mistake was made?"

I grimaced. I wished the prince widnae drag me into this discussion, but I skimmed the tally sheet, nonetheless. It was just a simple mistake. "You have transposed these two numbers. That changes the whole sum down here." I pointed to where the viscount had made his mistake.

Rochester chuckled. "You see, Overbury. This is why you should have played. You always keep me in line."

Overbury, who had taken the seat Lady Isobel had vacated by the fire, stood immediately. "Forgive me, my lord. Shall I join now?"

"Nay, sir. It was a small error," I said. "There isnae reason for ye to bother yerself for such a simple mistake."

"Robert will keep you in line, my dear," Frances said. Her eyes slid to Overbury, who was still anxiously standing over the viscount.

"I had a feeling we could count on you, Cousin." The prince laughed the ordeal off, but there seemed to be a tension in the room that wisnae there moments before. "Robert," Henry continued, "you must drop the formalities if you are going to play with us. We are all equals at the gaming table."

"All except for you, Your Highness," Tom snickered.

"Hear, hear!" Rochester called out, lifting his cup in agreement. He appeared to be unaffected by my correction, so I allowed myself to relax a wee bit.

The play continued for several rounds, with each player taking their turn at being dealer.

"Edith, you forgot to record the points on your last turn," Isobel pointed out.

The maid's face ignited into a bloom of red. "Oh, my lady, I am sorry. I must have gotten carried away with the excitement."

"Do you need Robert to sit next to you to keep you on track as well, Edith?" Frances teased. "He is quite good at keeping the numbers in line."

Edith laughed softly. "Yes, perhaps," she said, touching my sleeve and flashing me a flirtatious smile. I stared at her, not bothering to return the gesture. I preferred to show my affections in private, not openly displayed for all to see.

"That won't be necessary," Isobel quipped. "Here, write this down. Tom had thirteen, Robert had six, Lord Rochester had eight, Lady Frances had twelve, and Prince Henry and I tied with eleven."

"That is amazing, Isobel. Ye have a mind for numbers." I truly meant to compliment her, but I could tell immediately I had caused offense.

"I have a good memory. And I would thank you to remember my title when you address me."

I blinked at her, feeling the chastisement burn on my ears. "Forgive me, Lady Isobel, I thought we were all equals at the gaming table."

"Come off your high horse, Issy," Tom scolded. "The prince himself invited Robert to drop the formalities."

The young woman pressed her lips together, as if fighting back harsh words. "Forgive me, I must have missed that invitation." She began gathering the cards quickly and shuffled them with record speed.

"I will call ye whatever ye wish, my lady," I said without heat. She nodded to me slightly but didnae speak. Instead, she dropped the deck of cards in front of Tom for him to deal.

"Robert, check the viscount's calculations again," Henry said. "I had thirteen last round, and he is showing me in last place. I am sure the only person ahead of me is Edith."

I looked at the viscount's tallies. He had transposed the numbers in three different places this time. I pointed to his mistakes, and he hurriedly scratched out the errors and rewrote them. When he switched the numbers on a correction, I pointed to it without word.

"You really must have your eyesight checked, my lord," Frances spoke up. Her eyes met mine, pleading with me to stay silent on what I had seen. But I kent what I had witnessed. The viscount had a bad habit of mixing up his numbers. I wondered how he managed to play secretary to King James with habits like these.

"I tire of this game," Lady Isobel complained. "Let us play something else."

"Charades?" Tom suggested, collecting all the cards, and putting them away.

"I pray ye'll excuse me, Yer Highness," I interrupted. "I have had a long, eventful day. I would like to retire to my chamber if it please ye."

"You do look as if you had an eventful day, Cousin. What happened to you, by the way? No doubt there were fisticuffs involved. Do tell."

I stood from the table. I had been wondering when this topic would come up. I kent from the looking glass in my bedchamber that I looked as if I had been thrown into a stone wall. My left eye was bruised and slightly swollen, and a large cut split my lip, making it twice its normal size.

I glanced around the table, gauging how much of the story I wanted to tell. "Just a little misunderstanding with a female patron at the Seven Stars. Or I should say, a misunderstanding with her suitor."

"I have half a mind to shut that place down," the prince said, standing to his feet.

"Dinnae bother, Yer Highness. The owner is an honorable fellow, though he did toss me head-first into the street. But I heard him tell the other man he wisnae welcome in his tavern anymore."

"I should say not," Tom blurted. "Did you keep your purse? Sometimes thieves do that to distract you from your coin."

"Aye."

"Well done, man," Tom slapped me on the back.

"Speaking of coin, I need to purchase a few pieces of clothing. Would you be available tomorrow to show me to a good tailor, Tom?"

"Of course," Tom said cheerfully. "But Issy is the real fashion expert. Perhaps we can persuade her to join us. She will have you looking like a fine popinjay along with the rest of us."

I slid a glance toward Lady Isobel who was in conversation with her maid. When she heard her name offered, her face blanched, and she looked as if she had just been asked to dress a corpse. "I believe Mother had something she wanted me to do on the morrow, Tom. I'm sure you can manage without me."

"Mother will understand," Tom said. "Besides, you owe me one, remember?" Tom exchanged a knowing look with his sister, and the aggravation could easily be read on her face.

"Fine," she spat out, then turned her attention back to Edith.

"It's settled then," Tom announced with a glowing smile on his face.

"Aye," I confirmed, resigned to the fact I would either be ignored or talked down to all day long. But I had dealt with insults my whole life. I could handle anything Isobel's pretty little lips could throw at me.

Chapter 8

Chadwyck House, London
February 1612
Isobel

As soon as Robert quit the room, the air seemed to lighten, and I could finally breathe. Everyone moved away from the table as the viscount poured himself and the countess a glass of wine. The prince still nursed his hippocras, and he grabbed his cup, bringing it with him as he seated himself beside me.

"You look lovely tonight, Lady Isobel." His blue eyes twinkled over the rim of his cup as he took a swig of his drink. "I don't think I have ever seen you wear that color before, but it looks beautiful on you."

I ran my hands over my lap, smoothing my skirts. I felt the heat burning on my cheeks and I couldn't look at the prince. Edith, bless her, spoke up in my place.

"I told her she would outshine any lady in that cream frock. The color blends so exquisitely with her milk-white skin."

"I concur." Prince Henry's words thrummed through me, and I finally found the courage to look up at him. His eyes burned with an emotion I had never seen there before, and I felt as if I were underwater, unable to take a breath.

"Edith, I think your purpose here is done," Tom suddenly said. "Our lady mother will be wanting your help putting Mary and Harry to bed."

My eyes shot to Tom, horrified. He was being rude to Edith. "The little ones have already been put to bed, Tom. Since when are you so concerned with our younger siblings?"

His brow furrowed. "Since you invited the servants to keep company with the prince and the viscount." My mouth fell open. This was not the first time Edith had joined us in an evening of games. Grant it, never with the prince.

But before I could reprimand him for his churlish behavior towards Edith, the maid spoke up. "I do have a few more tasks to complete before I retire for the evening. Thank you for inviting me to play." She curtsied to Tom then turned to our guests. "It was an honor to beat you at lansquenet, Your Highness." Edith's face glowed with amusement.

Prince Henry chuckled. "I'll pay you to keep that quiet, Edith. I don't think my reputation as a skilled military leader and learned prince of the realm could withstand the humiliation of losing to a... young maiden," he finished kindly. Edith giggled, a pretty blush coloring her cheeks.

After the maid departed, the viscount let out a breath. "Careful, Tom. You're trying a little too hard to be a brute." The company laughed, and Tom turned abruptly on the viscount.

"I assure you; I don't know what you mean."

"I think you do," the countess supplied. Tom opened his mouth, then shut it again, as if thinking twice about what he was going to say. It was obvious his boorish behavior toward Edith conflicted with the congenial personality he showed to everyone else.

"She forgets her place," he finally sputtered. "She hung on every word Robert said, then she started on the prince once Robert left. She couldn't keep her hands off Robert, touching his sleeve every time she spoke to him. I'll not have her pawing the crown prince as well."

"That's ridiculous," I scoffed, rolling my eyes.

Frances laughed one of her low, breathy chuckles. "Is it concern for your prince, or jealousy at the lack of her attention toward you? For I'm sure I saw her watching you most of the time."

Tom swiped a hand through his hair, shoving his dark locks away from his face. "That's absurd."

"Didn't your grandfather marry one of the Queen of Scots' maids?" The viscount teased. "Of course, he didn't have a title to worry about, but it wouldn't be the first time someone married below their station."

Everyone laughed again, and Prince Henry slapped Tom on the back, his blue eyes shining in merriment.

"What is happening here?" I cried. "Tom, what is he talking about?"

Tom swallowed, the sound of his gulp, pealing like a church bell. But instead of answering my question, he turned on me. "What is the meaning of your rude behavior toward Robert? He has been nothing but courteous to you since he stepped foot into our home, and you have treated him like a lecher."

I propped my hands on my hips in consternation. "I do not wish to speak of that man. I want to talk of Edith. What—"

"That discussion is closed," Tom cut in. I pressed my lips together. Anger burned in my chest, but I didn't want to argue with Tom in front of the prince.

Rochester spoke up. "Perhaps your sister has good reason to be wary of Robert Stewart. His father is a disgraced earl that tried to have His Majesty killed on several occasions."

Tom and I both gawked at the viscount.

"Killed?" Tom questioned.

"Disgraced earl?" I said at the same time.

"Indeed," Rochester answered.

"How do you know this?" Tom asked.

"I am the king's secretary, have you forgotten? It is my job to know everything about the king and those who put him in danger. Grant it, it was a very long time ago. When His Majesty was still king of only Scotland."

"Who is his father?" Tom spoke again.

"Francis Stewart, the fifth Earl of Bothwell."

"Of course." Tom shuddered, sinking into the chair next to me. "Father has spoken of Bothwell on several occasions. He almost got my father killed when they were younger."

I stared at Tom. The name Bothwell did sound familiar, but I couldn't really remember what I had heard about him. That would explain our parents' exchange of glances at supper.

I sat up straighter. I knew there was a reason I didn't like the man. Never mind that I am only now finding out the lecherous family he hails from. My treatment of this stranger was justified. If his family was an enemy of my family—of King James—then he deserved no kind gestures.

Prince Henry spoke up. "Surely, we mustn't judge the son based on the sins of his father. He seems like a decent fellow. I think we should give him a chance."

The countess moved to the prince's side. Lacing her arm around the prince's she said, "You have always been a just and wise prince, Your Highness. But do you really think he is not a threat here? Is Sir William and his family safe with him under their roof? And what about you? You have invited him to your court. Do you not think he has some sinister plan for being here in London?"

"I do not know his plans," Prince Henry said, disentangling himself from the countess's grasp. He moved to sit opposite Tom and stretched out his long legs in front of him. "But I think we do him a disservice to jump to conclusions. He has given no indication he has sinister intentions. Besides, if he is an enemy, isn't it safter to keep him close?"

"All the same," the viscount spoke up again. "It is best to be on your guard. The Earl of Bothwell was not only guilty of plotting to kidnap and overthrow the king on several occasions, but he is a known necromancer. His name came up often in the witch trials His Majesty oversaw in Scotland. How he managed to escape execution is a mystery. If he has passed his dalliances on to his children, then Robert is not only an enemy of the king but of the Almighty as well."

The countess and I gasped at the same time. "God forbid!" Frances breathed.

Lifting my chin, I focused my gaze on my brother. "Now do you understand why I don't like the man?"

Tom narrowed his eyes at me. "Oh, please! You are just now finding out all of these things about Robert's family. That doesn't explain why you have treated him like a leper since supper."

"It must have been her intuition," Frances offered. "We ladies know these things."

"I'm sure that's what it is. Besides, I don't have to have a reason. His wild, unrefined Scottish demeanor just irritates me," I said.

Tom's mouth fell open. "Careful, sister. Don't forget where you've come from."

Just then, the door opened, and for a moment I feared it was Robert Stewart returning. However, it was Edith again. Her eyes flitted about the room, and when they landed on Tom, she dipped her head and cast her eyes downward. "Forgive the intrusion my lord, but your lady mother wanted me to give this to Lady Isobel." He grunted in reply, then tilted his head in approval toward me. She handed me a folded note addressed to me in Mother's handwriting, then curtsied and backed away. I eyed my brother as Edith closed the door behind her, and the rest of our party snickered at Tom.

Pushing the possible implications aside, I opened Mother's missive. A huge smile split my face before I remembered to cover my mouth with my hand.

"It looks as though Lady Isobel has received some good news," Lady Frances said, watching me with her heavily lidded eyes.

"Yes," I replied, hopping to my feet. "It seems my brother is going to have to play nursemaid to our guest tomorrow all by himself. I am to leave with you. Father has approved for me to return to court."

"A wise decision," the countess spoke again. "It is probably best not to leave his lovely daughter shut away in this quaint house, especially with such a scoundrel as Robert Stewart."

"I hardly think we can call him a scoundrel just yet," the prince spoke up. "He has not given us reason to think his motives for being in London are anything but amicable."

"Well, it matters not to me," I said, still smiling. "I won't be here to worry about him."

Chapter 9

Palace of Whitehall, London
February 1612
Isobel

In the end, I did not return to court with Prince Henry and the rest of his party. Father wanted to deliver me to Whitehall Palace himself, for he had something he wanted to speak to the king about. I only let the disappointment of not travelling with the prince worry me a little while, for it was still good to be back at court, and I would let nothing steal my joy.

Mother accompanied me to my rooms, and I squealed with delight when we reached my chamber and found three new dresses awaiting me.

"Queen Anne is very good to ye," Mother commented, watching me with a leery eye as I held up one of the new dresses, a crimson frock in almost the same color as what Lady Frances had worn to our supper. I spun around in a circle, letting the bright ruffles and creamy lace flare out in an arch in front of me.

"Mother, I am a reflection of the queen's benevolence. If I am to be maid of honor to Princess Elizabeth, then I must be the best dressed lady at court, next to Her Highnesses themselves." I laid the crimson dress on my bed and motioned for one of my maids to help me undress. "I want to try this on, Betsy."

My mother watched as Betsy and another maid, Jane, helped me into the new frock. She sighed heavily before seating herself on the mauve sofa in front of the tall, narrow windows that adorned my chamber. "This whole idea of sending you to court was your father's. I wanted nothing to do with the scheme."

I glanced at Mother, keeping one eye on the looking glass as Jane adjusted my dress. "Well, thank the Almighty for a sensible father," I said, laughing lightly. Mother scowled, and I immediately realized the impertinency of my words. Pulling away from the maids, I hurried to my mother. Kneeling before her and taking her hands in mine, I said, "I am sorry. I meant no insolence. But surely you can see the wisdom in Father's decision. Here at court, I am seeing and doing a lot of things I could only dream about if I were cooped up at Chadwyck House. And when the time comes, I will be better able to find a suitable match."

My mother's eyes dampened with worry. "Chadwyck House is safe, dear. Here at court—" she paused, looking around my chamber then over her shoulder to the courtyard that sat below my window.

When she didn't finish, I spoke up. "Chadwyck House is not safe. Not while Robert Stewart is in residence there."

Her eyes shot back to mine. "What do ye mean?"

I rose and seated myself next to her on the sofa. "Mother, there is no sense in trying to protect me anymore. I am old enough that you and Father no longer need to keep secrets. I know all about who Robert is, and why Father should never have invited him to stay with us. Especially after finding out who Robert's father is."

Mother squeezed my hands, then lifted one of hers to lay it against my cheek. "Ye were always such a smart lass." She patted my cheek then dropped her hand to her lap. "Your father likes to see the best in people, likes to *believe* the best about people. He is a fair and just man and that quality has served him well since coming to England."

It certainly had served him well. Father and Mother had fled to

England before they were married, because of some disagreement between him and King James. He soon found himself at Queen Elizabeth's court, and he built a respectable practice pleading cases in the Queen's Bench and the Exchequer. Queen Elizabeth witnessed him plead a particularly difficult case against the crown which led him to being invited to the Queen's Counsel. His years of faithful and impressive service led to the title bestowed upon him as the Earl of Stratford, a rare honor few who were not born into nobility ever saw.

"Do you think Robert is a necromancer like his father?" I asked, getting right to the point.

Mother's eyes darkened. "I nay know. From what I understand, the Earl of Bothwell was exiled from Scotland before his last son was born. I doubt the young man has ever met his father."

A twinge of sympathy squeezed at my heart momentarily, but I tamped it down. I would not feel sorry for this man. I loved my father dearly and could not imagine growing up without knowing him. But my father wasn't an evil man. The Earl of Bothwell was a notoriously malicious man. No doubt his sinister blood ran through Robert's veins as well. Like father, like son.

"I'm glad Father sent me back to court. I have no desire to sup with that man every night," I said as I stood to my feet.

"I can tell ye," Mother said slowly from her seat in front of the window, "Robert is not the reason your father sent ye back to court."

I twirled away from where I admired my new dress in the looking glass. With anticipation surging through me, I said, "You know something you aren't telling me."

Mother looked away at that, busying herself with an imaginary piece of lint that clearly did not exist on her skirts. "What do ye mean?"

I ran back to her. "You are hiding something from me. What was the true reason Father sent me back to court? I thought he'd wait until spring to allow my return."

Mother's brows knit together as she folded layers into her skirts with antsy hands. It was unnerving to see my bold mother appear nervous. This was the same woman who never hesitated to speak her mind. In fact, I prided myself on the fact I inherited my boldness from this brave Scottish woman.

She opened her mouth to speak, then closed it once more. "Mother," I said sternly, feeling as if I were the parent and she the child keeping a secret.

"There are certain lords that have been urging your father to put your name forth as a possible wife for Prince Henry."

My heart began pounding in my chest. Could the one dream I had held so close to my heart become a reality? Could I really be the wife of the most beloved crown prince in all of Europe?

Mother stood and took my hands again. "I didn't want to say anything to ye, Isobel. I know how much the prince means to ye."

It was true. Stories of Prince Henry had filled my head since I was a small child. Stories of how lovely and smart he was. Stories about his devotion to the true faith. And of course, stories about how handsome he was. I had fancied myself in love with him before I ever even met him. And when I came to court at the age of twelve, we became friends even though we lived at different courts due to Their Majesties' living arrangements. But it wasn't until I saw him again at the Oberon masque that my feelings were made plain. He looked magnificent that night dressed as the faery prince, and I lost my heart from that day on. My joy could not be contained now. I hopped up and down and squealed, "Mother, don't you see, this would be a dream come true!"

My sensical mother kept her calm. "Isobel, ye have to realize the chances of the king accepting ye as a possible suitor are miniscule. And with the queen it is even less likely. She is very protective." She looked at me with such sympathy that I immediately pulled my hands away.

"But Queen Anne loves me. She is always buying me dresses and inviting me to sit at her side when the princess is occupied elsewhere. She even mentioned to me at Christmas time she had been considering possible suitors for me, for it was time to think about marriage."

Mother turned her nose up at that suggestion. "Ye are still young. There is plenty of time to find a suitor."

"But Mother, this is the perfect solution." I twirled once more in my dress, catching a glimpse of the crimson skirts in the looking glass as they twirled around me.

"Isobel," Mother stated coolly, "ye must recognize ye come from a family that is not as—noble—as others here in England. Your father has been given a courtesy title; your bloodline is not noble enough to be married to a prince of England. Not to mention, even after all these years, relations between your father and King James are still strained. I do not believe the king will ever allow the match." Anger suddenly surged through me. Of all people, my parents should believe in me and my capabilities. Did my own mother have no faith in me and my ability to win the king and queen's favor? She continued, "Besides, your father might have high expectations of your marriage prospects, but I just want ye to remain true to yourself. To be comfortable with the fibers that make ye who ye are and to not forget your roots."

I lifted my chin. "*This* is who I am. And it is uncharitable of you to doubt the ability of your first-born daughter to make a suitable match. I do not wish to discuss this subject with you any longer."

A mixture of hurt and irritation shown on my mother's face. But before she could reply, a knock sounded at the door. Betsy moved to open it, and to my surprise, the Countess of Essex stood on the other side.

"Lady Frances, how nice of you to greet me. When did you arrive?" I curtseyed to the countess then folded my hands and sat demurely on the divan as I had been taught.

The countess stepped into the room, and the whole atmosphere changed. The anger I felt at Mother's words melted away, and I suddenly felt hopeful. Lady Frances was so beautiful and graceful, and she had plied me with compliments all evening when she last supped with us. Surely, she could see the value in me and believe a match between me and the prince was a possibility.

"We've been back since this morning, Lady Isobel. It is your carriage that was slow to arrive," she said with a laugh.

"Yes," I said. "Father had some other business to take care of before we arrived at Whitehall. We have only just arrived."

Her eyes lit on my dress, and she stepped closer to me. "Lady Isobel, you look exquisite in crimson. You'll have a string of suitors unable to take their eyes off you."

I smiled, unable to help myself, before placing a hand over my mouth to hide my gap. "It is kind of you to say so." I slid my eyes toward my mother who was still standing behind me. "What about the prince? My mother seems to think I don't stand a chance with him."

"That is not what I said, Isobel. Do not twist my words." Her voice shook slightly, and I knew I risked her ire.

Frances tapped her chin in thought. "He does have a long list of possible brides, but I'm sure you can snag his attention with some help."

My mother spoke up again. "Not to mention, Isobel is only ten and seven. We should wait a few more years and visit this topic again."

"Oh pish," the countess said, waving Mother's concerns aside. "I was ten and five when I was wed. It's never too soon to start thinking about a young lady's future."

My brows lifted involuntarily. "You are married? I did not know."

She chuckled, deep and throaty. "Yes, well, it is a situation I am trying to remedy."

A strangled sound came from the direction of my mother, but I was fascinated. "Why are you trying to remedy that?"

My mother took a step forward. "Isobel, that is a private matter. Do not intrude on the countess's personal business."

Lady Frances regarded Mother. "It is all right. I've not kept it a secret that I do not like my husband, the Earl of Essex. He is not very dashing." She smiled broadly, showing all her teeth at once. I giggled, and she joined me in laughter.

"I hardly think looks determine the quality of a husband," Mother said, pressing her lips together in consternation.

"No, but they do make the marriage bed more enjoyable. Surely you can relate to that, Lady Stratford, for Lord Stratford is quite handsome, even if a little too old for my taste."

I sucked in a breath, feeling embarrassment burn on my face. My father was handsome, but I wasn't sure how I felt about a young, beautiful countess speaking of bedding him.

"Thank the Almighty for that," Mother shot back.

The look on Lady Frances's face was hard to read. She should have been insulted by my mother's words, by the tone of her voice. But instead, she appeared to be amused.

"Never fear, Lady Stratford. I have my eyes set on a more eligible man. Your husband is safe with me."

"I've never doubted my husband's fidelity, Lady Frances. He's had his chance at beautiful noble ladies before. Don't flatter yourself."

"Mother!" I gasped, appalled at my mother's behavior. "I'm sure Lady Frances meant no insult." My eyes shot to the countess. I expected her to be offended but instead a slight smile pulled at her mouth.

"Oh dear. I fear I've overstepped," said the countess.

Mother didn't reply, but the look on her face spoke volumes. In an effort to quell the growing awkwardness, I said, "Lady Frances, can you suggest what jewels to wear with this crimson frock? I think I might wear it to supper tonight." I pulled her over to my jewelry casket and opened the lid.

"I am going to find your father. I shall see ye at supper, Isobel." Mother moved toward the door, and Lady Frances glanced her way.

"It is best to stay close to your earl, Lady Stratford. Not every woman at court is as trustworthy as I." She batted her lashes at my mother.

"I've never had trouble keeping my earl satisfied," Mother shot back. "Perhaps you should just worry about your own." My mouth fell open at my mother's impudence. Was she making a reference to Lady Frances's own marriage? But before I could say anything, she swept out of the room in a rustle of silk skirts.

"I am so sorry, Lady Frances. Perhaps I should have warned you that my mother is a silver-tongued Scots' wife that will fillet you alive with her words, then apply an herbal remedy to nurse you back to health."

The corners of the countess's lips curled into a mischievous grin. "I do love a good spar." She picked up a cameo with a Greek motif of three women lounging around a solitary man who was sitting under a tree. The three fates were admiring the man, Princess Elizabeth had explained to me when she loaned the necklace to me. It was encompassed with tiny diamonds and seed pearls that stuck out around the circumference and was hung from a tiny gold chain that also hung from a larger pearl at the top. "Your mother is rather—" she paused then looked to me, apparently trying to gauge my tolerance for insults. "Feisty. And when it comes to the topic of marriage, she's a bit old-fashioned."

Relief flooded my chest. I had feared what she would say about my mother. But I was relieved we saw things the same way.

"I agree," I said, pulling out a large diamond and ruby necklace from the casket. "She doesn't understand what it means to live at court."

"Of course not. Isobel—may I call you Isobel? For I would love if you called me Frances." Sincerity oozed from her hazel eyes, and I was drawn to her even more.

"I would be honored," I said, feeling the warmth of her approval spreading over me.

"Isobel, your mother does not understand the pressures of looking your best and making the best impressions at court. She has never had to do that. She was fortunate in that way. And I don't mean to make you feel uncomfortable, but your father is a handsome man. She is lucky to have such a man give her his attentions. She doesn't have to worry about keeping his interest. Everyone knows the earl to be smitten with his countess, even after all these years." Frances held up two diamond drop earrings at my earlobes and studied the look.

"My mother was—is—a beautiful woman," I said, swallowing the knot in my throat. "I don't think it's difficult to believe my father would remain faithful to her." I shifted my feet as I stood under the countess's scrutiny. Talking of my parents in this way was a little unsettling.

"Don't get me wrong, love. The Countess of Stratford is an attractive woman, even if she is a little rough around the edges. I suspect that has to do with her Scottish upbringing. Your father was raised at King James's court from the time he was a boy. He has a more polished edge about him. Not to mention, he is extremely attractive, kind-hearted, and noble."

"You seemed to be enthralled with my father's good looks." I laughed, but I wasn't sure of the joke.

The countess threaded the diamond drop earrings into my ears and stood back to study me once more. "All I am saying is your mother does not understand the pressures we ladies at court are under. She has her earl. We, on the other hand, must do everything within our power to secure the best possible match." She laid her hands on my shoulders and turned me around to face the looking glass. I admired my figure wrapped in crimson silk and topped with diamonds. "You are going to be the most beautiful woman at court, Isobel," she whispered in my ear. "And the prince won't be able to take his eyes off you. You're sure to capture his heart wearing this dress."

"Are you sure I have a hope?" I asked, taking a deep breath. The unease that sat like a rock on my chest since Mother had voiced her doubts was finally starting to dissipate.

"Most certainly," Frances said, flashing me a wicked little smile. "Especially if you have my help." Excitement blossomed in my chest, and I returned her impish smile with one of my own. "But I may have to ask for your help with something in return."

"Me?" I asked, puzzled. "But what could I possibly help you with?"

"Oh, we'll talk of that later," she replied as she pinched my cheeks gently to bring color to my face.

Chapter 10

Richmond Palace, London
March 1612
Robert

I liked the men Henry kept at court. They were jovial and friendly and nothing like I expected the royal court to be. But more importantly, I liked the prince, and I found myself wondering, not for the first time since joining Henry at Richmond Palace, what it would be like to make a life here. Henry would be king one day and surprisingly, the thought of serving him didnae turn to ash in my stomach as the prospect of serving King James did. I listened to the men's banter as we readied our horses until something odd caught my attention.

"Yer Grace," I said, noticing his saddle looked awry. "Something is amiss." I peered closer. "One of yer buckles is broken. It is hanging limply. Unless ye forgot to buckle it." I pointed to one of the straps, and the prince hopped off his horse to investigate.

"It isn't the buckle. The girth is torn. How did I not notice that before? I'll have to replace the saddle." Henry began unbuckling all the straps he had just fastened. "It's going to be a few minutes gentlemen."

I slid off my horse to offer my assistance. "Where is yer hostler?" I said as I pulled a strip of leather back through the buckle. Two stable boys were meandering about the yard. One carried a bucket and the other a shovel, but there seemed to be no sense of urgency about their business. A couple of men leaned against the wall at the far end of the stables, laughing at something one of them had said. They didnae look busy. In fact, they looked quite at their leisure. There appeared to be no one in charge of the stables, nor seeing to the tasks that needed to be done.

"One has not been appointed since I gained my own court. My father promised me he would assist me in seeking out a Master of the Horse, but I fear the task was not a priority. I must speak to him about this though for I fear the stable hands are rather lost without the guidance of a master." He nodded toward the young men lounging at the other end of the yard as he loosened the last strap. "Even so," he said, pulling the saddle from his mount, "I should have recognized the faulty girth."

"Allow me," I said taking the saddle from his hands. I peered at the fastenings for a moment then said, "I'll be right back."

Moments later I returned with another saddle. It was less elaborate than the first but well-made and sturdy. I ran my hand over the supple leather as I crossed the stable yard. The smell of freshly rendered leather filled my nose, momentarily conjuring memories of Branxholme Castle and my childhood there. Horses had been my escape from torturous siblings that saw me as an easy target for their harassment. Lord Scott's hostler, an aged man with more patience than the coin he was compensated, allowed me to spend hours in the stables, bombarding him with questions and learning all I could about the ins and outs of stable life. And when Walter taught me how to ride, I rarely stayed home long enough to get under foot or become an older sibling's punching bag. I even held onto childish dreams of riding off to rescue my father. I would bring him home and be the hero of the family.

The beginnings of a scheme germinated in my mind as I tossed the new saddle onto Hercules' back. I needed a way to support myself and give me a reason to stay in England. If I was going to carry out my plan of seeking the king's mercy for my father, I also needed to build trust. I didnae want to give the king any reason to be suspicious of me or my request. Nor any reason to deny it. I would serve the crown as best I could, and when he saw me as a loyal, Scottish subject, hopefully he would grant my petition. It had worked for Viscount Rochester. He had come up from Scotland, attended a joust and broken his leg while he was here, and now he was the king's secretary. I had been hoping I could find a position at court that could keep me close to the king. But without injury to my person.

"The girth is split clean in two," I explained as I began strapping the saddle to the prince's horse. "Ye are going to need a man skilled in leatherworks to mend it." I then added, "Even so, ye shouldnae use that saddle on this horse."

A thin line creased between Henry's brows. "Why is that?"

"The saddle tree width is too wide for this steed, making the saddle rest too close to the withers. Ye will hurt the horse by putting too much pressure on his back." I slid my hand under the top of the saddle. "A good fitting saddle doesnae touch the withers, neither does it sit too high."

"You know a good deal about horses, I see," the prince said with true interest in his voice. When I didnae concur, he said, "Where did you find this saddle, Cousin? I've never seen it before." He ran a hand over the saddle in appreciation. "I like it."

"In the tack room. Ye've got another one hanging in there similar to this one, in a deep mahogany. But it willnae fit yer horse's gullet either."

"No?" he said as he watched me at my task.

"Perhaps another steed but nay Hercules." I finished fastening it on and took a step back. "Try it out, Yer Grace."

He mounted himself Tonya and grabbed the reins. "That could have ended very badly for me—and Hercules. Thank you, dear cousin."

I ignored the swelling in my chest at the simple compliment. As the youngest child in a houseful of fatherless children, I had had my fair share of grappling for attention and seeking approval from a man who gave his praise sparingly. Only my mother saw the good in me, what little there was.

"Yer Grace." I seated myself once again on my mount. "May I seek a boon from ye without ye thinking my assistance held some ulterior motive?"

The prince cast a mischievous look toward me. "If you are seeking recompense for saving your prince's life, I should think I might be worth at least a little reward."

"I would help without compensation, Yer Grace. But what I seek only entered my head upon learning ye have no Master of the Horse."

Understanding seemed to light up Henry's face. "And you seek to place yourself in such a position?" His eyes flashed with a teasing not unlike that which I had experienced at the hands of my siblings. Yet, he was a fair prince, and I sensed no sinister motive in him.

"You would be perfect for the position!" Tom beamed at me. "Then you could stay on in London a while longer."

"It would be an honor I am nay worthy of obtaining. Yet, I am an excellent choice, raised and trained to ride by one of the best horsemen in Scotland, the Lord Buccleuch of Branxholme Castle. Nay man can fault my skill with horses, and my riding is unmatched. I would serve ye with fervor."

Henry assessed me judiciously. It wisnae the first time I had been weighed in the balances, yet I wondered what a prince such as he must think of a begging ruffian such as myself. I made many mistakes in my life. As a reiver I stole cattle and supplies and wreaked havoc. I even murdered three men. And I failed to protect the woman I loved. I didnae always measure up to my brother's expectations, nor my own, but a horse was the one thing I was confident in. So, I stood up straighter and held his gaze, sure of this one ability at which I was extremely adept.

"So, you plan to make a life here in England then?" A fat drop of rain splattered on Henry's sleeve, and he brushed it off absent-mindedly.

I liked—respected even—my princely cousin, but there were things about my purpose here I wisnae ready to share just yet. Instead, I said, "I have some business in London that might require an extended stay. I will gladly give up the position, should ye find someone better suited for the position than me." I swiped my hand through my damp hair, then adjusted Boudica's reins.

"I am quite curious about this business you speak of." It was Harington. He had been friendly enough to me since our first meeting a couple of weeks ago, but he eyed me now as if he thought I was a danger. Good for him. He was right to question my motives. And I understood his protection of the prince, but that didnae mean I wanted to give him any more information than I had already given.

"Harington does have a point," said the prince. "And if I am taking you into my court, then I have a right to demand knowledge of it. My father would. But for the moment, I will respect your privacy. And give you this one concession."

"That is kind of ye, Yer Grace," I said, refusing to look away from his eyes that seemed to miss nothing.

"This is a lofty position you aspire to," the prince said. "Historically, the Master of the Horse has been appointed from the most prestigious families in England. Men of great esteem who have shown themselves worthy of such a title. And to that, I am not sure what my father would make of me setting the appointment without his knowledge or input."

I ran a hand over my chin before speaking. "Ye ken it doesnae get much more noble than the House of Stewart," I said, watching his reaction. His mouth quirked up as he considered my words. "And forgive me, but I would think ye have the authority to make changes to yer own court, Yer Grace. After all, His Majesty the king saw fit to make ye lord of yer own household. Surely, he trusts ye to make the right choices for yerself and yer subjects."

"Careful there, Robert," Harington cut in. "Or you'll be accused of promoting the prince's authority over His Majesty's." His eyes danced with amusement.

"We certainly cannot have that," Tom added. "That accusation has already been tossed around more than I care to recall."

Henry didnae speak, but I could see his well-trained eyes assessing my every quality and all my lack.

"I'll not have you living in the mews. I must insist you live within the palace walls," he finally said.

I cocked my head. "Surely it would make the most sense to live within the mews with the rest of the staff."

"I cannot deny it has been nicely furnished and is a fine place for the Master of the Horse to dwell. But I have only just met you, dear cousin. You are family, and I have already come to value your friendship. I must insist you stay close by my side. It would make me most happy."

"Verra well," I said, bowing my head to him. My mare struck at the ground with her hoof, impatient to get moving. "I dinnae wish to be a burden to ye. I only desire to make myself useful. But if that is yer wish, then I must yield to yer command."

Henry's eyes lit up, as if he had just struck a valuable bargain. "Good," he said, "it is settled then." And he adjusted the reins of his black steed and turned him about in the direction in which he wished him to go.

The prince struck a magnificent pose atop his mount. He was the epitome of a goodly prince with his lean torso and narrow shoulders. His spine was as straight as a branding rod, and he held his head high. I observed the same pride and sense of purpose in him that could be seen in Walter. It was the persona of a man who kent his destiny and his place in this world.

Those were the traits ingrained in him. He was also blessed with a straight nose and a fair brow, strawberry blonde hair that fell to his shoulders and clear blue eyes. His features, coupled with his confidence, made him the desire of half the courts of Europe. I might have been jealous of such a man, if he didnae have a fairness of mind and strength of spirit, that made him such a likeable prince.

"You're gawking, Robert." Tom eased up beside me with a ridiculous smirk on his face. "We have a hard enough time keeping His Highness humble as it is. If he thinks he's handsome as well, his head will swell, and he'll never fit through the door of the Boar's Head."

The others laughed, and Prince Henry smiled sheepishly. "I am grateful for the life and limb with which our Creator has blessed me." The men groaned, and I watched as my companions for the day, excluding the prince, brushed the back of their right hands over their left shoulders three times in unison.

My face must have shown my confusion because Harington explained, "We brush off the prince's faux humility lest we too become infected with its nocuous venom."

"They taunt me so," Henry lamented, but the smile on his face led me to ken it was all in good fun.

"Congratulations, Robert. I am glad you have decided to stay on in England for a spell," Tom said. He genuinely looked pleased with my arrangements. Then looking around, he said, "I say, where is Essex?"

"He'll be here," Harington explained. "He is always late."

"Fashionably late, mind you," said a voice from behind us.

I turned in my seat to see another man sauntering toward us on his black steed with the grace and agility of a well-trained rider. He was rawboned with a gaunt face and large, dark, sunken eyes. He had a head full of dark hair, and he was dressed fully in black from sleeve to boot, with a starched, white ruff fastened round his neck, and lace cuffs, curling above the sleeves of his doublet. A large, teardrop pearl dangled from his left ear.

"Of course," Harington acknowledged, pulling up on the reins of his bay to widen our circle and allow the man and his horse entrance. "Essex, may I introduce to you, Robert Stewart, the king's cousin. Robert Stewart, this is Robert Devereaux, the Earl of Essex."

Essex blinked at me slowly then nodded. "It's a pleasure," he murmured.

"Essex. Any relation to the Countess of Essex?"

The laughter that had rang out just moments before the earl's arrival seemed to have dissipated in the wind. The awkward silence was almost palpable, and I immediately perceived I had said something out of turn.

"If you mean that loathsome, pompion-kissing giglet, then yes. She is my wife."

My eyebrows shot up in amusement. From what I remembered of Lady Essex, she was a pleasant enough woman. Albeit she was a little flirtatious and generous with her praise of Rochester. And she hid nae spoken of a husband at all.

Harington leaned into me again. "That is a touchy subject. The less said on her, the better."

"Gentlemen, shall we ride?" Henry called. "I have a meeting with a man I am considering for the position as headmaster of my new riding school. And I'm sure we can find some diversions that will get our minds off the Festering Wound."

"The countess, Lady Essex," Harington whispered to me by way of explanation as we maneuvered our horses out of the courtyard and onto the main thoroughfare. When I looked to him for clarification, he said, "She is referred to as the Festering Wound. We do not say her name."

I shook my head, chuckling. This was an interesting lot I had found myself attached to. And one I widnae have dreamed of two months earlier. But I wisnae mad about it. In fact, I was rather pleased with myself for having landed such a situation. What would Lord Buccleuch think if he could see me now?

Chapter 11

Eastcheap
March 1612
Robert

Eastcheap was far different from the area of Westminster where Tom had taken me for a new suit of clothes. Instead of fine shops of porcelain and jewelry and rich fabrics, Eastcheap offered weaponry, leatherworks, and woolen goods. The air was foul here, and the streets were choked with people who trudged along in the muddy quagmire of melting snow and ill-drained gutters. Copper pots for cooking and other sorts of crockery were displayed alongside lengths of ribbon and lace that danced happily in the early spring breeze. We lumbered our way along the street until the prince stopped outside a white-washed structure enforced with black, tar-covered beams. In fact, many of the structures in this part of London were built in the same fashion: timber-framed edifices painted in some shade of white. It was a slightly cheerier contrast to the gray stones that made up the streets and buildings of Edinburgh, but less appealing than the wealthier end of London on the other side of the bridge.

The building towering before us had two jettied floors and held a large black sign pinned above the door, where the shape of a boar's head, painted red, graced the entrance. Prince Henry dismounted, followed by the others. I was the last to unseat myself as I took in the surrounding buildings. Tom patted me heartily on the shoulder. "You ready?"

"How many taverns does this city have?" I questioned, counting three just within the short distance from where we stood.

"Twenty-nine, to be exact," the prince said.

"Are we counting inns and brothels?" asked John Harington.

"Too many to count," said Tom.

They all spoke at once. I looked to Essex for his two pence worth, but he just stood there observing the tavern sign, looking a little unsure of his decision to come.

"If she makes an appearance, we shall leave," Henry said, coming to stand next to Essex.

"I wasn't thinking about the babbling dish cloth," Essex replied. I chuckled at the earl's chosen names for his estranged wife. "I say, do you think Lucy is still in service here?"

"Only one way to find out," Harington said, motioning toward the tavern door.

We were immediately hit with the strong yeasty smell of ale. The brightness of the sun reflecting off the melting snow outside didnae prepare us for the darkness that enveloped us as we stepped into the tavern. I squinted at the large fire that burned in a hearth set in the middle of the room. The fire was the only source of light, as the windows that lined the front of the tavern were too small and dingy to let sunlight in. Tables, both long and round, with rectangular benches were dispersed haphazardly across the room. Almost every available seat was taken by a man with a mug of ale in hand and a wench on his knee.

Henry led us toward the back of the tavern where another group of men were drinking. From the sounds of it, they had been here for quite some time and were already in their cups. I marveled at the prince's choice of company, as the men here looked a bit rough around the edges. I felt right at home.

"Prince Hal!" A dark-haired man with a receding hairline and locks that fell to his shoulders shouted, lifting his cup in salute. He looked to be about the age of Lord Stratford, but without his impeccable taste in clothing. Two other men sat with him, all about the same age, and all looked as though they had been in the middle of a writing frenzy. Pages of foolscap lay scattered about, and their fingers were stained with black ink. The man with the receding hairline even had smudges on the ruffle of his tunic that stuck out from beneath a brown leather jerkin. It didnae take long to realize these men wurnae in their cups, they were drunk on the wine of their words.

Henry smiled widely as he reached the men and patted the ink-stained man on the shoulder. "Behold, what hath the feline craftily conveyed!"

"Ha!" the man cried. "Henceforth let thine moggies play!"

Henry laughed heartily as we seated ourselves round the table. I watched once again the intercourse between the prince and his friends. He had a presence that set those around him at ease. And amongst his friends there seemed to be a comradery only they could understand.

John Harington, seeing the confusion written all over my face, leaned toward me once again. "The Bard is rarely in London these days. He is a favorite of His Highness, and they always speak to each other in poetic verse whenever they meet. They usually try to out-soliloquize one another."

"The Bard?" I whispered back, not wanting to draw attention to my ignorance. I had only been in England a short time, and I already felt like a fish out of water.

"Surely, you've heard of Master Shakespeare. Poet and playwright."

I nodded. "Of course. Venus and Adonis."

He tilted his head, impressed. "Ah, you like poetry then? I mean no offense, but I would not have pegged you as a lover of poetry."

I stared at him, unwilling to give him the satisfaction of kenning me, even a wee bit. The fact was, I hid nae been a lover of poetry. Nay until I met Moira. But she had a way of making me look at the world in a different way. She saw the good in things, in people, and she tried to share that sight with me. I had been raised by a hard man, and saw little use for frivolities, until I met her.

"There is a good deal ye dinnae ken about me, Harington. But ye arnae missing much, so I'll spare ye the details."

Something dark came over his face. He looked as if he had a great many things he wanted to say but settled on only one. "If you plan on spending much time at the king's court, or even the prince's, you will be found out. No one comes as close to the king as you have, without all his secrets being laid bare." He took a swig of the ale that had been placed before him, not taking his eyes off me.

I resisted the urge to shift in my seat. He sounded as if he kent all about my situation and about my father. How the Earl of Bothwell had positioned himself time and again within King James's court. How he made himself available to the king, sacrificed his family, committed his men to the king's cause, and even donated his coin. Only to be labeled a traitor in the end and driven from his home. Made penniless in his exile and humiliated in his homeland.

"To what do we owe the pleasure of the Great Bard's company?" I heard Henry ask, drawing me away from Harington's covert accusations.

"A lawsuit," Shakespeare said in short.

"So, your wily ways have finally caught up with you?" It was Essex this time. He had been rather quiet on our ride to Eastcheap and not much more talkative since we arrived.

The Bard laughed dryly. "Not against me, believe it or not. I am a witness in a lawsuit for a marriage match I arranged a few years ago. The son-in-law is suing the father of his bride for payment of the dowry." He laid down the pen he had been using and sank back in his seat, rubbing his palm across his forehead. "Remind me to never again get involved in other people's love affairs."

Tom spoke up. "So, you don't want to help His Royal Highness find a wife?"

Shakespeare perked up. "Is Prince Hal finally going to put on the old ball and chain?"

"Finally?" Henry grinned. "I'm only ten and eight. I have plenty of time to decide on a bride."

"All he need do is put on a Roman suit of armor." This came from a big man with dark hair and a clammy face who already sat at the table. "He had maidens falling at his feet all night when he portrayed Oberon the Faery Prince."

"I did look rather stunning in that armor, didn't I?" asked the prince. "But of course, the designer could make a sea monster look like a god." He laid a hand on the shoulder of a third man with sandy-colored hair and patted in appreciation. Our riding companions choked out a laugh and brushed their fingers over their left shoulders in unison once more, causing the prince to hang his head in mock shame.

The third man shook his head. "My prince is too kind. Yet, the Oberon masque was exquisite if I do say so. And the stage and constructed props—" He laid a hand over his heart, enraptured in thought.

"I heard that masque was a smashing success," Shakespeare said, impressed.

"It was one of the best," the prince replied. "It is hard to believe it has been a year since we performed it. I should have liked to perform Oberon again for my birthday, but Her Majesty wants to do Hymenaei."

A choking noise came from Essex, and he spat out, "I think I just vomited in my mouth."

I was staring at him when Harington leaned in and whispered, "Hymenaei is the masque that was performed at the wedding ceremony of Essex and the Festering Wound. He is supposed to play one of the Humors this time around at the prince's celebration, but don't be surprised if he doesn't show at all. Lady Essex is also performing, and it is dangerous to be in the same room as they."

"Why?" I dared to inquire.

"Explosions and such." Harington moved his hands about as if indicating an explosion of gun powder. I wondered if there was bodily harm involved, or if it was just an explosion of insults.

I turned my focus back on the prince's conversation.

"I think it wise you do not perform Oberon again, Your Grace," Tom said.

"Yes, it will not do for the moon to steal the sun's glory," Harington added.

The Bard rubbed his chin slowly. "Ah, so the prince has overshadowed His Majesty's popularity. You must be careful, my prince. A father's love will only go so far. Choose a masque that will highlight the king's genius. And forget how high your star rose in Oberon the Faery Prince."

"I would not risk my father's ire. Still, you cannot go wrong with Jonson and Jones at the helm," Henry said. "Their talent will make a pauper look like a prince."

"And your money, Your Grace," the big man added.

"Aye, coin will make anything look good," I added involuntarily and immediately wanted to kick myself. I hid nae meant to say that out loud.

Silence fell on the table, and all eyes turned to me. I did shift in my seat this time but refused to drop my gaze. I fixed my eyes on the prince and flashed him my most innocent smile. I had much practice at casting suspicion away from myself. I did it all the time when I was a lad.

Henry laughed loudly. "Indeed, dear cousin! Coin is the best kind of companion, next to a woman."

"Hear, hear!" the others chanted, raising their cups in agreement.

"Fellows, forgive me, but I have failed to introduce you to my newly discovered cousin, Robert Stewart. He is visiting from Scotland, so be sure to show him your best English hospitality."

The three new men nodded toward me in acknowledgement. "Welcome," the Bard said as he gathered up several sheets of foolscap and straightened them into a neat pile. "A round of ale in honor of the

Stuarts, on Prince Hal's tab of course." The merriment began again, and the awkward moment had passed. I took a deep breath. I had managed to divert the focus away from me once again. A skill I had mastered, living in Lord Scott's household.

"Robert, allow me to introduce you to two of the most esteemed playwrights and poets in England, William Shakespeare and Ben Jonson." He motioned to the Bard and to the big man with the clammy face. "And this man," he said, motioning to the third, a fellow with sandy-colored hair, "is a genius architect who is currently laying plans for a grand house for my mother. When she is through with him, I will recruit him to build a house for me. His classical Italian designs are amongst the greatest in all of Europe." The architect bowed his head and pressed his palms together, motioning a thank you toward the prince in humble appreciation.

The prince certainly was an enigma. His birth put him at the highest echelons of English society. He dined nightly with dukes and other princes. He was a connoisseur of fine art and a student of philosophies and military maneuvering. He would marry another king's daughter and rule one of the greatest Protestant countries of Europe once his father was gone. Yet he enjoyed the company of the lowly working class. He had a way of making people feel valued—and wanted—and that would work well in his favor when he eventually became king. It was something King James was terrible at and was probably the reason for so many plots to exterminate him.

Amidst the lively conversation, a young man with flaxen hair and bloodshot eyes had materialized behind us, nursing a cup of ale. "Your Grace," he said loudly before flitting his eyes around the table at the rest of us.

"George Preston," the prince announced. "Can we find another chair somewhere?" he said, looking around.

Essex let out a heavy breath next to me. "I think I need a whisky." He stood and straightened his doublet. "You can have my seat," he mumbled, and I wondered if he had met the man before. "If anyone sees my darling stewed prune, tell her I left the country," he said before sauntering over to the bar.

I chanced a glance at Harington. "Does he refer to Lady Essex?"

"Indeed," Harington confirmed with a chuckle.

"I am surprised the prince allows such disparaging of his friends."

Harington's brows shot up. "Friends? Lady Essex? She is not a friend."

I gawked at him. "Forgive me. I misunderstood. She attended a dinner at Lord Stratford's house along with the Viscount Rochester and his friend Thomas Overbury. They traveled with the prince. We even played cards together. I wrongly assumed they were all friends."

Harington shrugged his shoulders. "Perhaps it was some official business of the king's. Rochester is the king's secretary and a favorite. And Lady Essex is a favorite of Rochester's. Henry may have accompanied them because he enjoys the company at Chadwyck House, and he has a particular interest in Lord Stratford's oldest daughter."

Isobel. I had no idea my cousin had an interest in Stratford's daughter. She was the most exquisite creature I had ever beheld. But my understanding of English politics led me to believe Stratford's title was honorary, not hereditary. I would find it unbelievable if the king and queen agreed to a match with his daughter. I was sure the queen had higher aspirations. At least, that is what court gossip had led me to believe.

George swaggered over to the chair Essex had vacated. Turning it around backward, he straddled it as he sat down. "Your Grace, I am enjoying this establishment. Thank you for inviting me." He reached across the table and grabbed a handful of shelled walnuts and popped them into his mouth.

"Allow me to introduce George Preston," Henry said, watching the man carefully. "I am opening a riding school at Richmond Palace and would like George to be my headmaster."

George's head jerked back, and he jumped to his feet. He brushed his soiled fingers down the front of this black doublet and stuck out his hand toward Henry. "I am honored, Your Highness."

Henry smiled kindly but didnae offer his hand. "You have been highly recommended to me, Preston. I hear you have a talent with horses. My cousin here is also extremely knowledgeable of horses. I have just appointed him as my Master of the Horse at Richmond. Perhaps you two will get along well. Maybe even learn a thing of two from each other." Henry nodded in my direction, and George's eyes fell on me.

"There is not much I do not already know," George said dryly. "But I'll teach you if you'd like." He swiped a bony hand through his yellow locks before seating himself once more.

"That willnae be necessary," I said with a sneer. This muckle-mouth actually thought he was going to teach me something new about horses.

Introductions were made all round and the men fell into a lively discussion about the Puritan problem. I refrained from the religious conversation, but my silence caught George's attention. He looked me up and down then leaned toward me and spoke lowly.

"I am jealous of your position."

Did he speak of the Master of the Horse? I widnae feel guilty about that. I was well qualified. I eyed him wearily. "To what do ye refer?"

"The king's cousin. Close friend of the prince. Such a prestigious appointment. It must be a comfortable living to move so close to the throne."

Alarm bells clanged in my ears. Was he looking for trouble? Was it worth risking his employment with the prince? This reeked of treasonous behavior, and I needed to be careful. I wisnae beyond doing what I must to get the king's pardon for my father. But this man was careless in his conversation.

"I suppose you are an Anglican as well," he continued.

"What?" I said a little too harshly.

"All the court favorites are Anglicans," he continued. "They fawn after the king with honeyed lips, telling His Majesty what he wants to hear."

Devil take him. Was he a Puritan? He sure didnae dress the part and certainly didnae act the part. But no other excuse explained why he spoke with such vehemence against the Church of England. Unless he was a Catholic—or a reprobate. In that case, I was in good company.

But I didnae want trouble. I had a purpose here and couldnae afford to bungle it by getting involved with the wrong people. "Are ye drunk?" I said, feeling the distaste for his company the longer we talked. "I widnae voice my complaints too loudly, especially not in front of the Prince of Wales, and especially not about the Church of England. From my understanding, His Grace is devoted to the English faith."

He lifted an eyebrow at me, and his glassy eyes stared at me momentarily. "You're a Scot. Have you switched sides then?"

"I dinnae ken what ye mean. I'm just as Scottish now as I was when I left my homeland six weeks ago."

"But you aren't Anglican." He paused, taking another drag from his cup. "Presbyterian then?" He sounded almost hopeful, and it was my pleasure to disappoint him.

"Catholic."

I had been sorely mistaken. A look of pure relief enveloped his face. "Brother," he said, spreading his hands out in a gesture of supplication. Then he reached into his tunic and pulled out a leather string. At the end of the string was a pewter crucifix. He held it between his thumb and forefinger, hidden within his cupped palm.

"Put that away," I hissed. The air in the tavern had grown stale and thick with the sweat of a hundred drinking men. I was glad for the bodies, for the noise made private conversations more difficult to eavesdrop. But the heat was stifling, and I needed air. I looked about the tavern for the exit. I wanted rid of George Preston.

"You know then of the king's dealings with the Catholics?" He tucked the cross back into his tunic. "We had hoped he would show some kindness given his mother's Catholic faith. But unfortunately, his charity has not been forthcoming. Perhaps you can use your familial connections and aid our cause."

I swung my head back to him, irritated. "I'm nay here for the

Catholics, nor the Presbyterians, nor the Puritans. I serve Robert Stewart," I said with vehemence, pointing to myself. "I havenae patience for the trifles of religion. I'll leave that to men more learned and righteous than I. And as for any privilege ye perceive I have, ye can rest assured I cut my teeth on horsehair, not a silver spoon."

His eyes widened at that, and his lips curved upward. "Good to know you are loyal to *someone*," he said, leaning back in his seat once more. "I am curious to see where that loyalty will get you."

"'Tis no concern of yers," I said, knocking back the remainder of my ale. The prince had risen from his seat, and the others in my party were moving as if to depart. I also stood, and George crooked his neck to look up at me.

"It was good chatting with you, Robert Stewart." He stuck out his hand for me to shake. I straitened my doublet and swiped my hand through my hair instead.

"Likewise," I said, then left the blackguard sitting with his ale, hoping I widnae have to work with him too closely.

Chapter 12

Banqueting House, Palace of Whitehall, London
March 1612
Isobel

My costume for the Hymenaei masque was woven from the finest cloth of silver and beset with tiny seed pearls and chips of iridescent seashell that shimmered when I moved. An azure underskirt hung below the hemline to cover my carnation-colored satin slippers. It was decadent and head-turning, and although I wasn't the only woman costumed in such an exquisite gown, I felt like a princess when I donned it.

I was nervously waiting for the performance to begin when Prince Henry appeared at the entranceway of the hall. I felt my pulse quicken at the sight of him. Dressed in a turmeric robe and a laurel wreath accented with marjoram and roses encircling his rose-gold locks, he was breathtaking as the role of Hymen, the Roman god of marriage.

A look of concern knit his brow, and he glanced about hurriedly as if searching for someone. When his eyes landed on me, he swept a glance over me, and I felt the heat of the approval that registered on his face. I smiled encouragingly at him, and he immediately made his way in my direction, weaving in and out of the throng of dancers and other participants that were readying for the masque.

"You are breathtaking," he said, stopping abruptly and leaving a space between us so he could look at me again. "You," he paused and wetted his lips. "You look beautiful, Isobel."

His words were like a caress against my skin, making me breathless. "As do you, Your Grace," I said, feeling my heart flutter. I couldn't seem to catch my breath, so I lowered my lashes and studied my red slippers against the contrast of the black and white tiles of the banquet floor.

Clearing his throat as if remembering what he came to me for, the prince asked, "Have you seen Essex?"

Lifting my eyes back to his, I said, "No, what is amiss?"

Henry ran a hand over his creased brow, as if easing a pain there. "Your brother warned me he might do this."

"Do what? Which brother? Tom?" I said, trying to follow the conversation.

The prince forced a heavy breath through his nose. "Tom warned me Essex was threatening to not perform tonight. The last I saw him he was already half in his cups."

Alarm set my heart pounding. "But Essex is my dance partner!" I cried. "Why would he not participate?"

Henry looked about the hall, his tall height giving him an advantage above a great deal of the crowd already gathered. "Hymenaei is the same masque that was performed at his wedding six years ago. I suppose it brings back bad memories."

I swallowed another cry and bit my lip to hold back the tears. I had already faced humiliation in the last masque in which I performed by fainting in the middle of the dance. This degradation couldn't be happening to me again. "But what am I to do if Essex doesn't show?" Henry didn't answer, apparently too consumed with how to solve this problem. So, I said, "Lady Essex doesn't seem to hold the same persuasion as her husband. Why can't he just grow up and be civil about it?"

A slight smile hinted on the prince's lips. "Because it is Essex we are talking about," he said. "And you really have no idea how much he cannot stand his wife."

His words shocked me, though I knew Lady Frances was not too taken with her husband either. I hadn't even known she was married the first time I met her, so enamored was she with Viscount Rochester. But did their hatred for each other go that deep? I opened my mouth with yet another question when Henry said, "I see Ben Jonson on the stage. Let me go speak with him and see what he suggests." And with that, the prince left me standing in the middle of the hall feeling a little out of sorts.

Before I knew it, Inigo Jones was clapping his hands and instructing all the players to get into their places. I looked around, panicked and not sure how this would all play out.

I spotted the princess seated with her parents. I wished she was participating in this masque, for she always had a knack for calming my nerves. But she had begged to be excused in favor of entertaining the attentions of Prince Otto of Hesse-Kassel. They sat closely, shoulders touching, and heads bent toward one another. Elizabeth pointed at something on the stage and the prince laughed, eyes sparkling in delight with his company.

The wail of a violin pierced the air, pulling my attention away from Elizabeth and her suitor. I wondered if Henry had located the Earl of Essex, for I saw neither of them as the players took their places and prepared for the performance. I gathered my skirts and made my way toward the stage, where a great cluster of clouds had been designed, fashioned of the whitest fleece, and hiding the gaggle of eight ladies that were to appear with Juno the goddess queen as her eight Powers.

"Have you seen the bride," whispered Lady Bedford, a blonde slip of a woman who was one of the eight dancing women.

"It's scandalous," the darker-haired Lady Montgomery said with a hiss. "But then again, everything that woman does is a scandal."

I had no idea what they were talking about. There was to be a young man and woman acting out the part of a happy bride and groom at the end of the masque. The young woman who had played the faux bride during our practices was the sweet young daughter of the Dutch ambassador who was visiting with her father. I hadn't caught a whiff of scandal surrounding her since she never left her father's side the whole time she was in England.

The chittering of ladies lowered to a soft hum as the practice notes of music swelled. I had just gotten into position when Lady Lucy Barrington, the young woman slated to portray Juno, made her appearance. A nauseous jealousy churned in my stomach at the sight of the beautiful woman, and I watched as two men assisted her with getting into her place on the stage.

A golden throne had been fashioned for her to sit upon, with a peacock placed on each side of her. Her gown was woven of silvery gossamer silk, and she wore a white diadem on her head. Roses and lilies were woven into the top of her crown and from the crown flowed layers of colorful silk, inlaid with jewels. The costume shone against her olive skin and dark hair, and she looked like a true goddess seated upon her throne. Once she was seated, her assistants handed her a scepter to hold in her right hand and a timbrel to carry in her left. She would make a dramatic entrance when the time came, and I wondered not for the first-time what Prince Henry thought of this dark beauty. Her mother was an Italian nobleman's daughter, but her father was the Duke of Cumberland. There was no doubt they had come to court seeking an offer of marriage for their daughter.

I pushed the sickening thoughts down and slid my mask into place. I could not afford to think on the prince's marriage prospects at the moment. I needed to pay close attention to what I was doing, as these dance steps were a little more complicated than the ones I had performed for the Masque of Oberon. The eight dancing ladies, and the eight dancing men, portraying the four Humors and four Affections, were all to wear masks. This added an air of mystery and excitement to the performance. Yet, it also made dancing a bit complicated. Each of the ladies had been matched with a gentleman. But since we couldn't see each other's faces, we had to look for their colored masks. My mask was lavender, which meant the Earl of Essex's mask would be lavender too. I twisted my hands in nervousness at the thought of performing my steps without a partner. I prayed Henry had found him.

Ben Jonson strode to the front of the stage to make his customary announcement before the masque began. Some of the candles were dimmed in preparation for the performance. Then, from the other side of the stage, a lutist strummed out the first notes on the musical score.

As soon as the clouds had been pushed aside, I could see Henry clearly. The worry that had creased his brow minutes before had disappeared and in its place sat a relaxed and happy demeanor. That made me relax too, for that meant he had found Essex and all would be well.

The first players entered the stage, and I immediately realized something was not as it should be. Viscount Rochester, who had been chosen to portray the bridegroom, stood in his place in his garments of purple and white with colorful ribbons wrapped about his head. Following him was Prince Henry as Hymen, carrying a torch of pine branch.

After him came my little brother, Harry, dressed all in white and carrying another torch made of white thorn. He carried a basket under his arm. Following Harry came the final three for this tableau; two little girls dressed all in white, one carrying a distaff and the other a spindle. But it was the woman who strode between the girls who caught all attention. The personated bride in this masque was dressed all in white with a garland of roses wrapped upon her head like a turret. An awkward hush fell on the other cast members. For this was not Lady Marie Van den Berg, the appointed bride, but Lady Frances Devereux, the Countess of Essex.

Now I understood what the other women had been whispering about. Lady Montgomery had called her scandalous. She had been speaking of Lady Frances. I was a little annoyed those gossiping women had been talking about my friend.

But there was no time to dwell on this. Soon, the performance was moving forward, and Hymen was speaking his lines. Henry delivered his soliloquy with perfection and the bride and groom moved into their places on the stage once more. More words were spoken, but I hardly heard the lines. I was merely waiting for the signal that would beckon the dancers forward for our entrance.

I laid a hand on my stomach and took a deep breath. Then, on the designated high note of the score, we ladies stepped out from behind the clouds and swept our way across the stage to our partners.

I nearly tripped over my feet when I reached my partner with the lavender mask.

It was not Essex.

The man behind the mask was slightly taller than Essex. He also did not share the lithe build of the earl but carried a more athletic physique. Instead of the dark locks of the earl, there was a tuft of russet hair protruding from his cap. I narrowed my eyes at him. With his mask in place, I could not make out who the mystery man was, and the dance was moving too fast to study him overmuch.

"Who are you," I whispered just loud enough for him to hear me over the music as we stepped together. He crooked a smile at me with teasing lips but did not respond. I watched as he stepped away from me and turned in a circle before coming back to me and lifting his hands to touch mine, as the dance required.

His hands were warm and rough, not the hands of a gentleman but of one who was used to labor. I frowned slightly. A common laborer would not be asked to dance in the prince's masque. And worse, why would the rough touch of such a man send a jolt of energy straight to my belly? I watched him as he stepped away from me again and spun around the couple dancing next to us. Whoever he was, he knew the steps fairly well, especially for having not practiced with us the days prior. When he stepped in front of me again, his mouth was set in a hard line. His smile had fallen away, and he looked to be in deep concentration. In the low candlelight, his eyes looked to be a gray green, the color of ocean water before a storm. His eyes watched me intently through his mask, holding me in a phantasm I didn't understand.

"Where is Essex?" I tried again. He tilted his head slightly but still did not speak. We had reached the most intimate part of the dance. He slid his arm around my waist and turned me away from him before pulling me against his chest. I stiffened my back and tried not to lean into him too closely. His scent of cedar and wood smoke enveloped me and his breath against my neck made the fine hairs at my nape stand on end. His hands around my waist were firm yet gentle, and my skin felt afire where he touched me. Fortunately, the move was only momentary, and I stepped away from him and turned to face him once more.

I felt breathless, and I didn't like my body's response to this stranger's nearness. "Do you speak English?" I questioned, trying to keep my mind on the issue at hand. Perhaps he was another foreign dignitary that had been roped into participating in tonight's entertainment. That would explain his lack of conversation and this persona that seemed to be a contradiction to everything a typical nobleman would be. He dipped his head in assent but uttered no words. He wouldn't take his eyes off me, and I felt my pulse quickening under his scrutiny.

My brother Tom stepped forth next. He was Order, the servant of Reason, who was portrayed by the prince's good friend, John Harington. As Order, Tom was dressed in a robe of cobalt blue which was covered with an outer garment of white, with all manner of geometrical and arithmetical figures covering it. He bore a star upon his forehead and carried in his hand a geometrical staff. Order had no lines to speak, but he looked magnificent and received Reason's instructions with great alacrity.

Here another dance began. The device used in this movement was beautiful, yet complicated, and I had to concentrate on my feet and the steps I was taking. At one point, my enigmatic partner took a step off, which quickly could have turned into a series of misfortunate steps. But I took his hand, forcing him to follow my steps, and in the end, all was well. The dance ended with all the dancers linking hands into a great "golden chain" as Reason pronounced it that reached the length of the stage.

As we stood with hands linked, Reason spoke his next lines. My lavender-masked partner was breathing heavily. Apparently, for all his swift footwork, he was not accustomed to such lengthy and quick dancing. I preened, taking a little satisfaction at this thought. Suits him right, trying to step into a role for which he wasn't entirely prepared. I risked a glance at him, and he turned his head toward me. Beads of perspiration wetted his forehead, dampening the hair that fell over his brow. I smiled at him and nodded, indicating I was impressed with his ability to keep up with the complicated dance. He didn't smile back, but I was sure I felt the slight pressure of his hand on mine as he squeezed gently, then swiped his thumb across the top of my hand. The shock of that intimate gesture startled me, and I jerked my hand away instinctively. But our time on stage was over for the time being, and I quickly exited the stage, leaving my partner behind to find his own way back.

My pulse was racing, but it wasn't from the dancing. I slipped into the corridor where I could have a moment's peace and examine what had just happened. I placed my hand on my chest, willing my heart to stop pounding. I didn't know why I felt off balance, nor why I had reacted so forcefully to the stranger's touch. Not only did I not know who this man was, but to feel drawn to him in such a way was a danger I was not willing to risk.

I wasn't gone long when Lady Bedford made an appearance. "All dancers on stage immediately!" she instructed. I pulled my mask back into place and straightened my gown. Pushing off the wall I had been leaning on, I stepped to the edge of the stage. The final notes were being sung, and I found myself scanning the opposite side of the stage for my lavender masked partner. We would be expected to stand together and take a bow together, along with the rest of the dancers at the end of the masque.

When it was time, Juno's Powers flitted back across the stage, reunited with the Humors and Affections. I spotted the lavender mask yet still hesitated when he held out his hand to take mine. The dancers were removing their masks to reveal themselves, and I deliberately refused to take my partner's hand until he had unmasked himself. But my partner appeared to be as stubborn as I. He remained masked, and even took a bow then turned slightly to me as if waiting for my next move.

I smiled broadly, fully masked and gloating that he had not gotten the best of me.

In all we took three bows before the music faded, and the candles were lit once more. The dancers were leaving the stage when I turned to the man who still stood beside me.

"Who are you?" I asked again. He shook his head slightly, indicating his refusal to answer my questions, and stepped closer to me. I tried to take a step back, feeling as if his presence was consuming all the air in the room. But the crush of people who had converged onto the open floor of the banqueting hall prevented me from moving away from him. He was taller than me, and with his face still partially covered, he was intimidating. The gray green of his eyes had darkened, and he looked as if he might devour me. I had never felt threatened in my life. I had been raised in a loving home with caring parents and protective brothers. And when I had been sent to court to be Princess Elizabeth's lady-in-waiting, every kindness had been afforded me. So, I didn't understand why every bump of gooseflesh that pebbled my skin screamed of a danger in which I had never found myself before.

He stood too close, looked at me too hard. "Sir, I demand you remove your mask this instant and reveal your identity to me."

He lifted his hand at my command. But instead of removing his own mask, he reached behind my head and pulled on the string that kept my mask intact. The soft material fell away, and I suddenly felt naked in front of him, as if all my secrets had just been revealed to him. I opened my mouth to protest but just then something caught my attention across the hall. The stranger must have noticed a change in my demeanor, for he too turned and looked in the direction of my gaze.

In the shadows of the corridor at the far end of the hall, Henry leaned against the wall, hovering over a demure Lady Lucy Barrington. He tilted toward her and whispered something in her ear. She laughed in response, but I couldn't hear it from where I stood.

The heat of embarrassment bloomed on my face. If I had ever thought Henry had looked at me with admiration, I questioned that now. He didn't take his eyes off Lucy. In fact, he gazed at her as if he wanted to eat her alive. I watched as he brushed a curl out of her eyes and tucked it behind her ear. The gesture was intimate, and I felt the heat on my cheeks seep downward, coloring my neck and chest in splotchy crimson patches. How could I think there was any hope for me with the crown prince of England? I was only the daughter of an earl with a courtesy title. Lucy's bloodline ran red with hundreds of years of nobility. Of course, he would want the most noble of women to be the mother of his future heirs. My mother was right. I was out of my element here.

The stranger turned back to me. His lips parted as if he were finally going to say something. But I felt like I was on fire. And the buzzing in my ears and the stinging of tears in my eyes forced my feet into motion. Before I realized what I was doing, I was fleeing the banqueting hall. While I had been exchanging glances with the lavender-masked stranger, Lucy had been busily sinking her claws into the prince. I was such a fool.

All right, I wasn't being completely fair. Lucy was a sweet girl. It was understandable how she could catch the prince's attention without much effort on her part. That thought triggered a twisting sensation in my chest, even more than the envious thoughts I had of her just a moment earlier. It was easy to play the game against a malicious opponent. But how could I compete with a woman who was truly likeable and in whom I could find no fault?

The tears came just as I reached the cold night air. But the sting on my cheeks was nothing compared to the pain of the rending in my chest.

Chapter 13

Palace of Whitehall, London
March 1612
Isobel

I *can't breathe. I can't breathe. I can't breathe.* The mantra pounded through my head as I ran out into the darkness. Voluminous torches burned brightly around the palace courtyard, illuminating the gardens and the path that led to the stables in rich light. But I sought darkness. Somewhere I could hide, where my humiliation could not be seen, and my sobs would not be heard.

I fled to the stables. The horses would be resting at this time of night, and I would be undisturbed. No one would think to look for me there.

But when I entered the barn, it was immediately obvious something was amiss. Stable hands were scurrying about, and shouts for assistance were coming from the far end of the mews. A lone lantern spilled light across the floor of the barn. A horse, whether angry or injured, I knew not, shrieked out a dreadful neigh, kicking the stall and releasing specks of dust into the air.

I darted into the nearest empty stall to avoid being seen. Only, it wasn't a stall at all, it was a small room filled with saddles and tools and other equipment pertaining to horses.

I sank to the floor with my back against the wall. I knew I was ruining my beautiful costume, but I didn't care. My feet hurt and my back ached, and the disturbing scene that had chased me into the darkness was now suffocating me.

I loved Henry and had for as long as I could remember. It was common knowledge my parents had fled to England when they were younger, and father had worked his way up into the old queen's favor. He had performed his duties well—more than well, actually—and she had rewarded him with the Earl of Stratford title. Father and Mother had never pretended to be anything other than the grateful and humble subjects of a generous sovereign. But they did have high hopes for their children. And I had been raised with the intent that I would marry well. I had been instructed in all the fine arts a lady of our status was expected to perform. But no matter how much I tried to put our Scottish roots behind me, it was always in the back of my mind and seemed to taint everything I had tried to accomplish. And now Mother's words that I am not high-born enough to pursue the prince's favor, when all along I was led to believe it was possible, was like a slap in my face.

And I had believed, despite all of this, that I *had* secured the prince's favor. I thought he had feelings for me. I thought about the way he always asked after my well-being. He would include me in any parties he planned or masques he was organizing. He always made a point to talk to me whenever we saw each other at courtly functions. And I couldn't forget the concern in his eyes when I fainted during the Oberon masque. He showed me as much attention and care as he did Elizabeth, and I felt more than attended to with his compliments and kindness whenever I saw him. But I had never seen him look at me like he looked at Lucy Barrington tonight.

Pulling my legs up and hugging them against me, I buried my head in my knees and wept. I wept for all the Latin lessons and mathematical sums I had endured. I wept for the needle pokes from embroidery and the dull, endless hours of stately dinners I had been forced to sit through. All for the sake of making me the darling of the English court.

I lost track of time until a noise at the door of the little room in which I sat eventually pulled me from my misery. However, the figure that stood in the doorway did nothing to sooth me. For standing there staring at me, was the king's cousin, Robert Stewart.

He didn't speak for a moment but just stood there with a strange expression on his face.

"Please stop staring at me. It's unsettling." Those misty green eyes that studied me so intently at supper that night at Chadwyck House seemed to bore into me now. I wiped my eyes with the fleshy part of my palms, then sniffed. "Have you never seen a woman cry before?"

He dipped his chin slightly. "Aye, I have three sisters. Tears arnae an entirely foreign occurrence." It was my turn to stare. I hadn't expected such an ordinary response from him. When I didn't respond, he continued, "Forgive me, my lady. I dinnae mean to disturb ye."

The look of pity that filled his eyes sparked annoyance in me. It was one thing to feel sorry for myself, but I wasn't about to let him stand there pitying me.

"Well, you did," I snapped. I didn't mean to speak so harshly, but for some reason this man's nearness always unsettled me. He watched more than spoke, and the habit made me feel as if he could see right into me and judge all my faults. "How long have I been out here?" I asked, as I patted my hair, checking that all was in order.

He hesitated then said, "The masque ended two hours ago."

"Oh. Help me up." I held out a hand for his assistance, and he dropped the satchel he was holding and stepped forward.

He took my hand, and a calloused thumb brushed softly over my fingers. It reminded me of my masked dance partner from earlier this evening. His hands were rough as well, and the sensation had sent a spark through me. But that man was a gentleman, and a fine dancer, not some shamed earl's son raised in the backwoods of the wild Scottish countryside.

I was distracted with my thoughts and did not notice my mishap until it was too late. As I stood, my foot caught in the hem of my gown, and suddenly pitched me forward. Robert released my hand and caught me by the arms, preventing me from falling on my face. Instead, I fell into him with only my hands against his chest to give me leverage.

His all-seeing eyes searched my face. "Why have ye been crying?"

I pushed against him in an effort to release myself, but he held fast. "It is no concern of yours."

"Is it the prince that brings those tears?"

I started. "What? No," I said, trying once more to free myself from his grip. If he had been at the masque, I hadn't seen him. So, how would he know it might be the prince I was upset about? Now I was sure he could read my secrets. I remembered Viscount Rochester telling us Robert's father was a necromancer. I wondered if that is where he got his power of perception. "Sir, I demand you let me go at once. I want to return to the palace."

But he didn't release me. Instead, he said, "Ye may want to wait. Yer cheeks are flushed, and yer nose is red. From my experience, ladies like to look their best when in the prince's company."

Logic told me he spoke truth, but his advice irritated me like a bee sting. "And from my experience," I said, biting out the words, "a lady does not like to be told by a gentleman that she is unattractive."

"That is not what I said, my lady. Ye are putting words in my mouth." At his statement, my eyes fell instinctively to his mouth where a serious line set his perfectly shaped lips into a wicked little stance. The space between us seemed to have grown smaller, and I could feel his breath on my cheek. "I would be hard pressed to see ye as anything but beautiful, no matter how red yer nose was," he continued. "And the lavender scent ye bathe in is a bonny addition."

His words curled in my stomach, like the blooming tendrils of a vine, spreading warmth to all my limbs. It was an unwelcome feeling, and I attempted once again to jerk away from him, finally breaking free from his grasp.

"Well, you smell like horse," I said, lifting my chin. I stared up at him, hoping to see a reaction but felt irritation when a teasing smirk parted his lips.

"That is the greatest compliment ye could give me," he said. Taking a step away from me, he went to the satchel he had dropped on the floor and picked it up. "I just helped birth a foal who was having a difficult time of it. I am glad I could be of service to the king, for I am told the mare is one of His Majesty's favorites." He hung the bag on a hook that stuck out from the wall, then pulled it open. "Perhaps now I can get an audience with him." The last was spoken under his breath, more to himself than to me. But I heard it just the same, and my interest was piqued.

"If you seek an audience with the king, why don't you just ask Prince Henry to arrange it?" I watched as he began removing items from his bag and putting them away in their designated places.

He twisted his body to look at me, and I noticed how his crinkled brow created a crease above his nose. "Now why didnae I think of that?" I detected the bitterness in his voice and recognized his cynicism. The flash in his eyes warned me I shouldn't poke this bear, but I couldn't seem to help myself.

I drew up beside him. "I would think that would be an easy solution. Unless you are keeping something from the prince you don't wish him to know about. In that case, then yes, it might be a little more difficult."

His green eyes flashed. "Ye are meddling in things too dangerous for ye, woman. Just trust me when I say I have attempted to speak to the king already and have been unable to do so. His Majesty is being hard-headed and widnae grant me audience. The prince nay need ken all my business."

My mouth fell open. "You dare to insult His Majesty? Your words will get you hanged."

He turned toward me. His face had darkened into an angry mien. In my few interactions with him, he had been reserved and careful with his answers. This reaction set my pulse thrumming with excitement, though I didn't know why.

"And will ye be the informant? My insults hardly compare to the wrong he has done to my family. If it is mere words that bring him injury, then I would hate to see what else his future might hold, should I be forced to take what I want."

I felt my eyes widen in response. "So, you admit you have come to London to seek retribution on the king?" Now I knew my reasons for mistrusting him were not in vain.

He dropped the tool that was in his hand and moved toward me so quickly I barely had time to move away. He hovered over me, forcing me to take a step back until I was backed against the wall.

"I have admitted no such thing to ye." He leaned a hand against the wall behind me, drawing himself closer still. "And if ye try to blackmail me, ye will regret it."

The low, umbral of his voice prickled my skin into gooseflesh. I had expected another angry outburst, but this time he spoke with a controlled, even tone that carried with it more threat than any heated words ever could. He took another step closer to me until our noses were practically touching, and for a split second I thought he was going to kiss me. My breath caught, and I watched him in anticipation of what wrath he would bring upon me. A thousand swarming bumble bees seemed to buzz in my stomach, and I was disgusted by my body's reaction to his nearness.

"I wouldn't dream of it." I said, feeling as if all the air had been sucked from the room.

"There you are." A voice pierced the dimly lit room. I jumped as if I had been caught doing something I shouldn't, but Robert just took a step back slowly, as if he were in no hurry to disentangle himself from this situation.

"Lady Frances," I started. "What are you doing here?" I smoothed my skirts and stepped away from Robert, in a hurry to distance myself from him.

A mischievous grin curved her lips. "I could ask you the same."

"I mean, how did you find me here?"

Her eyes swept over Robert, assessing the man quickly. I gathered by the sparkle that seemed to light her eyes that he met her approval. "Sir Robert." She bowed her head slightly toward him. "Are you holding my little protégé captive? This is hardly the place for a clandestine meeting."

I gasped at her insinuation. "I assure you," I said, shocked at what she was suggesting, "this is no clandestine meeting." Then rethinking what she had just said, I added, "Why do you call him sir? His father was stripped of his title years ago. I hardly think it proper to address him by a title his family has been denied."

The countess's eyes sparked. "Ouch. You do have a sharp tongue in your mouth, Lady Isobel. It hardly seems fair to hold the father's sins against the son, don't you think?"

Her gentle rebuke made me realize the rudeness of my words. But before I could apologize, Robert spoke up. "You can call me just Robert, my lady." He bowed to the countess, then putting away the last of the tools he was holding, said, "I am in no need of titles to remind me from whence I came."

"Self-assurance, I like that." Her voice sounded like a purr. She stood in front of the door, and for a moment, I thought she wasn't going to let Robert leave.

"I'm glad I meet with yer approval, Lady Essex," he said, standing in front of her now.

"Indeed," she said. There was an awkward silence in the air.

"If ye will excuse me, I need to see to Lady Luck." He motioned toward the stables and Frances slowly stepped out of his way.

"Who is this lucky lady?" she asked, tossing me a knowing look.

"A horse," Robert said. "Lady Luck is the mare who just birthed a foal. She will need to be checked on. I shall leave ye both to talk about whatever it is that women talk about." And with that, he was gone.

Frances turned to me. "My, my. I would have never guessed you and Robert would be meeting here in the stables. And here I thought you fled to the mews, heartbroken over the possibility of Henry's new love interest."

I fought back the tears that suddenly stung my eyes. "I was not meeting Robert. He found me crying here and started a conversation with me."

"Is that what I just saw? That did not look like a conversation. At least, not the kind spoken with words." She grinned wider, as if she had happened upon some great secret.

"I assure you, there was nothing but words being spoken. He asked me why I was crying and wouldn't let me leave until my nose had returned to its natural color."

Her brows arched in scandal. "How gentlemanly of him."

I pressed my lips together to keep from saying what I really wanted to say. He was no gentleman. What's more, she seemed to *like* Robert, and had no issue with the things we had been told about him. But I took issue with her thinking there would be anything between me and the disgraced earl's son.

I moved toward the door. I was through with this conversation.

"You are upset with me," she said. "Forgive me. I sometimes forget you are innocent in the ways of men."

I felt like a child at her words. I may not have a lot of experience with men, but I knew what I wanted, or rather who I wanted, and who I did not.

"I do not like what you are implying with Robert Stewart. I do not like that man," I blurted out.

One perfectly drawn eyebrow arched. "I don't understand what you have against him. He is sinfully attractive." Her lips curved into a playful little smile. "And he comes from a noble family. Not to mention, he practically worships the ground you walk on. It doesn't get any better than that."

"What?" I felt my stomach do a somersault. But whether it was excitement or terror at that thought was a matter I didn't care to examine too closely.

"Come now, Isobel. Surely you have noticed how closely the man watches you. And he hangs on your every word—no matter how little you say to him."

I shook my head. "That man sees too much. It unsettles me. It is a known fact that the man's father dabbled in witchcraft. He has been exiled, and the family has been humiliated and left with nothing, as they should be. And his father was the cause of great trouble for my father when they lived in Scotland many years ago. I'm sure my father wouldn't hear of his oldest daughter attaching herself to that rogue. Besides, he is unrefined and uneducated. I could never see myself with a man like him."

"*That man,* as you call him, comes from a long line of nobility. His great-grandfather was the fifth King James of Scotland. And the fact that the prince keeps him so close at hand leads me to believe he is more intelligent than what you give him credit for, for Henry doesn't surround himself with fools—or witches. Forgive me for saying so, but you would be lucky to have him, for his blood is far nobler than yours."

Humiliation burned on my face. Although I knew the sentiment was always there, not many people had the nerve to bring up my father's honorary title and our family's benefit from it. Some noble families thought it a disgrace for a person of lower birth like my father to be given such an honor as was given to him by Queen Elizabeth.

I blinked hard, trying to hold back the tears. I took a deep breath before speaking, but I could feel the quaver in my voice before I even opened my mouth. "Lady Frances, I am aware of the nobility's thoughts on my family's social standing. But no matter what others may think of me or my family, all that matters to me is what Prince Henry thinks. For he is the man I want."

"Good girl," the countess cooed, laying a hand on my shoulder. "That is the kind of attitude you will need to survive at the Stuart court. Do not show your weaknesses. Any little injury, even to your emotions or your ego, will draw blood, and blood draws sharks. And we both know what happens when a shark takes notice of you."

I sniffled and dabbed at my eyes with the tips of my fingers. "At this rate, I would almost welcome a shark or anything to get Henry's attention." I glanced back to the countess to gauge her reaction. She studied me closely but waited for me to continue. "I don't know how to make him want me. I thought he had feelings for me. He shows me the highest regard when we interact with each other, as much as he does his own sister. But—" I broke off here, not sure how to continue. My nose was starting to run, and I pinched it closed, in a most unladylike fashion. I was not prepared for watery eyes and a runny nose, for the night had not gone as I had expected.

The countess chuckled, then clicked her tongue. "There, there, dear heart. Don't cry. Tears never won a man's affection. And you are too beautiful for tears." She pulled a piece of cloth from her sleeve and handed it to me. "First, we must determine how serious his regard is for that Lucy Barrington trollop." She pinched my cheeks to bring color to them and tucked a stray hair back into place.

"But Lady Lucy isn't a trollop. She is the sweetest of girls. She wouldn't harm a housefly."

Frances pursed her lips. "Sweetling, any woman who is stealing the attention of the man you want is a trollop." Her voice was as smooth as honey, but I detected a danger there that made me glad I was her friend and not her opponent.

I took another deep breath, noticing for the first time the smell of manure mixed with earth. The odor, coupled with thoughts of Henry and Lucy together, turned my stomach sour. "I think it is serious. The way he looks at her—I have never seen him look at me like that."

She stopped fussing with my hair and considered my words. "Then we must redirect his attentions and assist him with seeing what he is missing in you."

"But that's just it. Up until this evening, I enjoyed his attentions. He is always quick to include me in strolls with Elizabeth or for an evening of entertainment with his family. I think he enjoys my company and truly likes to be with me."

The countess looked like the cat who stole the cream. The expression on her face was almost comical if the subject matter was not so heart-wrenching.

"My dear, therein lies your problem," she said, holding me at arm's length and looking me over once more. "The prince thinks of you as just another sister. We need him to think of you as a lover, not a friend."

I caught myself staring at her in disbelief. "But I want to be his friend."

"No, you want to be his princess and one day his queen. You're going to need to add a little more seduction to your repertoire dear." She took a step away, sweeping her eyes over me in consideration. Then she tugged at the bodice of my costume, stretching the neckline lower and pushing my breasts upward. "Hmm, we might need to work on the wardrobe a little. Come, I think I have a few gowns you can start with until we can have something made." She crooked a finger at me, and I found myself following her without question. But just as we reached the threshold, she turned back. "Oh, I almost forgot. I am going to need a small favor from you as well."

"Of course," I said, without hesitation. "It would be my pleasure and the least I could do."

"Oh dear, this is a little embarrassing." She looked over her shoulder, then leaned closer, as if there were someone close by to hear the conversation. "I would appreciate discretion in this small matter, Isobel."

I couldn't imagine what could be so humiliating to the countess as to be sworn to secrecy. But I would do whatever it took to gain her assistance. I couldn't go to Mother in this matter, and Elizabeth wouldn't understand. Lady Frances was my only hope.

"I will be as discreet as necessary, my lady."

Her brow smoothed, and her eyes cleared in almost relief. "I have a small rat problem."

I blinked at her. "A small rat problem?"

"Yes, the castle is full of these pests, but sometimes the efforts made by the servants are not adequate. I need a small amount of poison to rid myself of this problem."

I didn't understand. Surely this was something the chambermaids could see to. "I am not sure I comprehend my role in this."

She chuckled. "Your mother has a great deal of knowledge in herbs and poisons, does she not?"

Understanding finally struck me. "You want me to ask my mother for poison. For your rat problem."

"You're going to have to be a little more discreet than that, Isobel. Your mother must not find out who the poison is for. It would be hugely humiliating, you see. All she need be told is that a friend has need of it."

She was correct. My mother did have a great deal of knowledge concerning herbs. And although I knew her to be well versed in poisons, she tended to use her herbs for medicinal purposes to help people. But this wasn't for a person. It was for rats, I reminded myself.

"She will need to know what it is for. There are different poisons for different purposes."

When I was a little girl, I had worked with my mother in her apothecary, a dark, dungeon-like room tucked away in a far corner of Chadwyck House. But the space was dreary, and the air was tinged with strange odors, and I eventually lost interest in her work there. But I knew enough from my time spent with her to know at least that much.

"You may tell her it is for a rat problem. But truly, you mustn't say anything more."

"All right," I promised. "I will simply tell her a friend is in need of something to rid herself of rats."

"That's perfect." There was that silky tone in her voice again. It sent a shiver down my spine, that I promptly ignored. I needed Lady Frances's help. And if this is all I had to do, then so be it. "Remember, complete discretion." I nodded, wide-eyed as if she had just asked for some sacred oath like my first-born child. "Now come, we have work to do."

I followed her out into the crisp night air, her hips swinging in a way that caught every stable hand's attention. I was about to start my lessons in seduction, and Lady Essex was just the woman to give them.

Chapter 14

Palace of Whitehall, London
March 1612
Robert

It only took a day for King James to summon me.

Lady Luck truly did have a lucky streak, for I wisnae even supposed to be at the Palace of Whitehall. Henry's stables had suffered in the months following the last Master of the Horse's employ, and I had begged him to allow me to forego the festivities in order to finish setting the place to rights. But he was having none of it. "It's my birthday!" He would always toss out whenever someone suggested something contrary to his wishes.

But it had worked in my favor. My knowledge of horseflesh, accompanied with my availability immediately after the masque had ended, had allowed me to assist in the mare's delivery, sparing her life and making the king happy in return.

My attendance at the masque was a stroke of luck for the prince as well.

"I am going to hang Essex," he had gritted out as he approached me in the banqueting hall.

"What has he done this time?" Essex was a moody fellow, and I didnae understand the dynamics of the prince's relationship with him. Where the prince was sunshine and friendliness, the Earl of Essex was a brooding storm cloud. It was puzzling they managed to find anything to agree on enough to have a friendship.

"He has deserted me. He is nowhere to be found, and I just received his missive that he has found himself indisposed this evening and will not be able to join us." The prince smacked the wall with the flat of his hand, the most loss of control he would allow himself.

"Tom warned ye he would. He doesnae like his wife."

"He wasn't even dancing with Lady Essex. I made sure they didn't have to be near each other. He was supposed to be Isobel's dance partner." He stopped suddenly. "Devil take him! Isobel will be devasted!" The prince turned away from me and paced a short distance down the corridor. I watched as his mind raced, looking for a solution. He continued in this vein for several minutes until he stopped suddenly and turned on his heels. "Cousin, you know the steps."

Startled by this exclamation, I found myself sputtering, "I dinnae ken what ye mean."

He came toward me, excitement written all over his face. "You've been here every day we have practiced. You even told me the dance reminded you of one you danced in Scotland. You can take Essex's place."

I shook my head soundly. "Nay. Ye arnae dragging me into this melee."

Henry's eyes shone with hope. "It doesn't have to be a melee, Cousin. But it will be if we can't find a replacement for Essex. The masque starts in ten minutes."

"We should focus our efforts on finding Essex. We can drag him here to dance and then beat the living daylights out of him for putting ye in this predicament when it's all over."

The prince laughed. "If I know Essex—and I do—he is long gone by now. Probably making merry at the Boar's Head right about now. He won't show his face around here for some time. And it better be a very long time."

"We are about the same height, but he is much slimmer than I. His costume willnae fit me."

"We'll figure out something. Robert, please. I can't put Isobel through another humiliation. She had such a hard time of it the last time she performed in a masque. She might never do it again if this falls through."

And that is how I found myself dancing with the most beautiful woman at King James's court.

But Isobel didnae like me. That was evident from the first time I met her at Chadwyck House and from the handful of times I had seen her since coming to Prince Henry's court. She was part of the queen's court, and I was part of Henry's. Although the opportunities had been few, they had been there. And every time I saw her, she either barely spoke to me, or did so with such disdain, it left me feeling raw and inadequate.

Which is why I chose not to speak when we were finally thrown together during the Hymenaei dance.

If I said one word to her, she would hear my Scots brogue and recognize my voice. She would figure out who her new dance partner was and balk. I widnae put it past her to turn her back on me and walk away.

So, I was determined not to reveal my identity. At least, not during the dance. If she found out afterwards, then let her rail. The chit was a fiery little sprite and seemed to take great pleasure in abusing me whenever she saw me. But I was saved from having to make myself kent to her.

I had replayed those last few moments with her in my head a million times since the night before. The feel of her satin-soft skin against my palms, the scent of lavender on her skin. The urge to run her beautiful hair through my fingertips. And the sensation of her breathy voice, gentle like a songbird, but firm like steady rain, brushing over my skin and igniting my blood. All because she didnae ken who I was. For had she kent, the interaction would have been much different.

And when I unmasked her, the flutter of her delicate, translucent eyelids, with tiny blue veins painted on her pale lids like a portrait, made my breath catch and almost did me in. And then she had spotted the prince with Lady Lucy Barrington.

I kent she was upset, and I deduced it had to do with the prince. But when I found her crying in the stables two hours later, I was still surprised. And I couldnae explain what the sight of her tears did to me. Whenever I would see Moira cry, I wanted to move mountains. I wanted to fix whatever had upset her or rage against whomever had hurt her. But that was understandable. She was the sweetest lass I had ever met, and she loved me freely, without expecting anything in return. She was easy to love. But Isobel—there was no logical explanation as to why I felt protective of her. And no earthly reason why I reacted so strongly to her proximity. She was a puzzle I was still working out.

I rubbed a thumb over the lavender mask in my pocket. I had kept it after I pulled it from Isobel's face and stuffed it into my pocket this morning before leaving my rooms. It was soft and supple, like the feel of her cheek when my hand had brushed against it. I would savor the memory from now on, for I reminded myself Lady Isobel Broune wisnae for me. She had set her eyes on a high prize, and I wisnae prize at all.

However, I had some luck of my own now, for the king had agreed to talk with me. Or more like, he had heard of my deeds with the mare, and wanted to meet me.

I stuffed Walter's letter of recommendation into my pocket and made my way from my chamber to the king's privy chamber. I hid nae needed the letter to convince the prince to invite me to court, but the king was a different creature. I rehearsed what I would say to him, for although I had this conversation planned for a very long time, I wanted to make sure I said it exactly the way it needed to be said.

A servant announced my arrival and motioned for me to enter the king's presence. James sat in a large chair tucked into the corner of the room with his spindly legs stretched out in front of him. A healthy fire blazed in the hearth beside him, making the room stuffy for the unseasonably warm spring day. Robert Carr, Viscount Rochester, sat at a desk next to the king, and I dipped my head to him in greeting. I had met the man on my first night in London but hid nae seen much of him since, until we came to Whitehall in preparations for the prince's birthday celebrations. From what I understood, he rarely left the king's side.

I bowed low to the king, but he didnae look at me. He held a book in his hands, and he turned the pages gently, keeping one soiled and darkened finger between the subsequent pages. I didnae speak but waited for James to acknowledge me. He continued to read, and the longer I stood there waiting, the more I could feel my blood beginning to boil.

I tried to imagine what might have been going through my father's mind, each time he would have interactions with this man. He had told me in a letter once, the king was strong-willed but easily manipulated, and that it was much easier to gain forgiveness from him than to obtain permission. Of course, that was until my father had gone one step too far. He would never tell me exactly what that had been, but I could read between the lines. And armed with the information from my mother's conversation, and my own childhood memories, I gathered it had something to do with the witch trials my father had been involved with nay long after the king had married Anne. King James was a deeply religious man, viewing himself as the protector of Christianity and the Devil's greatest enemy. How difficult would it be to convince him to lift my father's exile?

Rochester cleared his throat. "Your Grace, your cousin, Robert Stewart, has come at your request." He motioned toward me, giving a wave of his hand for me to come closer.

For a moment, James still didnae speak. Then, without looking up from his book, he finally said, "You wish some favor of me." It wisnae a question. But it was understandable for him to guess my purpose here, even if he were the one to summon me. I would venture that most people who requested an audience with the king had some favor to ask. But before I could answer him, he spoke again. "You wish your father's exile to be lifted."

I choked. I hadn't expected to get right to the point so quickly. And to be honest, I half-wondered if the king had forgotten about my father altogether. Now I understood he hid nae forgotten but rather chose to let him rot away in poverty in Italy. That thought sent a jolt of pure anger through me. I reached for my sgian dubh but forgot I had left it outside the privy chamber, for the king was a paranoid man and widnae allow weapons into his presence. It was nay wonder. He had a knack for making people want to hurt him.

I touched the lavender mask in my pocket, seeking a calmness I didnae feel in the king's company. "Yer Grace." The words scratched past my tongue, "I have indeed come to speak to ye of my father." James grunted in my direction but didnae look up, so I continued.

"As ye ken, my father, the Earl of Bothwell, has—"

The king cut me off. "Your father is no longer the Earl of Bothwell. He forfeited the right to that title when he attempted to kidnap me and steal my throne for himself."

I licked my lips, giving myself some time to calm my aggression and speak reasonably to the king. Walter had pounded self-control into me since I was a wee lad, for he said I had a temper that could make a wildcat quake. It hid nae stuck, but it widnae do my cause any good to forget myself now.

"I believe my father always had yer best interest in mind."

"Oh, come now, Robert." His words dripped with disdain. "Your father was an instrument of evil and had an influence on a great deal of people in Scotland. If the investigations are to be believed, and I think there is evidence to support the claims, he inspired fealty from a great many people and influenced a great many more to denounce their God and follow his father, the Devil. And on top of all that, he tried to gain my throne every chance he could. I finally had to step in and force him out of Scotland before he brought the whole forsaken country down."

I took a step toward him, grappling for the phantom dagger that didnae appear at my side. When my nails bit into my palm, fisting air instead of my weapon, I drew up.

"Robert, please step back and remember in whose presence you graciously stand." It was Rochester, trying to talk sense into me. He had stood from his seat behind the desk, apparently ready to defend the king.

A deep crease dented his brow, and his jovial blue eyes had turned serious. A shaft of sunlight glinted through the heavy, drawn curtains and lighted his ginger hair. Tiny specks of dust floated about him, as if the Almighty was sprinkling some kind of holy approval on him. It contrasted with the darkness I felt filling my chest and crumpling whatever heart I had left. I stiffened my back but didnae step back.

"I humbly ask," I said, gritting my teeth, "for the sake of my mother who was left destitute and friendless, that ye allow my father to return to his ancestral home—"

"Crichton Castle has been given to another," the king interrupted again.

"Allow him to return to his homeland, to his family then. He can figure out the rest when he returns." My jaw hurt from clenching my teeth so hard.

"And figure out how to overthrow the king of Britain? Figure out how to drag more innocent souls to hell with him?" At this, the king finally looked at me, his watery blue eyes spitting poison.

I closed my eyes, blocking out his words and thinking only of the mask stuffed in my pocket. Smooth, satiny pleasure met my fingertips, and I imagined the material set against the soft skin of Isobel's rosy cheeks. The thought calmed me. Then another thought followed on its heels. If Isobel were here, she would think me too stupid to string two complete sentences together. And she would be sure to tell me. That thought brought me back to reality. I took a deep breath for one last attempt at persuasion. This conversation hid nae gone as planned, and I was quickly losing control of the situation.

I swore to myself I would never beg this man. But scrounging up a plea and feeling it stick in my throat, I said, "Please, Yer Grace. My father has learned his lesson. I dinnae believe ye will have any trouble from him again. I beg of ye, let him come home."

He chewed on his words for a moment before answering. Rising from his seat, he took the book he had been reading and walked to a shelf that lined the wall behind his chair. Tucking it back onto the shelf, he perused the books, running his ink-blackened finger along the spines until it came to a stop on a time-worn volume bound in brown leather. He pulled it from the shelf and turned to me.

"You know, my own mother was driven out of Scotland when I was just a babe. I never knew her, not really. I only knew the woman she shared with me in her letters." He gripped the book in his hand and walked toward me, the flat of his other hand lying against the volume as if he were holding the cover in place.

"My father loved yer mother," I reminded him, feeling little air in my lungs. "She was kind to him when he was a lad."

"Aye, my mother was a kind woman who liked to shower gifts on her friends." He stared at me, and I resisted the urge to shift on my feet. "But she made poor choices in her life, choices I would have sworn she had the good sense not to make, yet time and again she proved me wrong. And in the end, those choices got her killed."

I watched the king, trying to gauge where he was going with this conversation. "Aye, and my father would have defended her to the death. He wanted to avenge her execution. But he told me ye widnae allow it."

The king flinched. It wasnae obvious, but I noticed it just the same. But if he felt regret for not taking action against Elizabeth when his mother was beheaded, he didnae voice it now. Instead, he said, "I think you are missing my point, dear cousin. Though we love our parents, we do not always know them as well as we think we do. Rarely do we get a real glimpse into who they truly are. They show us who they want us to see. And sometimes it is not in our best interest to believe them."

It sounded as if he believed his mother to be guilty of all the accusations that were leveled against her. But I didnae have time to evaluate the king's feelings about his mother. What mattered to me was what he was going to do with my father.

"Surely, ye do not think it is in my best interest for my father to rot away, penniless in some hovel somewhere. He deserves to be at home with his wife—my mother—and with his children."

"What he deserves is God's judgement," James barked. It was the first time I heard him lift his voice above the monotone notes that usually modulated his voice.

Hatred, pure and undiluted rushed through my veins. My vision clouded, and I felt nothing but rage coursing through me. "Has the Almighty appointed ye as judge then?" I spat out.

The king's brows shot up in shock. Rochester rounded his desk and sputtered, "Shall I call for the guards, Your Grace?"

But the king held up a hand. "My cousin is angry. It is hard to hear the truth when it pertains to our own flesh and blood." He pinned me with an almost sympathetic look when he spoke, and it made me hate him all the more.

The heat that filled the king's private chamber was stifling, and I suddenly couldnae breathe. I had to get out of this room, where fire raged, and the king's words burned hotter than the hearth itself. I turned, staggering toward the door, and feeling as if I had been drugged with poppy tears.

"Your Grace?" I heard Rochester question behind me.

"Leave him be. It will take some time to digest that his father was the Devil incarnate."

I left the king's presence, not caring that I had turned my back on him and hid nae requested leave. When I reached the hallway, the cool air that surrounded me did nothing to enliven me. Instead, it sent a chill down my spine and reinforced a decision I had already come to but hid nae fully admitted yet. If the king widnae grant me this simple request, I would have to take matters into my own hands. I would show him the devil incarnate. And I didnae mean my father. I was the devil living right under his nose within his son's court. If he thought my father was a threat, he needed to take another look at me.

Chapter 15

Palace of Whitehall, London
March 1612
Robert

I was so angry I could barely see my feet in front of me. I grabbed my sgian dubh from where I had left it and took a left outside of the king's privy chamber, determined to retreat to my rooms and nay come out until I had finalized a plan. But low voices emanating from the green drawing room kept me from my destination. I slowed my steps when I heard the voice of Henry carrying into the corridor.

"My father is pressuring me to make a choice."

"You have such fine choices, Your Grace," said the teasing tone of Tom. "But I don't envy you the decision."

"You don't have to make a choice right now. His Majesty just wants the security of his coffers and his progeny. Do not let him pressure you into a decision you will regret the rest of your life. Take it from me."

Essex's shrewd advice delivered with a dose of reality. They must be speaking of the prince's marriage prospects. I wisnae much for eaves-dropping, so I stepped into the room, wondering if the prince was any closer to making a decision.

Henry sat behind a massive, ebony desk that stood in the middle of the room. Gilded, high-backed chairs covered in silver velvet sat around the desk and contained the bodies of Tom, Essex, and Harington, the three men Henry was almost never without. But a fourth contained a person I never expected to see: George Preston, the man Henry had employed to oversee his riding school in London.

I stopped inside the threshold, taking in the mossy green damask walls and the larger-than-life oil paintings that stretched from floor to ceiling. Portraits that contained scenes of hunters on horseback and hounds at bay, adorned the silk-papered walls. Behind the prince, was an enormous hearth that looked to be framed in ivory with motifs of fruits and flowers carved along the edges.

"Cousin! Come join us." He motioned me into the room and set another glass tumbler on the desk. "We are discussing brides and my choices on the marriage market." He poured a dram of amber liquid into the tumbler and pushed it toward me.

I reached for the whisky and threw it back, slamming the glass down on the table in front of me. It burned like hellfire all the way down my throat, and I motioned for him to pour me another.

"I agree with Essex," I said, swallowing my second dram and wiping my mouth with the back of my hand before setting my glass back on the table. "Ye are barely ten and eight. Ye have plenty of time to make a decision."

Essex cast a faint smile toward me, dipping his head in agreement.

"Yes, but my father wants to see the matter settled. I have a list of three names—correction—four names, but only one of them appeals to me. Unfortunately, my father, and especially my mother, will never agree to the last one."

I ticked off the women in my head. "The princesses from Savoy, Tuscany, and France, correct? Who is the fourth? Lucy Barrington?"

I watched the prince turn an interesting shade of pink. Harington coughed, fighting back a smile, and Henry cleared his throat. "No, but she is another one of whom my parents would never approve."

"It's my sister, Isobel," Tom blurted, sounding a little more than irritated.

I turned to look at him. He was wearing a cobalt blue doublet and trunks that brought out the bright blue of his eyes. The same piercing color of eyes I had looked into last night when I found his sister crying in the stables.

"Ye dinnae like that idea?" I asked Tom, looking from him to Henry. I would think a marriage between his sister and the prince would elevate his family even higher.

"My father's title is not heredity. There are many who will scorn her simply because she does not have the bloodline required to be a princess of England. I know this, the prince knows this, and Their Majesties know this. I am angry my father even brought up the idea in the first place. My sister will be the laughingstock of the English court. Our names will be dragged through the mud, and Isobel will be scrutinized to no end. Even her virtue will be called into question." He shoved himself away from the table and strode across the room, stopping to lean on the mantle and kick a protracted log back into the grate.

"Surely, her virtue can withstand," I said, watching him. "And I cannae imagine any fault could be found in such a lovely creature."

"Isobel is without guile," the prince said, leaning back in his chair. "She is exquisite in looks and manners. Nay-sayers will be hard-pressed to find any fault in her, except for the bloodline, as you have said. And it is for that reason, I fear my father and mother will not even entertain the idea."

John Harington spoke up. "The one important thing Lady Isobel has on her side, is her staunch Protestant upbringing."

"Yes, but she has no connections, no international ties that would make her a benefit to the English throne," Essex tossed in.

Tom turned on him. "Thank you for making it so plain, Essex." They may have been friends, but the rancor in Tom's eyes proved his loyalty lay entirely with his sister.

The earl shrugged and poured himself another dram of whisky. "I speak truth, Tom. Sometimes the truth is hard to hear."

Tom cursed under his breath, then turned back to the hearth.

God's teeth. Essex sounded like the king now. If I had to hear one more person talk about how hard the truth is to hear, I would throw myself on my dagger and be done with it.

"You may have to settle for a Catholic princess after all, Your Grace." It was Harington this time.

"According to my father's Basilikon Doron, one should not mix marriage and religion."

"Clearly, he has changed his mind," Harington said.

"He sees the benefit of bringing together the two religious persuasions," Essex interjected. "You have the power to wield the religious sword and bend them to your liking. Just think, if you choose the French princess, you can mold her into whatever little Protestant queen you want her to be." He rose and walked around the table to where the prince was sitting. Opening a drawer tucked under the desk, he pulled out a deck of cards, then slammed the drawer shut.

"Christina is only nine years old," the prince protested, picking up the cards Essex had begun to deal.

"Plenty of time to prolong the marriage then," Essex said. "Are you in, Tom?" He dealt cards to the spot Tom had vacated, evidently knowing he could lure him into a game. "Besides, my wife and I were still children when we got married. It does happen."

"And look how that turned out," Tom sniped as he took his seat at the large desk.

Essex raised an eyebrow. "It's highly unlikely the little French princess is a vixen like I was tied to."

"I want Isobel," the prince said softly as he picked up the rest of his cards. "She is a pure English rose. She is intelligent, and beautiful, and would make the marriage bed enjoyable."

"That's enough of that," Tom said, his voice sounding like a snarl.

"That milk-white skin..." Essex trailed off as he dragged a hard breath through his nose.

"And that gorgeous blonde hair," Harington tossed in. "I could wrap my hands into those luscious locks and..."

"That's enough!" Tom slammed his palm down on the table, and the empty whisky bottle wobbled.

Harington laughed and Essex smirked. The prince had a smile on his face too, but I wisnae sure how he felt about their words until he said, "You are trying to get under Tom's skin, but please keep in mind, if anyone will be feeling those silky tresses between their fingers, it's me."

If Tom could do bodily harm with just the look on his face, all three men would be in serious pain. Which is why I was surprised when George, with a stupid grin on his face, said, "I'd like to meet this Lady Isobel Broune."

"Over my dead body," I said with a growl. Something like venom surged through my blood, and I fought back the urge to knock his ridiculous teeth out. The banter between these friends as they teased Tom about Isobel was bad enough, but to add George Preston to the list of men itching to get their hands on her sent white hot heat searing through me. I didnae understand this overprotectiveness I felt for a woman who obviously loathed me, but it was there nonetheless. I hated to see what lengths one of these men might drive me to should the banter continue in this fashion.

Tom's eyebrows shot up. "My sentiments exactly."

Essex toyed with me. "How noble of you to take up our fine prince's cause and defend the honor of the woman who may rule us all one day."

Tom groaned. Feeling the irritation still rumbling through me, I turned to Essex. "What are ye even doing here? I thought ye would be in hiding a few days after that little stunt ye pulled last night at the masque."

A slight smile pulled at the corner of one side of his mouth. "I heard it went smashingly, and you didn't even need me. And thanks to me, you are a shining star."

I chuckled. "A shining star. If it hid nae been for me, the prince's birthday celebration would have been a disaster."

"You could have at least done so without sending my sister fleeing in tears," Tom harped. My, but he was in a foul mood today, it seemed.

"I am nay the one who sent her fleeing into the darkness in tears," I said, straightening my cards in my hand.

"So, you have met the stunning Lady Isobel?" George gawked at me, eyes bulging. "I have heard she is a delight."

"I'll thank you to stop talking about my sister like she is a piece of flesh at the market square," Tom bit out.

"Let us have no more talk of Isobel," Henry advised, a tone of warning in his voice.

We played six rounds of Maw before a footman at the door interrupted us. "What is it, Cummings?" Henry motioned to the man in the scarlet and gold livery to come closer.

"A missive for Sir Tom," the man said, bowing at the waist as he presented Tom a letter.

"Thank you, Cummings," Tom said, taking the missive and tearing the seal to open it. He shoved back from his seat, alarm darkening his features.

"Is everything all right, Tom?" Henry asked, pausing his shuffling for the next round of Maw.

"It seems my mother and father are leaving for Chadwyck House early. Father received notification that my sister's horse, Honeycomb, is in dire straits."

"The one she received for her birthday?" Henry asked, resuming the deal.

"Yes. Apparently, they are leaving at once and have asked if I wanted to leave with them. I must be back at St Andrews in a few days, and there were some things Father needed me to take care of before my departure." He turned his attention back to the letter and continued reading. "He requested His Majesty's Master of the Horse to assist, but your father told him he was needed here with the new foal." He looked up at that, concern written in the creases between his brows.

Henry shook his head, bewildered. "The foal will be fine. He over worries." Then, as if a light turned on inside his head, he said, "I can loan you my Master of the Horse." He patted me on the back, then said, "That is, if he doesn't mind. He can work wonders."

Tom looked toward me, hopeful. "My father will pay well, Robert. It is my sister's favorite horse."

I had things I needed to do here, or at Richmond, wherever the prince's fancy took us next. I needed to focus on how I was going to get the king to see things my way. I had a few ideas in mind, but I needed to hash some things out. But I couldnae seem to refuse anything that had to do with Isobel. No doubt she would spew her venom when she saw me. But her ire was like fuel to my fire. I was a glutton for this kind of punishment, and I relished it like some kind of monster.

"I am at yer disposal, sir." I threw my cards down on the table and stood to go.

"If you can save the horse, I will be forever in your debt." Tom too tossed his cards and drank the last bit of whisky in his glass before standing.

Chapter 16

Chadwyck House, London
March 1612
Isobel

I was more than a little irritated to find Robert standing with Tom
when I arrived at the carriage that would take us from Whitehall.
Father had sent word that Honeycomb was ill, and he was requesting a
favor from the king in the form of his Master of the Horse. We needed
someone with a better knowledge of horses than he, and Father had
hoped the king would oblige.

But the king had refused, and we were saddled with Prince
Henry's man instead. Which would not have been a problem if it had
been anyone other than Robert Stewart.

It didn't help matters he had discarded his perfectly good English
trunks for a Scottish plaid. The scarlet kilt woven with black stripes of
varying degrees of thickness, fell to the top of his knees and hung a little
lower in the back. It was paired with a black leather jerkin and boots
that covered his calves. "He looks ridiculous," I mumbled to myself. Yet
I couldn't keep my eyes from wandering to his plaid covered thighs. I

felt the embarrassment burn on my cheeks when I glanced at Tom and caught him grinning at me.

"You might want to tell your friend there is no great sympathy for the Scots here in England." I felt the words hiss past my lips when we exited the carriage three quarters of an hour later.

Tom's eyes danced with delight. "I noticed you can't keep your eyes off his knees. I think it's an excellent way to attract the female sex. I might ask Father if I can borrow one of his old kilts."

"You will do no such thing!" I gasped. "He looks absurd. What on earth is he thinking? Doesn't he know it was the king's Scottish roots that almost got him blown to bits in the Gunpower Plot? He's going to get himself killed."

Tom's eyes widened. "You know nothing of which you speak, Isobel. It was more than his Scottish roots that endangered the king. It was the Catholics who wanted him and the prince dead because of his Protestant leanings, not just because he was Scottish."

"All the more reason to distance ourselves from him. His Catholic ties could endanger us all," I whispered, loud enough for only Tom to hear.

Tom let out an exasperated sigh. "I don't understand your hatred for him," he whispered back. "He has been nothing but respectful and kind to you since dining with us the first night he was in London. He has shown you more kindness than you have shown him, and much more than you deserve. Ah, thank you, Robert" Tom said, speaking louder. He reached to take a satchel that Robert handed him as he joined us on the steps.

I stopped and turned aside as well. "I'm going to the stables to see Honeycomb," I said, leaving both men standing at the front door.

"I'll accompany ye," Robert said, moving to match my steps. "Do ye mind seeing that my things reach my chambers, Tom?"

"Not at all," Tom said, that irritating grin pulling at his mouth again. "By all means, see to Honeycomb." He motioned toward the stables before turning back to the footmen and giving instructions concerning our trunks. "Oh, and Isobel," he called, a note of teasing in his voice, "don't get your slippers dirty."

I stuck my tongue out at him like I used to do when I was just a girl. He threw his head back and laughed heartily before slipping into the house.

I led Robert to the stables, refusing to look at him, nor speak to him, until we came upon Father and my brother Will, standing in the middle of the stables. Father turned, and a look of relief spread over his face when he saw Robert. I fought the urge to pout, for I was usually the center of my father's universe, and he didn't even give me a second glance. But the look of worry that covered his face after his greeting led me to understand Honeycomb was truly in a dire situation.

"She's in here." He motioned to us to follow him, and I noticed Honeycomb had been moved into a different stall. "She isn't eating. Her flanks are sunken, but her abdomen is distended. She won't let anyone near her."

She would let me near her, I just knew she would. Without thinking, I ducked under the wooden bar that crossed her door and immediately made my way to her.

"Isobel, no!" I heard Father yell. But it was too late. In the instant it had taken me to cross the threshold, Honeycomb had reared up on her back legs and let out a horrendous neigh. Shock and fear stupefied me, and it wasn't until a strong arm had snaked around my waist and pulled me backward that I realized what was happening. In an instant I found myself pulled flush against a hard wall at my back. The arm that had pulled me backward, tightened around me, and flipped me onto my stomach, shielding me from Honeycomb's hooves as they came crashing down on top of us both. The sound of shouts and running feet reached me, along with the distressed cries of my mare. We lay motionless for a moment, and the sound of a groan and labored breaths flooded my ears. Will had been injured. I could hear it in his breathing. But I couldn't seem to move, so shaken was I at my mare's reaction to me.

"Are ye hurt, lass?" a voice heaved. A tremor jolted through me. It wasn't Will who had pulled me to safety and sheltered me with his body. It was Robert. My brain urged me to remove myself from beneath him. But the trembling of my limbs found comfort beneath the hard, unmoving muscle of his chest and legs that protected me.

His arm constricted tighter around me, and his ragged breath brushed lightly against the nape of my neck. The sensation prickled the skin down my arms, and I reflexively gripped his upper arm, clinging to him like a wet leaf to a skirt hem.

"I'm all right," I said, a little out of breath. After a moment, I wiggled in an effort to free myself, but it wasn't until he shifted his weight slightly that I was able to move. Warmth brushed across my calf under my bundled skirts, and I recognized the sensation of skin on skin as his thigh brushed against my leg, setting off a fluttering in my belly that I was sure turned my cheeks red. I pushed myself up onto my knees in the most unladylike position in which I had ever found myself. Robert climbed to his feet first and held out a hand to assist me. I narrowed my eyes at him, as if he had planned the whole thing just to get me on the ground.

He forced a polite tone. "My lady." He bowed slightly before the painful expression overtook his face. I took his hand for assistance and allowed him to pull me to my feet.

"Thank you," I said, knowing it was the civil thing to say.

"My pleasure," came his labored reply. His words caressed my skin and made me shiver.

"Isobel, you are hurt!" Will pointed to a spot on my dress. "There's blood." I looked down at my dress, then at my hands, where I found my right hand stained with a little more blood. I didn't feel injured, and I had no idea where the blood had come from, until I looked at Robert and noticed his face had lost all its color.

"Are you injured, Robert?" I could barely get the question out. I didn't particularly care if he was injured, but if he had taken an injury for me, I would feel a little guilty.

My father pointed toward the back of Robert's head, where a darkened spot soaked his coppery brown hair. "I think Honeycomb got you, Robert."

"Aye," he said, reaching up and gingerly touching the back of his head again. He winced slightly before his eyes sought mine. "My apologies." He pointed to my skirts.

"Apologies?" Father scoffed. "We owe you our deepest gratitude." Father reached for me and pulled me to him, wrapping his comforting arms around me, and I felt safe once again. "Thank you, Robert. We are indebted to you." He planted a kiss on the top of my head before Will handed me a handkerchief to wipe my hands.

"You wouldn't know it to look at her, but our mother is a skilled healer. Allow me to take you to her so she can have a look at that injury," Will offered. "You might need a stitch or two."

"Nay, not yet," Robert responded. "Give me a minute to look at yer mare."

"But you are bleeding," Will objected.

"I'll survive," he said, turning to look at Honeycomb. He slid himself along the wall of the stall, moving unhurriedly so as not to frighten the horse. When he reached her head once more, he slowly picked up a handful of straw and rubbed it between his fingers. He then spoke gently to her, shushing her and reaching a tentative hand toward her. "Easy, lass," he cooed, inching close enough until she finally allowed him to lay his hand against her muzzle. She huffed out a harsh breath, then leaned into his touch. He continued to speak quietly to her, moving with great patience toward her flank.

A few minutes later, Robert turned back to us. "This mare is in foal."

"What?" my father choked out. "But—" he paused momentarily, "she usually keeps to herself in the fields. And we only allow her runs with the other mares. How did this happen?" He looked to Will with exasperation.

Robert's forehead crinkled as amusement covered his face. "Well, sir—"

"Please don't indulge me with a lesson about the procreation activities of horses," Father said dryly. Robert chuckled, then sobered.

"She is starving, sir. I have a special concoction we used with my brother's mares. It seems to entice their taste buds and increase their appetites. With yer permission, I'd like to try it with Honeycomb. But a word of warning. The foal might already be sickly. Sometimes nature has a way of working these things out."

I stifled a cry. Was Honeycomb starving herself to rid herself of a sick foal? I shuddered at that thought.

Father ran a hand across his brow. "Let my hostler know what you need, and he'll see to it. We appreciate any help you can give her."

Robert leaned against the railing of the stall. He looked pale, and a sheen of perspiration covered his face. "I'll draw up the list immediately. Ye will want to start the mixture right away."

"I care about our horses, Robert, but Honeycomb can wait a little longer. That injury cannot." Father motioned toward Robert's head. "Will, take Robert to your mother and see what she can do for him."

"Yes, Father." Will laid a hand on Robert's shoulder and led him out of the stables.

"Perhaps you can assist your mother," Father suggested after they had left.

I swallowed hard. "You know I'm not very good at healing things." Not to mention I didn't want to think about my role in Robert obtaining that injury.

Father was silent for a moment. "Aye, and I also know that you don't like Robert much. But that man just took a kick in the head for you. At least check in on him and show your gratitude." I bit the inside of my lip to keep it from trembling. My recklessness was the cause of this fiasco, but I couldn't face him. Especially not after what happened on the floor of Honeycomb's stall. "I'm going to find Briggs," he finally said when I didn't answer. Father turned to fetch the hostler, but I lingered a little longer watching Honeycomb. I would give mother time to nurse Robert, then I would talk to her about the poison for Frances. And then later, when the memory of Robert's skin no longer burned against mine, just maybe then I would find him and tell him thank you. Maybe.

Chapter 17

Chadwyck House, London
March 1612
Isobel

I pushed open the heavy wooden door to Mother's apothecary and immediately inhaled the pungent odor of valerian. Stalks of the fetid plant with its pink and white flowers stripped from their stems, hung along the far wall, along with the more tolerable stems of fading white yarrow and the soft, sweet floral scent of purple violets. Dark glass bottles with dome-shaped lids and small, red clay amphoras littered the oak tabletops. Phials filled with the dried leaves, stems, and petals of various medicinal concoctions Mother had prepared and stored filled the shelves. All were arranged in order by its use, with plants used for pain relief or bruising and swelling, being separated from those used for settling upset stomachs, or inducing vomit, and so forth.

The golden yellow glow of the late afternoon sun shone through the tiny, stained windows of Mother's workroom, spilling sunlight onto her fiery, auburn curls. But it did very little to drive back the shadows that always seemed to cling to the walls. It was for this reason I never enjoyed coming here as a child. I preferred pretty frocks, delicate hair ribbons, and exquisite slippers, not a fusty room filled with cobwebs and noxious herbs.

Mother wore a linen caul on her head and a simple woad apron over a russet kirtle, her typical attire when she was at work in her apothecary. She was bent over a table, pulling dainty white flowers from a stalk, and separating the petals and leaves into distinct mounds.

I watched her for a moment, memories of my childhood clogging my throat and choking me with long-forgotten emotion. Thoughts of a time when I would sit at her knee, and she would instruct me on the ways of the herbal garden and the many remedies we can find for healing from the earth filled me with conflicted nostalgia. Her book of herbs, Tractatus de Herbis, still lay on the table beside her, along with another book in which she would record measurements so she could keep track of her supplies.

"How's your patient?" I finally asked, turning over the lid from one of her clay pots and spinning it like a top.

Mother eyed me as she continued pulling the leaves and petals off the stems of a chickweed plant. "Don't sound so concerned, Isobel," she said dryly.

I lifted my chin. "You are mistaken," I defended. "You think I haven't a heart, but I'm not so calloused as to wish ill upon the man who prevented me from coming to injury."

She brushed a wisp of hair from her eye with the back of her wrist. "He quite possibly saved your life."

"Oh, please," I said, rolling my eyes. "Whatever injury he sustained is the same injury I would have suffered. And *he* isn't dead. I don't think we can claim he saved my life."

Truth be told, Honeycomb's violent reaction had shaken me. But I wasn't about to admit that to anyone, especially Robert, and I certainly wasn't going to act as if I owed him my life.

"That horse could have done some real damage to ye. Robert had a deep gash and needed several stitches. I doused his stitched wound with aloe vera, gave him some ginger for the pain, and then sent him to bed to rest. I was able to stay the bleeding somewhat, but he could easily tear the stitches open if he isn't careful." I watched her in silence for several more minutes until she finally said, "Is there something ye wanted, Isobel? For I doubt ye came to inquire about Robert, seeing how ye cannot tolerate the man."

I started. First my father mentioned it and now my mother. I didn't realize I had made my dislike for him so apparent. That is, Tom had noticed because he had been around us both at court, but had I really been so obvious that night at dinner too?

"What I don't understand," I said, pushing myself off the counter against which I leaned and stepping closer to Mother, "is why no one is talking about the history this man's family seems to share with ours."

My mother's eyes shot to mine. "Of what do ye speak, Isobel? What is it that ye think ye know?"

I hated the way our parents still tried to protect us from things, especially information they thought we didn't need to know. I had tried to broach this subject with her before, but we had been interrupted by Lady Frances. Hopefully now I could get answers.

"Robert's father and mine did not like each other. His father is a necromancer. Father was an inquisitor. Did Father arrest and interrogate the Earl of Bothwell? I saw you and him exchange looks over the supper table that first night Robert was here. You obviously don't trust him, so why do you continue to allow him into our home?"

Mother stopped what she was doing and looked at me. Setting the chickweed leaves aside, she said, "Ye have become more inquisitive than ye used to be."

I narrowed my eyes at her. "I'm not a dunderhead, Mother. I do have good questions sometimes."

Mother's shoulders sagged. "Don't get me wrong, dear. I am well aware of how intelligent ye are. But ye are usually more interested in the latest fashions than the well-being of your family."

I could feel her chastisement burn on my cheeks. But what hurt even more was the truth she spoke. I could not deny I tended to be more caught up in myself than the suffering of those around me. I felt a hot tear stinging my cheek, and I turned from her quickly to brush it away. I pinched my lips together to stay their trembling.

Mother stepped closer and slid her arm around my shoulder. "I am sorry. I did not mean to hurt your feelings."

I sniffed then lifted my chin. "The truth hurts, doesn't it?"

Silence hung in the air for an awkward moment with only the *drip, drip, drip* of a late afternoon rain shower tapping against the windowsill. "The Earl of Bothwell was known for his scheming against his cousin, the king," Mother began. "He plotted several kidnapping attempts in the early years of King James's reign. He would attempt an attack on the king, then come back with his tail between his legs, begging for mercy and forgiveness. The king would always let him back into his good graces. But as the witch interrogations intensified, more and more evidence came to light concerning Robert's father. Your father had evidence against him and had to use it to clear his own name when he found himself thrown into the tolbooth and facing accusations of treason."

My heart jumped. "Father was arrested for treason? Was that because of the earl?"

Mother tilted her head slightly. "Somewhat," she said. "There was another man who wanted your father out of the way to get to me. He had a lot to do with your father's arrest. But the earl had tried to recruit your father to his cause, and in the process, incriminated him further."

"Another man wanted him out of the way to get to you?" I shrieked. "You have *got* to tell me all about that." I purposefully pouted, but she waved me off with an embarrassed smile playing at her lips.

"The fact remains, that Robert is not his father," she concluded. "He's never even met his father. 'Tis nay fair to hold the earl's sins against Robert when he had no part in them." I chewed on my bottom lip, considering her words. "Besides," she continued, "he has given us no reason not to trust him. Now, I would appreciate if my oldest daughter would remember the manners she was instructed in and treat the man decently while he is a guest in our home. Once ye are back at court, then I shall be blissfully ignorant of how ye treat him."

A small smile pulled at the corner of my mouth. "I'll take that as permission to treat him abominably," I said, feeling my smile widen.

She shook her head at me and my nonsense, then said, "Now, are ye going to tell me why ye are really here?"

I took a deep breath, searching for how to approach her about the poison Lady Frances needed. I bit my bottom lip in nervousness then said, "I have a favor to ask of you."

Mother stopped what she was doing and looked up at me. Her eyes reflected something there that almost pained me to see. She loved it when I asked her for advice, or even help. We had been at odds so often over the past few years, that she always looked elated when I was in need of something from her.

She schooled her features, then said, "It must be of grave importance for my independent and all-knowing daughter to ask something of me."

I frowned. This was exactly why I hated asking her for anything. But this *was* of grave importance, and I would have to put my own feelings aside for the time being to get what I needed.

I spun the makeshift top again and watched it wobble to a complete stop before speaking. I opened my mouth, then paused, thinking about how exactly I wanted to phrase my request. "I have a friend who has had some trouble with rodents in her bedchambers. She asked my advice on a type of poison that could be used to rid her of the pests."

Mother brushed the tiny chickweed flowers into a bowl then set them aside with the leaves. She dipped her pen into her inkpot and jotted something down in her book. Her face was void of any expression, and I was beginning to think she hadn't heard a word I said. I spotted a stray bud and plucked it from the table, dropping it into the bowl with the others, then looked to her again, waiting for her response.

She laid her pen down and ran her hands down both sides of her apron, smoothing her skirt. She pressed her lips together in thought then finally said, "Why doesn't she ask the chambermaids for assistance? Is that not their job?"

Irritation burned into me. Why did she always have to question everything? "She is embarrassed about the situation. She thought with your knowledge of herbs I might be able to help her obtain something based on your recommendations."

A confused expression overtook her face. "What is there to be embarrassed about? It's a natural enough occurrence, even in a palace." I didn't have an answer for that, so I just stared at her. When I didn't answer she let out a sigh, then looked around the room, her hands propped on her hips in her best thinking position. She looked like just another maid standing there, in her homespun apron and kirtle, not like the earl's wife most people knew her to be. I had always been a little embarrassed by the way she clung to her old Scottish way of life, even after Father had been granted his title, and they had become so wealthy. But in this moment, she was the key to helping me get what I wanted, and what I wanted was help catching Prince Henry's attention. Her Scottish housewifery might finally benefit me.

She went to a shelf at the other end of the room. Scanning the bottles and vials there, she said, "There are a few things that come to mind." She pulled down a short, round amphora with a lid that fastened on both sides. Lifting the metal rings, she pulled the lid off and peered inside. "*Solanaceae*, or rather, the berries from a *Solanaceae* plant." She shook the jar, allowing the berries to roll around inside, knocking against each other, then held the jar out for me to see them.

They were a shiny, black berry. "Those look innocent enough," I said, glancing at the innocuous-looking berries.

"Don't be fooled," Mother said. "They are called nightshade. They can induce hallucinations, convulsions and trouble breathing, to name a few symptoms." She replaced the lid and put the container back on the shelf. Running a fingertip over her pots and jars, she pulled another off the shelf. Shaking it, she removed the lid and showed it to me. "*Conium maculatum*, better known as hemlock."

I peered inside the jar at the small, brown, tear-shaped seeds. "Isn't that what Socrates ingested as his punishment for corrupting the minds of the youth of Athens?"

"A form of it, aye." She pulled another jar off the shelf. "All parts of the plant are poisonous. These are the leaves." She showed me the contents. "However, the roots and seeds are the most toxic."

"What happens to the person or animal that falls victim to hemlock?" I asked, feeling a sick bile rising in my throat at the harmful possibilities.

"The victim can't breathe," she said simply. Mother put the lid back on and turned back to the shelf. "Ye must be very careful when handling poisons, but hemlock can be especially dangerous as it can be poisonous just by touching it. Ye don't even have to swallow it."

I had no idea my mother knew so much about poisons. She had generally only used her herbal knowledge for good, or so I thought. But her knowledge of deadly herbs was impressive, and a little frightening.

She picked up a small, black pot and peered inside. "Ah, cantharides. I don't know a lot about this. It was given to me by a woman with a less-than-stellar reputation, with whom I would never admit to speaking." She chuckled lightly. "'Tis also known as Spanish Fly, a type of beetle."

My instinct was to jerk away. "Eww." I hated bugs.

Mother chuckled again at my reaction. "Nay, it's ground into a fine powder." She pulled the lid off once more and held it out for me to look.

I peered inside. It had indeed been ground into a fine powder of shimmering metallic green. "It's beautiful though," I said, stepping away.

"'Tis green," she pointed out, and I understood her insinuation. She was quite aware of my repugnance of the color.

"But it's shiny. It's very pretty."

"Hmm," she said as she replaced the lid. "Apparently 'tis deadly as well, but I know very little about it." She put the jars back on the shelf and pulled off another. Inside were flat, brownish-gray, disks with tiny hairlike coverings.

"I've seen those before," I said, almost excitedly.

"Do ye remember what they are called?" Mother quizzed.

I searched my memory for some knowledge of it. I had never been good at remembering the names of all the herbs mother had taught me over the years. I shook my head.

She rattled the contents, causing the flat disks to clink against each other. "Nux vomica. Another highly poisonous seed that can cause sickness even from touching it. This one is toxic to all vermin, so 'tis especially good for rats."

She put the lid back on top of the container but left it sitting in front of her, then looked up at me.

"My word, mother! I didn't know you knew so much about poisons. Is this all you've got?" I posed the question in a jest, but she put a finger to her chin, deep in thought.

Walking to the other side of the room, she pulled a small phial from the shelf that sat behind several much larger bottles. It was a clear bottle, and the contents were visible without opening it.

"This is called arsenic. I didn't make this, for it comes from a mineral and not from a plant. But it is deadly too. The frightening thing about arsenic is that it is virtually invisible in food and drink. The victim never knows it's there."

I swallowed hard, feeling like I had eaten sand. "That is frightening," I said, not taking my eyes from hers. "What does that do to the victim?" I asked again, not sure I wanted to continue hearing the results.

"Vomiting, abdominal pain, diarrhea," she said matter-of-factly. She shook the white, powdery substance within the small bottle before replacing it on the shelf.

"How did humans discover such atrocious means of eliminating one another?" I asked, my voice barely above a whisper. The thought of administering a poison to someone and inflicting so much pain on them was disgusting.

"Hmm," was my mother's wordless response once more. She turned and came back to the table. "It's a good thing it's only for rats, right? Those disgusting creatures deserve to die. They carry diseases and are a nuisance." She visibly shivered, wrapping her arms around herself as if there were a sudden chill in the air. "Ye must tell your friend to be very careful when handling poisons. Ye don't want her to make herself sick." I nodded in understanding, but then she said, "Who is the friend that needs this poison?"

I hesitated. Lady Frances was quite embarrassed at her little rat problem. And she had specifically said I mustn't tell Mother who the poison was for.

"She is too embarrassed and asked me not to tell," I said, hoping that would be enough of an answer that she wouldn't pry further.

Mother's brows knit together, and she placed her hands on her hips again. I knew my mother, and I knew that look. She wasn't going to budge unless I told her who it was for.

As if reading my mind, she said, "'Tis not she who should feel embarrassed. The king should take care of his rat problem." Her eyes hardened into the amber gemstones her eye color resembled, revealing her feelings concerning His Majesty. "All the same, I do not feel comfortable giving ye such a dangerous item without knowing who is receiving it," she continued. "Ye either tell me who it is for, or ye can forget getting any help from me."

I could feel the panic rising in my chest. I had promised Lady Frances I wouldn't give away her secret. But I also desperately needed her help. I would just have to explain to her my mother wouldn't help without knowing to whom she was giving the poison.

"You mustn't tell anyone, Mother. She is very embarrassed by it."

Mother let out a long sigh. "I am nothing if not discreet, Isobel."

We stared each other down for a moment before I finally broke. "The poison is for Lady Frances," I said, feeling a tinge of guilt for betraying her trust.

"Absolutely not," Mother said immediately, turning to put the nux vomica back on the shelf.

I was offended for the sake of my friend. "Why not?" I said, hearing my voice go a little higher than I intended.

"Isobel, I do not trust the Countess of Essex. I wouldn't put it past her to use the poison on an enemy."

I gasped. "Mother! What a horrible thing to say!"

Mother raised one eyebrow and shrugged a shoulder. "Well, I said it, nonetheless. And I stand by my decision. Ye can give her the information I shared with ye, and she can take it to an apothecary and ask for it. But she'll not be getting her poison from me."

"Mother!" The word came as an angry plea. I crossed my arms in front of my chest to show my displeasure and stared her down with all the daggers I could muster. "Why do you always have to be so difficult?"

Her eyebrows shot up, but she didn't speak for a moment while she cleaned up her work area. She closed the book she kept her notes in but left her Tractatus de Herbis open on the table. With a heavy sigh she finally answered my accusation.

"Before I was a countess, before I was a mother—nay—before I was even a wife, I was a healer. I hold a vast amount of knowledge in this head of mine. I can stop blood flow or bring on bleeding. I can settle an upset stomach or ease the pain of a broken bone. I can prescribe tinctures that will make a woman fertile, or help a man be the best lover he can be. I have the power of life or death in my hands. And I take that responsibility very, *very* seriously." She paused and licked her lips. "I will share my wisdom willingly, freely even, to anyone who asks. I do not hoard my knowledge if I can help someone else in need. But I will not," she poked the tabletop with her index finger, stressing her words, "enable someone whom I judge to be uncharitable and supply them with the tools to bring about their sinister intents." She stopped finally, taking a deep breath through her mouth, and blowing it out through her nostrils. She was quite calm for her passionate soliloquy, but her words stirred even more anger within me.

"Speaking of uncharitable," I shouted. "It is uncharitable of you to determine Lady Frances's intent when you aren't acquainted with her. She is young and beautiful and powerful, and you are jealous of her. You make her out to be some monster when secretly you probably wish you could be just like her." I was crying now, and I swiped at my tears angrily and tried to catch my breath.

Mother's eyes flared, and I could tell I hit a nerve. "That woman ogled my husband then had the audacity to tell me I was lucky to have the affections of such a handsome man!" She swiped her hand through the air in jerky, furious movements. "If I didn't know any better, I would say *she* was jealous of *me*." Her voice warbled on her last words, and she took a shaky breath.

"So that is it. Your pride was hurt because of her words, and now you are withholding your assistance as payback."

Throwing up her hands she said, "I can't do this, Isobel. Ye always want to fight, and I just don't have the strength left in me to indulge ye." She then removed her apron and hurriedly folded it before tossing it onto the tabletop and stalking for the door. When she reached the threshold, she turned back toward me. "Share the information with the countess if ye will, but I will not share my herbs with her. Do not ask me again."

I tried to school my features and not allow myself to glare at her. How dare she accuse me of always wanting to argue? She was the one who was always so contrary. I crossed my arms over my chest and fumed silently, trying to calm myself. My heart was beating wildly, and I took several deep breaths, willing my mind to think.

"It's time for supper," she finally said. "Let us be done with this argument and enjoy a peaceable meal."

I had to bring something back for Frances. She was my friend, but she meant what she said. If she was to help me, I had to help her in return. And if I came back empty-handed, there would be no help for me with Henry.

I swiped at my remaining tears, wiping my face dry. I followed my mother out of her apothecary, and she closed the door behind us. I said no more to her as we made our way to the supper room. Within minutes my mother's face was relaxed, but I was stewing inside. Mother was wrong about Lady Frances; I was sure of it. And I could not let the countess down. One way or another, I had to get my hands on some poison. It wouldn't take much. Mother would never know. That is, she would never know as long as she didn't catch me when I returned to the apothecary later, while she was occupied with other matters.

And if I did get caught, I told myself, I would deal with the consequences later.

~

Mother kept a stack of fresh linen bandages handy; it was just a matter of remembering where she stored them. I shuffled through several baskets and shelves until I found what I was searching for. I removed two squares of cloth from a small basket, then went to the shelf where she had put the poisons.

Now that I needed a specific container, they all looked similar. I picked up one and removed the lid to peer inside. It looked molded and smelled horrendous. I threw the lid back on top and replaced it on the shelf. Keeping one eye on the door, I hurried through the clay pots, looking for the hemlock or the nux vomica.

I didn't know if Mother planned to return to her apothecary this evening, but I couldn't take any chances. I needed to get what I was looking for and make my departure before she decided to return. I took a step back and studied the shelf, second-guessing where I thought she had placed the jars. It would have been much easier to take the bottle of arsenic. It was easy to see. But it would have been much easier to notice when it was missing as well, for I would have had to take the whole bottle since I had nothing to put the powder in.

My hands shook as I rifled through the jars, pulling off lids and looking inside each container. Frustration built as I opened every jar. Prickly leaves, withered flower peddles, dried nettles and stems. Nothing looked like the seeds she had shown me.

A scratching noise behind me had me turning on my heels. But there was no one at the door. And another glance about the room confirmed there was no one else in the room with me. My heart pounded a little faster, and I took a deep breath, turning back to my search. I reached for another jar, but in my haste, I knocked it over. The container crashed to the floor, sending tiny seeds scattering in every direction.

"Devil take it," I cursed under my breath. I didn't have time for this.

Grabbing a broom of husks tied together with a short handle, I fell to my knees and began sweeping the seeds into a pile. Once I had gathered them all, I reached to scoop them up to place them back in the jar. But fear suddenly gripped me. I had no idea what these seeds were, nor what they were used for. And given the nature of some of the poisons Mother had described to me, it was probably best not to touch them. Instead, I took the cloths I had found and scooped them up, being careful not to come in contact with the small, round seeds.

I had wasted too much time. I set the jar back on the shelf and reached for another, but this time a scurrying to my left caused me to practically jump out of my skin.

"God's teeth, Juniper, you scared the life out of me." Mother's cat peered up at me, his golden eyes glowering at me from his hiding place in the corner of the room. He crept closer to me, sniffing the floor where I had just swept, like a hound on the hunt.

"Shoo," I said, motioning to the long-haired black and gray feline that had been relegated to the apothecary to keep Mother company. Father had a severe sneezing reaction whenever Juniper was around, so Mother thought it best if the cat just stayed in here with her. The cat, not being a friendly creature, didn't seem to mind the seclusion. In fact, right now he was staring at me as if I were an interloper in his lair. "Shoo, Juniper. That's all I need is for you to consume something poisonous I might have spilled on the floor. Mother would have my head if that happened."

The cat lifted his nose into the air, strutted to the other side of the room, and settled himself in front of the hearth, where the embers from the previous fire still glowed. I turned back to my task. But the relief I felt at finding Juniper was the intruder, only morphed into panic the longer it took me to find what I needed.

Finally, I found the object I was looking for. The large, flat discs clanked together in their protective cocoon of a jar. I could have sworn

I had already opened this jar once, but no matter. I wrapped the cloth about my fingers then hurriedly plucked the seeds from their sarcophagus and gently placed them in the other cloth. I wrapped the seeds tightly and replaced the lid, pushing the jar toward the back of the shelf, out of sight. With one more glance toward Juniper, as if seeking his silence on the matter, I made my exit, the tightness in my chest only amplifying.

Chapter 18

Chadwyck House, London
March 1612
Robert

My head hurt like Hades. Lady Stratford had a gentle hand, and I was thankful for her assistance with the stitching. But by the time I had made it back to my rooms, I had already forgotten what she had told me to do with the ginger root she had given me. Chew on it? Drink it in tea? I couldnae remember what she said.

My shirt was bloody, so I decided to wash and change clothes before venturing back to the apothecary to get the instructions again. Mayhap I would have her write it down, for not only was my head pounding like a drum, but I felt like my mind was in a fog, and I wisnae stringing my thoughts together too easily.

I poured water into the basin beside my bed then washed my hands, face, and the back of my neck. The water was pink by the time I had finished, so I tossed the dirty water out the window before filling the basin with fresh water again. A small bar of soap sat on the table, and I worked it into a good lather and washed the rest of my body, ridding myself of the smell of horse dung and dirt.

But after all that effort, I could barely keep my eyes open. Lady Stratford had advised me to nay sleep just yet, but after cleaning myself up, there wisnae energy left to even go to supper. So, I disregarded her advice and had a lie-down. When I awoke, I felt a wee refreshed, but I could tell by the position of the sun in the sky that the day was well spent. I vaguely remembered Will coming to my bedchamber to call me to supper, but I had sent him away. Now I was famished.

I donned my plaid and a fresh tunic. My skin heated as I recalled Isobel's eyes roving over my kilt this morning. She hated me, there was no mistaking that, but I wisnae simple. I recognized a lass's appreciative gaze when I saw one. And there was heat in her eyes as she appraised my choice of clothing before turning her face away.

I tucked my sgian dubh against my right leg, then adjusted my hose snuggly around the hilt. I ran a hand through my wet hair before stepping into the corridor, being careful not to touch the spot where my stitches were. I hoped I could find my way back to the apothecary. Chadwyck House was nowhere near the size of Richmond Palace, but the many halls and rooms were still unfamiliar to me. And in my dazed state, I widnae be surprised if I found myself lost within its winding halls.

After wondering aimlessly for ten minutes, I finally broke down and asked the pretty little maid that had played cards with us the first night I visited Chadwyck. She had been friendly to me, despite her mistress's chagrin, and we had enjoyed lively conversation in the intervals between rounds.

She was escorting a cherub with auburn curls bouncing wildly around apple-rounded cheeks and big blue eyes. I believed her to be the youngest child of Lord and Lady Stratford, but I couldnae recall her name.

"Edith, can I trouble ye to point me in the direction of the apothecary? Lady Stratford prescribed a remedy for me, but I cannae seem to recall what I am to do with it."

The maid's eyes lit up. "Certainly, my lord. Lady Mary and I are heading in a similar direction. We will show you the way."

"I am nay a lord, Edith. There is nay need to show me such deference," I said, as I turned to walk with her and the wee lass, Mary.

We hid nae walked two steps when the child blurted, "Sir, you have on a dress."

I smiled at the sound of her sweet wee voice, perpetuating her angelic persona. Edith on the other hand, turned an embarrassed shade of red.

"Hush now, Lady Mary," the maid scolded. "That is not a dress but a kilt. It is common attire for the Scots, is it not, Sir Robert?"

"Aye," I said, nodding in agreement. I dropped to one knee in front of the child and whispered, "'Tisn't fair us men are bound by those confounded trunks while ye ladies have the freedom of a dress, is it?" Lady Mary giggled and covered her mouth with a chubby hand. The gesture reminded me of her older sister, and I wondered if that is where she picked up the adorable habit. I continued, "While we dinnae call them dresses in Scotland, we enjoy the freedom of movement all the same." I winked at her, and her face went slack with awe from my explanation.

We made several turns, and I was already twisted about although we had barely taken more than twenty steps. "Why are there so many twists and turns in this house?" I asked, noticing every hall had portraits of former lords and ladies, their children, pets, and all the accoutrements of a great manor house such as Chadwyck.

Edith chuckled. "Oh, it is quite easy to get lost in Chadwyck House. It took me over a year before I could find my way from the kitchen to my room without getting lost at least once." We took another turn. This hallway was painted in a dark green, but the paintings all looked the same. *I bet Isobel hates this corridor.* I smiled smugly at the intrusive thought. The maid continued, "Chadwyck House was built by George Cary in the later years of the reign of Henry the Eighth. It was in the care of the Cary family until the last Cary died without an heir." Here her voice dropped to a little above a whisper even with no one else around. "The Carys were known papists." She eyed me as if expecting me to give a reaction. When I didn't respond, she said, "The

Catholics have had a time of it in England for a while now. This house was built with several trick walls and hidden doors. The doors lead to secret rooms, where the manor priest could hide, should the king's soldiers come knocking."

"Priest holes?" I asked. I had heard of the sad lengths the Catholics had to resort to in order to protect themselves during the latter years of the Tudor dynasty.

Edith nodded. "Apparently, they made for great fun when the earl's children were younger. A game of hide and seek took on a whole other meaning, if you knew where the priest holes were." At this she stopped and pointed down a corridor to the right. "Walk to the end of this hallway, then turn left. Go past the Great Hall and when the hallway comes to another dead end, turn right. The apothecary is down the spiral steps, on the right."

I was usually good with directions, but my head was spinning with those instructions. "All right," I said, deciding I would find it eventually. "Thank ye for yer assistance."

"Good luck," the maid said with a compassionate look on her face.

"Goodbye," the wee Lady Mary called, waving frantically at me with her free hand. "We'll say a prayer for you."

I smiled at the child and dipped my head in thanks, then set off in the direction Edith had said.

The directions sounded complicated, but I found the spiral staircase in no time. I made my way down, flattening my hand against the wall to hold myself upright. The pain was increasing, and my head was feeling lighter.

I had just stepped off the last stone when I saw Isobel coming out of the door Edith spoke of. She was looking in my direction but turned her head as I rounded the corner, so I didnae think she saw me. She was gripping a wad of cloth in her hands, guarding it carefully, and the look on her face made me think of someone who was sneaking away.

I opened the door to the apothecary, but there was no one inside, save the feisty feline I had seen in there earlier with the countess. I shut the door behind me when I left and decided to see if I could find where

Isobel had gone. Perhaps she could direct me to her mother. I headed in the direction that I had watched her go. Of course, the hallway ended at another, and I was forced to choose a direction. I looked to my right and the hallway was empty, but when I turned to the left, I saw a sliver of a pale blue frock disappearing around the corner.

I hurried to catch up with her. She had a good lead on me, but I moved faster and soon I was within shouting distance.

"Lady Isobel, may I have a word?"

She heard me, for I could tell by the turn of her head. But the frightened look on her face as she hurried on made my heart sink. Surely, she didnae think I would harm her. She ran a little further, then turned into a little alcove. I recognized the nook, for this was the direction from which I had come earlier when the countess brought me to her apothecary. But as I stood in the middle of the alcove now—alone— I blessed Edith for her tidbit of information that she had shared with me earlier.

I stepped to the wall and looked at it closely. It looked like any other wall in the old house with nothing out of the ordinary apparent. The red bricks were old, but sturdy, and the masonry work was exceptional. But there was a portion of the wall that looked newer, where the brick work ended and a plaster, not unlike the wattle and daub houses in Scotland, began. It was here that I focused my attention, and I reached up and touched the wall, running my hand along the breadth and height of it. I closed my eyes and felt with my fingertips, feeling for any cracks or crevices or anything that would give an indication the wall opened. When my fingers moved over a slight variation in the wall, I opened my eyes.

After I felt the irregularity, the signs were obvious. A portrait of a young lass, sitting on a grassy knoll and holding a lamb, hung on the wall. But the frame was crooked and the dust around the corners had been smudged. I leaned on the wall to put my ear to it, when suddenly it gave way, casting me into the chamber on the other side. The wall immediately returned to its original position, plunging me into utter darkness.

A gasp from within led me to ken I had found my prize. "My lady," I whispered, as if the darkness demanded silence. There was no response, but I could hear her soft breathing as I used my other senses to find her. "I ken ye are in here lass. Dinnae be frightened. I merely need yer help." A scrape of her slipper against the wood floor guided me in her direction. But as I stretched out my arms to feel my way in the darkness, I was surprised to find that the walls were quite narrow, and I could reach them both by extending my arms completely. A thump and a rattle came from the direction of Isobel, then a soft curse. I smiled in the darkness at her words, for I was sure she would have never uttered such sentiments in broad daylight.

I had only taken one step when the sound of flint striking a fire steel echoed in the darkness. Tiny sparks fell onto what looked like char cloth. Isobel blew onto it and a dull flame ignited enough to spark a small candle to life. The single flame illuminated the lovely face of the earl's daughter, revealing she was right in front of me.

"Hello," I said, amused, but she didnae answer. Instead, she rolled her eyes as she held the candle up between us. She still clutched the bunched cloth in her hands, making it difficult for her to do much else.

"There is only room for one priest in here," she said through gritted teeth.

"Good thing I'm nay a priest then."

She harumphed, then placed her fisted hand on her hip. "This is a tight space. There is not room for the both of us in here."

The closeness of the walls and blackness of the room closed in on us like a suffocating shroud. Yet she smelled of lemons with a hint of sugar, and it made me want to pull her even closer. My hands itched to be on her again, and I ran a finger over the calloused spot on my left hand. The spot that always reminded me she wisnae for me. The monster never gets the maiden.

"There is plenty of room, unless ye had something else in mind besides talking."

Her eyes widened in the flickering light, and I could almost read her thoughts before she spoke them.

"Sir, if you are looking for a repeat of what happened in the stables, I can assure you, that will not be happening."

My hand went instinctively to the back of my head. "I could do without the kick in the head, but the rest of it was rather enjoyable." I really was being a beast, but her reaction was worth it.

"Your bare leg brushed against mine," she hissed. "And what is the meaning of this choice of garment anyway? You are not in Scotland anymore. It is a disgrace."

Liquid heat began to pump through my veins. The excitement of the picture she painted of the incident in the stables, clashing with the insult to my homeland and my heritage. There was barely any room in this little priest hole, but I took a step closer to her anyway.

"I see ye have been thinking about our skin touching as much as I have," I said softly. I stood so close to her now that my breath brushed against a curl that rested against her cheek. I watched as a tiny amethyst, set within a thistle that hung from a silver chain about her neck, rose and fell with her shutter, and the candle flame flickered under her quickened breath. "And as for yer insult, let us get one thing straight. I wear my plaid with pride, and no matter what English airs ye try to put on, Scots blood will always flow through yer veins as well. Ye are no better than I."

She put up her fisted hand and laid it against my chest. She still held onto the cloth, and it made me wonder what she clutched so tightly that she couldnae let it go.

"You are mistaken," she said breathlessly, pushing against me with very little resistance.

"About which part?" I held her gaze in mine, and she licked her lips then swallowed as if choking down her words. She then withdrew her hand suddenly, clutching her little bundle to her chest. "What are ye clinging to in that little bundle of yers, Isobel?"

In the light of that one small flame, I saw her face drain of color. The rosy cheeks that shone with warmth only a moment before, now appeared void of any life blood.

"It's nothing," she snapped, shoving her hand behind her back.

I cocked my head. "Ye will need to lie a wee better than that if ye expect anyone to believe ye."

Her mouth fell open, but she recovered quickly, changing the subject. "Why were you following me?" Her voice held an air of contempt; the same tone in which she always addressed me.

"Why were ye running from me?" I asked. "Does it have anything to do with that bundle of cloth ye are hiding behind yer back?"

"I'm not hiding anything," she insisted, her words coming out harshly. "Now, if we are finished here, I demand you let me go."

"I am nay holding ye here, my lady. I merely wished for ye to direct me to where I might find yer Lady Mother. She gave me some ginger root for the pain in my head, but I couldnae remember what she said to do with it."

She closed her eyes momentarily and shook her head slightly. "Cut a piece of the root off and boil it in water, then drink it." She shoved the candle into my hand then pushed past me. But when she pressed against the wall it widnae budge. "What have you done?" she cried, her voice echoing off the close confines of the narrow hole we stood within. "It won't open." She pushed on the wall again and came to the same conclusion. "It won't open," she repeated, panic in her voice.

I turned to inspect the wall. "Is there a locking mechanism of some sort?"

"Yes, but it hasn't worked in years. That's why you were able to get in, I couldn't lock it shut. But now it won't open." She shoved on the wall once more before pounding on it with her fists.

Her cries became more frantic and soon she was kicking the wall with a slipper-covered foot.

"Ye are going to injure yerself," I said gently, trying to calm her down. But at this point she was mad with panic and widnae move out of the way. "Isobel, please. Allow me." I tried to hand the candle back to her so I could try my hand at the wall. But in her terrified state she ignored me. I reached up to stay her hand and in all the commotion, she dropped the wad of cloth she had protected so carefully in her hand.

Large, gray seeds spilled from the cloth, and I knelt to help her pick them up.

"No!" she shouted, grabbing my arm and gripping so tightly it felt like it was in a vice.

"Let me help ye, ye stubborn woman," I said, finally becoming a little irritated with her.

"You mustn't touch them!" she warned once more. But it was too late, I had already picked two up off the floor.

"Robert!" she cried, then knocked the seeds from my grasp and began wiping the palm of my hand with her cloth, as if I were a wee child. "Those are poisonous!"

I didnae answer for a moment, only let her words sink in. Her gasp filled the silence and her eyes darted to mine when she realized what she had said.

"Oh," she said, her lips trembling. A fresh round of tears filled her eyes, and I set the candle down on the floor and swiped the thumb of my unsoiled hand across her cheek to wipe away a stray tear. "I'm sorry," she said softly.

"Shouldnae one consume the poison to be deadly?" I questioned.

"Mother said simply touching it can cause illness."

"What is it? And more importantly, why are ye carrying around poison?" The question hung in the air. She didnae want to answer, but if I was going to become ill from this mishap, I deserved to ken. "Isobel?" I said, when she didnae answer.

She spread a piece of cloth out and began plucking the oval seeds off the floor one by one with her other piece of cloth. She carefully wrapped them up again and tucked them into her fist. "I suppose I am at risk as well, since I touched the cloth where the seeds were stored." She didnae look at me again but turned her head and wept into her shoulder.

I picked the candle up and stood to my feet. "Why are ye carrying around poison?" I asked again. "Dinnae ignore my question. If I am about to die, I deserve to ken."

She jerked her head toward me with her mouth agape. "I—I was getting it for a friend."

"For a friend," I repeated. "Who is putting ye up to obtaining poison for them?"

When she ignored my question again, I grabbed her firmly under her arm and pulled her to her feet. "Who is the poison for?" I gritted my teeth.

"Lady Frances," she gulped. "She has a rat problem."

I narrowed my eyes on her. "I bet she does."

She lifted her chin. "I speak the truth. She asked me to ask my mother about some poison for a rat problem she is having at Whitehall. This is nux vomica. I was taking it to her."

"And yer mother just gave ye poison to give to Lady Frances?" I said, incredulous. Once again, she didnae answer. I was beginning to feel like I was speaking to a brick wall. "Yer mother gave ye the poison for Lady Frances?"

"No!" She spat out. "If you must know, my mother said she doesn't trust the countess and refused to give me anything to take to her. But the countess is my friend. And she has promised to help me with something if I do something for her in return."

"That doesnae sound like friendship. That sounds like trickery." She furrowed her brow at me, and her pretty little mouth turned downward. I continued anyway. "What could ye possibly need that only the countess can provide?"

She sighed heavily. "I need her help with the prince." When I simply stared at her, she continued, "You wouldn't understand."

Oh, I understood all right. But the disappointment that curled in my stomach prevented me from saying so. She was in love with the prince. That had been obvious since the night of the Hymenaei masque. If only she kent the power she had. That man was on the verge of defying the king and queen for her. But I couldnae bring myself to offer her such hope. Instead, I said, "So ye took the seeds when yer mother wisnae looking." I shook my head.

"Don't you dare judge me, Robert Stewart."

The acid in her tone was scalding. Bile rose in my throat when I thought about her reason. "Do ye really think there is no other way to get the prince's attention than by whatever means the countess was going to share with ye?"

She turned back to the wall and began pushing on it again, indicating this conversation was finished. I stepped up behind her and gently pushed her out of the way, then leaned my hand on the edge of the wall. It opened right up, immediately spilling late afternoon sunlight into the little priest hole. I turned back to get a good look at the little chamber in which we were just hiding. I was amazed to find it really was just a hole in the wall, large enough for a desperate priest to hide in, should the need arise.

"You must wash your hands at—" Her voice caught, and for a moment I thought more tears would come. "At the first chance you get. And come find me immediately if you start feeling nauseous."

I nodded in affirmation. "Ye do the same," I said, motioning to her seeds.

I turned to make my way down the hall. I might get lost, but I wisnae about to ask her for any more help. But her pale voice stopped me and had me turning back to her.

"Will you promise not to mention this to my mother?"

I shook my head in disbelief. "I dinnae make promises. But I have nay reason to tell yer mother and nay intentions of doing so."

She tilted her head at me, as if trying to understand my reasoning, then her shoulders sagged. "All right," came her small reply, then she turned her back on me and walked in the other direction. The intelligent thing to do would have been to follow her, to find my way back without having to wander the great house all evening. But instead, I just stood and watched her go, thinking about what wiles the Lady Frances would teach her in order to get the prince's attention.

Chapter 19

Chadwyck House, London
March 1612
Isobel

E dith was in a pother the next day.

"Your Lady Mother will not breakfast with you this morning," she said, as she tightened my stays and helped me don a pink and cream frock. "She was up half the night, tending to the poor Scotsman."

I brushed my hands over my waistline to smooth my skirts but froze at the mention of Robert. A jolt of fear gripped my chest. "Why does he need tending to?" My mind raced. Had he become sick from touching the nux vomica?

Her delicate brows arched into two thin lines. "Apparently, he was vomiting during the night. Sir Will heard him behind his chamber door and called for your Lady Mother."

A coiling sensation twisted in the pit of my stomach. Vomiting was one of the symptoms of poisoning by nux vomica. I wondered what the legal ramifications would be if my actions caused Robert's death. And if he didn't die, but had become deathly sick, would he be out for my blood? Vengeance and violence seemed to run in his family.

I shoved the unpleasant thoughts aside. "I'm going to visit Honeycomb after breakfast," I said, deciding not to ask any more questions about Robert. "I think I'd like to wear my black and white taffeta frock instead of the pink. I don't want to wear the lace cuffs. Will you see if it is in my trunk? I believe I instructed Betsy to pack it."

Edith scurried off to search my trunk, but I paced my chamber, treading the faded path that had been worn into the crimson and gold carpet from years of use. If Robert was sick enough to require my mother's assistance, had he told her about the poison? She would probably need to be made aware so he could receive the proper treatment.

"I could not find the dress you spoke of, but there was this honey-colored frock with the cream rosettes. It has a narrow, three-quarters length sleeve without cuffs." She shook the dress out and laid it on my bed, brushing away any wrinkles or stray lint that might be clinging to it.

"Yes, that will do," I said absent-mindedly. I needed to see Robert and make sure my secret was safe. When the new dress was in place, she turned me about to look in the looking glass before setting my silk slippers at my feet. "I'll need my boots instead, Edith," I said, waving the slippers away. "I'm going to see Honeycomb and don't want to spoil another pair of shoes." She moved quickly to heed my request.

"Do you want the pearl necklace? It complements the cream so nicely." Edith held up a string of pearls.

"No, I want my amethyst," I said, pointing toward my jewelry cask. "I need all the luck I can get."

Edith's brow crinkled. "Is Honeycomb really that bad off?" She slid the dainty, thistle-shaped jewel around my neck and fastened the clasp.

Lost in thought, I shook my head. "She is not well," I said. But I had not been thinking about Honeycomb. I needed luck concerning Robert Stewart. If I had poisoned him, or if Mother had discovered my thievery, I might as well bid my life at court a fond adieu.

"Does this amethyst really bring you luck?" the maid asked dreamily. Her eyes shone like jewels of her own when she looked at it. "I have never seen a purple gem before. Then again, I've not seen too many gems at all, until I came to Chadwyck House."

"No," I admitted. "I just like to imagine it. But it is my favorite, since it was a gift from my father. And if anything ever happened to it, I would be devastated." I reached up and touched the amethyst, clasping it in my fist. It was my most prized possession, from my most favorite person in the world.

Edith took a step back and looked at me. "I believe you are ready, my lady."

I took one last look in the looking glass and went to breakfast.

Edith was correct, Mother did not breakfast with me. In fact, when I entered the dining hall, the only other person in there was Will. His auburn hair, the same shade as Mother's, fell across his forehead in a tussled fashion. My heart warmed when he looked up at me, chewing a piece of food, then swallowing. I remembered Edith said he had been the one to discover Robert's illness. Perhaps he had been up late as well. He looked a little tired.

"I'm afraid you are on your own for breakfast this morning, Issy," Will said as he drank something from his cup. "I'm to check on Grandfather, then I'm off to town with Father. Oh, that reminds me, he asked me to give you this." He handed over a missive addressed to me in Father's hand.

I unfolded it and read his neatly printed script. "I'm to return to Whitehall," I read aloud. "The princess will be entertaining a suitor soon: the Count Palatine."

"Well, it's probably a good thing," Will said as he gathered his things to go. "There is a lot going on here right now. You would just be in the way." He winked at me to indicate he was teasing, but I threw my napkin at him anyway.

"I can be of use at times," I said, lifting my chin. "Perhaps Mother might have need of me."

Will looked at me, incredulous. "We both know that will not be happening. Although, you might be able to help nurse Robert back to health. He doesn't seem to be doing too well," he said as he stood. "He had an extremely fitful night. Although Mother has left him resting finally. I hope he gets better. He sure will leave a lot of broken hearts behind if anything happens to him."

"Your concern for his well-being is moving," I said wryly.

Will chuckled, his amber eyes dancing with mirth. "I think he is past the worst of it, or I might be more concerned. Mother went to lie down and rest and said to call her if he should need her. She would not have left him, if she thought he was still in danger."

I said nothing more as Will departed, and I sat nibbling on a slice of apple. I thought about the information he had given to me. The most important, of course, was that Mother had left Robert to rest and was not in the room with him. Now might be the only chance for me to speak with him in private.

I knocked quietly on the door of Robert's bedchamber. But when no answer came, I twisted the knob gently and slipped inside. The heavy curtains were drawn over the high windows leaving a sliver of light in which to see the patient.

I tiptoed to the side of his bed. Robert lay in a twist of linens with a heavy dove gray counterpane almost falling off the end of the bed. One sun-kissed leg covered with fine, russet-colored hair, stuck out from beneath the blanket. My eyes roved over his form, from the tone shape of his calf, over his perfectly shaped kneecap and up to the whiter part of his muscular thigh. The linens covered him at the waist, but his chest was bare, apart from the auburn hair sprinkled across the rounded knots and corded muscles of his abdomen. The hair was thicker there and made a path that pointed downward, leading to the unknown parts of him which I couldn't see beneath the linen. Suddenly my mouth was dry, and I jerked my eyes upward before letting my imagination get away from me. The bulge of his shoulders and upper arms spoke to the physical labor he was accustomed to. His skin was brushed with the faint markings of copper freckles. He was so unlike the prince in practically every way that it was hard to find any familial similarities. And although I had certainly never seen the prince without his clothes, it was easy to discern his lithe, athletic frame and pale skin. A far cry from Robert's muscular, bronze physique.

A funny sensation prickled my skin, warning me I should look away. I was infringing on his privacy and had no right to look my fill. I moved to pull the falling blanket up, telling myself that it was all right, if I was making myself useful. But as I gathered the corner of the counterpane into my hand, a voice sounding as if it had been dragged over broken glass, spoke to me.

"Come to finish the job?" he said with more than a little acrimony.

My eyes shot to his. His face was pale, and even the bronze freckles looked as if they had been drained of color. His russet hair was damp and mussed, with a strand stuck against his forehead. Even his perfect, boyish lips were wan. The sharp cut of his jaw was still intact though, and I focused on that while he spoke.

"How are you feeling?" The words felt hollow, given my part in his demise.

"Like I've been run over by twenty draft horses." He stretched his bare leg out then pulled it back under the blanket. He closed his eyes and ran his tongue over his dry lips.

I moved to his table and poured a bit of red wine from a flask. He made an effort to sit up but winced when he lifted his head from the pillow. I slid my arm under his shoulders and assisted him, holding the cup to his lips.

He drank deeply and did not immediately speak when finished. I set the cup on the table and stood over him, wringing my hands.

He lifted his cloudy gaze to me. "If ye have come to see if I have spilled yer secrets, then ye can rest assured nay a word has passed my lips."

I eyed him before pulling up a chair to sit beside him. "How did my mother treat you, if she didn't know what poison you had been in contact with?"

He pushed himself up further in the bed and motioned for another drink. "Do ye have anything stronger than wine?"

"I don't know," I confessed, glancing around his room.

He sat up further and made to swing his legs over the side of the bed but then stopped. "I seemed to have lost my clothes. Do ye mind bringing me that bottle from the cabinet there?" He pointed toward a cellarette that stood on the other side of the room.

I went to the cabinet and found a lone bottle of whisky sitting inside. "Would my mother approve of this?"

He took the bottle and pulled the top off. Splashing a dram into his cup he said, "If I am dying does it really make a difference?"

I forced my throat to work, swallowing the emotions lodged there. My contumacious behavior had led to this unfortunate ordeal. Guilt pecked at my mind like an angry hen, yet I couldn't bring myself to be sorry for what I had done. If the countess could teach me what I needed to do to win the prince's favor, then the risk would be worth it. Still, I felt bad for Robert. He was innocent, and I did not wish to see him dead.

He downed two glasses of whisky, and I had to admit some of the color had returned to his face. His smokey green eyes had darkened though, and he watched me with a heavy-lidded gaze.

I took a deep breath in anticipation of the demand I was about to make. "I have somewhat to talk with you about."

He poured himself another two fingers' full of whisky before I took the bottle from his hand and moved his cup away. His stare bore into me momentarily until he held his hand out to me. "Speak," he said. He sounded amused.

I cleared my throat. "I think it is only fair that you share a secret with me, since you know one of mine."

He blinked at me, then threw his head back and laughed.

Irritation scratched at me. "You find something amusing?"

He leveled his gaze at me, his green eyes the color of a North Sea storm. "What makes ye think I have secrets to tell?"

"Of course you have secrets to tell. You admitted you are a reiver, and everyone knows they are a ruthless, murderous lot. Plundering innocent people's homes and stealing whatever catches their fancy. No doubt you've killed a few people who have gotten in your way. Probably taken what you will from a few women as well. And now what? You've come to London to see what delights you can steal here? And don't get me started about your traitorous father."

The amused smile fell from his face, and his eyes turned a menacing black. He moved so quickly that I had no time to protect myself. Before I knew it, he was in my face, his lips hovering dangerously close to mine.

"Ye ken nothing of what ye speak," he said, his breath hot with the whisky he drank. "While ye sit down here in London in yer ivory towers and filling yer bellies with all manner of delectables, people are scratching out an existence along the border. The king has no worry for his fellow countrymen. He's yet to show his face again in Scotland since coming to the throne of England. We do what we can to survive. And mark my words, I may have killed a few scoundrels in the process, but I have never laid a finger on a woman. Neither have I taken anything that wisnae freely and gladly given." Here his lips curled into a mischievous grin, but there was a threat hidden there. I didn't miss the warning he was doling out. "And as for my father," he shoved the counterpane to the floor and fisted the linen in his hand as he moved to stand, "I may have never met the man, but I love him just as much as ye love yers, and I will do anything in my power to defend him." He swung the linen around his waist and stood.

I shrieked. "What are you doing? You are naked beneath the bedclothes!"

The wicked turn of his lips had not disappeared. "I would think it 'tis obvious. I am going to get dressed. Now, if ye dinnae care to watch, ye may want to leave." He strode to the wardrobe and flung open the door.

I followed him to the wardrobe. "I cannot trust you if you do not give me some token to prove you would not incriminate me to get what you want."

He motioned with a finger for me to turn around. I did as instructed, feeling the heat burn on my cheeks at the sound of the linen dropping to the floor as he pulled on a pair of leather pants.

He sighed heavily. "I owe ye nothing, but I will tell ye this: I came to London to ask the king to lift my father's exile."

I dared a look over my shoulder to confirm he was decent before turning to face him. He was *not* decent, and I looked away, but not before I got another look at his bare chest. "Well, your father's release would be dangerous for the king and the rest of the country, but it's hardly secret worthy."

His lip curled into a sardonic smile. "I willnae give up until he has restored my father's title and lands, or he pays for what he has done to my family."

My eyes widened at that. "You would hurt the king?" He didn't respond, but I could tell by the look on his face no good thing would come of this. "And what of Prince Henry? He loves you like a brother. Your actions would devastate him." Robert looked away from me. I took a little comfort, at least, in knowing his friendship with the prince was not all a charade. He turned his attention to the wardrobe and began rummaging for something more to wear. "Well, we'll just have to make sure he doesn't refuse you," I said with finality, as if the matter was really that simple.

"He already has," he said, pinning me with a look full of promise. And I had no doubt he would keep his word.

I swallowed hard but didn't know what to say to that. This man came from a family who felt they had been deeply wronged by the king. He had been raised on hatred and fueled by thieving, plundering, and murder. I always suspected he was dangerous, but I had no idea this danger extended to the king of England.

My mother's voice could be heard in the hallway, just outside Robert's room.

"Edith, see if ye can find Isobel. Her father is ready to leave for Whitehall. She is to go with him, but I cannot find her anywhere."

There was a muffled response, presumably from the maid, before the door to Robert's chamber opened.

Just as quickly as he had shielded me from Honeycomb, Robert wrapped an arm around my waist and pulled me to him. With his other hand he pulled the wardrobe door toward us to block my mother's view.

"Oh." Mother stopped short when she did not see Robert lying in his bed where she had left him. "Robert?" she called tentatively.

"I was feeling a wee better, Lady Stratford, and thus decided to get dressed. Can ye give me a few minutes?"

"Certainly," Mother sounded flustered. "I've got to find Isobel anyway. I'll come back in twenty minutes. I just wanted to check your stitches and see how ye were feeling. I've got some more ginger tea for your nausea."

"That would be fine," Robert said, still holding me against him.

Mother closed the door behind her, but he did not release me. He did, however, release his grip on the wardrobe door and placed his other hand on my hip. He moved his hand upward and for a moment I thought he was going to grope me. My heart was beating wildly within my chest, but he slid his hand between my breasts and gently grasped the amethyst that hung around my neck.

"Do ye want to ken another secret, Isobel?" His breath was warm in my ear and sent a delicious shiver down my spine. I cursed my body's reaction to him but nodded my head all the same.

"Yes," I could hear myself say, though it felt as if all the air had left my lungs.

"I wisnae poisoned. I have a concussion. The injury to my head from yer mare has caused vomiting and dizziness. I am nay dying."

Aggravation jolted my senses, and I turned in his arms to face him. "You are a blackguard," I said, squirming to disentangle myself and my necklace from his grasp. "How dare you take advantage of my kindness?"

He tightened his grip on me, and his gaze fell to my mouth. I bit my bottom lip in an effort to keep him from seeing how he affected me. The heat of his hand burned into me, setting my skin on fire.

"Oh, ye have been anything but kind, my lady. Ye have looked down yer nose at me from the first day we met. Ye have tried to poison me. And ye have insulted my intelligence, my clothing, and my father. I'd say this is just a wee example of reaping what ye sow."

I scowled at him.

"I didn't try to poison you. You intruded where you weren't wanted. You shouldn't have been following me."

"I needed help," he said, voice rising.

"I know that now. And keep your voice down," I said, looking over my shoulder. "Now, I'd say we are even. Kindly unhand me."

A low chuckle rumbled from his throat. "We are nay even," he argued, tightening his grip around my necklace, and pulling me closer.

Understanding dawned on me. "You said you've never taken from a woman without her consent. Will you force me now? Is that what this is about?"

"There's a first time for everything." There was a playfulness to his voice, but his stormy eyes led me to believe he wasn't jesting. "My secrets come at a cost." I started to protest when he jerked the delicate chain of my necklace, breaking the clasp and tightening his grip on the amethyst as it slid into his hand. I gasped, reaching for the flesh that now felt bare before him. "This will be my payment," he said, a wicked smirk jerking his mouth upward. "Unless ye care to indulge my baser desires."

My mouth fell open. "I do not," I said firmly.

"Then ye best be on yer way, Lady Isobel. Yer mother is looking for ye."

"My father gave me that necklace," I said, panic causing my voice to warble. "It is very dear to me."

"Then I shall keep it safe." He tucked the necklace gently into his pocket and looked down at me. "Ye may go." And with that he dismissed me, as if we were not in my own house and he was not the guest.

Chapter 20

Palace of Whitehall, London
March 1612
Isobel

My neck felt bare. Humiliation and anger still bubbled under the surface of my skin every time I thought about how Robert Stewart had broken the chain and stolen the necklace my father had given me. The audacity of that man to take my most prized possession from me, without a second thought, was astonishing.

But I had thought he was going to kiss me. I saw the way his eyes fell to my lips. The intensity of his hands on my hips, and the way he pulled me close to him—

I shook my head as if I could settle some sense back into my brain. I couldn't determine what I was most irritated about. The stolen necklace, or the fact he didn't kiss me as I had thought he would. "What is wrong with me?" I berated myself. "Of course, I don't want that rake to kiss me."

"You're kissing rakes now?" I started at the voice that drew me out of my woolgathering. Lady Frances stood at the threshold of my door with a coy smile brightening her eyes.

"Gah! No." I turned and looked at myself in the mirror before adjusting my ruff and swiping a stray hair from my eyes. She stepped into my chamber, closing the door behind her, and looking all the while like she had just discovered some great secret.

"Someone tried to kiss you," she guessed.

The countess looked exquisite today in a gown of cerulean blue. She had discarded the stiff, fan-shaped rebato collar, and it gave a soft, uninhibited look to the low-cut neckline of her bodice.

"No one tried to kiss me," I said, going to my jewelry cask. I opened it and perused, trying to find a necklace that would fill the void of my missing purple amethyst.

"Oh, that's too bad." She crossed the room and stood behind me, looking at our reflections in the mirror.

"Why is that bad? You know I want the prince. Shouldn't he be my focus?" I watched as she admired herself in the reflection of my mirror.

"No one said you couldn't have your cake and eat it too, dear." She reached up and untied the small ruff that was wrapped around my neck.

"What are you doing?" The movement startled me, and I reached for the ruff as it fell from my neck.

Innocence shone in her widened eyes. "You want to attract the prince, do you not? Here is lesson number one: make yourself desirable."

"By leaving nothing to the imagination?"

She laughed. "Make yourself noticeable. When others notice you, take advantage of the attention. The prince will wonder what he is missing and start paying closer attention. He is very intelligent. He will want a piece of what everyone else is having." She pulled the neckline of my bodice down, exposing the very top of my shoulders. I resisted the urge to pull it back up. My father would have an apoplectic fit if he saw me, and my mother would probably fall into hysterics.

"Lady Frances, I think you have misunderstood. I do not wish to draw the attention of every man at court. I merely wish for the prince to take notice. Surely there are other ways—"

"Isobel, you are young and inexperienced. Take it from a woman who has been forced into a marriage she did not want and made to find her own happiness with her own bounty. Take the attention you get and use it for your own benefit, even if only for your own enjoyment."

"Forgive my ignorance, but won't that be a sure way of hurting my chances with Prince Henry? I do not wish to be his mistress; I want to be his wife."

"And you shall." She adjusted my sleeves one more time and stepped back to look me over. "This is all wrong. Your bodice and stomacher are all wrong. Let us remove the gown and start from the foundation." She motioned toward my wardrobe. "Let us see what we have to work with."

"But my maids, I dismissed them."

"We don't need them. I will assist you." She rummaged through my undergarments, pulling out stays I had never even seen before.

"Where did that come from?" I stood like a statue as she unlaced the stays I was currently wearing.

"I took it upon myself to have some of my old things brought to your room. But don't worry, they are all very much still in fashion. I just don't wear them anymore." She pulled the stays off me, and a chill ran up my spine as the cold air brushed through my chemise. "Oh, there *are* breasts under there!" She laughed at her own joke, and mortification burned on my cheeks.

"Just because I am not," I paused to choose my words carefully, "as endowed as you, does not mean I do not have any assets at all." The words came out with a bite, and the countess took a step back to look into my eyes.

"Of course, dear. I did not mean to offend you. But you have done an excellent job of hiding those assets. It is time we bring them to light," she waved her fingers around as if she were working some magic spell. "Not literally, of course." She chuckled again, and I got the impression she was having too much fun at my expense.

She tightened the new stays, and the movement pushed my breasts up higher, making them look much larger than they were. I stared at myself in the looking glass. The awkwardness of this new look was overshadowed by a much stronger sensation—empowerment. As a girl, I had counted on my pretty face and social graces to attract attention. And it had worked to my advantage to get what I wanted, for the most part. But using other body parts to get what I wanted had never occurred to me. I was a woman now, and it was time I use my womanly resources.

Frances went to the wardrobe once more and pulled out another garment. It was a cream gown embroidered with purple lilacs with bronze colored lace at the cuffs. The sleeves were designed to set off the shoulder, and the neckline was cut extremely low, much lower than I had ever worn before. Once the gown was in place, it was easy to see all my best features.

"What kind of collar will look best?" I asked, noticing the vast amounts of skin exposed above my décolletage.

The countess eyed me with her heavy-lidded gaze. "No collar, love. This dress is designed to be worn just like this. Collars are on their way out. But a nice jewel at your throat couldn't hurt, to draw the prince's eyes right here." She ran the tip of her finger down my chest and pointed toward the cleft between my breasts. "How about that lovely amethyst you always wear?" She moved toward my jewelry casket and opened it.

"I lost it," I said, a little too quickly. She turned her gaze on me again and watched me for a moment. Then she said slowly, "What a shame."

There was no way she could know Robert had taken it from me, but I felt the embarrassment of the situation just the same and tried to change the subject. "I have a pretty pearl necklace the princess gifted me on my birthday." I stepped in front of her and began sifting through my jewelry.

A strange silence hung over us. Then the countess said, "It really is a shame you lost your amethyst. I got the impression it meant a great deal to you. You wore it quite often."

I ignored her comment and pulled the pearl from the casket. It was larger than I usually wore, which is why I didn't wear it often, but it was a pretty piece, fashioned in the shape of a star, with the pearl set in the middle and tiny diamonds adorning each point. I held it up to my neck. "Do you mind?" I asked her, not meeting her eyes in the mirror.

She clasped the necklace around my neck without a sound. Then as if I hadn't tried to ignore her question, she said, "Do you have any idea where you might have lost your amethyst?"

"You seem to be concerned about it more than I." I laughed nervously. "I'm sure I'll find it eventually." I ran my hands over my waist and took a deep breath. Smiling, I said, "You are a magician, Lady Frances." I looked at her in the mirror before she turned me about to face her. She held me at arm's length and perused me from head to toe.

"You look lovely. You can wear this gown today, and tomorrow we will go to the dressmaker. Your gowns will need to be a little narrower in the bust than mine, so you'll want your own. Mistress Turner will be able to accommodate you nicely." She pulled on the bodice again and fiddled with the sleeves at the shoulder. "The prince has returned to Richmond Palace but will be back for Elizabeth's supper party to greet the count. Mistress Turner is a wonder at her ability to prepare a gown in a timely manner. I'm sure if you throw in a little something extra, she can have a dress ready for you in no time."

"Thank you, Frances. Your help is appreciated."

"Ah, but my assistance does come at a price, if you recall. And on that note, do you have something for me, Isobel?"

I nodded and went to the trunk that had been deposited at the foot of my bed. I moved the garments aside and dug to the bottom of the trunk, feeling around until my fingers brushed against the black velvet pouch I had wrapped the seeds in.

"You must be very careful. These nux vomica seeds can be extremely dangerous. Even contact with your skin can make you sick. Handle with care." I held out the pouch to her, and she took it carefully.

She loosened the cord and pulled the pouch open. Peering inside, she said, "And what am I to do with them? Do I just set it out and let the rat eat it?"

I bit my lip nervously. I never thought to ask my mother that. "I'm not sure if the rat would eat it just like that. You might want to grind it up into something that will entice the rat. Stick a little bit inside a piece of cheese or something."

She nodded and hurriedly pulled the cord on the pouch to close it up. "This will do," she said, as if what she was doing for me was of far more value than what I had given her. But the cost of disobeying my mother, and stealing from her, weighed on me far heavier than the gown she had given to me.

"Whatever you do, do not touch it. Wear gloves when you are handling the seeds," I warned. "And keep the seeds hidden so there is no chance of other people coming in contact with them."

She gave me a demure nod. "Of course. Now, I really must be off. I want to finish the needlepoint I started in the evening drawing room before the queen takes it over. It is her favorite room, and she doesn't like me. I like to stay out of her way when she is at Whitehall."

Elizabeth had mentioned once that her mother rarely cared for the people King James kept at his court. And in turn, the queen tended to attract those with whom the king took issue. Since the queen and king rarely stayed at the same palace anymore, it usually wasn't a problem. But when they were forced into the same proximity due to something involving one of their children, or some state affair, there was always potential for drama.

"Perhaps you should move your needlepoint to a different room. The queen will probably be here a lot more, as Elizabeth's suitors make more and more appearances," I advised.

"But that is my favorite room as well," she said, her eyes flashing with mischief. "Thank you for the advice, though. I will keep it in mind."

Chapter 21

Richmond Palace, London
October 1612
Isobel

"Let us move closer so we can see better," Elizabeth said as she nudged my elbow. We were picnicking at Richmond Palace, where Henry was hosting festivities in honor of his sister's betrothal to a young count named Frederick, Palatine of the Rhine. The prince had just challenged his cousin to barriers, a sport Robert apparently had never participated in. This should be interesting.

Frederick held out a hand to assist Elizabeth to her feet, then she turned to me and extended her hand. I set my cup aside and took her hand, brushing my skirts into place. I knew Henry to be an excellent swordsman. And no one ever beat him at barriers. I couldn't wait to see him get the best of the Scotsman.

Most of the onlookers made their way to the barriers, but I held back, trying to allow the princess and her betrothed a little privacy. I went to the table and picked over a piece of cake topped with clotted cream and strawberries that I had left there earlier. I had just stuck a slice of strawberry into my mouth and licked the cream from my thumb, when a voice spoke up from behind.

"I do not see ladies licking their fingers very often at the court of King James," it said. I turned to see a pair of porcine eyes studying me. It was Viscount Rochester's friend, Thomas Overbury.

"I, I," I couldn't seem to get my excuses out.

He chuckled, the sort of laugh that burrows under the skin and creeps along the veins. "I meant no insult, Lady Isobel. I merely meant it is nice to see someone that is not taken with such formality all the time. The court can be full of such sycophants."

Sir Thomas was not unattractive. He looked to be about thirty years of age. His pale skin was free from wrinkles and his closely cropped, dark curly hair showed no signs of graying. He wore his beard trimmed in the latest fashion, shorn close, and combed to a point at his chin. But it was his eyes that unnerved me. His eyes of pale, watery blue, closely set and always watching, as if taking inventory of everyone's accounts. It was his eyes that made me uncomfortable around him when he visited Chadwyck House with the prince last year, and it was those same, pinhole eyes that sent a surge of awkward discomfort through me now.

The cake turned to sand in my mouth, and I swallowed hard, forcing it down. "I assure you, Sir Thomas, I have the utmost concern for formality and manners. You caught me in a moment of weakness, I suppose."

"Oh, no doubt," he said, eyes boring into me as if he were trying to find some other fault. "You remind me a lot of the countess." He licked his lips and stuck a piece of roasted duck into his mouth. The grease from the fowl dribbled down his chin, but he didn't seem to notice.

"Yes, I am told quite often I have my mother's mannerisms," I began.

"Oh, no. Not that countess. I speak of the Countess of Essex." His shrewd eyes seemed to darken into obsidian. "You even have her look about you. I notice your manner of dress is quite like hers. Does she advise you?"

The cake I had eaten now sat heavily in my stomach, feeling like I had swallowed a rock. Why was he speaking to me about the way the countess dressed? It was highly inappropriate.

"She has given me a few pointers. She is the fairest flower of the court, is she not?" I laughed nervously and laid a hand on the bare skin of my chest as if to cover the space my bodice used to fill. His eyes fell to my hand before drifting back to my face.

"She is something," he said vaguely. He popped another bite of duck into his mouth, and I suddenly realized how uncouth it was to stand at the table eating as if we were beggars scrounging for food. "Of course, her Howard family has always been the seedbed of scandal, I suppose the countess is no different."

Cold fear tightened my chest. It was true. It seemed the Howards had been at the heart of many a scandal that spanned over the reign of several kings and queens. But I had only known her as Lady Frances Devereux, the Countess of Essex. I had almost forgotten she had been a Howard before her marriage to the earl.

I didn't see what that had to do with the current conversation, nor what scandal he spoke of. I felt a danger in this discussion that had started out so innocently. "Are you alluding to something particular, Sir Thomas?" I regretted my words as soon as I spoke them, for I did not want to hear him impugn Lady Frances.

He looked at me in surprise, as if he hadn't meant anything by the words he had spoken. The streak of grease still clung to his chin, and I couldn't seem to draw my attention away from it. He waved my question away. "I'm simply thinking aloud, my lady." He smiled, and I fought back the urge to cringe as his lips pulled back to reveal a piece of duck stuck between his teeth.

"You haven't mentioned how your trip to France was, Sir Thomas." I flashed my brightest smile at him. It was common knowledge he had been sent away because of some offense he had caused the queen, and he was not happy to be separated from his friend, Rochester.

The innocent smile fell from his face. "Anyone could have done the job I was sent to do. The queen wished to punish me by insisting I be the one to take care of it. She wanted rid of me."

"Perhaps you should not speak so openly about the debts the queen has accrued. What is it the King's Bible says?" I laid a finger on my chin in thought. "Ah, yes, '*A fool uttereth all his mind.*' Sometimes it is best to keep your own council. If I have learned anything from my father, it is that if you have a complaint, there is a proper chain of command by which to express your concerns. Publicly airing them about like a flag for all to see is not wise."

Anger darkened his pale eyes, giving them an even more sinister mien. "Leave the theology to the clerics and the philosophy to learned men, my lady. It does not become a woman of your position to lecture her equal."

My brows lifted in shock. *My equal?* I may have been the daughter of an earl with a courtesy title, but at least my father had earned that title with heartfelt thanks from Queen Elizabeth. Overbury only had his status because he was friends with the king's favorite, Rochester.

He took a step closer to me, and it took all my strength not to move away. "And let me give you a little bit of advice as well." He leaned closer and said in a low voice, "Be careful of Frances Devereux. She plays the innocent lamb, but in reality, she is the raging wolf. She is a witch, capable of casting spells on people. She did it to Essex, causing him to be impotent in her bed. And she did it to Rochester, making him fall in love with her."

These were outrageous claims, so ridiculous they hardly warranted a response. But I weighed my words carefully. It would not do to make an enemy at the court of King James, especially when I was trying so desperately to prove I was worthy of Prince Henry's attentions. There was so much more I could have said to this sorry little man. But I decided to take the higher road.

Instead, I said, "I happen to be a good friend of the countess, Sir Thomas. And I have seen no sign of the witchery of which you speak. Be careful. The Howards are a powerful family. And the Viscount Rochester is the king's favorite who happens to be in love with the countess. You will find yourself in much difficulty if you continue spreading these lies. Now, if you'll forgive me, I was just heading over to watch the barriers."

He frowned. "I try to avoid such displays of athleticism. The last time I watched sport, Rochester broke his leg, and the king had to rescue him."

"But that brought good fortune to the both of you, did it not?" I asked innocently, hoping my jab at his unearned title hit him where I intended. "Isn't that how you came to be at King James's court?"

He lifted his chin in defiance. "That is true. It pays to be at the right place at the right time." He flashed a smile with gritted teeth. That duck was still hanging on for dear life.

"Indeed. Now, if you'll excuse me," I cooed, and turned to go.

"And I suppose sometimes it is bad luck to be at the wrong place and at the wrong time."

"Excuse me?" I peered at him over my shoulder, not sure I followed his line of thought.

"Oh, I was just thinking about that poor maid of Lady Frances's. She was certainly at the wrong place at the wrong time."

"I'm sorry," I said, shaking my head. "Lady Frances's maid?" I had no idea what he was referring to.

"Haven't you heard? Yes, well, I suppose it is probably not common knowledge. But Rochester and I are good friends. He tells me everything. That is how I found out Frances's maid died this morning after several days of sickness. Most gruesome ordeal it was. They say she was poisoned."

I choked on thin air. "Poisoned?" I tried to maintain my composure. "No, I had not heard she had even lost a maid, let alone something as dastardly as poison. I hope you don't mind me asking, sir, but who are *they*, and why do *they* say she was poisoned?"

"The palace staff. It was the manner in which she passed that invited suspicion. She had been sick with vomiting and diarrhea for several days. The poor chit was finally put out of her misery, may she rest in peace." His greasy lips turned down in a regretful frown, and I almost believed he was sincere.

"Yes, God rest her soul," I said absentmindedly. My mind examined my interactions with Lady Frances at the supper party today. She hadn't seemed a bit mournful or distraught. I would be beside myself if I had lost a maid in such a fashion. She had been as jovial and flirtatious as ever, maybe even more so just to spite the queen. For she was sure Queen Anne hated her.

"And there is yet another maid who is sick as well. She has not died —yet. Perhaps there is hope for her," Overbury continued.

My eyes shot to his. "Who are these women? What are their names?"

"Alice Graves and Lenora...," he paused here and pursed his lips as if he were trying to remember the other maid's name. But I had no doubt he approached me specifically to share with me this news. "Lawson. Yes, that is it."

"Is Lenora the maid that is still sick?" I asked.

"I believe so." He tilted his head at me questioningly. "Are you acquainted with her? Since you and the countess are such good friends."

I ignored his pointed slight. "The countess and I are friends, but I do not know these women. However, I hope for Lenora's sake she has a quick recovery. Now, if you'll excuse me. I believe the princess is waiting for me. I'll be sure to give my condolences to Lady Frances." I motioned toward the barriers, and he dipped his chin to me in dismissal.

I twisted my ankle trying to make my way quickly across the lawn. One of Frances's maids has died? Of poison? How could that be? Had she handled the nux vomica to help the countess with her rat problem and been careless? I tried to warn Frances.

But what of the other maid? I bit my bottom lip and wrung my hands together. This had to be a misunderstanding. Surely, this wasn't a poisoning. And it wasn't related to the poison I had given Frances. It couldn't be.

By the time I reached the barriers, I felt faint. When Elizabeth saw me, she braced my arms to steady me. "You do not look well, Issy. I think the sun has gotten to you, although you look more like a ghost than a sun-stroked maiden. Are you all right?"

I nodded but couldn't seem to form words on my tongue. I tried to breathe deep breaths, but it didn't help. I changed my mind and shook my head. Finally, I managed to say, "I do not feel well."

"I can tell. Why don't you go have a lie-down, and I'll send one of the maids to check on you."

"One of the maids," I muttered under my breath.

"What?" Elizabeth questioned.

"Nothing," I said, as I turned away. On shaky legs I made my way back to my chamber. I did feel a little lightheaded. I would have a glass of wine and lie down. That was if I could keep my composure until I reached my rooms.

When I reached the top of the winding white, marble staircase I had a thought. Instead of turning toward my bedchamber to my right, I turned left and walked along the gold and scarlet carpets until I reached another set of steps. I had only been inside Richmond Palace a handful of times, but I was sure this was the way to the servants' quarters. I glanced around to see who else might be in the corridor before ascending the service stairs.

The floor of the palace that held the servants' quarters was like stepping into another world. Instead of the regal rugs and gilded trappings of the lower levels, drab walls of yellowing plaster met my eyes. Cracked wainscoting and crumbling checkered tiles perpetuated the neglected atmosphere. There were only small, dirty windows on this level, letting in little light, and a darkness seemed to hover in the corridor like some strange miasma.

A maid exiting a chamber stopped short when she saw me on the landing. "May I help you, my lady?" Dark smudges beneath her gray eyes gave her pallid skin an eerie, sickly appearance. Limp, ashy brown tendrils escaped her caul, and she looked as if she had not slept in days.

I hoped for her sake she was not sick with the same illness that afflicted Alice and Lenora.

I twisted my rose-colored skirts in my hand, feeling over-dressed and conspicuous with my plunging neckline and tight bodice. I ran my tongue over my dry lips and swallowed hard.

"I am looking for the chamber of Lenora Lawson," I said, barely above a whisper. My eyes were finally adjusting to the darkness that lurked there, and I could see the maid's brow pull together into a tight, downward arch.

"Please, my lady. She has made it through the worst part. There may be hope for her yet. I pray, do not afflict her again. I assure you; she has learned her lesson."

My mouth gaped. Learned her lesson? "I'm sorry, but what do you mean?"

The young maid's eyes darted to and fro. "Forgive me, I misspoke. Right this way, my lady." She turned and practically fled down the hallway, and it was a task keeping up with her. When she finally stopped outside a door on the other end of the corridor, she turned abruptly. "Please, my lady, forget what you have heard." Her voice warbled, and her chin began to quiver.

"I cannot," I said gently. Touching her gingerly on the sleeve, I added, "Tell me, what has happened here." Just then, the door opened and an aged man with a head of unruly red hair and a bushy beard of the same color stood on the threshold. Perfectly symmetrical lines were traced into his wide forehead, and a thick, protruding brow bone seemed to hover over his dark eyes. He looked as surprised as we were.

"Oh, good. There you are. Hester, please bring us more hot water and clean cloths. And we will take another bottle of brandy."

Hester curtsied then turned to fetch the man's request but not before stealing a glance at me. I nodded to her and watched as she hurried off down the hallway, then I turned my attention to the man who I presumed to be the doctor.

"How is the patient?" I asked, laying a hand against the door, and catching it before he could close it in my face.

"Who is inquiring?" His eyes were bloodshot and half hidden beneath his drooping eyelids.

"My name is Lady Isobel Broune. I am the daughter of the Earl and Countess of Stratford and a friend of the Countess of Essex."

He studied me momentarily before scratching his shaggy whiskers in thought. A murmur from within had him turning his head to listen, then he finally opened the door slightly. "Take care, my lady. Sickness lurks herein."

I could see right through his theatrics. "I assure you I am not afraid." I pushed the door completely open and stepped inside.

I may not have been afraid of whatever disease may lurk within, but I was unprepared for what I saw in the small form that lay upon the bed.

A fire blazed high in the hearth, raising the temperature to stifling degrees. Dozens of candles were set in various parts of the chamber, but the room still felt dark and underlit. And the smell! I pulled a piece of cloth from my sleeve and covered my mouth and nose. It smelled of feces and vomit, and a strange, foreign odor I could not place.

Lenora looked like a marble effigy lying so still on the bed. Her skin was pale, and her hands were folded over her chest as if she had already been laid to her eternal rest. Her dark hair was damp and mussed and looked as if it had been swiped across her forehead with a wet cloth. Delicate, black eyelashes framed translucent lids, and lips of a blueish tint parted slightly as she slept. At least, I hoped it was sleep.

"Hester said she is over the worst of it," I whispered, fearing I might disturb the invalid.

The doctor shuffled his feet but did not answer. It was a voice from the shadows that spoke instead.

"It is too soon to tell."

The voice sounded familiar, and I jumped when I saw Mistress Turner, the court dressmaker sitting in the darkness of the room's corner.

"Mistress Turner," I said, startled. "Why are you here?" I didn't mean to sound impertinent, but the woman was not my equal, so I shoved the tinge of guilt aside.

"Did Lady Frances send you?" she asked, disregarding my question, and coming to stand beside the bed.

I got the feeling if I told her the truth, that the countess had not sent me, I would be dispelled from the room. So instead, I said, "She wishes to know the condition of the patient."

The dressmaker sighed. "I sent her word only an hour ago. Does she really think there will be much change in that short amount of time?"

"Perhaps." I shrugged my shoulders, and the woman crossed her arms in front of her chest. "This room needs cleaned," I blurted, and the two occupants that were still awake gawked at me.

"Are those Lady Frances's orders?" the woman asked with suspicion in her voice.

"Those are my orders," I said. I didn't hold authority over a countess, but surely Frances would be appalled if she saw the state of this room.

"She's right." The doctor finally spoke up. "Her father is an expert in the law, so she probably knows what's what as well."

What did my father's law training have to do with anything? This was a matter of common decency. It didn't take a law degree to recognize the chamber needed to be kept clean.

"Well, I am not cleaning it," she said with a huff. "We'll have to get a maid in here to do it." Mistress Turner fisted her hands on her hips and scowled at the doctor.

A slight movement from the direction of the bed caught my attention. Lenora pulled her eyes open, and the doctor rushed to her side. She turned her head and looked in my direction, and I watched as her eyes focused on me. Her mouth moved as if she were speaking, but no sound came out.

"Here's the sedative, Doctor Forman." Mistress Turner handed the doctor a small phial, and I watched as he unstopped the bottle. *Doctor*

Forman. I had heard of him. The man had gained renown for his ability to heal the plague and detect other illnesses in the body.

"Is that poppy seed oil?" I asked, curious as to why they were treating her with such an elixir. The doctor stopped and looked at me. Mistress Turner rushed to reply.

"I think it is time for you to go, dear. We don't want to overtax the poor girl. Please tell Lady Frances that Lenora is awake."

The dressmaker gently, yet firmly, tried to guide me to the door. But not before Lenore reached out a hand and grabbed my wrist. Her touch was clammy and cold, and her nails bit into my flesh as if in desperation.

"Please, my lady. I am not sick," she said in a voice that sounded like crushed rock. If her touch had not turned my blood to ice, her words would have.

"What do you mean, Lenora?"

Mistress Turner laughed and broke Lenora's grasp on me by pulling her hand free. "Poor thing. She is delusional. Anyone with two eyes can see she is sick." She placed the girl's hands across her heart once more and patted them as if to make them stay in place. "All right. Be off with you, Lady Isobel."

"Please, my l—" Lenora tried again, but whatever the doctor had given her was already taking effect. She couldn't even finish her sentence.

"What is that, Doctor Forman?" I tried again. He replaced the stopper on the phial and turned his back on me to put the bottle away. "I know a bit about remedies. My mother is a healer."

"I know your mother," the doctor mumbled. "She would not wish you to be tangled up in this."

"Excuse me?" Tangled up in what?

"Leave the doctor to his work now," Mistress Turner said, all the niceties gone from her tone. "Be sure to relay our message to Lady Frances and ask her to send a maid to clean the room." And with that the dressmaker shoved me out the door and closed it behind me. A click of the lock told me there would be no getting back in.

I stood in the corridor for a moment longer, contemplating what to do. Something about this situation did not sit well with me. Mistress Turner was acting strangely. Someone must be told what was going on with Lenora.

But then another thought hit me. If this was the poison I had given to Frances, was I responsible for Lenora's sickness? And Alice's death? A sick feeling curled in my belly causing the lunch I had consumed to roil hotly.

When I returned to the supper party, the men were through fighting at barriers, and everyone was playing jeu de mail on the lawn. Everyone except Lady Frances. Even Rochester had disappeared, and no one seemed to know where they had gone.

"No doubt they are off mollycoddling one another somewhere," the Earl of Essex retorted as he hit the ball with his mallet as hard as he could. "Have you tried the barn?" He leveled his gaze at me, and I blinked at him.

"Sir, you jest," I said, not sure what to think of his comment. This was his wife we spoke of, after all.

"I assure you, I do not." He swung his mallet over his shoulder and walked off in the direction that he had hit the ball. I looked to the nearest player for explanation.

"It is a sensitive subject," the prince's friend, John Harington explained, although it wasn't much of an explanation at all.

"My head hurts," I said to no one in particular. "I'll be in my chamber if anyone needs me."

"My brother was looking for you," Elizabeth called from behind me. She was setting her ball on the ground and positioning herself to give it a swift hit. "But I told him you weren't feeling well, so he went for a walk around the grounds with Lady Barrington. I'm sorry, Issy, I didn't think you would be back for quite a while."

Lady Barrington. My lip curled at the mention of her name, and I felt my eyes narrow as I looked off into the distance to see if I could spot them.

"Careful now," Robert said softly into my ear as he came up behind me. "That ugly green-eyed monster called Envy is rearing her ugly head. And we all ken how much ye despise the color green." The breath of his words tickled the hairs at the nape of my neck and sent a chill down my back. I resisted the urge to turn and shove him away. He walked around me but stopped short when he got in front of me. He gazed at me a moment before his eyes fell to my lips. Then he pointed to my mouth.

"Ye have—" He reached toward me and brushed a thumb over the corner of my mouth.

"What are you doing? I yelped, stepping away from him.

"Clotted cream," he said, in all innocence. "Ye wear it well."

I hurriedly wiped the corner of my mouth with the back of my fingers, feeling the spot Robert touched burn beneath my hand. "You're —" I bit my tongue, realizing I was about to say something rude, when all he was doing was trying to help me. "Thank you."

"Ye are welcome," he said, brushing his hands together before running one hand over his jaw. The sound of the coppery whiskers that stubbled his jawline scratched across his palm. For a split second I had the urge to tell Robert about the poisoned maids. Someone should be told. And he already knew my secret.

But just then young Prince Charles came trotting up. His feathery light hair shone in the autumn sunlight, making him the living image of his older brother. "It's your turn, Robert," the younger prince said, holding up a long-handled mallet for Robert to take. I had almost forgotten they had been playing jeu de mail.

"Thank ye, Yer Grace," Robert said, taking the mallet from the prince's hand. Prince Charles glanced at me and stood up straighter.

"Forgive me for the interruption, Lady Isobel," he said with impeccable manners, then bowed to me.

I tilted my head in acceptance of the interruption and watched Robert walk away with Prince Charles. It was probably best I didn't tell Robert about the poison anyway. The less incriminating evidence he had against me, the better. Instead, I turned my attention toward finding the countess. I wanted answers, and she was the only person who could give me an explanation. But whether she told me the truth remained to be seen.

Chapter 22

Richmond Palace, London
October 1612
Robert

I sat in the shadow of the blue drawing room at Richmond, dealing myself a hand of solitaire. The dark blue of the walls and the silver trim of cushions and furniture were peaceful after an afternoon of glaring sun and raucous play. When I closed my eyes all I could see were bright reds and oranges, and the sensation made me feel anxious and irritated. Shutting myself into a dark room always seemed to help calm me when my senses felt overloaded.

My body hurt all over. It had only taken one game of hitting a ball across the lawn playing jeu de mail to see that playing at barriers had exercised muscles I didnae even ken I had. I had to admire Henry, or any man for that matter, who could put on such heavy, constricting armor and swing a sword. And if they could strike a foe, that surely deserved a reward. To think that men went into battle girded with such protection was baffling. We certainly didnae fight like that in Scotland. At least not along the border. Padded doublets and a protective breast-plate perhaps. But I preferred my unrestricted plaid and the free form fighting of my forefathers to the stiff, weighted feel of heavy armor. Then again, I had never fought in a battle of such magnitude that would call for that kind of protection. All my fighting experience came at the Scottish border fending off thieves and protecting my own plunder. Often a woman or child would need protection as well. I was all too happy to oblige. That was how I met Moira, after all.

I was pulled from my reverie by the sensation of someone sitting down beside me. I turned to see George Preston taking a swig of his ale. He winked at me as he dropped his cup to the table, and I fought the urge to slug him. I didnae like this man. But he had just enough ire for the king that gave me the notion he might be willing to help me with my plan.

"You wanted to talk to me?" he slurred, apparently half in his cups.

"I wanted to talk to ye sober," I said with irritation. "Ye are no good to me if ye willnae even remember this conversation in the morning."

He swiped a sleeve across his mouth. "I'm fine," he said, opening his eyes wider and looking at me. "I've been much drunker before and for much prettier company."

I ran a hand over my face, hoping I hid nae made a mistake in asking for his help. Picking up the bottle of whisky I had carried with me into the drawing room, I poured myself another dram and threw it back quickly. Setting the glass down hard onto the table, I shook my head and resumed my card game.

I glanced over my shoulder to ensure we were alone. "How satisfied with the King's policies are ye?" I asked, my voice low. I laid down a card on the table and studied the spread before me.

George shifted in his seat. "That is a very private question, is it not, my lord?"

"I'm not a lord, George. I have His Majesty to thank for that." I laid another card on the table and finished my round.

"I," he paused, picking up the discarded cards from the table. "I did not know that." He shuffled the cards quickly and began dealing a two-player game. "I, err—"

"Just answer the question," I demanded, picking up the cards he had dealt me. The sun was quickly sinking in the west, casting shadows across the table. I had lit no candles, but there was enough light left in the room to see the hesitancy in his eyes. "I'm not here to entrap ye. I need yer assistance, but I need to ken ye willnae be a turncoat."

"He has turned his back on the one true religion. Trampled underfoot the teachings of the Church and all that his sweet mother, our queen, Mary of Scotland held dear. He has made promises to the Catholics he has not kept, and if he were to continue to be allowed in this vein, he will destroy what little we Catholics have left here in England." He spoke with such vehemence; I almost admired his dedication to his faith. I lost that dedication long ago if I had ever possessed it at all. "He is a reprobate."

"What are we playing?" I asked as he finished dealing and picked up his hand.

"Maw?" He offered. I nodded and played my first card.

"Well, perhaps ye should ken, it isnae for love of God nor faith that I make my plans. It isnae even to put another monarch on the throne, for indeed the next in line would be another Protestant, and I am nay about to bring harm to my cousin, Henry." I pinned him with a look that told him I meant what I said, and absolutely no harm was to come to my cousin. "What I do is solely out of revenge. Revenge for my father, who was wronged. Revenge for my mother, who was humiliated. And revenge for me, who has been left without a name or identity I can be proud of."

We finished out the round with me taking the trick. I took the cards and began to shuffle them again.

"I understand," George said. "My grandfather was implicated in the Gunpowder Plot. So, I guess I have a reason to want revenge as well."

I stopped dealing the cards and looked at him. "Ye never said as much before."

He shrugged. "We do not talk about it in my family and certainly not in public. He nearly ruined my mother's brother and his family. My uncle was the heir to his small estate. It was confiscated when my grandfather was executed. My mother will allow no talk of it. She was angry at her father for a long time afterwards. She will not speak my grandfather's name in conversation, although she does allow us to talk of him now, at least."

I picked up the whisky to pour another dram. George held out his cup to me, expecting me to pour some for him.

"I need ye to be clear-headed," I said, holding my bottle aloft.

"I am as clear-headed as a nun saying prayers." He cast me an innocent look and I caved, pouring him just enough to satisfy his aching. He threw the swallow back and choked. "I never understood the love you Scots have for your whisky," he said with a strangled breath. He swiped the back of a finger across his watering eyes and leaned back in his chair, exchanging his cup for his cards. "Now what is this plan of yours you need help with? And be warned, my services do not come cheaply. I know you have the coin to compensate, being the prince's Master of the Horse and all." He bared his teeth at me in an attempt at a charming smile, then perused his hand for a card to play, and tossed it on the table.

I threw down my first card. Irritation thrummed through me at the thought of having to trust a man I barely ken to such a dangerous task. But it couldnae be helped. I didnae have one friend in this forsaken city that would see things my way and be willing to help. My aggravation came out in a growl. "Dinnae fash yerself. Ye will be paid well."

He laid down another card then looked at me pointedly. "Well?"

I took a swig of whisky directly from the bottle this time and felt the liquor buzzing in my veins. I laid down another card, winning another round then said with arrogance, "We are going to kidnap the king."

Chapter 23

Richmond Palace, London
October 1612
Isobel

My head still ached from this afternoon's events, but I made my way to the blue drawing room anyway. I had not been able to locate the countess all afternoon, and I hoped she and Rochester would decide to join this evening's entertainment, since they were both apparently fond of games.

But before I made it even a quarter of the way down the corridor, a footman approached me. He bowed slightly, then inquired, "Lady Isobel?"

"Yes," I answered, studying his blue and white uniform, the colors of the prince's livery. He looked to be no older than me, but his face was set like a stone and his eyes darkened, as though he had lived a much harder life than his years should have allowed.

He didn't speak again but held out a small, folded piece of paper to me. With darting eyes, he looked about him like he was afraid we might be discovered in the hallway.

"What's this?" I asked, but he merely bowed again and turned quickly away without another word. I looked at the folded piece of parchment. It was not sealed or marked in any way on the outside. When I unfolded it, I noticed it looked as if it had been torn from a larger piece of parchment. It read:

Meet me in the library.
Tell no one.
H

My heart leapt in my chest. It wasn't the neat, illustrious writing of the prince, but I could think of no one else who bore the initial "H." I turned the sliver of paper over in my hand and studied the outside of it. Most of my correspondence with the prince was sealed with wax and his signet. Still, excitement trilled through me at the clandestine invitation.

There was only one problem. I had no idea where the library was here at Richmond. I looked down the corridor, hoping the footman who had brought me the note was still close by, but the hallway was empty.

I walked in the direction in which the footman had disappeared, hoping to come upon someone in the prince's service who could direct me where I wanted to go. It didn't take long until I came upon two maids whispering in the hallway that led to the great hall.

"Direct me to the library, please," I said, too excited at first to notice the looks on their faces. Perhaps they feared I would chastise them for their idle gossip.

"Down that hall and on the right," the older of the two maids said, pointing in the direction she had just described. "Shall I light a fire there for you, my lady?"

"No," I said, already walking where she indicated. I ran a fingertip behind my ear, sure to tuck any stray strands of hair back into my coiffure and looked down at my bodice and the low neckline the countess had instructed Mistress Turner to create for me. Her tips for catching the prince's attention must be working.

When I reached the library door, I paused, taking a deep breath, and glancing once again down the hall for busybodies who like to report all they see to the king or queen. Although these servants were employed for the prince's comfort, it was Their Majesties who controlled the comings and goings at all the estates in the crown's trust. I needed to stay in the queen's good graces, if I were to ever convince her I was worthy of her son's attentions.

I pushed the door gently open and stepped inside. The fireplace was indeed dark, and a cold draft seemed to creep along the floor. It was a strange place for a rendezvous, if he had not taken pains to make it comfortable.

But the voice that greeted me was not the prince. Instead, from out of the shadows, a figure stepped, startling me with its urgency.

"My lady," the feminine voice said hurriedly. It was Hester, the maid I had met in the servant's quarters earlier that afternoon.

"What is the meaning of this?" I asked, my disappointment and worry hardening my tone.

"Forgive me for the secrecy. But I must speak with you regarding Lenora." The girl's voice quaked as she wrung her hands together.

"What of Lenora? How does she fare?"

"She is dead," Hester said, her voice on the edge of breaking.

"Dead?" I repeated, shock and disbelief pinning me to my spot. "How can that be? I thought she was on the mend?"

"She, she was," the woman stuttered. "Or so I thought." Her lips quivered uncontrollably, and she brought a shaky hand to her face, covering her mouth.

"Tell me everything," I urged, moving closer to the girl, and laying a hand on her arm. She was a pretty girl, but the weight of her knowledge, and the loss of her friends made her eyes droop in a pitiful expression.

"All right," she said, wiping her nose with a piece of cloth. "When I arrived at her room after you had left, I heard the doctor and Mistress Turner talking about your visit. I heard how you had commanded them to have Lenora's room cleaned, and they argued whether the countess had sent you to check on them. The doctor seemed to think you could be trusted, he believed the countess had sent you. But Mistress Turner disagreed. She said you were oblivious, and they should not allow you access to the room again. Then, she said something about locking the door to any further intrusions until the deed was done."

I furrowed my brow. "Until the deed was done? What deed?"

"I think they were poisoning Lenora. She and Alice had recently been caught discussing the countess's affair with the Viscount Rochester. Alice said the king would never allow the countess her divorce from the Earl of Essex because she wasn't a maiden. Lenora asked her how she knew Frances wasn't virtuous, and Alice said she saw it with her own eyes. Then Lenora laughed and said she had heard that the countess had bewitched her husband, so he was unable to have marital relations with her. She thought it would be great fun if the countess had bewitched the king to get him to grant her the divorce."

I sucked in a breath in shock. Not only were the maids questioning Frances's chastity but accusing her of witchcraft. That was dangerous talk indeed! Accusations such as those could very well prevent Frances from getting what she wanted: her divorce from Essex.

"You said they were recently caught talking. Caught by whom? Was it the countess?"

The maid shook her head. "No, my lady. Mistress Turner discovered them."

"I see," I said, dropping my hand from her arm. "Hester, who else thinks Lady Frances has bewitched her husband?"

The girl sniffled and raised her head to meet my stare. "Everyone, my lady. All the prince's servants and many of the queen's. Even some of the king's footmen have heard the rumors."

"And has no one told the king?" I asked, shocked so many were privy to the information, yet none had made it known to the king.

"I believe he knows," Hester said, wringing her skirts in her hands.

"No, I do not believe he knows," I argued. I knew the king's history of witch hunting. My father, mother, and grandmother had been caught up in his witch trials in Scotland many years ago. If the king smelled witches, he would act with swiftness. "Who helped Lady Frances bewitch her husband? How does she know of such things?"

The maid shifted on her feet. "I know not."

"Well, what makes you think Lenora and Alice have been poisoned? What proof do you have?"

The girl bit her lip. "Forgive me, my lady, but I haven't much proof. It is just a gut feeling and the observance of things that feel a little off."

A cloud moved over the full moon that glowed in the sky outside the library window. It cast darker shadows across the maid's face, making her look even more dreary. "Like what?" I swallowed the bile that rose to my throat. Even without such proof, I knew the countess was equipped with the poison she needed to perform such a task. I knew because I was the one who provided it for her. It was all thanks to me.

Hester lowered her voice, as if there was still a possibility we could be overheard. Leaning in closer, she said, "The countess was very angry when Mistress Turner revealed her maids had been talking about her. A few weeks later, on a particularly warm day, the countess had invited Alice and Lenora to sit and have refreshment with her. I thought that was strange because ladies of yours and the countess's station do not socialize with their maids like that." I chewed on my bottom lip, thinking of how I had sat and chatted with Edith many times and all the lectures I had received from our housekeeper, Mistress Hunt, because of it. "I was appointed to bring a tray of cakes to her chamber. When I entered, the countess was arranging three chalices on the table. She appeared a little put out that I had returned so quickly. '*Back so soon?*' she had asked me, and she hurriedly tucked a small black bag into the folds of her skirt, as if she didn't want me to see it. I moved the cups aside to set the cakes down, and the countess became very upset when I almost mixed up the order of the cups. She peered into the cups before arranging them again then waved me away. By that evening, both girls had fallen ill."

My blood went cold. "What did the black bag look like?"

"It was a beautiful black velvet satchel. It was embroidered with silver thread, but I didn't get a good look at the design."

My satchel. The one I had kept the nux vomica in and had given to Lady Frances when I handed over the poison. It bore my initials.

I squeezed my eyes shut in humiliation. *How could you be so stupid?* I chided inwardly. Then again, I never dreamed she would use it to harm a human.

My supper roiled in the bottom of my stomach, feeling as if it wouldn't stay put. If anyone were to find out I had given the poison to Frances, my life would be ruined. It didn't matter that I was not aware of her intentions. My mother's words came rushing back to me: *I do not trust the Countess of Essex. I wouldn't put it past her to use the poison on an enemy.* I didn't know everything Frances was up to, but I had a sickening feeling my mother was correct. The floor seemed to tilt beneath my feet. I felt myself sway and laid my hand on a nearby book-shelf to steady myself.

"Are you all right, my lady?" I could hear Hester saying. "You look a little pale."

I took a deep breath and licked my lips. "Of course," I said, managing a weak smile. "But Hester, why have you come to me with this information? What makes you think I am not a part of this scheme and that I won't have you poisoned next?" I don't know why I asked the question. Perhaps it was to gauge if any suspicion had been cast upon me.

The maid's eyes widened as if she had not even thought of this possibility. She ran a shaking hand over her forehead. "I could sense a kindness in you, my lady. And the fact the doctor and Mistress Turner didn't know what to think of you, made me to believe that you were not in league with them." She paused momentarily. "Am I mistaken?" Her voice quavered, and a look of fear filled her eyes.

I reached out a shaky hand and touched her elbow. "You are not. Thank you for the information. I will look into it." I straightened my back and studied the maid for a long moment. "You must speak of this to no one, do you understand?"

She nodded her head vigorously then curtseyed. "Yes, my lady."

"These are dangerous accusations and if we are not careful, the wrong people could get hurt."

"I understand."

But she didn't. She had no idea just who exactly could get hurt. I turned toward the door, trying to appear unruffled. "I have a gaming party to attend. Do not leave this room until you have counted to one hundred. And do not step out into the hallway until you have made sure there is no one in it to see you departing."

"Yes, my lady." She curtseyed to me again, and when she lifted her head, I could still see the silvery tears gathered at the corners of her eyes.

"And wipe your eyes," I said. "We must not let on we are suspicious of anything." And with that, I departed the library and made my way to where the games were being played. I made sure to lift my head high and appear as if I was still the naïve girl who had no idea that I had aided in the murder of two maids. But I could not shake the trepidation that lurked in the back of my mind.

When I arrived at the blue drawing room, it appeared all the party had already assembled. Elizabeth and Count Frederick, Prince Henry and his close friends, Essex and Harington, minus my brother Tom who was away at school. Robert sat to the right of Henry and Lady Barrington to his left. As I took in the party of players, I nearly stopped breathing when I spotted Lady Frances and saw she and Rochester had rejoined the festivities. My thoughts turned to the two young women now dead and my velvet bag still in the countess's clutches. I tried to reason that there must be an explanation, and that neither the countess nor I were guilty of such a dreadful charge. But my mother's words replayed in my mind, and something told me that she was right.

The Earl of Essex slipped past me, drawing me out of my thoughts. He bowed to me slightly and I noticed not for the first time how well suited he was. Frances had once said he wasn't very dashing. But I found his Delphic features intriguing. His dark, deep-set eyes held a bit of mystery, and his mouth, set perpetually into a dreadful scowl, spoke only when he had something extremely important to say. Or, when he doled out insults to the countess. I'm sure to him those were one and the same. And then there was that pearl drop earring that always dangled from his ear, giving him a dashing air.

"Leaving so soon, my lord?" I asked.

"I regret that I will not be able to enjoy your lovely company this evening, Lady Isobel. I seemed to have lost my appetite for fraternizing with loathsome, boil-brained varlets and their viperous doxies." He looked past me, and I followed his gaze to the other side of the room where Frances and Rochester were sitting next to one another, leaning in closely and lost in each other's words. I felt the color leave my face, and I was suddenly filled with pity for Essex and his reputation. If the rumors about Frances bewitching him were true, the poor man never stood a chance.

"That is a pity," I replied coyly. "I have a need to repel one man's attentions and attract another's, and I was hoping for a handsome escort to help me do that." I smiled at him, and his eyes fell to my lips before drifting back up slowly.

A sly expression crossed his face, lifting his darkened brow slightly. "Who am I to leave a maiden in distress to fend for herself?" He extended an arm to me, and I took it with alacrity.

He led me to the table where everyone, except for Thomas Over-bury, was seated and waiting for the games to begin. There was a young man sitting between two empty chairs and when we reached the table Essex barked an order at him.

"Move," he said, not bothering to ask nicely. The young man, I believe he had once been introduced to me as George, fell over himself to vacate the seat in which he sat. He moved to the empty seat to his left, leaving two seats together for Essex and me to be seated together. It wasn't until the earl had assisted me with my seat, that Lady Frances looked up from her conversation with Rochester and noticed the change in seating. Her eyes darkened as she took in first Essex, then me, and the slight lifting of her brow made me to know she was not pleased.

"Lady Isobel," Prince Henry announced as he shuffled a deck of cards in this hand. "I have been looking for you all afternoon." His eyes shone with a mischievous glint, the kind that usually made my belly flutter. But whether it was the disappointment of my earlier imagined tryst, or his disappearance earlier in the day, for some reason unbeknownst to me, I did not flirt back.

"It was my understanding you were occupied elsewhere, Your Grace." My eyes drifted to Lady Barrington, who had conveniently seated herself next the Henry. Essex chuckled, and from the corner of my eye, I could see Frances cock her head at me in interest. Everyone seemed intent on my conversation with the prince. But there was only one set of eyes that seemed to burn a hole through me, and I was sure to avoid his misty green gaze at all costs. Robert said not a word, just leaned back in his chair, watching me, and nursing a bottle of what looked to be whisky. He drank directly from the bottle, and I made a conscious effort not to watch the knot in his throat bob when he swallowed the amber liquid.

The prince studied me, and I finally smiled shyly at him. When he was satisfied I wasn't mad at him, he began dealing the cards.

"What are we playing, Your Grace?" I asked, watching his long, graceful fingers slide each card off the deck.

"Primero," he said, and a groan drifted from the other side of the table. It was the countess.

"Why must we even play cards at all? I am bored with the game. Let us play charades, or some other game that requires movement."

The prince stopped in the middle of his deal. "But Rochester wanted to win his pin money back. This is the fastest way." John Harington hooted at that, and the other men at the table guffawed as well. Even Essex seemed visibly pleased at what could almost be interpreted as a slight toward the Viscount Rochester.

"By the beard," Rochester said under his breath. "Pin money is for women. Are you challenging my manhood, Your Grace?" His tone was light, but it was hard not to hear the slight irritation in his voice.

"By no means," said the prince, smiling. "But you were complaining of losing a small fortune the night before last. I told you we would give you an opportunity to win it back."

"I for one would love to see a show of your manhood," Essex said in a low drawl. I shot a glance at him, amused that he would voice his hatred of the man who cuckolded him so openly.

"Lower your feathers, peacocks," the countess said coolly, addressing both men. "This is not the time nor place for this." She laid a hand on Rochester's sleeve, and the gesture released a growl from beside me. Essex was practically vibrating with anger.

I had no particular dislike for the viscount and no wish to make an enemy of the countess. But the more I thought of the predicament she had placed me in, the angrier I became. I also felt sorry for the Earl of Essex, especially if he had been unknowingly bewitched. So, with a need for redress flowing through my veins, I leaned into Essex and with my voice smooth as silk, said into his ear, "She is right, my lord. Why don't you challenge him to a duel? If he has wronged you, you deserve that vindication. But right now, if you want to get them both back, put your arm across the back of my chair and laugh at the ridiculous thing I have just said."

He pulled back from me, searching my face for explanation. A smile pulled at my lips, but I covered it with my hand before the small gap between my teeth could show. "I do not know what game you are playing at, Lady Isobel, but it is a very dangerous game indeed. You do not want that foul hag for an enemy."

"Come now, my lord. It is just a bit of fun." I took a sip of the red wine that had been placed before me, studying him from beneath heavy lashes. Then, playing along like a true genius, he shook his head and laughed.

From across the table, the countess narrowed her eyes at me in suspicion. I laughed along with the Earl of Essex, to make the joke seem more real, but I couldn't ignore the cold chill that Frances's glare sent down my spine. Was this truly the way I wanted to handle Frances's betrayal? She came from a powerful family, and she had evidence against me. Both were very good reasons to try to stay on her good side. Perhaps I should rethink how I wanted to play this game of revenge. Besides, if I took the friendly approach, I might be able to ask her for my black satchel back. She doesn't know I know about the murder of the maids. I could explain that the satchel was a gift and I needed it back.

"Place your bets," Henry called from his end of the table, and the game began.

"I have nothing with which to gamble," I said, taking another sip of wine. "My most valuable jewel is lost to me." I moved a hand over my throat, where my amethyst used to hang.

A look of satisfaction glazed over Robert's face as he watched me. He took another swig from his bottle but did not say a word.

"I noticed you haven't been wearing your favorite necklace, Issy," Elizabeth said as she arranged her cards on the table without picking them up. "What happened to it? I am surprised you never mentioned losing it. It was a gift from your father. I know how much you adored it."

"Yes, it means the world to me," I said to the Princess, then finally leveled my gaze on Robert. "Where would you look for it, Robert? You look as if you have knowledge of the matter." It was not wise to call Robert out for his thievery here in front of everyone, especially the prince. And even more so since he knew my secret about stealing the poison from my mother's apothecary. But I seemed to be doing all manner of unintelligent things this evening. And his smug expression made my blood boil. I would get my necklace back somehow.

"How would Robert have knowledge of it, Lady Isobel?" John Harington spoke up. "Purple does not seem to be his color." Everyone chuckled at Harington's jest. Everyone except for Robert and me.

"Indeed." Robert placed his bet on the table. "But if I had lost something very important to me, I'd start by clearing away all my other distractions, until I got what I wanted."

You could hear a pin drop in the drawing room as everyone listened to our conversation. Robert spoke of the king, I knew, and it made me wonder what he was planning. He had already confessed to me the reason he had come to England and that he would do anything to avenge his father.

"All right," Harington drawled. "I am not sure what this conversation is about anymore. Shall we play cards?"

"I'll spot Lady Isobel," Essex said from beside me. He spoke of covering my bet, but I had almost forgotten he was there. I could feel the intensity of Robert's gaze on me, and it made any lucid thoughts slip right out of my brain.

"When I have children," Frances spoke up from across the table, "I want them to each have a token of my love, as the Earl of Stratford has given to Lady Isobel. I think that is a beautiful gesture."

"But if someone stole that token from me, I would want revenge," Robert said, throwing down his first card.

The countess gasped. "Do you think someone stole Lady Isobel's necklace? Who would dare?" Her voice was a low purr, and I wondered if she had a suspicion.

It was the prince's turn to play, but instead of laying down a card, he sorted through the hand he held, shuffling the cards into different spots. The prince was studying his cards closely, and I knew from playing with him before that he wasn't much for conversation when there was a serious game at hand, especially if the bets were high. But he looked up at the countess when she spoke, and I could tell he was thinking about what had been said.

When he finally spoke, it was not of my necklace, nor thievery, but of something far heavier weighing on his mind. "Revenge is a bitter root that strangles the life out of any seed of happiness," he said. "I should not want to die seeking revenge but rather in giving my life for the glory for my king and my country. I hope that my good deeds would live on in those around me, in the people whose lives I have touched." He finished his turn by throwing a card on the table and looking to Robert. "Your turn, Cousin."

I swallowed hard. Had Robert spoken to the prince as well about his desire to avenge his father and reestablish his title and lands? Surely, he would not have mentioned doing harm to Henry's father to get what he wanted.

"What a horrible thing to talk of, Your Grace," Frances said. "To speak of one's own death must surely be a bad omen."

Nothing more was said of death or revenge, or even my necklace. When the round ended, the prince scooted his chair back and stood.

"I have just the activity for us. Let us play hide and seek in the maze and leave this weighty conversation behind us. We are supposed to be celebrating my sister's betrothal."

There was a general cry of excitement at his suggestion, but Princess Elizabeth spoke up above all the exclamations. "But brother, it is getting quite chilled outside, and it is dark."

"That is the fun of it, Bess," the prince explained. "The gardens are lit, and there is a full moon. We will see well enough. And you ladies can bundle up if you need to. We will give you a minute to prepare yourselves."

Everyone immediately began moving about, and I couldn't help the twinge of jealousy that knotted in my stomach as Lady Barrington took a step closer to the prince and said something to him. The prince answered her but looked a little distracted. Probably because he was watching me.

Chapter 24

Richmond Palace, London
October 1612
Isobel

The torches that lined the gardens were lit, casting a radiant glow across the maze and surrounding grounds. The vibrant pinks and yellows of dahlias, and the rich sunburst of marigolds that were planted along the footpath that led to the maze could still be seen under the burning flames of the torches and the full silver moon that hung in the inky sky. We drew straws to see who the seeker would be. Essex pulled the short straw and bowed to me before making his way to the designated safe spot, to hide his eyes and count. No water flowed in the large stone fountain that stood in the middle of the terrace, and all one would have to do is touch the deep, empty bowl of the fountain to be considered safe.

I wrapped my arms about myself, feeling the coolness of the evening after the loss of Essex's body heat next to me. But what the Earl of Essex gave me in heat, the Countess of Essex gave me a hundred-fold in ice.

Her slippers crunched the stones beneath her feet as she drew up beside me. "I wasn't aware you were such close allies with my husband," she said coolly, eyeing me. She wore a mink stole wrapped around her shoulders and held together with a sharp diamond and pearl broch that glinted in the light of the full moon. I suddenly had a sickening vision of her scratching my eyes out with the pointed jewel.

"Allies against whom?" I asked with reciprocated coolness. "Am *I* your enemy now?" I held my breath, unsure why I was picking this fight and even more uncertain if I had the ammunition to win.

She stared at me: her mouth slightly agape. "Of course not," she laughed, but the sound came out strained. "We women must stick together. This is a man's world, and if we are not careful, they will take everything we have to give and then some and leave us with nothing but a shell of our former selves."

"Is that what happened to you and Essex? Did he take advantage of you, steal your identity and freedom, and make you a puppet in return?" I was shivering now, but I knew not if it was the night air or the foolishness of my words that made me shake.

Her shrewd eyes bore into me. Had she never looked at me like that before, or was I just noticing it for the first time? "You know nothing of which you speak, *girl*." She hurled the word with such aversion that it felt as if she had slapped me with it. "You know nothing of what it is like to be married off at the age of ten and three, having no choice in the man you must share your bed—your *body*—with, and having no hope of ever feeling true love." Her lips quivered as she spoke the words, and I could practically feel the desperation in her voice. "So, yes, I suppose he did steal my identity and my freedom. But I will never be his puppet. I have too much avarice for that."

A sharp wind picked up, rustling the leaves in the Sycamore trees that lined the garden surrounding us. It shook the foliage and my common sense. In turn, I said, "Is that why you bewitched him? To free yourself from your perceived prison?"

If it were possible to see the color slip from her face in the dark, I was sure I would have. She glared at me; her eyes reduced to small slits. "Who told you that?"

"From what I hear, it is common knowledge. But I don't believe all the gossip I hear. So, tell me true: have you used witchcraft on the Earl of Essex?"

She laughed at that, a cold, calculating sound slipping from her mouth. "Why would I tell you anything? The daughter of the king's infamous inquisitor. Do you think me that stupid as to incriminate myself with such admissions? You will be hard-pressed to find evidence of such accusations, and you would be imprudent to even try."

"Why? Will you poison me like you poisoned those maids?" I hadn't meant to say it. I hadn't meant to hurl the accusation so churlishly. I slapped a hand over my mouth to keep myself from saying any other foolish things.

The countess stepped closer to me. "Again, you do not know of what you speak. But the poison *you* provided me has come in quite handy. So much so I will be needing more. And you are going to get it for me."

I watched her pinkened lips move as she spoke. It was as if she were a disembodied oracle spewing some abstruse prophecy and not a real woman whom I had considered my friend. I shook my head. "I will not be a part of your wicked undertakings," I said, fighting back the urge to cry.

"Oh, it is too late for that, my dear. You are already entangled. And if you want to keep your reputation untarnished, and worthy of a prince's affections, you will do exactly as I bid."

Essex's voice came drifting across the veranda. "Hide yourselves, for I am coming to find you!" he called.

But before I could say anything more to the countess, a hand reached out and grabbed my wrist, pulling me away. "Come, Issy, you don't want to be found. The earl is a presumptuous braggard when he wins." I turned to see Prince Henry smiling as he pulled me along behind him.

We ran into the maze. At every sharp corner, the prince knew exactly which way to turn. Right then left, then right then left. On and on we ran as he pulled me deeper into the tangle of shrubs. There was no time to think, no time to ponder whether we were going in the right direction. All I could do was trust the prince. The bushes extended several feet above our heads, with no way to see the end and no way out except to solve the puzzle and work our way through. I imagined he had walked the maze a thousand times, for he never made a wrong turn. Yet, as the greenery rose up around us, a sickening feeling wrapped itself around my throat. I gasped for air until the prince slowed and finally came to a stop. Pulling me into a small alcove where the maze came to a dead end, he slid his hand into mine, intertwining our fingers. His were cool and smooth, and his feather-light touch sent a pulse of satisfaction straight to my belly.

He stepped closer to me, pulling my hands to his chest. "I have been looking for you all day," he said again. "You look beautiful in your rose-colored frock. You take my breath away." His eyes dropped to my dress, and I could feel the ardency of his gaze as it swept every inch of me.

"You cannot fool me," I teased. "You were with Lady Barrington all afternoon. I surmise you probably told her the same thing." I resisted the urge to lean into him. It was colder out here than I imagined it would be, and even the tall hedges did not fully block the wind.

Merriment danced in his eyes. "Your jealousy is misplaced, Issy. Lady Barrington is engaged to be married to Baron Longfellow. And I refuse to impose on another man's possession."

Possession. My conversation with Lady Frances came rushing back to me along with her words about losing her freedom. Is that how the prince felt about marriage as well? That a wife was someone to be owned and controlled? I supposed if I were to be his queen one day, that is exactly how it would be.

The shrubbery was too close; their limbs, though stretching upward, seemed to reach for me. Green. Green! I was surrounded by green, and the feeling was suffocating. An uneasiness twisted in my stomach, and the back of my neck prickled. Memories of the Oberon masque and the green dye that created the sensation of bugs crawling under my skin smothered me. Even the older memories of being forced to eat my green vegetables as a child, then dispelling the food in a nauseous bodily reaction, haunted me. This crippling fear of green things had tormented me since childhood, making it difficult to touch, or taste, or want to be near anything of such coloring. It was as if I feared the color itself were a living thing and would seep into my skin and crawl beneath the surface and eat me from the inside out.

Perspiration pebbled on my brow, and the cool night air brushed against my face, sending a shiver over me. But I couldn't pull away. I couldn't run for fear the prince would take my escape from the hedges as an escape from him. Not that I could ever find my way out of the maze by myself. Instead, I stayed right there, clinging to his hands, and carefully dragging quiet breaths through my lungs.

And when he leaned toward me and laid his lips against mine, I wasn't sure if it was the hovering bushes or the pleasure of his kiss that stole my breath completely. "Issy," he whispered, sounding as if he too could not breathe. "I've been wanting to tell you—"

"Your Grace!" someone called from beyond the hedge. "Your Grace, His Majesty has sent for you!" The voice sounded closer now, though I knew it must be a footman, standing on the outside of the maze. "Your Grace?"

"Here I am." Henry called back. "I am coming." He stared at me, still holding my hands but quickly pulling away.

"What have you wanted to tell me?" I said in a rush, feeling the moment quickly slipping away.

"I must go. We will talk later," he said, dropping my hands and stepping away.

"Tell me now," I urged. "I will not be able to sleep for fear of what you have to say." I took a step closer to him, realizing if he left, I would be all alone, lost in the hedges.

"I," he paused, looking over his shoulder as the voice called out for him again. "I hope what I have to say will not be a cause for fear," he said in a teasing response to my words. His finely formed brows arched into a crinkled line across his forehead. I could not see the color of his eyes in the darkened maze, but the familiar sky blue of his gaze seared me, nonetheless. "I want to marry you. I want you to be my wife, my queen, when the time comes. Although, it is not right to speak of that right now since that would mean the death of my father."

I stared at him in disbelief. "Your wife? I wasn't aware you felt that way. You've never said anything about your feelings for me." I rubbed my hands over my arms, realizing the foolish mistake I made by coming outside without a cloak.

He looked over his shoulder again. "My father and mother want me to marry a Catholic princess. But I cannot. My wife must be a Protestant. You are beautiful and come from a titled family. I will have my way in this. You shall see."

"Your Grace!" the voice called once more as the prince began unbuttoning his coat.

"Here," he said, wrapping his doublet around my shoulders. "I must go." He kissed me on the forehead, then said, "We will talk more of this later." He took a step then turned back to me. "Don't let Essex find you." He flashed a boyish smile at me and was gone.

I stood there frozen in fear. Or was it excitement? He wanted to marry me. I waited for the happiness that surely follows such declarations. But it didn't come. Where was the euphoria? The giddiness? All the emotions I had imagined over and over again each night when I laid my head upon my pillow. The thrill of seeing Queen Anne in her crown and imagining it sitting atop my head one day. Gone. And in its place: dread.

I gasped a breath, looking up at the surrounding hedges. I usually didn't have such reactions to the bushes. Trees and bushes were everywhere, just part of nature. But standing here, lost in this maze, and feeling like the shrubbery was closing in on me, I panicked. And then I began to scream.

I squeezed my eyes shut. "Help!" I cried "Somebody please help me." I felt my composure slip away, and hysteria reared its crippling head.

I do not know how long I cried. But eventually a sound in the darkness arrested me. "Hush!" a harsh voice whispered in my ear, as strong arms wrapped around me, pulling me to my feet. At some point I had sunk to the ground and lay there in a heap of skirts with my knees pulled up to my chest like a babe newly come into the world. "Ye dinnae want Essex to find ye." I didn't even have to open my eyes to realize it was Robert. My pounding heart sped faster, and I threw my arms around his neck in relief. The smoky-sweet aroma of whisky on his breath centered my nerves and warmed my skin.

"Hush now," he said again, but this time his tone was softer. "Ye are all right." He laid his hands on my hips and pulled me closer. I pressed against him, burying my face in the crook of his neck, and squeezing him tighter.

I couldn't stop shaking. Whether it was the cold night air skimming across my skin, or the terror of my green prison, I did not know. Whatever the reason, I could not seem to get control of my shaking limbs.

Robert brushed his hand across my back, whispering soothing words in my ear. The sensation of his hands on me and the gentleness of his breath brushing against my ear sent strange tingles through my body. This was different from the prince's hurried kiss. When Henry kissed me, I felt disheveled, like all my pent-up emotions were jumbling about in my brain. It was unexpected and forced. Like I was his only appealing option, and he was settling on me.

But with Robert I felt—safe. Like I could be myself and had nothing to prove. I had spent my whole life trying to separate myself from my heritage. The Scots were an undignified nation of miscreants according to most English. And although my father had found favor with the former queen, I would have very little to recommend me. I needed to prove to the English court I was a woman worthy of notice. An English woman, born in London and covered in satins and silks and embroidered flowers, and not some backwater lass who would rather run barefoot through the heather-covered mountainsides of Scotland.

I didn't understand it, and the feeling frustrated me. I did not like this man. He irritated me and teased me relentlessly. He was uncultured and untitled. He wore kilts at the English court and didn't care what people thought of him. And with all the other foolish things I had already done this evening, I decided I would do one more.

I moved my hands upward and twisted my fingers into the coppery locks of his hair. He watched me with those stormy green eyes and the depths of that storm reached right into my belly, sending tiny shivers through my limbs. I bit my bottom lip momentarily, contemplating my next move.

His eyes fell to my mouth. "Well, dinnae stop now," he drawled, the whisper fanning over me in soft ripples of desire.

I stared at the smooth fullness of his bottom lip, then let my eyes wander to the short whiskers that stubbled his sharp jawline. A muscle twitched in his jaw, and I couldn't tell if he was fighting a smile or some baser need.

I pulled his head down and kissed him. It was slow and soft at first, and the feel of his lips on mine sent fire shooting to my core. He let me lead, though I was extremely inexperienced. But soon he reached up and laid a hand on the side of my face, brushing a calloused thumb across my cheek and deepening the kiss. He ran his other hand down the side of my leg and fisted my skirt, pulling it upward. I was only slightly aware of the sensation, but when cool air touched my thigh, and the warm skin of his palm lit me aflame, I gasped.

He stopped his hand and pulled back. "I've gone too far," he said, releasing my skirt. The cambric cascaded down my leg and his hand moved back to my hip and settled there.

"We both have," I said, disentangling my fingers from his hair and pulling away. The scruff on his jaw scraped over my palm and felt like fine grains of sand against my skin. I ran my fingers over my swollen lips, then cleared my throat.

"I—"

"Well, this is a surprise," said a voice from behind us. We both turned our heads to see Essex standing in the path. "I am going to forget I just saw that and slowly back away."

"Leave us be," Robert said sharply, and Essex bowed his head to us, as if he weren't the highest ranked person standing there.

"Do not ask me to vouch for you, Robert," he said, turning his back on us.

"Nay need," Robert responded. His voice sounded hard.

"I am certain the prince would not agree," he retorted, turning the corner out of our sight. I ran my hands down my bodice, making sure all was in order. What had I just done? The prince declared his intentions of marriage, and this is how I repay him? My stomach felt like a bottomless pit now. I wanted the prince. I *loved* the prince. So why did I just kiss Robert?

"Get me out of here," I commanded, walking in the direction that Essex had retreated. Of all the foolish things I've done in my lifetime, and several of them just today, this was the most fatuous. I couldn't even look at Robert as he stepped up beside me and handed me the prince's doublet that must have slipped from my shoulders. I hadn't even noticed.

"Thank you," I said, making sure I didn't touch him. He didn't respond, and we continued walking, all the green hedges looking like one another and still making sweat bead on my forehead.

We walked in silence for several minutes. "You have a cut above your left eye," I pointed out finally, "and scratches on your cheeks." Then I noticed the greenery stuck in his auburn hair. I peered closer to get a better look, "You've got leaves in your hair." I reached up and pulled out a twig that was tangled in his locks. Then I noticed his jerkin and stopped walking in order to take in his state of dress. "Why are you covered in twigs and greenery?" I asked, brushing a leaf from his sleeve. "And your sleeve is torn."

"I cut through the shrubbery to get to ye."

I gawked at him. "You just pushed your way through all those tightly planted bushes?" I said, forming a barrier with my hands and pushing outward from my chest. "How is that possible?"

His eyes darkened and he stared back at me. "I heard yer cries and I thought ye were hurt."

I opened my mouth to speak but couldn't think what to say. He started walking again and I hurried to keep up with his long strides.

"So, you heard me crying and tore through the hedges like a madman to get to me?" I asked.

An unamused smile pulled at his lips. "I just said as much, did I nay?" He didn't look pleased with himself, but I tucked the confession away to think on later. "But when I found ye lying on the ground, squawking like a banshee," he continued, "I thought perhaps ye were just trying to get Essex's attention."

I scowled at him. "And why would I want to get caught just for the sake of getting caught?"

"The way ye were cozying up with him earlier, mayhap that is what ye wanted after all. For him to find ye in here, all alone, needing—rescued." He waved a hand in the air, motioning in the direction of Essex, wherever he may be.

My mouth fell open. He must think me a common doxy. "Don't be daft," I said severely, still feeling off balance. "That man is still in love with his wife, and she is in love with another man. I was only there for moral support."

Robert laughed bitterly. "That was some display of moral support ye showed earlier. But 'twill take more than ye pressing that lovely figure of yers against him for the earl to get over the embarrassment of his marriage. She has practically castrated the man with her infidelity."

I stopped walking again and looked at Robert in disbelief. Did he know about the claims that Frances had made the earl impotent with witchcraft? His father was a necromancer. Perhaps he knew of such spells.

"I did not press my body against him." I propped a hand on my hip. "And what do you know of their marriage anyway?" I said, irritated. "Did you help her create the charm?" I fished for information, hoping he might share what he knew.

He stared at me, confused. "I dinnae ken of what ye speak, but I assure ye, I havenae made any charms. What are ye yammering about?"

I stiffened. "I do not yammer." He didn't respond so I pressed on. "Do you mean to tell me you have not heard the rumors that the

Countess of Essex has made a wittol of the earl by means of witchcraft?"

"Witchcraft?" He laughed, the sound raking over my skin like sharp stones. "And ye think I had something to do with it because of rumors of my father."

"Do you deny the rumors of your father?" I asked, watching him closely.

He sighed heavily. "I suppose not." He looked away from me, and I felt for the first time a twinge of sympathy for this man who had grown up not knowing his father. He suffered the consequences of his father's choices. He began walking again, and we moved along the path as we tried to make our way through the maze. I felt a little more of my composure slip away each time we came upon a dead end. But Robert just turned us about without comment and kept walking. "I never kent my father was involved in the witchcraft trials of North Berwick," he said, looking straight ahead and calculating every turn we made. "My mother shared a lot of stories of my father while I was growing up. But she saved the most sinister one for the day I left home." He kicked a rock that had fallen into our path, and it went skittering into the trees. "And she still didnae share everything there was to ken about his escapades. If it hid nae been for yer father, I still widnae ken the half of what my father had done before he left Scotland."

I jerked my head to look at him. "My father?" I said, puzzled. "I'm sure he did not have good things to say about the Earl of Bothwell. Your father almost got mine killed." We came to another dead end in the maze, and my shoulders slumped in defeat. It was getting colder, and my feet were starting to hurt.

A contemplative smile touched Robert's lips. "He shared the truth about my father's exile, but he told me some good things about him as well. The Earl of Stratford is an honest man. Ye are fortunate to have him as a father."

I nodded, feeling a knot forming in my throat, and it made me want to cry. I suddenly missed my father greatly and wanted nothing more than to get out of here and write him a letter to tell him how much I love him. Then it hit me.

"And that is why you should return my necklace to me." I turned to look at him. "You stole it, and I want it back."

"I will give it back to ye when I am ready."

I crossed my arms over my chest, making it apparent I was not happy. But when we saw the light of the torches lining the garden seconds later, relief filled my chest, and I forgot all about the necklace.

Those players Essex had already found, Elizabeth, Frederick, and Harington, stood waiting by the fountain that stood in the middle of the gardens. Frances and Rochester were there too, although they sat on a step away from the others.

"I don't understand," Elizabeth said, her brows pushing into her forehead. "Did Essex find you two, or did you just stop playing?"

"He found us," Robert answered. "He was just in a hurry to find the next players." That was a reasonable excuse. Hopefully, they wouldn't ask more questions.

Harington called out to us. "It seems George Preston and Lady Barrington are the last two missing." He waggled his brows at us, and I wondered if the two were off hiding somewhere together.

From the corner of my eye, I could see the countess walking toward us. "Forgive me," I said to the party, "I am chilled to the bone and extremely tired. I think I'm going to retire for the evening." I turned before Frances had reached us and walked quickly into the palace.

I wanted to speak to Hester again. I wondered if I could recruit her to confiscate my black satchel. Perhaps if the price was right, she would consider it. She seemed to have access to Frances's rooms. However, that would also require me to confess that the bag was mine, and I wasn't sure I was ready to do that.

When I reached the top of the stairs in the servants' quarters, I realized how misguided my idea was. I stood at the top of the stairs, looking down the corridor at dozens of darkened doors, each of them with no distinguishing marks on them. Nothing to indicate to me which one might belong to Hester. I couldn't very well just start knocking on doors. I leaned against the wall, waiting—hoping—that someone would exit one of the rooms so I could ask them where I might find Hester. But the hallway was like a tomb, quiet and still, and I finally gave up my sentineling and headed back down the stairs. I would try to find her again tomorrow.

"Isobel."

The sound of Frances's voice calling out to me, surprised me, then sent a jolt of fear through me. Since she had practically confessed to me she had used me to poison those maids, I feared what she might do if I refused her demands. In my blindness and desperation for the prince's favor, I had thrown myself at her mercy and entangled myself in a dangerous game in which I didn't know the rules. And although I had foolishly thrown my accusations at her earlier, I now realized how much danger I was in and had no wish to speak to her again.

I picked up my pace, walking faster toward my chamber. But either her long legs carried her faster, or she had run after me, for within a few seconds she had apprehended me, grabbing my arm, and turning me about to face her.

"There you are, dear," she cooed, as if we had not spoken of murder only an hour earlier. "Why are you running from me?"

"I wasn't running. I merely have a headache and wish to retire to my chamber. It has been a long day. Perhaps we could talk tomorrow."

She looked at me, her left brow arched suspiciously at me once again. "We both know that will not happen. You will hide in your chamber, and I will be forced to send you missives to which you will not respond. It is much easier this way."

"Easier? For whom? I already told you I will not assist you any further." I tried to twist away from her, but her grasp tightened, soliciting a cry of pain from my lips.

"I do not think you understand, love. You no longer have a choice in the matter. It would have been much better for you if you had just stayed ignorant of the whole affair. But now that you know, I have a proposition for you. One in which you will not need to obtain any poison for me, thus easing your conscience and still satisfying your debt to me."

I frowned. "My debt to you? Of what do you speak?"

"Why, the debt in which I assist you in becoming the prince's darling. I am helping you obtain his favor. And when he eventually proposes to you, and you become his wife, and then queen someday, you will thank me."

I laughed bitterly and tried to jerk my arm free from her grasp once more. "I believe that debt was paid when I provided you poison. Besides, I already have the prince's favor. He told me this very night that he wishes to marry me. I do not need your help any further."

Her eyes widened into round saucers. A moment later, a slight smile lifted her lips, and she eased her grip on me. "That is good news."

"You speak as if you truly have an interest in what is best for me," I said tartly. "You lied to me. You played on my emotions, my feelings for the prince. You told me you had a rat problem and convinced me to get poison for you. You then proceeded to use that poison to harm innocent people. I will not be an accomplice in your murderous plans any further. You should be glad that I will keep your secret and not go to the king about it."

"And that my friend, is where your mistake lies. Do not bite the hand that feeds you. I have made you what you are. You are beholden to me now. Do not threaten me or you will find yourself in a worse situation than the one in which you presently find yourself. Take my advice and use it for your benefit. But if you cross me, you will be sorry."

I stared at her in horror. The beautiful face of the woman I had thought was my friend had turned into a monster I did not recognize. I swallowed hard. I did not want to help her any further, but I didn't trust that she wouldn't stab me in the back the first chance she could.

"What do you want from me?" I asked steadily, trying to keep my voice from shaking.

She smiled broadly now. "That's more like it. We can still be friends, Isobel." I said nothing in response, but she chuckled as if I had said something funny. "As you are aware, I am in the process of trying to obtain a divorce from that loathsome Essex."

"I do not find him loathsome," I said, casting her a look of disdain. "I found him to be charming."

The smile fell from her face, but she continued. "Regardless, of your feelings for the earl, I want to marry the Viscount Rochester, and the Earl of Essex stands in my way."

"Well, he is your lawfully wedded husband," I reminded her.

The countess pressed her lips together, appearing as though she was quickly losing patience. Ignoring my comments, she continued, "In order for me to obtain the divorce, I must submit to a physical examination to have my maidenhood proven."

I laughed out loud at this, but the heat that emanated from her glare kept me from another snide comment. Instead, I said, "And what does this have to do with me?"

"I want you to go in my place."

I stared at her. "Go in your place."

She looked over her shoulder. "Keep your voice down, you silly girl. Yes, go in my place. There may be reasons why my virginity might be hard to prove in such an examination. I need someone I trust can pass the test to ensure my divorce is granted."

"You mean, you are not a virgin," I said, letting all the judgement eek out of my voice. "Tell me true, did you consummate your marriage with the earl?"

"I do not see how that is your business, but no, we did not have intimate relations."

"You told me that you had given your body to him. Now you are telling me you did not consummate the marriage. I am confused."

She sighed heavily. "I made myself available to him. That man has been trying for eight years to make our marriage official but has failed to do so. I am ready to move on."

The maids' deadly conversation came back to my mind. "So, did you bewitch him, to prevent that from happening? Did you *make* him incapable?" I asked.

Her eyes bulged. "That question does not warrant an answer. What matters most right now is whether you are a virgin. You are, aren't you?"

Heat flushed my face though I hardly knew why. "Yes," I said, lifting my chin.

She understood my gesture entirely. With a bitter laugh she said, "That is good. You are just as you should be." She looked down her nose at me as if I was the one caught in a compromising situation. "Now, I will send you a missive when it gets closer to time and give you specific instructions. And remember, you must tell no one, is that clear?"

"How do you honestly think I could pose as you? Our hair is not the same color, and your eyes are much darker than mine." I was grasping for anything that would prevent me from being stuck in this agreement.

"No one will pay attention to the shade of your eyes," she lectured. "And you can keep your hair tucked into a caul. Your face will be covered with a piece of lace for modesty's sake. You and I are about the same height, even if my bosom is bigger than yours. No one will know."

I rolled my eyes at that. I knew from wearing her dresses that I filled her bodice just as nicely as she did. She sounded so sure of her plan. I wanted to ask what I should do if somehow I was still discovered, even after all her scheming. But she cut the conversation short.

"Do not fret, Isobel. All will be well. I will have my viscount, and you will have your prince. We shall all live happily ever after." She tapped my cheek lightly as if I were her favorite pet, then turned and retreated down the hall.

Resentment coiled in my chest, spurring me to call out to her. "I did not agree to this arrangement."

She turned back. A wicked little smile tilted her lips. "You will," she said, then resumed walking.

Chapter 25

Richmond Palace, London
October 1612
Robert

He sat on the edge of my bed, staring down at me with something akin to hope in his soulless eyes. "Son," the apparition said, his breath feeling like fire as it swept across my face. I rubbed my eyes, trying to make sense of what I was seeing. It was dark, the middle of the night still, and there was a man sitting on my bed, speaking to me. I peered closer, trying to decipher who he was. He chuckled, a low, sinister laugh that sent ripples across my flesh and vibrated through my veins. "Ye ken me," he said, smiling.

Was he my father or the Devil? I didnae ken. I shoved myself up to lean against the wall and study him. He looked a lot like the portrait my mother had given me. His hair was the color of mine, and so was the shape of his face. But his eyes were black and bottomless, and when I opened my mouth to speak to him, I found my tongue was tied.

"Ye have a good plan laid out in order to avenge me. I am impressed with the details. If ye carry it out exactly as planned, ye will not fail." He stared at me, eyes burning black and sending a shiver through me.

Isobel's father, the Earl of Stratford, had told me many things about my father in the days that I had spent at Chadwyck House caring for Honeycomb. Things my mother had failed to share. He told me how my father had plotted against the king on several occasions, and how he was accused of witchcraft by several witches who had been tried and executed for the same crime. He mentioned many of the accused specifically identified my father as the "Devil" who came to them during their Sabbaths and exacted payment from them in several hideous forms. I didnae want to believe him, but after my conversation with my mother before I left Branxholm Castle, it left little doubt that his accusations were true.

"Are ye willing to pay the price for yer actions?" the specter was asking, as I drew my attention back to him. I kent the price was possible execution. 'Twas the chance I had to take, if I were to bring justice to my father, my family. "I dinnae mean with the sacrificing of yer body, my son." Sweat beaded on my forehead at his words. I hid nae spoken aloud. I hid nae been able to speak since he awoke me from a sound sleep. He was reading my mind, or my heart or some such witchcraft, and I found the thought frightening. "All who serve me will find great reward in this life. I have many who serve me, my son." I wished he would stop calling me son. This wisnae the man I spent my life extolling. I thought back to the last missive I had received from my father just days before. I had written to him to tell him of my plan to kidnap King James. Father had given me some advice on the king's habits and written some warnings by sharing a few of the plans he had used against James that had failed. Between the lines of his words, I sensed he wisnae well. I wisnae sure if it was physically or emotionally. But whatever my plan, I must do it quickly.

"I have many who serve me," he said again. "And at times they do so on their own volition." He chuckled, looking quite pleased with himself. "It makes no difference to me. They will find ruin one way or another. But beware. My use for ye is much greater than my need for him. I cannae see ye fail, and if ye arnae careful, he could ruin yer plans completely. That would make me verra angry."

He who? Of whom was he speaking? Who was serving him with their own plan that wisnae quite as important as mine? I didnae speak this, but he heard my thoughts just the same.

"Just continue with yer intentions carefully. The King of England must be brought low. Do what ye must to see it done." The apparition laid his fiery hand on my chest, sending invisible flames shooting through my abdomen and flowing through my limbs to my very fingertips. My body was on fire, and I opened my mouth to scream, but no sound would come out. I gasped for breath and thrashed about on my bed, entangled in the bed linens that widnae release me. I dinnae ken how long the terror lasted for the next thing I realized, my eyes were open, and the faint glow of morning sunlight radiated from behind the heavy curtains on my window. A fine sheen of sweat coated my body. I would swear the flames still licked at my skin, even as I came to my senses and realized it was all a dream. At least, I think it was. The man that visited me, whether human or demon, felt so real I could still hear the words he said to me, and I understood the implications of all that he spoke.

I was tempted to believe this was all a result of the alcohol I consumed the evening before. I was a wee off balance after my kiss with Isobel and had sought comfort in a bottle of whisky and a lass in my bed. Yet deep down I understood this dream had deeper implications than my short-lived tryst with Isobel or the crapulence I was experiencing now.

My throat was parched, and my head ached. I felt rough. It had been a long time since I had drunk enough to wake up like this. But was this the result of drink or of the apparition that visited me?

The events that had unfolded within the hidden passages of the maze last night had left me reeling. But I had bigger concerns at the moment, and that was the carrying out of my plan to kidnap the king. I made a mental note to send George Preston a missive to meet later in the day to finalize the plans we laid out last night. I ran a hand over my scratchy jaw and rubbed my tongue over my teeth. I reached for the bottle of wine on my bedside to rinse my mouth, but it was empty.

Tossing the bottle onto the table, I threw the linens back and swung my legs over the side of the bed. The cold morning air hit my body, raising my skin into gooseflesh, and sending a chill down my spine. The sensation reminded me once again of that moment when Isobel had laid her lips to mine. That too had pimpled my flesh, but a searing heat had shot through me then, not this cold chill.

When I first heard her cries, I thought some danger had befallen her. I didnae even think. I just reacted, tearing through bushes and shrubs, breaking branches, and chafing skin. I followed the sound of her voice until I spotted her on the ground, crumpled into a heap of silky skirts and satiny blonde curls. The sight of her sent a rush of relief, then a twinge of aggravation, for she wisnae hurt after all. I spoke roughly to her at first, a fact I immediately regretted. But I thought she was being infantile, crying out like a spoilt child because she had become lost, as if the party would leave her there in the maze to freeze.

But when I lifted her from the ground, and she clung to me like a drowning kitten, all sharp claws and soft hair, I kent I was mistaken. She buried her face in my neck and drenched me with tears. It was then that I recognized the feeling of terror that caused her limbs to shake and her heart to pound like a wild pony. And it was then that I realized where we were and how her aversion to green affected her so violently.

She was petrified, and her body thrummed as I rubbed the palm of my hand across her back. Her spine knotted under my fingertips, and her ribs dipped into the little rivulets that softened under my touch. And the relief in her eyes when she drew back and looked at me was like the warmest summer sunshine radiating down on the darkest pit of my soul. My lungs clenched, and the satisfaction of being the one to find her in that condition—and save her—gave me immense pleasure.

But nothing could prepare me for what happened next.

She was scared, and she was relieved, I kept telling myself. It was the only explanation that made sense. She wanted Henry, and my cousin wanted her. I didnae ken if he loved her, but it was obvious he cared about her and wanted her for his wife. But devil take me. When she pressed her sweet mouth to mine and kissed me like a starving beggar, I lost my mind, and I didnae care who she belonged to, nor who was in love with whom. I wanted her, and not even the Gates of Hell would keep me from having her. Or so I thought.

Her breathy gasp when my hand touched her thigh stopped me cold. And for some odd reason—a reason I am still trying to examine—Henry's charitable face floated before me, and I couldnae go further.

I was a sinner. Henry had been nothing but good to me. He took me in without question. Not only into his court but into his inner circle. He trusted me with his life. And this is how I repaid him.

And then there was Isobel. She despised me. That was glaringly obvious. And I usually widnae care. She was too high above me, or mayhap I was just too far beneath her. If I learned anything from the catechism, it was that angels and devils dinnae mix.

Which is why, when Isobel made such a speedy departure as soon as we found our way out of the maze, I was reeling. And when I happened upon another damsel in distress later on, this time a maid under my cousin's employ, I was primed and ready to rescue.

I rinsed my face with the ice-cold water from the pitcher on the table and smoothed my hair back with wet hands. I dressed quietly in the pallid daylight, allowing the maid I had brought to bed last night just a little more sleep. Hattie? Henrietta? I couldnae remember her name. She was mildly attractive with full, sensuous lips and a nicely shaped nose. God's teeth. Was that all I could say about her? Yet she was sweet, and she kept me company and helped me forget about the unsolicited kiss inside the maze earlier that evening and the lass who had given it.

Her light brown hair lay crumpled upon the pillow as I observed her momentarily. She stirred and a sleepy smile spread across her face before she came fully awake.

"Good morning," I said slowly, waiting for her to realize where she was. A second later her eyes shot open, and a blush colored her cheeks. Pulling the linens up to her chin, she said shyly, "So that wasn't a dream?"

I grunted at that and handed her the gown she had deposited on the floor the night before. "Get dressed. I have things to do, and yer mistress will be looking for ye." She took the dress from my hand and dressed quietly.

"Are ye going to be all right?" I asked, pulling on my boots.

"I am a grown woman, sir. I do not need to be coddled. I know this tryst was a singular occurrence. You have other women on your mind." She laced her apron over her gown and smoothed her skirts.

I straightened, looking at her. "What do ye mean?"

Without looking at me she said, "You were quite drunk last night, sir. You kept calling me *my lady*."

God's teeth. I ran a hand through my hair, dragging in a ragged breath. What else had I foolishly uttered? "Is that all?" I asked. She was quiet for a moment then simply said, "Yes." I wisnae convinced but decided to let it go. "What of yer friend? Are ye safe?" 'Tis possible I wisnae completely coherent last night, but I remembered she had been distraught when I came upon her in the kitchen, and she had shared with me the circumstances of her friend's mysterious death. And that was the business I needed to take care of this morning. I needed to speak to Isobel. I didnae want to believe she was involved, but the details were too much of a coincidence.

Her brows arched in concern. "I think so. As far as I know, the countess doesn't have it out for me."

I watched her as she swept her mousy hair up and pinned it into place. "Ye can tell me if ye are in danger. I will help."

The happiness she had awoken with was gone now, and she lifted her sad eyes to mine. "Yes, thank you."

My mind was still a bit befuddled, and the disturbing dream still vivid in my memory when I opened the door. I noticed nothing as I ushered the maid through before me. But she stopped dead in front of me.

"My, my lady," she stammered out, and I looked up to see Isobel standing in the hallway, gaping at us.

"Hester," she said, tilting her head slightly in acknowledgement.

Then her eyes drifted to mine. I couldnae read her expression. Her cheeks were devoid of the rosy shade that usually colored her milk-white skin, and her bright blue eyes were bloodshot, as if she had been crying. Had the guilt of her involvement in the poisonings been too much for her? Or did she truly nay ken of the countess's plan and was feeling the weight of her mistake?

The awkwardness of our situation hung over us like a hideous tapestry. I cleared my throat, then leaned toward the maid. *Hester*, Isobel had called her.

"Please tell me if ye need anything," I said. She nodded, then scurried down the hall without another word.

Unfortunately, she didnae carry the uncomfortable silence with her. Isobel stared at me a moment longer until I grabbed her arm and pulled her along behind me. "We need to talk."

"Unhand me," she squeaked, but I continued to pull her down the hallway, looking for an empty room where we could speak privately. She fought me the whole way down the hall and gave me an earful when I finally pulled her into the library. "How dare you put your hands on me?"

I smirked. "Ye didnae seem to mind my hands on ye last night." I was a cad that didnae deserve the roof over my head. But I couldnae help it. I was rattled, and I wanted her to be rattled too.

Heat bloomed on her cheeks, giving the first sign of emotion other than dread. "We will not speak of what happened last night. I was distraught, and you took advantage of me."

I laughed out loud. "More like ye took advantage of me," I said, moving closer. "Let us not forget who kissed whom?"

Fury pursed her lips. "Do not act as though you could be seduced. We both know who spent the night with a nice warm body in their bed."

I crossed my arms in front of me and leaned against the back of a chair. "Does that bother ye?"

She rolled her eyes. "Is this what you dragged me in here to talk about?"

Nay, but this was a much more enjoyable topic. She seemed a little flustered, and I couldnae recall a time since first meeting her that she wisnae completely composed. But we could talk about that later. Right now, we needed to speak of the Countess of Essex.

"I can admit we made a mistake, but ye arnae going to place all the blame on me." Isobel opened her mouth to retort, but I cut her off. "There is something more important I wish to speak with ye about." She propped her hands on her nice, round hips and glared at me, but I continued. "Does yer father ken ye are poisoning people at the court of Prince Henry?"

The color drained from her face, and her lips began to tremble. I had chosen true on my plan of attack. So why did I feel like a blackguard?

She bit her bottom lip and took a moment to compose herself. My eyes fell to those soft, pink lips and the adorable little gap between her teeth as she bit down. I could feel the effect she had on me, from the heating of my blood to the hardening of my muscles. She was a siren, and I was a sailor adrift. If I wisnae careful, she would call, and I would throw myself into the sea in answer.

"I had nothing to do with the poisoning," she said, sounding strangled. I wanted verra much to believe her. Yet she had stolen from her mother to give the countess what she wanted. What else was she willing to do?

I uncrossed my arms and stepped closer to her. "Ye mean to tell me ye honestly didnae ken what the countess had planned when she asked ye to obtain the poison?" My heart was pounding, and I realized I feared what her answer might be.

A choked cry escaped her, and she pinched her lips together to stifle it. She dragged in a ragged breath. "I don't know what hurts more," she said, her voice raw with emotion. "The fact that someone has died because of my ignorance, or that you don't believe my innocence."

I blinked at her, stunned. Why did she care what *I* thought? More importantly, why was I taking the moral high ground and trying to shame her for any involvement? The thought of me being the honorable man in this drama was laughable. However, my concern came out of a worry that she would get caught. And if that happened, the noose would be the only thing hanging around that pretty neck of hers.

"If ye tell me ye had no knowledge of her scheme then I believe ye," I said, not moving a muscle. Her troubled eyes shot to mine. "And if ye tell me ye kent her plans and did it anyway, then I'll lie for ye."

Her lips parted as if surprised. "On my grandmother's grave, I knew nothing about it."

I nodded and my mind raced, trying to formulate a plan of action. "All right, let's make a list of who ye think is involved in the poisonings." I strode to the desk that sat in the corner of the room and shoved some things around, looking for a pen and ink.

"Frances wanted me to help her obtain more poison. There must be someone else she wants to be rid of." Isobel drew closer to the desk and watched as I shuffled items around.

"Who else might she want to slough off?"

"Essex," she blurted without hesitation.

I stopped rummaging for a moment and looked at her. "Aye, Essex would be the logical choice. But she would be daft to attempt to murder him. She would be the first suspect."

Isobel leaned over the desk while I continued my search. "Hmm, you're probably right. Not to mention the scandal she would cause between the two noble families. I'm not sure her Howard blood could save her from such a crime."

"What did ye tell her when she asked for yer help again?" I finally located a pot of ink and peered inside the bottle to see if it was empty.

"I told her I would not assist her any longer."

I pulled a drawer out, looking for something to write on. "Why do I get the feeling she didnae take too kindly to that?"

"She wasn't pleased. She told me I was involved whether I wanted to be or not, and if I didn't comply, I would find myself in a worse situation than the one I'm currently in. She said if I cross her, I would be sorry."

I stopped rummaging through the drawers and looked at her. "She threatened you?"

"Yes."

I pulled a piece of foolscap out of a drawer, but still couldnae locate a pen. I gritted my teeth. "I kent Essex didnae like the woman, but I didnae realize she was such a deceitful jade. I thought it was his hurt ego that spurred all those insults." I slammed the drawer shut and stood up straight. "There isnae a pen to be found around here." Isobel turned her back on me and walked to the window. My eyes followed her and watched her throat constrict as she swallowed down her emotions.

"There's more," she said faintly, not turning from the window.

"What?" I asked, striding to stand behind her. "What else did she say?"

"She offered me a proposition. One that would release me from having to get more poison for her."

A strange apprehension filled me. Whatever the countess wanted from Isobel it couldnae be good. I stepped around so I could stand in front of her and see her face. "What is it?"

She proceeded to tell me Lady Frances's plan to have Isobel stand in for her physical examination. I listened in horror as the details just kept getting more and more bizarre. When she had finished, she looked up at me, and I felt the weight of the trust she had placed in me to help her.

"Ye have to do it," I instructed, recognizing the benefit in it.

"I cannot!" she said with a shriek. "How humiliating and deceptive!"

"I see. Ye draw the line of deception at stealing from yer mother." A choked cry escaped her, and she covered her mouth with both hands. That was harsh, and I immediately felt remorse. I placed my hands on her arms and turned her toward me. "Isobel, listen to me," I spoke softly, hoping to make amends for my cruel words. "No one will ken it is ye. And Frances will see to every detail and make sure no one finds out. She wants this divorce verra much. She willnae risk losing her chance to a trivial detail. Besides, the punishment for falsifying a physician's report cannae be worse than being an accomplice to murder."

Her voice shook. "My father would know. He knows the law and punishments."

I shook her gently. "Do ye really want to tell yer father about this?" When she didnae answer, I shook her again. "Isobel?"

"No," she answered. "No, he and my mother must never find out." She dragged her eyes to mine, and I felt my heart squeeze in fear for her. She continued, "My mother would be devastated if she found out I stole from her."

"Then it's settled," I said, dropping my hands from her arms.

Isobel didnae relent. She turned back to the window, and I wondered if she watched the robins that bathed themselves in the rainwater that sat at the bottom of the stone fountain, for her eyes seemed to be drawn to something in the garden down below.

I moved to the window to see what she watched. "Well, what are ye going to do?" I asked as I drew up beside her.

"I don't have a plan as of yet," she said. Her eyes darted, and I followed the path in the direction she looked. "But I will not be bowing to the countess's wishes." A far-off look came over her face and that is when I noticed what—or rather, who—she watched below.

Worry curled around my ribcage. She was going to get herself killed. For if she was tried for being an accomplice to murder, she would surely be hanged. In desperation I said, "Ye are walking a dangerous line, my lady. What will become of yer chances with the prince if he should hear of yer entanglement with this poisonous plot?" I nodded toward the man below, heading out on foot in the direction of the river.

Her eyes took on a dreamy expression. "Henry wants to marry me. He told me so last night in the maze. Once we are married, the countess will not be able to touch me."

Bile rose to my tongue. "Did he tell ye that before or after ye kissed me?"

A scowl dented her brow, but she didnae turn around. "I do not have to answer that."

I wisnae sure what kind of game she was playing, but I dinnae like being one of her pawns. With more than a little spite, I said, "He will have to get Their Majesties' approval first, and that will never happen."

She jerked her head toward me finally, and her eyes were full of scorn now. "You just think you know so much, don't you Robert Stewart?"

"I ken enough," I said roughly, not caring what emotion she measured in my tone. She made a face of irritation as she pushed past me.

"Well, we'll just see about that."

I watched her swaying hips as she walked away from me. "Good luck," I called out, as the library door slammed closed behind her. I ran a hand through my hair in irritation and blew out the breath I seemed to be holding. That woman's recklessness was going to be the death of her. And if I wasnae careful, she would take me down right along with her.

Chapter 26

Richmond Palace, London
October 1612
Isobel

My circumstances had not changed one iota, but I felt immeasurably lighter once I saw Prince Henry making his way across the gardens as if going for a morning walk. I left Robert in the library and hurried down the stairs, hoping I could catch up with Henry. I wanted to speak to him about us. I needed to feel his confidence and get his assurance that he would be able to convince Their Majesties I was the woman he should marry. I wanted him to tell me again that he wanted me, and I would tell him the feeling was mutual.

But by the time I reached the courtyard, he was nowhere in sight. I stood looking in the direction in which I had seen him walking and debated on whether I should follow. I was to meet Elizabeth and the queen later in the day for a dress fitting, but I had plenty of time.

A well-worn path cut across the back of the gardens into a line of Cypress trees that hedged the edge of the manicured grounds. I followed the path as it wound over a footbridge and out of sight of the palace gardens. Beyond the row of trees, the path petered out, leading to the riverbank. I followed the path until I came to the river's edge. The water gurgled along the shallow parts of the riverbed, where rocks covered with dark green algae and brown sludge and debris peppered the banks. I peered down into the river, listening to the bubbling water until a shiver brushed down my spine. I then took a step back, craning my neck to see where it was Henry could have gotten to in such a short amount of time.

A splash drew my attention. I tiptoed a little closer, feeling a little awkward, and hoping Henry didn't think I was spying on him. A cluster of shrubs sprang up along the river, allowing only a partial view of the water and the bank. The closer I drew, I could hear splashing like someone swimming and when I cleared the greenery, I spotted Henry.

He was wading in the river where the water came up to his chest. His chest was bare, and the buttery autumn sunlight glinted off his fair skin. He ran both hands through his hair, sweeping his golden strawberry locks back from his face. Little rivulets of water dripped from the ends of his hair onto his contoured shoulders. He was lean and lithe, but the muscles in his arms bulged at the movement, quickening my pulse, and sending blood rushing to my ears. Riding, sword play, and military maneuvering were his preferred forms of exercise, and they had honed his well-toned muscles into a graceful form.

Anticipation drove me forward as I stepped around the shrubbery, not taking my eyes off him. As careful as I was, I took a misstep, snapping a branch that lay on the ground. Henry's head shot up, but when he saw it was me that intruded, happiness spread across his face.

"Care to join me for a swim, my lady?"

My mouth fell open at the invitation. A sudden urge to cover myself came over me, though I hardly knew why, and I found that I could not get my tongue to work properly. When the prince chuckled, I drew in a quick breath.

"I, I cannot, Your Grace."

He waded to a shallower part of the river. All his clothing lay in a pile on the ground as if he had shed them in haste. I felt my mouth go dry at the sight of his hip bones breaching the water. I jerked my eyes away to keep from staring.

"It is just as well. It is cold today. Why do you have no wrap?"

I looked down at my state of dress. I was in such a hurry I had not thought to grab a shawl.

"I forgot," I murmured lamely.

The prince continued. "Harington and I just finished sparring. I came to the river to cool down." He extended his arms and ran the palms of his hands across the surface of the water, as if to feel the wetness there. Desire shown in his striking blue eyes, and he looked at me from beneath lowered lids. Holding out a wet hand, he said, "Come closer."

We had known each other half of our lives, and I had loved him from a distance for nearly as much time. But I had never seen him look at me like that. Curiosity pulled me toward him, and I glanced over my shoulder to see if we were being watched before following his command. I peered down into the shallow water that lapped at the stones at the edge of the bank.

"The water is green," I observed and looked to Henry for reassurance. He nodded slightly.

"Nothing will harm you, Issy," he said gently, still watching me. "I am right here." I swallowed down my fear, seating myself on the ground in order to remove my shoes. I set my satin slippers aside and looked to him again before reaching for the garters that held up my stockings.

Henry eyes flared before looking away, allowing me a modicum of privacy so I could shift my heavy skirts aside and bare my legs. My heart was pounding now, and I laid my stockings beside my shoes and pushed myself off the ground. I drew up to the water's edge and looked down. The algae made my stomach turn, and I felt perspiration beading on my brow. The memory of what happened in the maze the night before came rushing back, and I paused before stepping into the water.

"It's all right," Henry soothed, waiting patiently for me to dip my toes into the water. His reassuring words comforted me, and I curled my toes into the cold mud at the edge of the water. The soft, pliable silt calmed me momentarily, and I took a tiny step closer, holding out my hand.

"Will you take my hand?" I pleaded.

A naughty smile lifted the corners of his mouth. "I cannot come closer, my lady, for obvious reasons." He motioned to the pile of clothing that lay on the grass.

I licked my lips and took a deep breath, fortifying myself against the onslaught of panic bubbling in my chest. I edged my toes into the water and looked to the prince once more. He lifted his brows, waiting for my next move.

I stood without moving for several minutes. Somewhere nearby, a bird tittered across the expanse and another bird answered. A chilly autumn breeze blew against my cheek, and when I looked at Henry again, he appeared to be shivering. It was cold, much too cold for swimming, and I was keeping him from the exercise that kept his blood pumping. I looked down at the green rocks once more, and another wave of nausea rolled over me.

"You go on and swim, Your Grace. I can't walk across the slimy rocks to reach the deeper part of the water."

He studied the rocks momentarily, then looked back at me. "Are you sure?"

"Yes, yes, go swim." I laughed lightly, waving him away. I was thankful I wouldn't have to climb into the water after all. He took a deep breath, then pushed himself beneath the surface of the water, staying under for what seemed too long. I watched for movement beneath the water, but the river appeared murky today, and nothing could be seen moving beneath the surface. When he emerged further off toward the middle of the river, I sighed in relief then turned to retreat up the shallow bank.

Twenty minutes later, Henry called to me that he was finished and would retrieve his clothes. I drew my knees up and buried my face in my lap to allow him time to dress. When all was in order, he sat down beside me, pushing his wet hair out of his face. The coolness of the water radiated from his skin, sending a chill through me.

"You are sitting on the grass, Issy," he observed as he situated himself. "Forgive me, but I do not think I have ever seen you willingly touch anything green."

I lifted my chin. "I touched the Thames, didn't I?"

He cocked his head at me then looked out over the river. "Truthfully, that water is brown."

I crinkled up my nose. "It is disgusting, I do not understand how you can swim in that filth."

"The recent rains have stirred the sediment, giving the river a dirtier appearance," he said, not taking his eyes from the water. We fell silent for a moment as I tried to gather the courage to ask him about his plans for us. But then he turned his eyes on me, and I melted under the fervency of his gaze. "Why *are* you so afraid of green things, Issy? I've never understood."

I shifted under the weight of his scrutiny. I hated talking about this, but if we were to be married, then I guess it was something he ought to know. "I'm not exactly sure," I began, plucking a blade of grass from the ground to play with, as if trying to overcome the fears he spoke of. "I suspect it stems from an incident that happened when I was about five years old."

His brows arched. "That long ago?"

I dipped my head, embarrassed. "Yes. My grandmother Naomi was still alive, and she and I used to spend a lot of time together. She taught me how to make bread, and we would make biscuits and pies and such."

Henry listened intently, and his face lit up when I told him this. "It is hard to imagine such a fine lady as you, getting her hands dirty in the kitchen," he teased, giving me a little nudge with his shoulder.

A smile brooked my lips. "I was quite handy in the kitchen, if you must know," I said. "But my grandmother was sick. Not sick in the way that one's body breaks down and stops working. But her mind was sick. She was forgetful and did things absentmindedly." A flock of geese flew overhead, breaking the solitude of our conversation with obnoxious honking. When they had passed over, I continued. "One day we baked biscuits. They were very tasty with bits of walnuts and raisins in them. My grandmother got it into her head we should hide them in a crock someone had given her and save them just for us, no one else was to know about them. She put them on a high shelf, behind some other containers, out of everyone else's sight. But we never got to eat them. My grandmother passed away in her sleep the very next night and the biscuits were left on the shelf, forgotten.

"A few weeks later, I was feeling very sad. I was missing my grandmother and wanted to do something that reminded me of her. I ventured into the kitchen and dragged out all the ingredients it would take to bake some biscuits. I spilled the flour all over the table, had butter smeared all over the place, and dropped several eggs on the floor, breaking them. I made a horrible mess. When Mother came upon me, she broke down into a fit of crying and scolded me, telling me to get out of the kitchen and go to my room. Tom told me it took her over an hour to clean up the mess I had made."

"Good 'ole Tom," Henry said, smiling. "He probably took pleasure in rubbing that in your face."

I laughed. "You know my brother well. He never let me live it down." I finished breaking down the blade of grass that I had plucked and pulled another from the ground. It felt good to have something to occupy my hands as I relived this bitter childhood memory. "Well, I was angry at Mother for yelling at me and for ruining my baking. All I wanted was to feel close to my grandmother again, and she had foiled my plans. Then I remembered the biscuits she and I had hidden on the shelf. Later that night, after everyone had gone to bed, I snuck into the kitchen with my little candle, pulled a chair over to the shelf, and climbed up. I retrieved the crock with the hidden biscuits and opened it. There was a strange odor that emanated from the container, but I paid it no heed. I stuffed my belly with six of those biscuits." I paused, laughing in spite of myself. Shaking my head, I continued. "I snuck back to bed but was up again a little later, vomiting. Once I had confessed what I had done, Mother immediately went to the kitchen to see what I had eaten. When she showed me in the daylight what I had eaten in the dark, I was almost sick all over again. The biscuits had grown mold on them."

Henry laughed. "You ate moldy biscuits? How could you stand the taste?"

I scowled at him. "I was five!" I said, smacking him on the arm for teasing me. "I didn't know any better." I tamped down the amusement that pulled at my lips.

Henry tried to pull his features into a serious mien. "Oh yes, and you were in mourning. You poor thing. You just wanted to be near your grandmother."

I laughed at his words but searched his face, nonetheless. "Are you teasing me, Your Grace?"

The smile slipped from his face. "I would never tease about something as serious as death, Isobel." He plucked a blade of grass for himself and tore it into pieces, dropping little flakes onto the ground. "Two maids have died in the past couple of days here within the walls of Richmond Palace. While under my protection." I held my breath, afraid to answer him. What would he think if I told him I was aware? He continued, not waiting for a response. "I was told they died of sudden sickness, but I believe there might be something sinister at play. I am looking into it, but I cannot help but think about their families and how devastated they will be." He ran his hands over the ground, letting the grass brush between his fingers before plucking another blade. "The Holy Writ says life is but a vapor that appears for a little time and then vanishes. We need to hold close those who are important to us, for we never know how long we will have with them." He looked at me then and his eyes softened. To my surprise, he changed the subject. "You have the bluest eyes I have ever seen."

I laughed nervously. I wanted to ask him if he had looked in the mirror lately. But his gaze seemed to wrap itself around me and pull me in. "So do you," was all I managed to whisper.

He reached out and laid his cool hand on my cheek, then leaned closer to me. This time when he kissed me it was unhurried and full of emotion. His kiss was pleasant, but I couldn't help my mind from wandering. He knew about the poisonings, although he didn't know yet it was poison that killed them. If he was investigating the deaths, how long would it take for him to trace it back to me? Would I be able to convince him I knew nothing of the countess's plans? Would he hold it against me? Would it change his opinion of me?

He pulled away from me, eyes drowsy with longing. "You seem distracted. Perhaps you do not feel the same as I?"

"Please do not think that." I searched for an excuse that would sound believable. "I just," I paused, unsure of my response. "I just wonder what Their Majesties will think of your choice for a wife." I dropped my gaze. "I can't believe I'm saying this, but I'm not exactly on their list of acceptable brides for the future king of England."

He sat back, looking at me curiously. "Since when does Lady Isobel Broune care what is acceptable?" His eyes glinted, and I knew he found humor in his words, but they worried me. Did he think me too rebellious?

"I do not understand your meaning," I said, hesitantly.

He laughed. "It's not like you to care what others think. You usually do what you want, do you not?"

"You are mistaken. I care a great deal about what others think of me." I dipped my chin, a little embarrassed. "But I guess I do tend to be a little stubborn."

Henry wrapped his arm around my waist and pulled me closer. "You let me worry about my mother and father. They may not be happy with my choice. But I always get my way. I will convince them you are the right bride for me. And if they still have objections, then I will be forced to use my wits to make them see reason." He beamed at me then leaned in and kissed me again.

Was he that persuasive he could talk even the king and queen of England into whatever he wanted? He had certainly persuaded me.

I pulled away from him. "You haven't asked me to marry you."

He blinked at me, as if trying to clear his mind. "I already know you want to marry me,' he said innocently.

I was taken aback. "How?" I had barely had a chance to flirt with him since the countess had started helping me.

He grinned widely. "Tom told me."

"Devil take him." I cursed, and the prince's eyebrows raised in surprise. Embarrassment choked me. "I-I'm sorry, Your Grace. But leave it to Tom to open his big mouth." I covered my face with my hands, too humiliated to even look at him.

"Don't apologize, Issy. Besides, if it weren't for Tom, I would never have found a way out of my predicament. You certainly never gave me any hope. You would barely look at me when we were together in any social setting, let alone speak to me."

His predicament? The situation was becoming clearer. "You don't want to marry any of the women your parents have suggested for you. Better the devil you know than the devil you don't, right?"

Henry looked hurt. "Isobel, please don't say that." He took my hand and held it between his own. "It is true that I do not want to marry any of the princesses or duchesses from any of the other countries my father wants to pair me with. I want to marry a Protestant woman, and you are the loveliest one I have ever laid eyes on. You come from a good, loyal family, and you have a good head on your shoulders. You were practically raised at court and are familiar with all the protocol and expectations. You will make a wonderful queen one day."

I tried to swallow the bile that had suddenly risen to my throat. Only one question pounded in my mind, and although I feared his answer, I had to ask.

"Do you love me, Henry?"

He rubbed my hand faster. "Princes do not marry for love, Isobel. Unfortunately, it is a luxury we are rarely afforded." The injury must have shown on my face because he rushed to add, "But love will come in time. We will grow to love one another. I have the utmost respect for you, and I like you very much. I've no doubt we will be happy together.

My mother and father didn't know each other when they married, but they have much respect for one another."

"Your mother and father do not even live together in the same palace anymore," I said sardonically.

"But we have something they didn't have at the beginning. We have a friendship, and—attraction," he finished, quietly.

I had to admit he was right. Very few people in our positions married for love. And especially not kings and princes. The marriage of the last king of England that married for love did not end well for his wife. At least we were friends.

We sat quietly then. I ran the fingertips of my other hand over the top of Henry's knuckles. I loved him. I had for a very long time. But I wasn't sure if I could tell him that, knowing the sentiment would not be returned.

Finally, Henry moved to stand. "I must be on my way. I was going to ride to St. James Palace today to speak to my father before the next round of Elizabeth's engagement activities began. Am I wasting my time? Do you not want to marry me, Isobel?" His voice shook, and I could tell this meant a lot to him, even if he didn't love me—yet.

"You are not wasting your time," I said, looking up at him and taking the hand he had extended to me. "I do wish to marry you, Henry."

He smiled then, a bright, happy smile that made his blue eyes sparkle and his whole face light up in elation. Even the radiant sunlight that reflected off his rose-gold locks could not outshine his delighted countenance. "You have made me the happiest prince in all of Christendom, my lady." He bowed to me regally, then leaned in and kissed me one last time.

I was happy too, or at least that's what I told myself. But I couldn't help feeling like everything was about to change.

Chapter 27

Richmond Palace, London
October 1612
Robert

I leaned against a stool in the tack room of the prince's stables, looking over requests for purchases that were awaiting my approval. I was later than normal getting here, for I wanted to meet with George Preston one more time to finalize the plans for the kidnapping. I wanted to do it this evening, as the king had just left for St. James Palace this morning and would be off his guard, having just returned from the Richmond festivities. But George had in his head that it had to be on the anniversary of the Gunpowder Plot, the failed assassination attempt on James's life on the fifth of November, seven years earlier.

"Allow me this one concession, please!" he had exclaimed. "For my grandfather's revenge."

I didnae want to wait another three weeks. A sense of urgency had gotten hold of me concerning my father. His latest letter was melancholy, and he stated that he hid nae been well for several weeks. I was convinced the apparition that had appeared last night had been a bad omen. I wisnae too keen on delaying. But I conceded nonetheless, and we agreed we would wait a few more weeks. I certainly couldnae pull this off without George's help, so I agreed to keep him happy.

I had just signed off on a purchase for three more bridles and another saddle when a jovial voice met my ears.

"The pungent odor of manure and earth," Prince Henry said, dragging a deep breath through his nostrils. "It sure stings the eyes, but it never gets old, does it, Cousin?"

I instinctively took a breath, making a mental note to tell Joseph, the stable hostler, that the stables needed a good mucking.

"Ye are in a good mood, Yer Grace. What is afoot?"

"I need Hercules saddled. I ride to St. James today to speak to my father."

I pushed myself off the stool and motioned to a stable boy across the way. "Prepare Prince Henry's horse," I ordered.

"Yes, sir." The boy bowed, then ran to carry out my command.

I turned back to Henry. "Sounds important." I didnae want to question him, but he looked absolutely cock-a-hoop.

He smiled broadly. "It is. I am going to speak to my father about marrying Isobel."

He couldnae have knocked the air out of me more if he had punched me in the gut. "Marry Isobel," I repeated. "I thought ye decided Their Majesties widnae approve." I crossed my arms in front of me, trying desperately to refrain from knocking his block off.

"They won't. But that doesn't change my mind about her. She is the most enchanting creature, is she not?"

Of course, she was. But I couldnae tell him that. I clenched my fist together. This had always been the plan. Isobel told me she has loved Henry for a verra long time. There wisnae a man in all of England who deserved her more than the prince. But that didnae stop the jealousy from squeezing the life out of me. It didnae stop me from wanting to hit something either.

"Lady Isobel doesnae like me much," I said instead. "Our families have a history, and I think she holds that against me."

"Well, that family includes me, Cousin. And she likes me well enough." He clapped a hand on my back not realizing for every kindness he showed me, I was stabbing him in the back.

I forced a smile. "True enough."

The stable boy approached with Hercules on a lead. I stepped up and checked the saddle and the girth.

"I shall never forget how you saved my life, Robert. I am indebted to you." He watched as I tightened the straps just a little tighter and gave Hercules a little rub on the nose.

"Ye have already thanked me, Yer Grace, and repaid me with this position. I couldnae ask for more."

"And yet, you seem melancholy. You have not been happy here in London."

It was just like Henry to see right through my façade. I weighed how much I wanted to tell him. "The purpose for which I came his nae been accomplished. 'Tis disappointing." I couldnae share with him my feelings for Isobel. I wisnae even sure of them myself until he spoke of marrying her.

He stepped closer to me and laid his hand on my shoulder. "Let me talk to my father about your situation. I'm sure we can work something out." I blinked hard several times, trying to stay the water that stung my eyes. He was too good to me.

"I dinnae ken what to say, Yer Grace. If ye could talk His Majesty into just allowing my father to return, we would be grateful. Returning his title would be wonderful, but I would settle for just having him home."

"No, he must have his title returned to him. It is only right that a grandson of the fifth King James of Scotland be recognized thusly. I'll see what I can do." He mounted his horse and adjusted his seating. I hoped he was as good at twisting His Majesty's arm as he claimed to be. "And if you decide to return to Scotland," he continued, "you can lead my new riding school I plan to open there as well." He smiled, and I felt my chest squeeze in excitement.

"It would be my honor, Yer Grace," I said bowing. I then remembered something I wanted to take care of. I stuffed my hand into my pocket and drew out the sliver of lavender satin. I unrolled it, pinching the soft material between my finger and thumb. The object caught Henry's attention, and his curiosity was piqued.

"What have you there?" He dipped his chin in the direction of the mask as I continued to unroll it from around the object it protected.

"Would ye do me one more wee favor?" I asked, wadding the mask up in my fist and shoving it back into my pocket.

"Of course," Henry said, eyeing me.

I held out Isobel's necklace to him. "I took this from Isobel a while ago. I am a boor and feel bad about it now, although I meant no harm and had no intention of keeping it. Can ye see it is returned to her?"

The prince's mouth gaped. "The amethyst her father gave her. She will be elated. Does she know you are the one who took it?"

"Aye, we were playing a game one night while I was at Chadwyck House. She lost, and I took that as my reward. It is important to her. I want to give it back." I twisted the truth just a little. I found I couldnae tell him the full truth, especially if it put Isobel in danger.

Henry studied me. "Why don't you give it to her yourself when we meet at St. James Palace? We will all be there again in a few weeks for Elizabeth and Frederick's masque."

I swallowed hard. I would be there, but I widnae be seen. "I just want to get it out of my hands before something happens to it. I ken how anxious she is to have it back."

"All right," Henry said, reaching for the jewel. He tucked it into a pocket, then said, "You have probably made her happier in that gesture, than I will in making her my wife." I cocked my head at him, not fully understanding his words.

"Yer Grace?"

"Never mind," he said, then nodded at me and sauntered out of the stable yard before kicking Hercules into a full gallop.

"So long, my friend," I said to his back. If the prince thought me melancholy before, I was glad he couldnae see me now.

Chapter 28

Richmond Palace, London
October 1612
Robert

Hester finished stoking the fire and turned to me. "Would you like the rest of the candles lit, sir?"

I had written three letters by the light of the single candle that sat beside me on the large, mahogany desk in the blue drawing room. I wrote to my father to tell him the date George and I had decided on for kidnapping the king. I also informed him Henry was going to make one last-ditch effort to convince his father to change his mind. If the prince was unsuccessful, we would proceed with our plan. I also told my father of the apparition I had seen, and in jest, I asked if he had sent the specter to taunt me. I also wrote to Henry. After he left Richmond Palace that morning, there were other things I wish I had said to him. I wrote him mainly to ask that he notify me as soon as possible what the king's decision was on my request and whether he had been successful in convincing His Majesty of my cause.

The third letter was intended for Isobel. After I gave Henry the necklace this morning, I found out the queen's retinue had delayed their plans for one more day and widnae be leaving until the following morning. I could have given the necklace to Isobel myself. But I felt it was better this way. When she left me in the library this morning to chase after the prince, I had made up my mind I was through toying with her. I had allowed myself to get distracted from my purpose for being in London for much too long. I wrote to wish her and the prince much happiness and to tell her goodbye.

A slight clearing of the throat brought me back to the present, and I realized I hid nae answered Hester's question. "Nay, I have all the light I need." I upended the bottle of brandy I had pilfered from the kitchens, then dropped it back on the table when I realized it was empty. "Can ye find me a bottle of whisky in this god-forsaken palace?"

The maid moved closer. "I believe you have drunk it all, my lord." Her voice was low with a hint of suggestiveness. I kent she meant to tease me, but I wisnae in the mood for banter, nor for bed sport. At least not with her.

"Dinnae call me that," I said brusquely. "I am nay a lord."

She seated herself on my lap and reached up to brush a lock of hair from my face. I caught her wrist in my hand and growled, "I am not good company tonight. Leave me be, wench." Her eyes practically popped out of her head at my words, and she winced in pain as she struggled to release herself from my grasp.

"All right, then let me go!" she cried. The force of my release sent her scurrying from my lap. "What is wrong with you?" she spat, straightening her skirts, and tucking a stray strand of hair behind her ear. "We had fun together last night, and tonight you are a beast. What's the matter, are you not drunk enough yet?" The tears that rimmed her eyes made me feel like a blackguard, and I looked away from her in guilt.

"Perhaps," I said, nay looking at her again. "Now leave me be and go find that whisky I asked for." She huffed her displeasure but left in accordance with my request.

I sank back into the seat cushions of a large, velvet-covered chair. I watched the shadows dancing across the wall as the flames in the hearth crackled and popped. Running my fingertips over the smooth surface of the velvet, I imagined the delicate skin of Isobel. Her soft cheeks when I brushed my thumb across them in the maze. And the sweetness of her lips as she clung to me in anguish, then pressed her mouth to mine in desperate relief. I couldnae get her out of my mind.

I reached into my pocket and pulled out the mask I had taken from her at the Hymenaei masque. Though her scent had long ago faded, the softness remained. I held it to my nose, then rubbed it gently across my lips. I conjured the image of her flawless skin accented by beautiful, bright, sapphire eyes and lips the color of pink rose petals. My fingers itched to feel the soft strands of her waist-length hair. She was the complete opposite of Moira in not only looks but social status and disposition. Not to mention Moira loved me, and Isobel hated me. That should have been enough to squelch any attraction I held for her. But it didnae. I honestly didnae ken what it was about her that drew me to her. She was stubborn and headstrong, with a little bit of a rebellious streak. Nothing like the timid, shy Moira who would make the perfect wife. I would dare say she was even a little spoiled, although that wisnae her fault. She was a creature of her surroundings, being the daughter of an earl and raised in one of the greatest courts in Europe. But she was loyal. And she loved fiercely. I found she would do anything for her friends, if one was so lucky as to be counted among her friendships. And she paid nay heed to the classes, for I had seen her befriend maids at Chadwyck House and here at Richmond Palace. I seemed to be the only one whose lack of title met her disdain.

Hester strode into the drawing room and slammed a bottle of whisky onto the table. "I hope you can drown your misery. You are much more pleasant when you are drunk." She fisted her hands on her hips and stared down at me. I stared back but didnae respond. She finally turned on her heels and left me alone.

∿

When my whisky was almost gone, I found myself nodding off in my chair. I grabbed the bottle and the letters I had written. I would post the two outgoing missives in the morning. But Isobel's letter could easily be slipped under her door before I went to bed, and that is what I intended to do.

The corridor that led to Isobel's chamber was dark with only a few candles lit sporadically on the walls to cast flickering shadows across my path. My intention was to slip the letter under her door and be on my way. But when I drew up outside her chamber, the hair on my arms seemed to stand on end. I paused and pressed my ear to the door to listen.

It was quiet inside. I listened a moment longer, straining to hear any movement. I didnae want to appear the eavesdropper, but I couldnae shake the feeling something wisnae right. After satisfying my curiosity, and concluding there was nothing amiss, I bent to slide the letter under her door. It was then for the first time I caught the faint sound of a muffled cry.

I didnae delay. I pushed on the door, only to find it had been blocked with something. I leaned into it, thrusting all my weight against the door. But before I could get the door fully open, a crash sounded from within along with another feminine cry. I continued pushing until I was finally able to wedge the door ajar just enough to squeeze through the opening. Other than the banked fire, I was plunged into darkness.

I strained to see in the dark. Isobel's bed was empty, the linen's tossed aside as if she had been snatched from her bed. I looked around the room frantically, willing my eyes to adjust so I could see better. Another cry, some scuffling, and a crash of some piece of furniture sounded, letting me ken the intruder had dragged her into her antechamber.

My sgian dubh was already in hand when I found them. From the light of the moon, I could see the man had one arm wrapped about Isobel's neck and the other hand over her mouth, pulling her toward the window. Isobel hung suspended in the air, wide-eyed and thrashing about. She grappled with him, tearing the flesh on his forearms with her fingernails as her bare toes sought purchase beneath her. I was going to kill him. If I had to rip every limb from his body and shove them down his throat, I would. And I would start with the arm that he used to strangle her.

When they reached the other side of the room, he removed his hand momentarily from her mouth to open the window. Isobel tried to scream, but he was swift and quickly covered her mouth again once the window was open. She tried to bite his hand, but he restricted her throat tighter, choking off her airway so that her mouth gaped open in a gasp for air. He mumbled something about doing as she was told, and how he never kent a nice piece of virgin flesh could have more than one use. I had nay idea what he was yammering about, but before I could bound across the room, he had the window open and was struggling to bend Isobel over the sill. *Was he going to throw her over the ledge?* I felt my heart lurch in my chest.

"Now are you going to comply with the countess's wishes? Or am I going to have to toss you out the window and watch your brains spill out on the cobbles below?" he gritted out. His voice sounded familiar, but in all the commotion, and with my brain sloshed, I couldnae place the familiar intonation. Isobel, to her credit, fought him tooth and nail. She grabbed the jamb and held on, not allowing herself to be thrust through the open window.

"Frances can go to the devil," Isobel said, panting.

Good girl. I smirked at her sassy tongue. She fought like a rabid dog, and if there was more time, I would have admired her grit and determination. I ran up on them in their struggle, but before I could stick my sgian dubh into his back, he turned about to face me, pulling Isobel in front of him. *The coward.* He had released his hold around her neck, choosing to hold his dagger to her throat instead.

"If you want to see this pretty piece of flesh left alive, throw the knife down," the intruder said. His face was covered with some kind of makeshift mask: a black sack with holes cut into it to see and breathe and speak.

I squeezed my eyes shut then forced them open, straining to see him in the dark. If I had ever wished I hid nae consumed so much alcohol, 'twas now. I gripped my sgian dubh tighter, turning the handle over in my hand, and rubbing my thumb across the smooth surface of the pommel stone on the top of the handle.

"I said drop the knife," the familiar voice said again. "Now, Robert."

George Preston. The gowk was George Preston.

"Och. Ye dirty, sleekit blackguard. Now this be a braw kettle of fish." I gritted my teeth. "I didnae ken I threw my lot in with such a craven eejit."

George's eyes danced excitedly. "You see, that is what I love about you Scots. You have such colorful language. Although, I must admit, I barely understood a word you said." He laughed, and I took another step forward, ready to run him through if necessary.

"Ah, ah, ah," he warned, pressing the blade a little harder against Isobel's white neck. She sucked in a frightened breath and stilled. By the faint light of the moon my eye caught what looked to be a small drop of blood, pooling at the tip of his blade. I gritted my teeth and counted all the ways I would make this man suffer. I cursed, then tossed my sgian dubh away. It clattered across the floor, spinning until it came to a stop when it hit the edge of the doorway. The same light that illuminated her blood shimmered across Isobel's face and ignited her sapphire eyes. She may have been fighting George Preston with every thread of her existence, but in her eyes was more fear than I had ever seen. Even more so than that night in the maze when her terrified screams had drawn me to her. And when she looked at me with that fear, my heartbeat ceased.

"Why are ye doing this?" I asked. We had made a deal that he would help me kidnap the king. We drank to it, and I had even paid him an advance with the promise of the remainder when the deed was done. But I didnae care about that now. All that mattered was that he let Isobel go unharmed.

George chuckled like we were just sitting at the table playing cards. "I got a better offer. One that paid more and wouldn't get me executed for treason."

Isobel yelped in surprise, her blue eyes as big as robin eggs. But she didnae say anything. She appeared to understand the conversation and all its implications and for that I felt true regret.

I inched closer to him, ever so slowly as I spoke. "Lady Isobel has a powerful father and two older brothers that will make life miserable for ye if they ever find out what ye've done. Ye will probably wish for a quick and painless execution after they get done with ye." And that wisnae to mention what I was going to do to him.

"I'll have the power of the king's favorite behind me and of his Lady when this is all said and done. Lady Isobel just needs to comply with the countess and when her divorce is granted, I'll be richer than you can imagine. But the Lady needs to do her duty first." At that he pulled her against him and with knife still at her throat, he let his hands rove over her body.

Isobel began to cry. And I dinnae mean a whimper. She began to wail so loud, I couldnae believe that a footman or guard didnae come running to her chamber. George tried to shush her, but he couldnae hold the knife to her throat, keep another hand over her mouth, and continue to grope her all at the same time, so something had to give. His roaming hand went to her mouth and this time, Isobel's teeth didnae miss. George bellowed as her teeth sank into his flesh, but the cost of the distraction came at a price. With the knife still held to her throat, George jerked, and Isobel let out a true cry this time. "You witch!" he spat out, struggling to get control of her once again.

But he was too slow. As soon as Isobel bit him, I moved to knock the knife out of his hand. I wisnae sure if it was my movement or his that caused the blade to skim the surface of her skin. I would never forgive myself for the consequence.

"Are ye all right?" I asked as I wrestled with George, trying to get the knife from his grasp.

"It is just a scratch," she said, breathing heavily.

We fell to the floor, as George and I each took a turn getting the better of the other. When he was finally under me and I got my bearings, I drew back my fist and pummeled him, knocking him square in the nose. Blood spurted everywhere, but he didnae react. Instead, he took another swipe at me with his knife since I had still not managed to disarm him. He tried to throw a punch at me, but I had one arm pinned to the ground as I tried to avoid the blade. I pressed all my weight against his pinned arm and finally knocked the knife from his hand. It clanged to the floor, and from my peripheral vision, I saw Isobel pick it up.

I grabbed a fistful of hair on both sides of his head and smashed his head onto the stone floor. George managed to pull his knees up and pushed me forward with his feet, and the next thing I kent, he was on top of me once again. We somersaulted together for several more minutes until Isobel cried out, "Robert! He has a second knife!"

Her warning came too late. He swiped at my ribs, but I swiveled my hips, deflecting the blow just enough to avoid a punctured kidney. Instead, the knife skid across my hip, and the searing pain that erupted in my leg indicated he had cut flesh. I ignored the pain and grabbed his wrist, flipping him onto his back. I pulled the sack from his head, wanting to see the face of the man who dared to lay a hand on Isobel. The man I had paid to help me. The man I was about to kill.

I punched him in the face again, then in the ribs. I didnae care where the blows landed, I just wanted him down. Getting ahold of George long enough to bash his head against the floor again proved tricky. It was like wrestling an octopus. He wiggled and jerked beneath me until he managed to throw me off balance and had me on my back once again.

Employing his technique, I squirmed violently until he leaned forward, shoving his forearm against my throat. I gasped for breath, seeing a black haze forming at my peripheral vision. I tried to get my knee up enough to kick him off me. But with all his weight baring down on my throat, I was quickly running out of air. I braced myself for a stab wound. Would he plunge it into my chest to stop my heart, or would he go for a lung so I would thoroughly suffocate? With his arm on my throat, the most likely place he would strike was my side.

The thought of what he would do to Isobel once I was dead sent fury pulsing through me. But no matter how much I moved, I couldnae break free from his arm. My only recourse was to dig my fingers into his back and try to scratch at him. But his thick leather jerkin hindered that movement.

Suddenly, George's eyes went wide. A crimson stream spurted from his neck where the hilt of my sgian dubh protruded from him like a nail in a plank of wood. He slumped over onto me, pushing his weight further into my throat. The slight shift in pressure allowed me to take a gulp of air into my lungs, and I pushed him off with a heave.

It was so quiet, ye could hear the Thames burbling over the riverbed through the open window. Crickets chittered and the sound of frogs and other unidentified creatures sent a cacophony of night music drifting through the air. I looked at George as he lay motionless on the chamber floor, eyes still wide with shock, and his tunic drenched in blood. Then I looked at Isobel. She stood there with both arms held out in front of her as if she held a large, imaginary basket. Her hand and face were splattered with blood and the front of her dress was stained crimson.

"Isobel," I said gently so not to frighten her. She stared blankly as if studying the void. When she didnae answer, I moved closer to her. "Isobel." I waved a hand in front of her face, and the movement seemed to jolt her out of her shock. Her normally creamy skin had turned as white as milk glass, and her eyes were glassy orbs.

I stepped in front of her and took hold of her hands. They were cold as ice. I pushed them down to her sides, then ran my hands up her sleeves and gripped her arms firmly. I searched her face for recognition, some sign that she kent where she was and what she had done. "Issy," I said, tasting the strangeness of the name on my tongue. I didnae usually call her by the nickname those close to her used, but I thought the famil-iarity might draw her back to me. It appeared to work, for she finally blinked, stirring as if from slumber. I could see the moment she came to her senses, for her chest began to heave as she drew ragged breaths into her lungs. She pulled her eyes to my face and blinked again.

"You're alive," she said, taking in another shaky breath. I felt the corners of my mouth hitch up.

"Thanks to ye," I said, swiping a strand of moon-kissed hair out of her eye and tucking it behind her ear. When I pulled my hand away, my fingers were stained with George's blood.

A coppery tang of metal hung in the air. I lit two candlesticks that sat on the mantle, then grabbed a piece of linen from a nearby shelf and wiped her face clean. I then took her hand in mine and wiped it clean as well. She watched in silence as I rubbed the cloth over her long slender fingers, making sure not to miss a drop of blood. When I finished, I tossed the cloth aside. Still holding her hand, I grabbed one of the candles and led her into her bedchamber and away from the gruesome scene on the antechamber floor.

Her lips began to tremble. I deposited the candle, then pulled her into me, wrapping my arms around her. She buried her face in my chest and immediately started to cry. Her arms snaked around my waist, and she clung to me, sobbing into my shoulder. "'Tis all right," I said softly, rubbing my palms over her back in a soothing manner. "Ye did well." I moved a hand to the back of her neck and wrapped the loose wisps of hair from her plait around my fingers. We stood like that for a long moment until she lifted her head and looked at me. We stared at one another, her blue eyes still shining with unshed tears. My leg was weak, and the loss of blood was making me light-headed, but I refused to move while her hands were on me.

She peeked over my shoulder toward the antechamber where George's body lay crumpled on the floor. Relief swept over her countenance at the realization her life was no longer in danger. My eyes were drawn to the spot of crimson that beaded on her neck again. I ran a soiled hand over the place on her throat where George's blade had punctured her flesh.

"I cannae believe the blackguard drew blood," I said with labored breath, inspecting her porcelain skin.

"I'm all right," she said, though her voice shook, and her face was still pale. She drew back to look at me, resting her hand on my chest. "I killed him," she said, voice full of wonder.

"Aye." I watched her, pondering what kind of effect this would have on her. I remembered my first kill. A young man who had taunted me about my missing father and besmudged my mother's reputation. We were practically boys still. He had said ugly things about my mother, and when he didnae stop after several warnings, I had thrown the first punch. Walter was right. I have always had a bad temper. The lad was bigger than I, and when I couldnae get the best of him, I did the only thing I kent to do: pulled my sgian dubh on him. I hid nae meant to kill the man, but once it was done, I had no regrets. But Isobel wisnae a heathen like me. She wisnae a murderer. This kind of incident would haunt her the rest of her life. "Ye did what ye had to do." I tried to reassure her, but the strange look on her face had me second-guessing my assessment of her.

"Yes," she said, darkness shaping her word and turning her voice husky. She looked back at me, and there was no mistaking the look in her eyes. "I thought he was going to kill you."

Warmth flooded my veins. I was convinced she could feel the thundering of my heart beneath her palm. But would she ken it was her nearness and the sound of her voice that set my blood pumping more than the vigor of the fight with George Preston? Isobel had no idea what she did to me. Her touch made every muscle taut, every vein tighten, until I felt the pressure would make me explode. My body was on fire, and I wanted nothing more than to put my mouth on her and kiss her until she melted into me, and we burned together.

But she was Henry's. Her heart belonged to him, and he wanted her for a wife. Could I cross that line and take what didnae belong to me? Could I throw all of Henry's kindness back in his face and tread on his generosity to me? The one man who had never questioned my name, my abilities, nor my reputation.

The prince was noble and beyond reproach. He was just and kind and deserved every good thing that was offered him. The man was a saint.

But I wisnae.

Devil take me. I pulled Isobel against me and buried my face in her hair. She smelled of lavender and lemons, and I drank in her scent like a refreshing cup of spring water. The last time we kissed, she had initiated the encounter. What would she do if my lips sought hers? I inhaled, breathing in her essence once more, then ran my hands down her arms, feeling the delicate bones of her frame beneath my fingers. I wanted to fold her up like a warm blanket and squeeze her to my chest and never let her go.

I kissed the top of her head and stroked her hair, thrilled at the feel of those silvery blonde strands between my fingers. I brought the tip of one lock to my mouth and brushed it softly over my lips before inhaling the scent of lemons from her hair. I then kissed her temple. She didnae pull away, so I laid my lips on the lids of her eyes, the translucent skin where the faintest of blue veins spread delicately under her brows. I kissed her there as well. Her eyes were still closed and her face wet with tears. I kissed the salty rivers that ran down her cheeks. Then finally—*finally*—I put my mouth on hers.

Her lips were shaking. Her whole body was shaking. I was a rake for even taking advantage of her in this vulnerable situation. That was exactly what she had accused me of before. But I couldnae help myself. I never claimed to be a good man, and in this moment, I would make a trade with the devil if it would make her mine.

Isobel held on to the front of my jerkin as if I were the only thing keeping her alive. When my lips touched hers, she drew her hands up and laid her palms on both sides of my face. She opened to me, and I responded with fervor, all tongue, and teeth, and lips. Her mouth was warm, her lips soft, her tongue demanding. I laid my hands on both sides of her face, steadying and claiming her.

The night air was sweet, and the cool breeze brushed over us, blowing the tendrils of her hair against my cheek. The sensation lit a new fire within me, and I was intoxicated with the taste of her. She was sweeter than any port wine, and her touch burned hotter than the best whisky.

I had tried to stay away. I had written a letter to say good-bye with no intention of seeing Isobel again after my plan had come to fruition. But now my accomplice was dead, and Isobel was in more danger than ever before. How could I walk away? There was no future between us. But if I could be the eyes and ears for the prince, and for Isobel, to provide them protection and be their right-hand man, would I be satisfied? And what would happen if the prince couldnae talk the king into restoring my father's title? I would have failed my father, and my mission. Could I live with that?

The high-pitched screech of a barn owl sounded somewhere in the distance, making us aware of our surroundings. The realization of our situation was thrust upon us. Isobel pulled away from me, looking lost and...*guilty*. I understood the feeling. I should feel extreme shame for my behavior, especially in light of Henry. But I couldnae bring myself to regret my actions. I would do it all again if given the chance.

Isobel pulled me toward the antechamber. "We need to dispose of the body as soon as possible."

Anger brewed in my chest. The man hid nae double-crossed me per say, but the fact he had looked elsewhere for more coin and had found it in the skin of Lady Isobel Broune, made me seethe. He could rot right there for all I cared. But King James must be told of this assault. If Viscount Rochester was involved, he needed to be made aware. "We need to report this to the king," I finally said, as I shoved the man's body over onto his back with my foot.

"No," she said sharply. When I glanced at her, she softened her tone. "I don't want to involve the king. That will just make matters worse for me."

I frowned. "If ye think I had any intentions of letting ye take the blame for this, ye are mistaken. No one will ever ken of it. I will tell the king how I came upon George attacking ye in yer bedchamber, and I killed him when he tried to toss ye out the window."

Isobel shook her head. "The king can know of none of this. Frances is determined to get my help with this physical exam. George told me as much before you arrived. It's obvious she enlisted him to scare me into giving her what she wants. She has also made it more than clear that my involvement with the poisons will be made plain if I do not assist her."

I looked around for something to stop the bleeding on my leg. "Ye must not give her what she wants. I said before that ye didnae have a choice, but I've changed my mind. Lady Frances will stop at nothing. It is time to involve the king."

Isobel fisted her hands on her hips. "No, Robert. I will not tell His Majesty. It is my word against the word of Viscount Rochester's lover. He is the king's favorite and therefore, I cannot see how the king would side with me in this matter, even if you try to take the blame. If you have spent any time with my father, then you are aware there is an underlying current of animosity between my father and the king. That does not fare well for me. If I go to the king, Frances is likely to double her efforts to be rid of me, or worse, someone I love. Promise me you will say nothing of this. I will take care of her in my own way."

I listened to her reasoning as I grabbed another linen that was folded and laid on a nearby shelf. I pulled it from its nest and unfurled it, quickly finding the seam to tear the garment apart.

"That's my shift!" Isobel cried, storming over to where I stood ripping the cloth into strips.

"I'm bleeding," I said sheepishly. She tore her eyes from my face and let them rover over my body, looking for signs of injury. When her eyes landed on my bloody pantleg she inhaled loudly. "That's going to need cleaned."

I lifted a skeptical brow. "Ye want me to remove my trunks to have a look at it?"

She scowled. "No, but you need to have *someone* take a look at it. Hester perhaps?" The smug look on her face was ridiculous.

In two steps I stood before her, hovering with an intimidating glare of my own. "Are ye jealous, my lady? Because that sounds like a resentful snipe, if ye ask me."

Her mouth fell open. "I am not jealous!" she sputtered out.

"Good, because she doesnae hold a candle to ye. Now, if ye dinnae mind—" I reached to unfasten my trunks and her eyes practically bulged out of her head.

"You have mistaken what has happened here tonight," she said, scrambling to put space between us. "I," she paused, licking her lips nervously. "I'm engaged to the prince."

I snickered. "Are ye now? Ye dinnae kiss like a woman betrothed to another man."

She took in a sharp breath. "How dare you? We both know you took advantage of me in my vulnerability." Her eyes burned with fury as she swiped a stray strand of hair away from her face. My fingers itched to tuck it behind her ear once more.

I rolled my eyes at her instead. "Here we go again," I said, a mixture of ridicule and teasing leaking into my tone. I was getting tired of this game she seemed to be keen on playing. "What I find interesting is ye seem to be finding yerself in all manner of compromising situations and circumstances that continuously require ye to be rescued—by me."

She stamped her bare foot on the wood floor, the soft thud surely not having the effect she desired. "Rescued!" she shrieked. "I saved *you!*"

"True enough," I said, pausing my task. "Still, ye didnae quite have the matter under control when I came to yer room."

"I was not in need of rescuing." she said with a huff. "I just," she paused, sinking her teeth into her plump lower lip. "I just needed a little help." I watched her over my shoulder as she turned her face away from me. I didnae understand this desire of hers to do everything herself. Wurnae noble ladies used to having everything handed to them on a silver platter? She stiffened her spine and turned back to me. Taking a deep breath, she said, "Regardless of how things may appear, I am to marry Prince Henry. Nothing and no one will deter me."

I couldnae let it go, so I shrugged. "It was my understanding he his nae cleared that with Their Majesties yet. So, that makes ye a free little bird as far as I'm concerned." I continued to untie my laces, and she turned away from me quickly in a huff.

"Henry will talk them into it. He is very persuasive."

"I am counting on that," I said, remembering again his promise to me to speak to King James of my father.

An awkward silence hung in the air between us. I realized she probably thought I was referring to Henry persuading the king to allow them to marry.

"Why are you always in various stages of undress in front of me?"

"I widnae be if ye didnae insist on meeting in the bedchamber." I pulled my trunks down just enough to look at the stab wound. With a piece of the clean cloth, I dabbed at it, trying to see how deep the cut had gone.

"I thought you usually wore a kilt," she chattered nervously. "That would have made it easier to see your wound, don't you think?"

"Perhaps," I said, wiping the remaining blood from my skin. It was only a surface wound, but it sure hurt like the devil, and the bleeding widnae stop. "There are a lot of things that are easier to do in a kilt," I explained with the tone of a schoolmaster. "For instance, the ladies—"

"I don't care to hear about your exploits," she interrupted. "Are you finished yet?" She tapped that bare foot of hers on the floor impatiently, and I caught a glimpse of the bonniest toes I ever had the pleasure of seeing. I ran my tongue over my bottom lip in response and tasted blood.

"Ye didnae tell me my lip was bleeding, lass." I dabbed at my lip with the makeshift cloth I had created.

She turned abruptly, stopping shortly, and looking to see if I had dressed myself. "I didn't notice," she said, wiping at her bottom lip and sounding embarrassed. She watched as I retied my laces and adjusted my trunks, shoving my hand into my pocket and pulling out the lavender satin I always kept hidden there. I hoped it wisnae ruined by knife or blood.

When Isobel's eyes landed on the mask I held in my hand, a strangled noise escaped her lips. Her brows shot up so high, her forehead almost disappeared. "Where did you get that?" She looked at it as if it had three heads and mouths full of teeth.

I looked at her, sure the heat in my eyes burned a hole through her. "Ye ken exactly where it came from."

She took a step closer to me, never taking her eyes from the slip of fabric. "I did not ask where it came from. I asked where you got it."

I straightened to my full height and looked down at her. "Ye ken," I said, my voice rumbling out.

She stared at it a moment longer, and I watched her. I could see the exact moment when she finally fit all the pieces together. With more than a little awe, she said, "That was you."

Longing pulsed through me. A desire for her to truly see me and not the scoundrel she ken me to be. "Aye," I said, watching her intently. "'Twas me."

Chapter 29

Richmond Palace, London
October 1612
Isobel

So, it was Robert Stewart all along. The masked stranger at the Hymenaei ball that had intrigued me with his lightness of foot and his muted tongue.

"Why didn't you speak to me? I tried to talk to you, and you wouldn't say a word. It was frustrating," I said, letting a little too much irritation into my voice.

"Ye would have kent it was me as soon as I opened my mouth. I was afraid ye might flee and ruin the whole masque." His lips twitched as if amused, and he ran his thumbs over the piece of lavender cloth he clutched in his hands. I knew it was the one I had worn because the ladies' masks were finely detailed with French lace and tiny seed pearls. But it was only large enough to cover the eyes. It looked like a tiny scrap of paper in his large hands.

I dragged my eyes away from his hands. His fingers were large but well-manicured for a man who spent his days thieving and murdering people. These were the same hands that had brushed gently over my cheeks and curled wisps of my hair around his finger. The same fingers that stroked heat across my legs when we were locked in an embrace in the middle of the maze. My skin still burned from that touch. I shook my head to clear my addled brain of all those distracting thoughts.

"But after the masque, you were working in the stables with Lady Luck." I searched his face for understanding. "How did you manage that?"

His eyes bore into me. "I was called almost immediately after ye fled the banqueting hall. It truly was pure luck that I found ye after such a length of time still in the stables crying."

I shifted, mortified. I didn't want to talk about it anymore. I had obsessed over this stranger for days after the masque, wracking my brain, trying to figure out who he was. I would admit to anyone who asked that I was intrigued with him, but I would never admit the attraction I had felt.

Yet, that attraction didn't seem so disgusting to me now. Though it still bothered me. I was in love with Henry. Why did I have to keep reminding myself of that? And why did I keep throwing myself at Robert?

When he found me in the maze, I was hysterical. Paralyzed by my fear, and petrified of some unknown monster I created in my mind. I clung to him, desperate to get out. But somehow, we found ourselves in the most precarious of situations. I tried to tell myself he had taken advantage of me, but we both knew that was a lie. And tonight—I *killed* a man. George Preston tried to scare me by dangling me out the window, threatening if I did not help Lady Frances with her physical examination then there would be worse things to come. I was never so glad to see Robert than I was this evening when he surprised us in my antechamber. I wanted to kiss him again if for no other reason than for what he did to distract George. When I thought he was going to kill Robert, I just snapped.

Now I was in the biggest mess of my life. How did I keep finding trouble? Robert had once told me even if I had known of Frances's plan to poison the maids and assisted her willingly in carrying it out, he would have helped me cover up my involvement. Then tonight he offered to take the blame for George's murder. Why was he always helping me and without judgement? I had treated him terribly from the very start, yet he was willing to practically die for me.

"If I dispose of the body will ye be able to clean this blood up on yer own?" he asked, pulling me from my woolgathering. "Or do ye want my help?"

I licked my lips and tried to swallow, feeling like my mouth was stuffed with dandelion fluff. "I can, uh, I can clean up the blood," I said, glancing around at the wreck that was my privy chamber. George had pulled me straight from my bed and dragged me in here, presumably because it was more secluded. I had grabbed at anything I could get my hands on to try to prevent him from overpowering me, but it had been futile. Now there were gowns and shoes and undergarments strewn all over the floor. One of my favorite hats was trampled, and a painting that had hung on the wall had been knocked off and a hole torn in the canvas. Several of my dresses had spurts of blood on them, casualties of me stabbing George in the neck. I had never been allowed instruction in anatomy, but Will always taught me his lessons after his tutor, Doctor Fowler, concluded his. He had taught me if you cut someone in just the right place in the neck, they would bleed to death in a matter of seconds. He was right. I swallowed down the bile in my throat. I never thought I'd see a day when I would find that out.

Robert was stoking the fire, trying to rekindle it. "Be sure you burn anything that has blood on it," he was saying.

Alarm arrested me. "There are ways to remove bloodstain, Robert. Surely not all my dresses need be disposed of."

He straightened, pinning me with a severe look. "Ye cannae risk any evidence that there was a struggle here. Questions will be asked, ye must be without guilt." He strode to the painting that lay punctured on the floor. He scooped it up and tossed it on the grate, sending sparks flying and a great plume of dark smoke puffing into the air.

"I hope you realize that was a Botticelli you just sent up in flames," I said dryly. He looked at me, then back to the hearth.

Swiping his hand across the back of his neck, he said, "Guess we willnae be asking him to paint another then, seeing how he's been dead for a hundred years."

I bit my lip to tamp down the smile that fought to emerge. I always thought him to be some uneducated, drunken reiver, growing up in the Border region of Scotland. I had to remind myself he may have been the son of an exiled earl, but he was the son of an earl, nonetheless, and had probably been educated as one.

I watched as he pulled a bed linen from the shelf and laid it on the floor. He rolled George's body up in the linen, then looked around for something more. He walked to the window and inspected the coverings, then jerked one free from the hooks. "If anyone asks, tell them ye accidentally caught the curtain on fire with yer candle." He proceeded to roll George's linen-wrapped body in the second layer of material. Thankfully, the curtain was a deep blue, and the blood was not easily spotted.

In all, I burned four gowns, two shifts and a farthingale, one pair of shoes and my crushed hat, besides the painting Robert had tossed. I also burned all the linens used to clean up the blood and made a report to the housekeeper about the damaged window covering. By the next afternoon, I had new, cerulean blue curtains on all my windows. I rather liked the change in color, but it made no difference, we were leaving for St. James Palace onto the next leg of celebrations for Elizabeth and Frederick's betrothal.

I never found out what Robert did with George's body.

A mock sea battle was planned on the day we arrived at St. James Palace. Fortunately, unlike the ancient ones, known as naumachia, this was not a fight to the death, but merely a demonstration acted out between sea-faring ships.

Many a Londoner came to watch the show, for although the event was designed for the pleasure of the king and his court, anyone willing was welcome to attend.

The preparations for such a production were no small task. Upon the Thames was built three large castles which floated upon a total of eight barges. Ships of war and galleys had been brought to stage the mock battles. Beautiful flotillas with colorful banners of purple and blue streaming in the breeze floated lazily upon the water. One such flotilla was designed specifically for the royal household, with the future bride and groom positioned in seats of honor at the head. We lounged on carnation pink and crane blue cushions of crushed velvet, embroidered with gold thread, and monogrammed with Elizabeth and Frederick's initials. The boat was laden with furs, various pelts of mink, fox, and sable to make our seats most comfortable. We nibbled on candied fruits, flakey pastries, meat pies, and wedges of cheese as we waited. We held a most excellent view of the festivities and would practically feel a part of the action once the battle began.

Another faux castle had been built upon the northern shore of the river, and it was this castle which would be under siege by the Turks. Not real Turks, of course, but civilian and naval men alike had been recruited to play the piratical Turks who fought against the English Navy, a representation of Protestant Christendom, to steal their wealth and ruin their faith.

A large canon boomed, signally the start of the festivities. Happy melodies floated in the air, sung out by flutes and various other instruments, as onlookers watched the start of the show.

Just as he had two years earlier, at his investiture as Prince of Wales, Henry stood at the end of a large flotilla, moving rapidly down the river, and quickly coming into view. His rose-gold hair glowed in the autumn sunshine, dancing wildly about his face as the wind whipped violently about him. His imported Italian armor with its religious and military insignia shone brightly, polished to a brilliant shine matched only by the golden globe that hung in the midday sky. He looked magnificent, portraying the Lord High Admiral of the navy, a position he one day hoped to hold.

When he came into view, the crowd cheered to deafening levels, drowning out the flutes and nearly obliterating the sounds of a second round of canon fire. The people loved Henry, and rightly so. For he loved them in return. It was evident in every act he performed in his role as prince. Somehow Henry always managed to steal the show. For although this was a celebration of Elizabeth and her impending marriage, Henry became the center of attention.

My heart fluttered beneath my Parisian silk gown of midnight blue, and I felt my cheeks warm at the sight of him. I had not seen him since the queen's court had arrived at St. James Palace, for he had been busy with the sea battle preparations. However, he had replied to my letters and had informed me he had spoken to Their Majesties about our engagement. But he didn't tell me their answer. I knew what that meant. They had not agreed to the engagement, for if they had, he would have told me straightway. He said he was still speaking with them concerning it.

The music continued to play, and the laughter rang out. But something about Henry as he drew closer on his flotilla caught my attention. His hair and armor may have glowed in the

midday sun, but his complexion was wan. His usually bright blue eyes didn't sparkle, and his smile appeared forced. He stood with one knee bent on a wooden chest in front of him, his hand on the hilt of the sword hanging at his side. But he did not pull the sword and brandish it about as his form of showmanship. Instead, he waved meekly to the throngs of people gathered on both shores.

"Henry doesn't look well." I leaned in to speak in Elizabeth's ear. She sat at Frederick's side but leaned toward me as we sat with our knees bent touching each other. Her countenance fell, and she glanced across the river to where Henry's flotilla had just reached ours.

"He has not been himself," she said quietly, sneaking a glance toward the queen. "Yesterday, he and Frederick were touring the new Navy shipyard. Half-way through the tour, he told Frederick he wasn't feeling well and wanted to go have a lie-down. He left abruptly, and as you know, he wasn't at supper. And the day before that, he canceled a meeting with our father, claiming he had no energy and wanted to rest for a bit. They arranged to meet later, but he never showed." She stopped talking and looked at me, worry clouding her pale blue eyes. "He spreads himself too thin," she continued when I didn't speak. "He must stop taking on so many responsibilities, especially when there are others who can do the task just as easily."

I watched Henry as Elizabeth spoke. He smiled at the crowds of people before lifting his hand again and dropping it dramatically, signaling the firing of another canon. The shot was fired, and the boom shook the water, sending our flotilla rocking with the rolling waves.

"He's only ten and eight," I said, searching for an excuse to make myself feel better. Worry bloomed in my chest, unfurling like a rose opening under sunlight. I tamped it down. It was ridiculous to worry about a little cold, or fatigue, or whatever must be ailing him. "He is young and healthy. He's always active. But perhaps there is such a thing as too much activity."

"You must encourage him to get his rest and to start delegating his responsibilities, Isobel. If you two are to be married, it will be your job to keep him in check." She raised a knowing brow at me to accompany her lecture.

"You're marrying my brother?" It was Charles, the younger prince of the Stuart household. His voice sounded like the high-pitched chirp of a bird, having not gone through the change yet of boys his age. At twelve years old, he was precocious, but he held no sense of delicate matters nor any knowledge of when to bite his tongue.

"Hush, Charlie," Elizabeth chided. "Mother and Father have not given their blessing yet. Do not speak of it until you hear it announced."

The child jerked his head toward Their Majesties, observing them momentarily where they sat wrapped in ermine and watching the show, before looking back at me. He eyed me suspiciously but didn't speak again, then finally turned his head back toward the activity on the water without another word.

"He'll never shut up about it now," Elizabeth said, her mouth quirking to the side. "He secretly likes you and will therefore talk nonstop about you and Henry until my parents relent. It will work in your favor."

I stared at her, but she had already turned back toward the water as well. "When you say he likes me, what does that mean?"

She leaned toward me not taking her eyes from the water and the boats dueling thereon. In a whisper so the young prince couldn't hear, she said, "He draws pictures of the two of you getting married and scratches your names together all over parchment every chance he gets."

"Oh," was all I could manage. I wasn't expecting that. The child had barely spoken ten words to me in the time I'd known him, and that was almost all his life.

"He'll have to get in line," Elizabeth continued, teasing. "From what I understand, you break hearts everywhere you go."

Now I was thoroughly confused. "What?" I demanded. The duel on the water was completely forgotten.

"Rumor has it George Preston fled back to wherever he was from," she said, waving her hand in the air. "A little birdie told me he had set his cap toward you, but he heard Henry had his sights set on you, and he returned home, his tail between his legs like a scolded dog."

Well, that was an untruth, perpetuated by...whom? Perhaps Robert had told the tale to cast suspicion of George's disappearance away from us.

"And then there is the Scotsman," Elizabeth had continued.

"W-what?" I stammered, and her face took on a devilish mien.

"Robert Stewart. That man is so in love with you he can't see straight."

I scoffed. "Not true." My heart was pounding now. Why did the mere mention of his name solicit such a reaction from that traitorous organ? My hands began to itch as well, just thinking about the prickly stubble of his jaw against my palms. "We loath each other," I explained. "Our families have history together. Not good history either."

"Uh-huh," Elizabeth teased. "Well, someone needs to let Robert know. When you loath someone you don't stare at them from across the room with your tongue practically hanging out of your mouth."

I guffawed at that. "He doesn't stare at me like that. Does he?"

The princess nodded emphatically. "Every time you two are in a room together." She popped a grape into her mouth, and her teeth broke the tight flesh with a snap.

Panic was creeping up my chest. Any minute now it would spread across my neck like it always did when I found myself in these situations. The splotchy redness of my skin would scream at everyone how bothered I was. "But you realize I'm in love with Henry, correct? You recognize I haven't encouraged any amorous feelings from the Scot."

Elizabeth looked at me with a funny expression. "Of course not, silly. Everyone knows you are in love with my brother. Always have been, always will be, I presume." She squeezed my knee lovingly, then tossed another grape into her mouth before turning her attention back to the battle.

Henry did not come to supper again that night. And within a fortnight, my world was turned upside down.

Chapter 30

St. James Palace, London
November 6, 1612
Robert

The atmosphere at St. James Palace was somber.

Henry had stopped responding to my letters weeks ago. My responsibilities in the stables at Richmond Palace kept me occupied, so I hid nae realized his lack of letters, until I overheard a couple of maids gossiping about the prince being sick.

Weeks earlier, the prince had requested a pair of steeds he had purchased be brought to him at St. James Palace, where he was currently residing. We had made the arrangements well in advance, and although Henry was too ill to correspond, I followed through with the original plan, nonetheless.

I expected to see Elizabeth and Frederick's engagement festivities in full swing when I arrived at St. James. A masque had been planned, and perpetual suppers and balls, all of which Henry had been delighted to host at this second residence. The day before, the country had celebrated a national day of thanksgiving, for the sparing of His Majesty from a plot to rid the land of James altogether. The incident had been coined the Powder Plot, and Parliament had declared from thenceforth it would be a day of celebrations with the burning of bonfires and the searching of royal dwellings for more gunpowder in hopes of foiling another plot.

Even those celebrations had been curbed. At St. James Palace, the armory was bare, where in lieu of a great hall the stage which Inigo Jones had so meticulously crafted, stood unused. The kitchens which usually bustled with nonstop activity, and the court that teemed with lively entertainments was silent. It was as if the puppet master had tucked away his strings and folded up his stage and called it quits.

"God's teeth," I cursed under my breath as I made my way through the corridors. The ominous atmosphere hung in the air like a shroud and enveloped me as soon as I stepped foot within the walls of the palace. Even the brightly covered wall hangings, the Turkish carpets and gilded furniture dimmed under the cloak of darkness that permeated the halls. I shook my shoulders, trying to rid myself of that menacing milieu that clung to every nook and cranny of the place.

Even the guards seemed to be in a state of despair, for no one questioned me as I made my way through the palace looking for some familiar face so I could inquire about the prince's condition.

I finally came upon a small party in the library right outside the Chapel Royal. Harington, Essex and Isobel's brother, Tom, sat within, each lost in their own thoughts. Harington sat with a book in his lap, but he didnae read. Instead, he stared into an unknown abyss, neither scanning the pages, nor turning them forward. Essex stood with a tumbler of something amber clutched in his hand, staring out the window into the courtyard beyond. Tom sat at a small writing desk, playing some solitary card game, flipping cards over from a deck he held in his hand. None of them seemed to notice when I stepped into the room.

The fire in the hearth was dying. Like a foreshadowing omen, the look of it sent a chilling sensation skittering down my spine. I strode to the fireplace and stoked the flames, pushing the remaining portions of logs around until a spark ignited, setting the flame afire once more.

"What news have ye?" I asked, straightening my back, and hanging the poker back onto a hook strategically placed on the mantle.

As if noticing me for the first time, Harington roused himself, shuffling the book in his lap. His eyes were red, like he had been crying, and when he looked at me, all vigor seemed to have drained from his face.

"There is little change, if not for the worse. His speech is nonsensical when words come at all. In his delirium he cries out he has something to say, but then he cannot gather his words when asked to do so. He breaks forth in short bursts of song, cries out in agony, lies quiet and still at times, and thrashes upon his bed, tearing at the bedclothes on other occasions." Here Harington's voice broke, the sound reminiscent of crackling glass.

Tom took up the chronicle. "He called out desperately for his Master of the Wardrobe, David Murray last night, and David said when he reached his bedside, Henry could not even speak the words he wished to say to him. He had to signal what he wanted him to do." Tom turned another card over onto the table, adding it to a long string of discarded plays.

"They shaved his head. The doctors thought that would make him more comfortable— Thought it would balance his humors, or some such belief—" Harington tried once more to speak, but the words got tangled up in his throat. He stood and left the room abruptly. Essex's dark eyes followed Harington out of the room wordlessly.

"What did Henry want with David Murray?" I asked.

"His personal correspondence." Tom again. "There were some letters and other documents he wanted destroyed, others he wanted mailed."

My mind went to Isobel's necklace. I wondered if he had ever given it to her as I had asked him to do.

"Ever the protecting prince," Essex murmured. "He had many strange pursuits."

My brows drew together. "Strange pursuits?" I questioned.

"Pet projects, explorations, and grand ideas. He had many friends, and some of those friends had ideas of their own. Ideas that might not be welcomed by His Majesty. I imagine Henry's personal effects have a plethora of incriminating information in them, should they fall into the wrong hands. He would never endanger a friend if he could help it. He would want all of that destroyed." Essex's words hung in the air.

"Murray destroyed all his personal effects?" I ran my tongue over my lips. My mouth suddenly felt dry. "That sounds so verra...final."

We all stared at one another as my words sank in. A feeling of panic clawed at my throat, swelling my tongue, and making it hard to breathe. I swiped a hand through my hair and turned back to the hearth, leaning heavily on its mantle. I felt like a millstone had been laid upon me, squeezing my chest, and immobilizing me. The stillness of the room closed in as the *tick, tick, tick* of a clock somewhere close by counted out the seconds. Seconds that, had Henry been well, he would have filled with some prosperous pursuit. He was never one to waste a moment. He lived to the fullest, taking every opportunity presented to him to improve himself, and leave this world a better place.

With a strangled breath, I said, "Is there nothing that can be done?"

Another beat of silence before Essex cleared his throat. "Her Majesty sent for assistance from Sir Walter Raleigh, begging for some potion or wonder cure he could recommend." Essex drained his glass and set it on Tom's writing desk to pour another dram. "He sent back his special Balsam of Guiana with a note attached." He stopped, and with no further explanation, seated himself in the chair Harington had vacated, glass in hand.

I raised my brows. "Well?" I said, shaking my head. "What did it say?"

Tom once again came to the rescue. "He claims the elixir is a universal cure for ailments, with one exception—poison."

Poison. The word triggered a vice, clutching my gut. "Poison?" I swallowed hard. Dear God. Why did Lady Frances's face float before my eyes. "Is there a reason for us to believe he was poisoned?" I held my breath. Surely, the man must have made an enemy here or there, at some point in his life. But I was hard-pressed to think of any that could hate the prince that much. And Lady Frances was the only one I could think of that would be brave enough to wield that kind of nasty blow.

Essex shifted in his seat. "Let's just say the elixir had no effect."

I needed to talk to Isobel. Needed to see whether she had spoken to Frances since our unintended tryst the night George was killed. Might she ken something about a motive the countess might hold for wanting Henry dead?

"Doctor Mayerne does not think it is poison," Tom said.

"Old fool," the Earl of Essex spat out the words. "He also insists on bleeding our prince and turning him into a corpse before the spirit has even left his body."

Just then a commotion in the hallway silenced us. A moment later, the young prince, Charles, came into the library. He headed straight for a shelf behind us, where Henry kept a collection of small bronze statues of various sizes and shapes. His eyes locked onto something above his head where he reached but couldnae retrieve.

I stepped to his side. "Is there something with which I can help His Grace?"

He squinted up at me. "Are you my brother's Master of the Horse?"

"Indeed." I swallowed hard, remembering how I got that position. "Yer brother has been kind to me."

"Henry is kind to everyone. He is a goodly prince, and I—" His voice hitched as his bottom lip began to tremble. "And I hope to be just like him someday."

"'Tis a good aspiration to have," I said, watching him as he twisted his ankle, stepping on the side of his shoe.

"Will you be so kind as to hand me the pacing horse bronze?" he said, pointing to a statue of a beautiful brown horse with a front and back leg raised as if he were indeed trotting.

I pulled the statue from the shelf, noting the solid weight of it in my hand. "Is this a Tacca sculpture?" I queried.

"Yes," the prince said, taking the bronze in both of his hands. "It is one of mine and Henry's favorites, gifted to him by Grand Duke Cosimo. I'm going to give it to him and tell him to recover swiftly so we may go riding together again soon." A silvery rim of tears pooled around the prince's eyes. I looked away upon seeing his tears, for fear my own might be forced from my eyes.

"Come along, my son." King James stood in the doorway, holding out a shaky hand to the prince. The hollow look in his rheumy eyes sent a ripple of gooseflesh across my skin. Dark purple smudges hung beneath his eyes, and the buttons of his fine black woolen doublet were askew, having skipped a buttonhole and all the other buttons following suite. His spine curved forward a degree, giving his slight frame a withered look. I cursed under my breath for the measure of pity that began to take root in my chest.

The king was on the verge of losing his firstborn son.

I turned away. I was unable to look at this man who caused my family so much grief. I had hated him for so long, hated him still. Yet, for the sake of our mutual love for Henry, I fought to reconcile this compassion I felt for him now. It wisnae in my nature, to empathize with men of great power who refused to extend grace to those less fortunate than themselves. I had seen it with my own half-brother, Walter and many times over amongst the Scottish lords.

A dreary autumnal rain began to fall early in the afternoon, casting long shadows across the chevron pattern of the hardwood floor. The wind outside drove the rain down in sheets against the lead-lined windows and shook the eaves. I stoked the hearth two more times before a footman came to add more fuel. The fire burned bright, but nothing could drive away the chill from our bones. When a maid came to light the sconces that hung from the library walls, Essex drove her away. The maid fled in tears, leaving in her wake an awkward silence and a library as gloomy as a tomb.

~

"Hanson, light the candles in the library. We won't have our guests sitting around languishing in the dark. We have said our prayers, and the prince still lives. There is yet hope!"

The queen stood in the doorway of the library with her hand on Charles's shoulder. Queen Anne had always been a protective mother. So much so she had miscarried one unborn child years earlier, in her efforts to secure access to her firstborn son, whom the Scottish lords had removed from her care, as was custom. It was hard to tell if she held Charles protectively now, knowing her chances of losing Henry were so great, or if the younger prince simply served as a means of holding the grieving mother upright.

Her words were full of hope, but her countenance didnae portray the same belief. Her face was drawn, her cheeks sunken. The lines that accented her downturned mouth seemed to have grown deeper in the short amount of time since I had seen her last. And her eyes were rimmed in a pink line, giving the slightest indication she had been crying. She may have been holding it together, but the worry was starting to take its toll.

Elizabeth and Frederick stood behind her, and behind Elizabeth, Isobel stood in the shadows. She had been crying too. In fact, all the women standing there looked stricken. Isobel appeared to have even lost some weight, for her beautifully rounded cheeks were also drawn into a tight mien.

The queen moved on, Charles walking stiffly and slowly to uphold her. I wondered if the weight of the implications of Henry's death had occurred to the younger prince yet. Perhaps he was still too young to understand.

"I think I shall retire as well," Elizabeth said. "I want to be well rested when Henry asks for me again. Perhaps the next time, Doctor Mayerne will allow me entrance." The bitterness in her words didnae go undetected.

"I take the princess," Frederick said in his broken English. He bowed to us regally, then turned back to Elizabeth and offered his arm in escort.

"It's too bright in here for my liking," Essex growled. He too stood to depart, grabbing his tumbler which still held a swallow of whisky. He also took hold of the bottle to take with him, until my words stopped him short.

"Leave that," I said, motioning to the whisky.

His eyes narrowed on me. "Get your own bottle, friend. This one is needed elsewhere."

I strode to him and wrapped my hand around the neck of the bottle. "There isnae much left in this one. Ye are going to need another. Ye might as well get it now, ye were leaving anyway." I stared him down, daring him to make a move with the whisky I decided to claim. I wisnae above pummeling him. I was in no mood to negotiate, and I was sure he was too much of a gentleman to fight me for a few swallows of whisky. Besides he could barely stand up straight as it was.

He grunted and pushed the bottle toward me. "Sounds like you need it more than I do." Then knocking back his half-filled tumbler, he dropped the glass on the table and swayed toward the door. When he reached Isobel, he stopped. "I am truly sorry, my lady. You deserved all the happiness the prince could have given you." And with that, he stumbled away.

Isobel's eyes filled with more tears, and the color drained from her face. She let out a choked sob, then ran to Tom, who stood there waiting, with arms open to her. She buried her face into his shoulder, and I felt a thread of jealousy pulling into a tight knot in my chest. I didnae care he was her brother. I wanted to be the one to comfort her. For I longed for her comfort just as much.

Tom soothed her, running his hand over her back and shushing her with gentle, brotherly cooing. I lifted the bottle I had apprehended from Essex and tossed back its contents, draining it dry. I fought to keep it down, for the bile that rose in my throat was forceful. It was hard to watch the woman I wanted, in love with another man, mourn his imminent death.

After standing like that for some minutes, Isobel finally drew back and looked at Tom. "You look exhausted, Brother. How long have you been holding vigil here?"

Tom looked at the clock that sat on the mantle. "We've been here since yesterday afternoon."

Her mouth fell open, horrified. "Tom, you must get some rest. You are about to fall over."

He rubbed a hand over his face, squeezing the bridge of his nose before rubbing his eyes. "I just—can't leave."

"You must," Isobel insisted. She rubbed her hands up and down his arms to invigorate him. "Your presence here does nothing, and you will be of no use to the prince when he recovers, and you are laid up in your bed with exhaustion."

"Will he recover, Sister? Do you truly think he will ever leave that bed?"

Isobel didnae speak. The question hung, heavy and demanding, above us. Finally, she said, "I hope so, Tom." She reached up and ran a light finger through a lock of his hair that had fallen into his eye. "Now, go get some rest. I will wake you if there is a change in Henry's condition."

He blinked at her, then nodded, pulling away. "Yes, let me know when he awakens." He gave a quick, cursory look at the cards he had been playing with, then left them untouched on the desktop and departed.

Isobel stood with her back to me, unspeaking. Everything that had happened, all our secrets and even our sins, stretched between us. All the cruel words, the teasing, the hard feelings, seemed to congeal awkwardly as we stood before the chasm of possibility. The possibility of Henry's death. We both loved him. She for the lover he might never be to her, and me for the brother I had never had, despite the many I had back home in Scotland. And it was because of this love that I hated myself. For in Henry's death, I might have a chance at winning Isobel's love. And for that, I was truly depraved.

That thought constricted my throat, causing a strangling noise to escape my lips. Isobel turned, and with something I could only define as pity, her eyes roved over me.

"And how long have you been here, holed up in this library, waiting for news?" she asked.

"I arrived this morning. I was unaware he had regressed so far." Emotions I hid nae experienced constricted my throat. I had already said my goodbyes to Henry when I thought I was going to kill his father and flee to Scotland. I kent I widnae see him again unless it was as I swung from a noose. But this wisnae what I had expected. It wisnae supposed to be this way. "Have ye seen him?"

Her chin began to quiver. "No, they will not let us in. He even asked for Elizabeth, but those cursed doctors will not allow us entrance. If he dies without getting what he asked for, I hope they all rot in hell for their denial of a prince's final wish." She buried her face in her hands. "I'm sorry," she said through her muffled cries.

I moved toward her. I wanted to wrap my arms about her, console her, but I wisnae sure if my consolation would be welcomed. I clenched my hands into fists, then unclenched them, fighting the urge to cry right along with her.

When she finally got control of her emotions, she looked up at me. A wobbly smile crossed her face. "You look as if someone has stolen your favorite steer." A jest again about my reiving.

I swallowed hard, trying to choke down my emotions. "I love Henry, maybe not like ye do, but I love him. No one has ever accepted me without question, without thinking of what I could do for them, except him."

Her eyes softened, and she pressed her lips together as if holding back more tears. "Robert." She reached out and took one of my clenched hands in hers. I couldnae look at her, for fear I might grab her and never let her go. When I didnae speak, she released my hand and wrapped her arms around me, pulling me into her.

The tenderness with which she held me was unparalleled. Only my mother had ever comforted me thus. Moira certainly never had. She was the one who always needed comfort. The feeling was strange and wonderful and frightening as hellfire. I let my head drop to her shoulder, then buried my face into her neck. The tears came unbidden, scorching my face and soaking her skin, and in spite of the shame of showing such emotion, I couldnae stop them. Her fingers stroked through my hair, and she shushed me like a wee child. Angel and demon were at war for my soul, but I was sure I already kent the outcome.

They could damn my soul to hell, and I still widnae pull away. I would never let her go, no matter what happened with Henry.

But it seemed the heavens had already been working in my favor, curse it all. For the king had staggered to the door of the library and stood blubbering like a drunkard.

"Henry is dead. My son, my son," he wailed. "My Henry is dead."

PART II

"I have said, Ye are gods;
And all of you are children of the most High.
But ye shall die like men,
and fall like one of the princes."
Psalm 82: 6-7
Archbishop Abbot's eulogy
for Prince Henry

"...our Rising Sun is set ere scarcely he had shone,
and with him all our glory lies buried..."
Richard Sackville, 3rd Earl of Dorset
in a letter to Sir Thomas Edmondes
referring to Prince Henry.
23 November 1612

Chapter 31

Banqueting House, Palace of Whitehall, London
February 1613
Isobel

A flood of memories overwhelmed me as I stepped into the crowded banqueting hall at the Palace of Whitehall. The décor had been changed, yet the shape of the room, the smell of the air, and the golden candlelight flickering off the frescoed walls could not be forgotten. For a moment I was back in my cloth of silver gown at the Hymenaei masque and Henry in his turmeric-colored robe with a laurel wreath upon his head. I could see him still, as he strode across the dais, rose-gold locks brushing his shoulders and blue eyes blazing.

Three months. It had been three months since Henry's death, and at times, it felt like an eternity ago. Other times, like today, it felt as if I had just spoken to him, just felt the brush of his finger down my arm, or the whisper of his breath upon the shell of my ear. He was in every childhood memory as far back as my memory could go. His impression was upon every royal residence in London. In every painting he had chosen to add to his portrait collection in Richmond. In every scientific instrument or military map that adorned the library at St. James. Every card game, every sword play, every celebration.

He was here, even now.

I felt as if a hand had reached within my chest and clenched my heart, squeezing the organ until it would pop. My lungs too, for as I tried to take a breath, it was as if all the air had either been sucked from the room, or my lungs had collapsed. Either way, I could not take in enough air. It wasn't until a presence at my elbow drew me out of my imaginary bubble by speaking my name. I gasped, bursting the illusion, and pulling myself back to reality.

"Lady Isobel."

That familiar brogue. The sound like harsh rain yet caressing the skin with soft pelts. He stood beside me, staring down at me with his crinkled copper brow drawn together over those wintery, balsam-green eyes. Eyes that seemed to bore right to my soul. I always felt as if those eyes saw right through me, right to every secret, though I knew that to be impossible. It made no difference now. Robert Stewart knew all my secrets, every last, dirty one of them. From me stealing from my own mother, and my involuntary part in the poisoning of the maids, to George Preston's murder. From my unfulfilled desire to marry Henry to my willingness to do anything to see that happen. He knew them all. Yet here he stood beside me with the faintest touch of his palm against the small of my back, looking for all the world like he would whisk me away from this wretched place in an instant, if only I would ask him to.

A surge of relief flooded me. "Robert."

He bent his head and spoke into my ear. "At the risk of making an untimely jest, ye look as if ye could keel over at any moment. Shall we find ye a seat?"

I looked about the hall frantically. The place had been transformed from a rich masque to a sumptuous marriage feast. Festoons of bright pinks and deep purples hung from the walls. Crisp, white linens with the bride and groom's heraldry embroidered along the edges covered the tables. Porcelain vases with gold leaf patterns and gilded edges were arranged in the middle, brimming with pink and white carnations, red roses, and tiny sprays of white baby's breath. Delicate gold filigree baskets, overflowing with artisanal breads, cheese-filled pastries, and fresh fruits and other delectables. Crystal flutes filled with sweet wine were passed about to newcomers. All were aglow with what looked to be a thousand candles set upon thick, heavy golden candelabras.

"My family should be here somewhere," I said, still glancing about the room.

"I see them." Robert guided me through the maze of servants bearing trays of food and drink to the other side of the hall where my parents and siblings were already seated and beginning their feast. He pulled the chair out and seated me before bowing slightly to me. "Enjoy the rest of the celebrations," he said before turning to go.

I caught the sleeve of his black doublet. He had worn his scarlet and black kilt and tall, black boots. From the waist down he was all Scotsman. Above the waist, he looked like an English gentleman.

"There is room here for you," I said, motioning to the empty seat beside me. Now that Henry was gone, and Elizabeth married, I had never felt more alone in the world. I desperately wanted him to stay. "Or are you seated with the royal family?"

He scoffed. "His Majesty doesnae like to claim me as family." A wicked glint sparked in his eyes for a split second and then it was gone. It reminded me of his long-ago plan to take vengeance on the king. I wondered if that was still his plan. Henry's death seemed to have knocked the wind out of all our sails.

"But he asked you to stay on in your position at Richmond for a time, did he not? He must see some value in you. That is more than most of Henry's court can say. Most of them are scrambling for positions at the king's court now."

He shifted his stance. "I will finish the tasks I began under the prince's employ, then I will return to Scotland where I belong. I dinnae have plans of serving the king here in London."

I could not read his expression. There was a void there that made his eyes look hollow now. The light had gone out, leaving him cold and passionless.

"But what about your father and your quest to regain his title?" I twisted in my seat, gripping the back of the vacant chair beside me. It was my lifeline, for suddenly, I felt like I was drifting. First Henry, then Elizabeth, now Robert. This couldn't be happening.

"My father is dead."

He spoke the words without so much as a hitch in his voice. No wonder he looked as though the life had been drained out of him. *I willnae give up until he has restored my father's title and lands, or he pays for what he has done to my family.* I remembered his words so clearly. His whole life had been dedicated to that one thing, that one person. And now that person was gone.

"I-I'm so sorry, Robert. I didn't know."

He looked down at me, and the twinge of something primal flickered across his face. "Ye couldnae have kent. Dinnae fash yerself." I opened my mouth to say something more, though I knew not what, but he bowed to me again and turned and strode away. His broad shoulders seemed to list momentarily as he paused, then he lifted his head and continued across the banquet room with back straightened.

"Where is Robert going?" Tom asked, ripping a bite of chicken away from the bone with his teeth. "You should have invited him to sit with us, Issy."

Irritation surged through me. "I did, Tom. He doesn't want to." I spat out the words, regretting the sound of my frustration.

My hand shook as I took a drink of the wine that had been set before me. When I spilled a few drops down the front of my bodice, I almost lost all composure.

"Are ye all right, Isobel?" Of course, my mother would notice my demeanor. She missed nothing.

"I'm fine," I said bitingly. I pushed back my chair to find my maid and see if she could help with the stain. "I'm going to clean up." I excused myself from the table. But before I could make it halfway across the banqueting hall, another figure stood before me and stopped me short.

"Lady Isobel, you look devastatingly beautiful." Lady Frances appraised me with her keen eyes, and I almost felt a surge of pride in the way I looked. If I had gotten anything out of the friendship we once had, it was her advice on fashion.

But instead of a humble *thank you* rolling off my tongue, I said, "Now I know you are lying. I've spilled wine on myself. The only thing devastating is the condition of my bodice."

Frances smiled sweetly. "It's nothing a little vinegar can't remove."

"Well, I have plenty of that," I said, but I didn't mean the kind that came in a bottle.

She tilted her head at me slightly. "Isobel, I perceive you are angry with me. May we go somewhere and talk?"

I looked back toward the table where my family sat dining. My mother was watching us. She had stood as if she intended to come to my aid, but I started walking again before she could interfere. "I want to remove this stain before my gown is ruined."

"Allow me to assist." Frances followed me without waiting for a response. There were so many things I wanted to say to her, but I wasn't sure which topics were safe to discuss. Should I mention her sending George to my room to harass me? If I did, would she question what happened to him? He had disappeared completely, and no one seemed to question where he had gone. Perhaps it was safer not to mention him at all.

Before I could reach the exit, another person accosted me.

"Lady Isobel, you look ravishing." It was Thomas Overbury. I had not seen him since our talk in the palace gardens at Richmond months ago. Not that I had missed talking with him. He always made me feel uneasy. I was already feeling out of sorts, between my conversation with Robert and my run in with Lady Frances. I really didn't want to speak to him. But seeing Overbury standing here with his crimson stained cheeks to match his bloodshot eyes, he looked overly agitated. Not to mention, it appeared as though someone had tied his collar too tight. It made his dark, curly hair puff out on top of his head, and it made me want to laugh.

"Sir Thomas," I managed, keeping my composure. "I would love to chat, but I'm afraid Lady Frances has gotten to me first. Perhaps some other time?" I motioned behind me to where I assumed Frances stood waiting. A look of pure dread overtook his face until he glanced behind me, and his countenance cleared.

"She is speaking to the Duchess of Bouillon. It appears you are free after all." He grabbed a glass of wine from a passing tray and took a small sip. "Shall we?" Motioning with his free hand, he directed me out the nearest door and into a dark corridor.

"Sir Thomas, I really must see to this stain." I tried to extricate myself from a conversation with him, but he was having none of it.

"Forgive me for interrupting your evening, but I was hoping to ask for your assistance. I am seeking some legal counsel."

Amusement lifted my brow. "That is not my specialty, Sir Thomas. You need to speak to my father. He's the advocate."

One side of his mouth quirked up. "Indeed. That is exactly whom I wished to speak with. Could you arrange a meeting with him for me? As a favor?"

A favor? We were no more than passing acquaintances. Why would he ask me for a favor?

"My father is a busy man. And he doesn't take private cases anymore. He only deals with legal issues involving the crown."

Overbury's shoulders slumped. "No, of course. It was rather presumptuous of me to ask."

Devil take him. Why did he have to look so forlorn? I felt like I had just strangled a kitten. Knowing I would probably regret my decision to help, I asked, "What is it you need legal advice about?"

"I'd rather not say. It is a private matter, you see." He took another sip of wine and leveled me with a look that said, *it's too complicated for your woman's brain.* I really disliked this man, so it made no difference to me.

"Well, don't let me keep you," I said turning to indicate I was finished speaking with him. If he couldn't deign to tell me the problem, why would I bother my father with his issue?

He laughed a light, tinkling sound. "Forgive me, my lady. I am used to the king's court where everything you say and do is scrutinized and held against you."

What made him think I wouldn't do the same?

I was getting bored with this conversation. I glanced down and picked an imaginary speck of lint from my dress.

"My issue," he unfortunately continued, "is I have been offered an ambassadorship to Russia."

"Congratulations, that's wonderful."

"No, it is not. I do not wish to go. But I fear my refusal has solicited the king's ire. There have been whispers that if I do not relent, I will be forced to see reason with a little trip to the Tower of London."

"It doesn't take a law degree to realize it is not wise to refuse the king."

"The king cannot force me to leave my home. That would be exile. And I've done nothing wrong."

"Oh, I think the king could force you to do anything he wanted. But again, I'm not an advocate, so I really wouldn't know." I turned away from Overbury ready to make my escape. But it wouldn't hurt for me to at least speak with my father about his problem, so I said, "I'll ask Lord Stratford to call upon you, if he has the time."

I took one step away before Overbury hurriedly said, "Have you heard the rumors of poisoning?"

I sighed heavily. We had already discussed this once. If he continued to snoop, how close would he get to the truth? "Have you forgotten? We spoke of the poisoning of the maids last October, Sir Thomas."

"Not *that* poisoning," he purred, then took another sip of wine before looking over his shoulder to see if we were being watched.

"I'm afraid I do not understand. To what poisoning are you referring?"

"The poisoning of the prince."

I felt like my head had suddenly been shoved inside a bell tower, and someone was jerking on the ropes. Swinging from them, in fact. I felt off balance, like I had drunk too much wine and needed to have a lie-down.

"The poisoning of the prince?" I asked, not sure I heard him correctly.

He nodded. "There is a rumor that the prince was poisoned by someone close to the king."

I shook my head. Not true. It couldn't be true. Doctor Mayerne said Henry probably died after swimming in the infected waters of the Thames. Elizabeth had even praised me for not getting into the water that day that he had invited me. "Who knows what sickness you might have ended up with?" she had said through broken sobs. But I had never been certain. People swam in those waters all the time and never got sick, *didn't they?*

"What are you saying, Sir Thomas?" I ran my hand across my forehead, squeezing the spot where right this instant it felt like someone was touching a hot poker to my skull. "Who poisoned Prince Henry?"

He took another look over his shoulder, then leaned closer. "Rumor has it Viscount Rochester and his lover had something to do with it."

Bile, putrid and hot, rose in my throat. I felt the room tilt beneath my feet, and I reached out a hand to steady myself against the wall. Viscount Rochester? He never seemed hostile toward Henry. Why would he want him dead? This all seemed too preposterous. Not to mention, Rochester and Overbury were friends. Him telling this secret seemed suspicious. "Why would you betray Rochester? I thought the viscount was your closest friend."

"I am not sure of our friendship any longer. Lady Frances does not like me. She has turned the viscount against me as well. He seems to have forgotten it is I who helped him prosper. He would be nothing at the king's court without my knowledge and skills."

I tilted my head slightly and studied him. "You do all his work for him?"

"Practically. And he would do well to remember the exchanges I have seen between him and the king. Secret correspondence concerning affairs of the state. I could ruin him just by revealing information I am not supposed to know if I had half a mind to do so."

"Well, I wouldn't brandish that information, if I were you. Besides, it didn't help when you wrote that scathing poem about wives," I laughed weakly. "She took it personal." I spoke of the poem he had written several months before, extolling the virtues of a good wife, and pointing out all the poor qualities of a bad one. Lady Frances fit the bill for an unvirtuous wife perfectly, according to Overbury.

"*The Wife* was some of my best work yet. And holds much truth. I only wanted my friend to see the dire mistake he is making by attaching himself to an already married woman. No good can come of it. Not to mention, the woman is a man-eater."

If he only knew.

"You must be careful, Sir Thomas. You do not want to make an enemy of Lady Frances and the rest of her Howard family. They are extremely powerful." I felt obliged to warn him.

"The countess is the one who should be cautious. She has been seen associating with some disreputable people. Her family will not tolerate her bringing shame upon their family name with her choice of acquaintances."

"Disreputable? Of whom do you speak?"

"A woman by the name of Cunning Mary."

When I looked at him blankly, he explained. "Her real name is Mary Woods, but folks call her Cunning Mary because she is, in fact, cunning. She claims to read palms and tell fortunes. She has a knack for convincing people they are bewitched, then offers to relieve them of the sorcery wrought upon them. She will also help you bewitch whomever you desire for a price."

I felt my blood run cold. "Has she ever tried to bewitch the Earl of Essex?"

Overbury flashed a sickening smile. "Perhaps. Rumor has it, Frances gave Mary a diamond ring that Essex had given her as surety for her services. But the woman returned home to Norwich without fulfilling her end of the bargain. Frances sent a man to retrieve the ring, but it had already been sold."

I eyed him momentarily. "You certainly are free with your knowledge, aren't you? You do not like the countess."

"I loathe her," he said through gritted teeth.

"That still doesn't answer the question, why would you betray the viscount? And more importantly, why would they poison Henry?" I questioned.

Overbury hesitated, as if unsure of what to say next. Then with a slight shrug of his shoulders, he said, "Jealousy perhaps?"

"Jealousy? You're not making any sense. Jealous of what? Of whom?"

He stared at the ceiling, then into his glass. He even dug the toe of his shoe into the crevice between two tiles beneath our feet. The man would not look at me. I seized him by the arms and shook him.

"Jealous of what, Overbury?"

"Of the countess and the prince's affair."

Chapter 32

Banqueting House, Palace of Whitehall, London
February 1613
Isobel

Frances and Henry? Overbury's words left me temporarily speechless as I felt all the color drain from my face. It should not have come as a shock. She was beautiful and from an influential family. And he was—Henry. I was not aware there had ever been any dalliance between them. But Overbury's eagerness to tell his tale did not set right with me. And the apparent delight he displayed in sharing this bit of information had me tasting venom.

I always tried to be the very picture of decorum. Being the daughter of an earl who was not born into the gentry made me feel as if I had something to prove. And being the daughter of a feisty Scotswoman, had me striving to not be seen as a sharp-tongued shrew. But I had loved Henry desperately. And since his passing I found myself becoming even more protective of him and his memory. So, when Overbury basked in the gossip he so churlishly brandished about, I lost my last shred of composure and unleased on him.

"Who told you they were having an affair?" My voice was hard as I took a step closer to him. My eyes felt wild and my heart pounded in indignation. Overbury's mouth fell open at my sharp tone. I was being unreasonable, acting like a jealous wife when I was nothing but a scorned afterthought. But if Frances and Rochester truly did have something to do with Henry's death, I was going to get to the bottom of it.

"I, I—" He was having trouble forming his words now. "I hear rumors, that is all. A-a-and it was a couple of years ago. N-nothing recently. I'm sorry. I don't know it to be fact."

"Then perhaps you shouldn't repeat them as if they are fact," I said with scorn.

"Yes, my lady," he said, chastised.

"More importantly, who told you the prince might have been poisoned?" Once again, he avoided my gaze, looking everywhere but at me. "Who told you?" I repeated, feeling my voice rise in desperation. I took another step closer to him and he took a step back.

"Shh. My lady, please. It will not do to draw attention." He held up his hands as if to calm a feral animal, then he looked past me, his eyes darting to and fro in a nervous vigil.

I had backed him into a corner, and he looked frightened, as if he thought I might hurt him. However, he was correct: it would serve no purpose to draw attention to our conversation. And if I wanted answers I was going to need to be a little more discrete. So, I said nothing more, only stood with my hands propped on my hips like I had seen my mother do when trying to get information out of my youngest brother, Harry.

"Court gossip," he finally said with a strangled voice.

I let out an exasperated breath. "I assumed as much. But who is spreading such tales?"

"I couldn't say," was his only reply. When he shifted on his feet the slightest inkling of guilt niggled at the back of my mind. Overbury wasn't the culprit here, even if I was annoyed that he was so quick to tell what he knew. That was a poor inclination, and if he wasn't careful, he was going to get himself hurt.

I took a deep breath, trying to summon my patience. "Thank you for the information," I said calmly. His eyes were wide as goose eggs as if my calm demeanor frightened him more than my aggressive one. "Seek me out if you should find out more useful information." Then, remembering that Frances didn't take too kindly to gossip about herself, I felt the need to warn him. "And I would be careful, to whom you dispense your gossip. That kind of talk is liable to get you killed."

He nodded his head vigorously, then took another step away from me. He opened his mouth as if to say something, but no words came out, only a fearful mewing. His eyes searched mine, as if he were trying to work out my sincerity. Then he turned and fled the hallway.

What did it matter if Henry and Frances had indeed been in some kind of relationship at some point? I doubted it would have been within the last year, for Frances pawed all over Rochester something terrible. She was completely infatuated with him. But might that explain Henry's behavior toward the viscount on occasion? It was no secret the prince did not care for the viscount. But I always thought that was because the king treated Rochester like one of his sons and doted on him like a fawning schoolboy. If anyone would have been jealous, I would have thought it would have been Henry.

I turned about and strode back into the banqueting hall. Wine stain forgotten; I was thinking about this new information that Overbury had given me. I needed to get closer to Frances. With the princess married now, the two courts would be spending less time with each other. Which meant, I would go wherever Queen Anne led, and Frances would be wherever Rochester was. And he would be wherever King James resided. I would have very little contact with the countess if I didn't find a reason to be in her company.

"Lady Isobel, there you are." Frances called to me when I entered the room once more. She was right where I had left her, talking with the Duchess of Bouillon. The duchess had a knack for picking the gaudiest of gowns and complimenting them with hideous feathers and an overuse of heavy jewelry. Tonight, she looked as if she had put on every piece of jewelry she owned. With layers of pearls and diamonds and rubies, and a heavy dose of gold, I didn't understand how she could even move about the banqueting hall, let alone do it with an air of lightness. She waved at me as I approached her and Lady Frances, and I nodded toward her with a weak smile.

Frances continued, "Her Grace was just telling me about a pretty little sea-faring vessel her husband just christened with her name." She batted her lashes and flashed me a sugary smile. I wondered if she had used these tactics on a young Henry to lure him to her bed. And why was she being so nice to me? Did she honestly think I didn't know who sent George Preston to manhandle me into an agreement to help her? I blinked at her, then shook myself when I realized a response was desired.

"How quaint," I said, matching the countess's sweetness with a tone of my own. When Frances detected my faux sincerity, she cocked her head and studied me.

"Forgive me, Lady Elisabeth." I curtsied to the duchess, realizing I was being rude. "But as you can see, I had a mishap with my wine, and I'm on my way to request help from my mother."

"Nonsense," the countess said. "You requested my help, remember? There is no need to fetch your mother."

"By all means." The duchess waved a bejeweled finger in the air, dismissing us.

Feeling trapped, I turned and walked toward the other side of the banqueting hall. I wanted to speak to Frances, but I needed time to sort my thoughts. Instead, she grabbed my hand and led me down the hall into a little room used for storing linens and other napery. When she closed the door, she turned on me.

"You seem a little irritated. Have I done something to offend you?"

I resisted the urge to laugh outright. Did she honestly think we were still on friendly terms after all that had passed between us? I swallowed down all the biting words I wanted to say. I needed to maintain my composure, no matter how much I wanted to ruin her. Yet, this might be my only opportunity to get the truth out of her. I took a deep breath, willing my voice not to shake. "Did you poison the prince?"

She stared at me. "What?"

My stomach was tied into a million knots. My hands were also shaking, but I took another breath, trying to calm my heightened nerves. "Did you poison," I said slowly, as if she were a child, "or were you involved in the poisoning of the prince?"

Her eyes narrowed into daggers. "You and I both know Doctor Mayerne said it was bad miasma from swimming in the river."

"And you and I also know that poison is sometimes hard to detect. The doctor wouldn't look for signs of poisoning unless he had reason to believe the patient was poisoned." I stared back at her, daring her to contradict me.

"Well, the doctor evidently didn't think there was a reason to believe the prince would be poisoned. Besides, I don't know why you would think I had anything to do with it."

I gaped at her. "Oh, please. We both know you are capable of poisoning someone. I just never thought you would stoop so low as to harm the most treasured of princes." My voice caught, and I bit my bottom lip to keep it from trembling. I would not cry in front of this woman.

"I know how much you cared for Henry," she said almost kindly, and I quailed at the nicety in her tone. "And rightly so. There will never be a prince as chivalrous as he. But I had no reason to kill the prince. So, *if* he was poisoned, I had nothing to do with it."

I wanted so badly to ask her what, if anything, he had been to her. But I couldn't bring myself to ask about their relationship. I didn't know what I would do with that information if I had it.

I didn't speak until I was sure I had full composure. When I felt my resolve strengthened, I said, "You speak polite words. But I don't believe you. If anyone is a master of secrets, it's you."

Her back stiffened, and she lifted her chin. "I am not the only one with secrets here, Lady Isobel. What happened to George Preston?"

My stomach tightened, and I felt all my blood rushing to my ears. There is no way she could know I stabbed George Preston in the neck, and Robert hid his body. Unless Robert had been seen. He was a master thief, so I doubted it, but I couldn't be sure. The only thing I could do was feign ignorance.

I schooled my expression. "George Preston? Is he that young man who came to court to write poetry or some such endeavor?"

Her eyes stripped me bare. "You know full well who George Preston is. Rumor has it, he was seen entering your rooms very late on the night he disappeared. Never to be heard from again."

Lies. It was late, and he was sent to do me harm. I find it hard to believe he allowed himself to be seen sneaking into my chambers.

I chortled. "Why are you concerned with who may or may not be entering my chambers?" I knew Frances had sent George. He told me so outright. I don't know why we played this cat and mouse game, as if we were trying to get a feel for what the other person knew. I would not take the bait. "I wish I could spread my favors about like *some* women do." I sneered the word *some* in hopes she would take the insinuation. "But alas, my heart belonged to Henry, so whatever someone claims to have seen, George stealing into my chambers for a midnight rendezvous was not one of them." That part was true, at least.

Frances's eyes flared as her lips pulled together in a tight cinch. With a cold tone she said, "I would be careful where you toss your insults, Isobel. Have you forgotten who my family is?"

What I said was foolish. Her family's noble lineage went back much further than my father's courtesy title. They were a powerful and dangerous family. But I couldn't seem to stop talking. "Are you threatening me now? Will you poison me like you did those maids? Like you did Henry?"

"For the love of all that is holy!" she burst out. "I did not poison Henry." She ran a hand across her forehead as if her head ached. Letting out a sigh, she said, "Henry was a light in a dark place. I would never hurt him." Her voice sounded wan, as if she were trying not to cry. Once again, I was reminded that they may have been something to one another at one time. Perhaps the soft feelings were still there. And that made me even more determined to be her downfall.

"What about the viscount? Would he have just cause to poison him?"

She stopped rubbing her forehead and pulled her eyes to mine. "Don't drag my viscount into this mess."

Her viscount. She would confess nothing that might endanger her precious viscount. I needed to find another way to get information. The fact remained: if she hadn't used her poison to harm Henry, there was someone else she was planning to poison.

"Now if you're finished throwing accusations around, I've been wanting to speak with you." She pulled a small, folded piece of foolscap from her sleeve. "I've taken the liberty of making a quick list of things that will be required of you for the physical examination."

My heart began to pound violently, and a wave of nausea swept over me. "I never said I would help you. I suggest you look for another naïve maiden because I am finished being your blindly devoted sycophant."

The countess's eyes practically sparkled. "Have you forgotten you are obligated to me?" I had not. In fact, I had not ceased to dwell on it. "We've gone over this before, Isobel. Quite frankly, your resistance is getting tiresome." I opened my mouth with a retort, but suddenly a thought hit me. As appalling as the proposition was, perhaps I could use it as an opportunity to get my satchel back. One final word from Frances helped me make up my mind. "I would hate for someone else to get hurt simply because you are being stubborn."

Was that a threat toward me? Toward my family? "Well, I have a headstrong mother to thank for my stubbornness, or have you forgotten?" I stood up a little straighter, feeling my confidence in my freshly formed plan taking root. "How about we strike a bargain? If you agree to return my velvet bag, I'll help you out of your little predicament." Come to think of it, I rather enjoyed the thought of holding her future in my hands.

Frances's eyes flared. "Is that all it will take?" She chuckled softly. "Well, of course you can have your satchel back. I have no need for it." She reached out and laid a hand on my arm. It would have been a friendly gesture if it wasn't laced with cloying words. "I am so pleased we can work this out, friend to friend."

I resisted the urge to curl my lip at her. *Oh, make no mistake. We are not friends. You killed that friendship the day you decided to make me an unwilling participant in your murderous plans.* I bit my tongue to stay the words. I would have to use a different tactic with the countess, to get what I wanted. Instead, I said, "Send me the particulars and make sure no one ever finds out it is me in disguise." I opened the door to leave and came face to face with my mother.

Her face blanched as though she thought I was carrying out some clandestine meeting in the napery closet. But when she saw the countess behind me, her face shifted, and her eyes narrowed into suspicious slits.

"I was just looking for ye. Is everything all right?" She blocked my exit from the closet, trapping Frances and me in her reproving glare.

"Lady Stratford," Frances said, stepping around me and into my mother's line of view. "How nice of you to be concerned for Lady Isobel's well-being. It seems she has spilled wine down the front of her gown. I'm afraid I'm no help with such menial tasks. Perhaps *you* could assist her?"

I felt the sting of Frances's insult toward her and waited for my mother to sever her with her sharp tongue. But as the countess stepped around her, my mother remained silent. Frances turned back to me before she walked away. "We'll talk again soon," she said ambiguously, then departed.

We watched her walk away, and I was filled with a mixture of emotions. I almost wanted to see my mother lay the countess out with her quick wit. "I'm surprised you didn't put her in her place," I said, disappointed.

"Some people aren't worth the effort. Besides, I get the feeling that woman is up to no good, and I don't want to endanger ye by engaging in a battle of clever words. I told ye, I don't trust the woman, and neither should ye." She paused for a moment, studying me. "But it sounds like ye might have already discovered that. I don't hear the admiration for her in your voice anymore. And there seems to be tension in the air that was there even before that woman tossed her insult at me. What were ye two talking about?"

My mother's perception was arcane. I remembered her telling me once that her own mother had been arrested, having been falsely accused of being a witch before my father had helped obtain her release. If it were not for my father's sense of moral astuteness, I might have been suspicious of my own mother working some kind of magic, for she had a keen sense of people and situations that the average person did not possess. I suddenly found myself wanting more than anything to tell her about the poison and the predicament I had gotten myself into. But when I thought of the disappointment I was sure to cause her, I just couldn't bring myself to tell her. I couldn't confess how foolish I had been.

"We were speaking of the prince," I said instead. It wasn't the full truth, but at least I didn't feel like I was telling my mother an outright lie.

Mother watched me for another moment, and I wondered if she could sense that I wasn't being completely truthful. But instead, her eyes softened, and she took my hands in hers. "Isobel, I hope ye know that ye can always come talk to me. I remember what it was like to be young and in love, even if I have not suffered the tragedy that ye have. I'm a good listener." She squeezed my hands and gave me a small smile. I felt the tears threatening to spill from my eyes and I blinked hard to stay them. We may not have always seen eye to eye, but I knew she loved me and only wanted what was best for me. "And if ye are ever in trouble," she paused again, as if considering her words, "ye can tell me that too."

I pulled my hands from hers and clenched my skirts instead. "Thank you, Mother. I appreciate your concern. Truly." I looked down at my dress and the wine stain that was probably already set and now might never come out. "I think I'll go see if Betsy can save my dress. She can work miracles, but I'm not sure there is any hope left for this stain." I leaned in and gave my mother a peck on the cheek. Her soft skin and the smell of heather that seemed to be a natural part of her, filled me with nostalgic memories of happier times between us. "I love you,' I said, working down the knot that seemed to be lodged in my throat.

"I love ye too," she said, brushing my cheek gently with her palm. I took a deep breath and curtseyed to her out of politeness, then went to find Betsy to see about my gown.

Chapter 33

Palace of Whitehall, London
February 1613
Robert

I congratulated the bride and groom then made my departure. I couldnae stand one more minute in that banqueting hall. The flame of a thousand candles flickered against the gold framed mirrors, multiplying the light, and making it even brighter. A cacophony of sounds—music, conversation, and laughter—all competed for space within the crowded hall. Too many scents, too many colors. My senses were overloaded, and I felt the pain of it all pressing down on my brow and ruining the good mood I tried so hard to maintain. None of it set well with the whisky I drank before coming here.

The sight of Isobel, looking so lost amongst the sea of revelers, as if she were barely keeping it together, annoyed me for some reason. I was angry, but I didnae ken with whom. Angry at Henry for dying so young? Angry at Isobel for loving him and looking for all the world like she couldnae go on without him? Angry at myself for allowing both of them to chip away at my soul and take a piece of me with them? It hurt my chest, my heart perhaps, and I rubbed the fleshy part of my palm against my chest where the villainous organ lay beneath.

My foul temper did me no favors. When I came upon a young lord handling a maid a little too roughly and berating her at the end of the corridor, I *might* have overreacted.

I narrowed my eyes at him, approaching on light foot as I watched him twist his hands into the woman's hair, pulling hard and setting her cap askew. The maid looked nothing like Moira, but her innocent face flickered before me as I watched the man abuse this woman, and she whimpered in fear.

I quietly slid my sgian dubh from my boot and crept up behind him. The woman's eyes went wide when she saw me, but I motioned for her silence as I approached. When I was close enough, I forced my hand over his mouth and quickly pressed the edge of my blade against the sweaty flesh of his throat.

"Release the damsel's hair." I said calmly into his ear. He stilled beneath me, making a choking sound as if I had already pushed the blade through his skin. Slowly, he untangled his fingers from her hair and grappled at my hand instead. "Dinnae," I ground out. If he fought me it would just make the kill messier. He dropped his hand and sagged, his legs becoming like willowy reeds beneath him. "Give me one good reason not to slit ye open from gizzard to bollocks."

I had killed Moira's attackers, slit their throats for daring to lay a dirty finger on her unsoiled skin. One of them was the father of the bairn that grew in her belly, but it was hard to say which one. They had both taken their turn with her. It didnae pain me one bit to kill them both. In fact, the pleasure that coursed through my veins with the first pop of flesh beneath my blade, was something I had pondered long after the deed was done.

"Please, please, sir." The plea brought me back to my senses. But it wisnae the man begging for his life, but the woman with whom he had been arguing. "It was my fault, sir. I shouldn't have provoked him."

I looked at the woman, *really* looked at her, for the first time. Her brown hair was mussed from the man's assault and her small, blue-gray eyes were flooded with tears. Her lips quivered as she gawked at me. There was a plum-colored bruise on her left cheek.

"Ye want me to let this blackguard go?" I didnae comprehend what would make a woman beg for the life of her attacker.

"Please," she said again, nodding briskly. "Please don't hurt him." She twisted her skirts in her hands, wringing the fabric into a tight wad.

"Ye deserve better." I stared at her, willing her to allow me the pleasure of ridding the earth of such filth.

"Robert."

The voice behind me gave me pause. The sweet sound of an angel laced with threatening notes of a devil.

The maid drew in a harsh breath. "My lady, please!"

I didnae take my eyes from the damsel but watched her still, challenging her to convince me to let him go.

"Robert, I need to speak to you." Isobel's voice quavered, and I couldnae deny her. Like a well-trained dog, I would always come to heel for her.

I removed my blade from his neck and pushed him forward, away from me.

"How dare you?" He gasped. "Do you know who I am?" He straightened his doublet as he turned back to me. "Why, I ought to have you—"

That was all he got out. I drew back my fist and punched the man right between the eyes. The woman squeaked as the man fell hard, straight back onto the tessellated floor. I stood over him momentarily, wishing I had just killed the cad.

"Go to your room," Isobel said to the maid. "He's going to be quite angry when he awakens, and you don't want to receive the brunt of that anger. I'll find you later, and we will talk about your next course of action."

The maid nodded, wiping a tear from her blue-gray eyes. She then turned and hurried down the corridor, disappearing into the darkness.

Isobel pulled me away before I could do more damage and forced me down the corridor. I pulled my arm from her grip. "I am nay a mount needing bridled and led." The words came out more harshly than I intended.

"You were about to make a grave mistake. I saved your hide once again."

I let out a bark of irritated laughter. Rubbing my tongue against the inside of my cheek, I said, "Well, arnae we full of grandiose opinions of ourselves?" I stepped around her then turned down the corridor that led to my room. "He deserved to die."

"That may be so, but it will not be at your hand."

I opened my chamber door and stared down at her. "Was there something ye wanted to speak to me about?"

She pushed past me and stepped into my room. I glanced down the corridor before following her in and shutting the door. Drawing to the side of my bed as if she kent right where to go, she lit the taper, then lifted it, carrying it with her. "You are in rare form. I don't think I have ever seen you so angry."

"I've a lot on my mind," I said with a growl.

She eyed me with a curious stare then strode to the middle of my bedchamber, looking around the room with fascination. I watched as she walked to the small desk that sat in the corner and peered down at what I had written earlier.

It was a list of tasks that still needed to be completed at Richmond. Tasks that I had given my word to the prince that I would see to. And even though he was gone, I felt an obligation to complete them before I left, for his name's sake.

But the tasks were the furthest thing from my mind. Instead, all I could think about was how bonny Isobel looked tonight in her gown of peacock blue silk. It shimmered when she moved, reflecting a bluish purple at some angles, and greenish blue in others. I hid nae seen her in green—ever—and it looked stunning on her. I wondered if she realized the shifting colors from the angle at which she would look at it.

In the days since Henry's death, we had spoken verra little, and when we had, it had been painfully awkward. She was grieving. But it didnae matter how much I wanted to comfort her, how much I secretly hoped that with Henry gone, she might find some small affection for me. What mattered was that it was terribly obvious her thoughts were filled with nothing but Henry. Rightfully so, I supposed.

"Do you miss him?" she asked, voice hushed as if Henry's name were too holy to utter. I watched as she continued strolling around my chambers, brushing her fingers across the books on the shelf, looking at the paintings on the wall. I had barely noticed any of these trappings the whole of the time I'd been here. I found it gratifying that she took an interest.

My mouth had gone dry, and my throat felt as if I had swallowed rocks. I wanted to ask her what she saw in my chambers that prompted talk of the prince. But she needed no prompting. He was always on her mind, as he was on mine. Wetting my lips I finally answered, "Aye."

She took a deep breath. "His Majesty seems intent on forgetting him completely."

Neither king nor queen could find the fortitude to attend the funeral. They left the wee Prince Charles to be the chief mourner. I shook my head, not understanding that level of grief. However, Their Highnesses hid nae been needed there, for thousands of people trudged out into the snow on that cold December day to pay their respects one last time to the young prince whose life was cut short. The prince who would never be king.

It was all too much. Henry's death, the news of my father's passing while still in exile, Isobel's distancing of herself. The losses weighed heavy on my heart. My horse, Boudica, could have set herself down upon my chest, and it widnae have hurt as badly as these losses.

"How are ye holding up?" I watched intently as she walked around my room, taking in my measly possessions.

"Oh, I cry a lot," she said, so matter-of-factly it sounded as if we were talking about the weather. "At least thrice a day," she laughed dryly, but there was no humor in her words. When she reached the desk again, she glanced down at the foolscap. "How long will it take you to complete these tasks?"

I watched her from my spot by the door. I dared nay come closer, for fear of what I might do. Like the inescapable tow of the tide, I couldnae resist her pull.

"A month, possibly two."

She continued to read my list until she finally looked up at me. "I'm sorry about your father."

My lips parted, surprised at the change of subject. I wanted to thank her, to tell her I appreciated her show of concern. But I feared what might come out. I was coming apart at the seams and on the brink of an unmitigated disaster.

"Tell me about him." She sat down in the chair at my desk, adjusting her blue-green dress around her.

"My father?"

"Yes," she said, pulling another piece of foolscap out and dipping the quill I had been writing with into the pot of ink.

I stiffened. My father wisnae a good man. I had created a mythical version of him in my head during my childhood. One that deemed him worthy of redemption, one that drove me to questionable actions as a man. But after recent discussions with my mother and with the Earl of Stratford, I was beginning to get a clearer picture of him. I would have still done anything for him, but perhaps now I understood some of my actions were just foolish.

She must have sensed my hesitation because Isobel prompted me with another question. "Do you look like him?"

"Aye."

She continued to press pen to paper, spreading the ink across the page. She glanced at me occasionally before making another mark. "So, bronze skin with a dash of golden freckles splashed across your body for good measure. Enough to drive the ladies wild, I suppose." She looked at me again before resuming her task. "Russet locks that glint with flecks of copper when the sun hits them just right. Smokey green eyes, the color of a misty morning on the glen."

"Nay," I said shortly, swallowing hard. Her observations of me were dangerous. Her words drew me taut like a bow string, and with just enough pressure, I was sure to snap. "I get my green eyes from my mother." Her mouth formed a surprised "o", but she didnae respond. "The freckles too, are compliments of my lady mother."

She nodded in confirmation then said, "And the hard-headed determination?"

"My father."

"And was he as annoying as you?" A faint smile curled her lips, and I cocked my head at her.

"Ye dare disrespect my father and speak ill of the dead?" The low timbre in my voice sent a current of heat across the room. There was a time when a comment like that would have had me throwing punches. But I sensed she was trying to gently tease me, perhaps to make me forget my pain.

"No, I only meant to disrespect you." A flash of white teeth shown before a full smile spread across her face. "Forgive me, I meant no disrespect toward your father," she said, before covering her smile.

I finally got up the nerve to draw closer to her and look down at what she was writing. But it wisnae words that she had spread across the page, but a small sketch of my face looking back at me.

"Ye are verra good," I said, picking up the paper and looking at it closer.

"I'm tolerably adept. All ladies are taught some kind of skill to show off at dinner parties and the like. For some reason, my striking wit wasn't good enough. I had to learn to draw."

I handed the paper back to her. She blew on the page to dry the ink, then folded it and tucked it into her bodice. My eyes followed the movement, then drifted back to her face. The heat of my desire for her ignited in that one little motion, and it took all my control not to reach out and touch her. Being alone with her in my private chamber wisnae wise.

"Why are ye here, Isobel?" My voice was husky, as if I hid nae used it in months, and the skin on her arms visibly prickled when I spoke.

She stood and ran her tongue over her lips before speaking. "I heard a rumor. I wanted to share it with you. I didn't know who else to turn to."

I walked around her, just a hair's breadth away, observing the flush of her cheeks, the blonde curls of her hair twisted into knots on top of her head, and the rope of sapphires that bobbed as her chest rapidly rose and fell. The urge to caress her silky skin was so overpowering, I clenched my hands into fists to keep from touching her.

"And what rumor is that?" I stood so close behind her my breath stirred the little wisps of hair on the nape of her neck. A little tremble sent a shiver down her back that could be seen from where I stood.

"There are rumors that the prince was poisoned," she said without turning to look at me.

I froze. I hid nae expected that. Three ticks of the clock passed before I said, "And who is supposed to have done the poisoning?"

"Lady Frances and her lover, Viscount Rochester."

White hot anger shot through me. "Rochester." I growled. This wisnae the first time I heard talk of poison. I wisnae surprised the Countess of Essex might be involved. But Rochester?

"I'm going to kill him." In an instant I strode to the trunk at the foot of my bed and tossed it open. Not only was I angry enough to kill the man, but it saved me from making a grave mistake here in this chamber right this instant. I rummaged around inside until my fingers brushed against the cold metal of my pistol.

"What are you doing?" she said in alarm as she flew to where I knelt on the floor. I pulled the hem of my tunic out from my plaid and ran it over the barrel, bringing it to a shine. "Robert, you can't just kill him in cold blood."

With pistol in hand, I slammed the trunk lid closed. "I am a man without a home, without a father, and without a purpose." *A man without you.* "I have nothing left to lose, Isobel. Other than my father, who could only love me from a distance, Henry was the only man in my life who ever saw any good in me. Now they are both gone, and I am verra angry about that. If Rochester had something to do with that, then I'm going to make sure he pays." I stood and opened the barrel of the gun and blew into the chambers for good measure. It hid nae been shot in months.

She stood, drawing close to me, and laying a hand on my arm. With desperation she said, "This isn't something you can just sweep under the rug. Rochester is the king's favorite. You will surely be hung for such an act."

"I've been itching to plant my fist into something or jab my knife into someone for three months now." I gritted my teeth. "Putting a bullet into someone's head should do the trick."

She stifled a cry. "Robert, please! We don't know for sure. And I did not come here to recruit you to do something foolish. I have a plan."

I eyed her. "What kind of plan?"

"I've decided to help Lady Frances."

"Help her?" I ran a hand through my hair, trying to clear my thoughts. "Help her poison people?"

A grim line flattened her lips. "I am going to be her proxy." She didnae elaborate, but I kent exactly to what she referred. Ice crackled in my veins as I thought about the implications of her decision to pose as Frances for the countess's physical examination. All the whisky I consumed on an empty stomach this evening threatened to toss itself onto my chamber floor.

"'Tis a treacherous game ye play, Isobel."

"I will be a fly on the wall. I will listen, observe, and where possible, learn all her secrets. I will entrap her in her own game. Besides, she has agreed to give my satchel back in return for my assistance."

I fell back a step, feeling as if she had punched me in the gut. I would have much rather seen the whisky make another appearance. "God's teeth," I breathed, as the ramifications of her decision settled in. She still held the candle aloft, and I could see her blue eyes flash with something akin to revenge. "Do ye really think she will just hand over the only evidence that she has that might implicate ye in the murder of the maids?"

"I'm not sure she has thought of that. She said she had no need for it."

"Oh, believe me. She has certainly thought of it."

Isobel let out an exasperated breath. "Either way, I'm afraid I have no other choice. I have to at least try."

I might nay be leaving for Scotland after all. There wisnae a chance I could leave her now. That would be like throwing an innocent sheep to wolves. Well, perhaps not an *innocent* one but a defenseless one nonetheless. I watched her as she meandered across my chamber, biting the tip of her thumb, and flipping through a book that lay on my desk. Before I could stop the words, I found myself saying, "Tell me yer plans." I had a bad feeling about this. But I wisnae about to let her face the countess alone.

Chapter 34

Denmark House, London
April 1613
Isobel

I didn't know how we were going to get away with this.

Frances came to my room the night before, followed by Mistress Turner and two footmen, carrying a trunk with some of her personal items. Items I was to use to pretend to be her.

The biggest concern was my hair. Not many women had hair so blonde that it almost looked white. It was decided Mistress Turner would comb out my waist-length locks and pull them back into a tight chignon at the base of my neck. A linen caul would be tied about my head, covering my hair. I would wear a lace veil to mask my face. It wouldn't hide my blue eyes that were a few shades brighter than Frances's, but it would hide the unmistakable gap between my two front teeth, by which anyone would be able to tell did not belong to Frances.

"The veil is not so remarkable," Mistress Turner had explained. "In circumstances requiring modesty, it is acceptable to cover your face."

"I don't see how it matters, seeing how they will be seeing other, more secret parts of me instead." The words were crass, but I had never submitted to anything so violating, and I was beginning to regret my decision.

Mistress Turner crinkled her nose. "Well, it is necessary. It is the only way to hide your identity."

Frances moved in front of me, inspecting me from head to toe. We were about the same height and size, with the exception that her bosom was slightly larger than mine. But the modest dress she had chosen would cover that fact without someone thinking anything the wiser.

"Shall we practice your voice?" she asked, pulling at my bodice, and making final adjustments. Not that it would matter. We'd have to do this all over again in the morning.

"No," I said, looking at myself in the mirror. "I don't plan on talking."

Mistress Turner fisted her hands on her hips. "And how are you supposed to respond to the doctor's questions if you don't talk?"

"I thought I'd go with the shy, uncomfortable maiden," I said, turning to her. "I'll just nod and point."

She let out a guffaw. "No one would ever believe that."

"Why not? It would be the truth." There was an edge to my words I hoped they felt.

Frances turned her head from me to the other woman slowly. "I'll have you know," she said, pinching an inch of material between her forefinger and thumb, "I too would be very uncomfortable in these circumstances."

Mistress Turner suppressed a smirk, swallowing further comments. "Indeed," she said, pinning the extra material on the dress Frances held between her fingers.

"Isobel might be onto something, Anne," Frances continued. "Maybe you could accompany her and be her voice. Tell the doctor I'm feeling a little under the weather and my throat is sore. I'm trying to rest my voice and don't want to talk."

Horror surged through me. "What if he wants to examine my

throat next?" I squeaked. "This is too much. I refuse to be poked and prodded like an experiment. I should have never..."

"Oh, hush now," Mistress Turner lectured. "Let me take a look at you." She took a step back and observed me. "I think we might actually get away with this." She turned me fully toward the mirror as she fastened the finishing touch on the costume: the lace veil.

I stared at myself, trying to recognize the woman in the mirror. I still felt like Isobel Broune, daughter of the Earl and Countess of Stratford. The almost betrothed of a dead prince. Scheming courtesan of the Stuart court. Broken woman with broken dreams. *And a broken man at my side.* I wasn't sure where the last thought came from, but I took comfort in it. Robert had declared no intentions toward me. But I knew no matter what I attempted, how I failed or succeeded, he would be there, ready to catch me if or when I fell. That was a powerful feeling and one I wasn't entirely sure I deserved.

Frances went into hiding for the day and Mistress Turner led me down the hall to an unused bedchamber on the second floor. We did not speak, for we had already planned everything that would be said and didn't want to risk anyone overhearing me talk. When the door opened and a red-haired man with a predominant brow jutting over dark, sunken eyes greeted us, Mistress Turner took a step back in surprise.

"What are you doing here?" she asked, not entirely warmly. "Where is Doctor Mayerne?"

I recognized the man. He was the same doctor who had tended to Lenora. Doctor Forman. A sickening chill trickled through me. *The doctor who was there when she died.* I planted my feet at the threshold, unwilling or maybe unable to move forward.

Doctor Forman held the door open wider, as if the welcoming gesture would coax me in. "I'm merely here to assist." His voice was warm and soothing, yet it curdled the breakfast in my stomach. "Please, come in."

Mistress Turner put her hand on my shoulder. Gripping my clasped hands, she pushed and pulled me forward. "Come, Lady Frances," she said tightly. "Let's get this over with."

Forman led us behind a dressing screen where I was given instructions to remove my gown and put on the linen chemise provided for me. Mistress Turner assisted me.

"What are we going to do now?" I whispered frantically when we were alone again.

She began to undress me. "Just act natural," she hissed. "He doesn't know you're not the countess. Just don't speak." She barely spoke above a whisper, but her tone indicated she shouted as quietly as she could.

"But he," I paused, realizing what I was about to say included Mistress Turner as well. Were they not ultimately responsible for Lenora's death?

"What?" she whispered.

"Doctor Forman frightens me." I said as she removed my gown.

"Pah! You've nothing to worry about. He's a competent physicker, even if the College of Physicians fought the granting of his license. But his real skill is in reading stars. That's how he's found success."

"Reading stars?" I had never heard of such a thing.

"Yes. He's an astrologer. He can predict a person's future, tell them when their husband will return from his journey, and even tell a woman the best time to conceive a child, based on the map of their stars. He can also predict the best days to have physical examinations performed such as bloodletting and the like." She dropped the chemise over my head and adjusted it.

"Is that how Lady Frances knows him? Did he read her stars?"

Mistress Turner stood up straight, her hand paused on my chemise. She had a strange expression on her face, and I wondered if I had gone too far with my questioning. I wanted to glean as much information from this situation as I could. Since Forman was there when Lenora died, perhaps there was some important connection there.

"Lady Frances met Doctor Forman through me. I am," she paused, correcting herself, "I was a client of his."

"Did he read your stars?" I asked.

Her face turned a bright shade of red. "Quit asking so many questions," she whisper-shouted. I was sure she could be heard from the other room.

"But why is he here?" I risked once more. "I thought the king's physician, Doctor Mayerne, was performing the exam."

She motioned for me to sit on the nearby stool so she could remove my shoes. "Perhaps Lady Frances requested him. She trusts him. I just wish she would have warned us."

Before stepping out from the screen, Mistress Turner adjusted my veil and caul. "Leave the talking to me," she reminded me, though I needed no reminding.

Doctor Forman entered the room a few moments later. "Ah, I see you are ready, my lady. He led me to a bed on the other side of the room and indicated for me to lie down. It sat beside a wide window from which the dark red curtains had been pulled back. Early spring sunlight shone down, casting lead-lined shadows across the floor and the counterpane on the bed.

Panic seized me at the sight of the exposure, and I motioned nervously toward the window. Mistress Turner caught on immediately and said to Doctor Forman, "Surely, we will draw the curtains for such a delicate examination."

Doctor Forman stood at a table next to the bed, wiping off a long, metal instrument. I do believe my heart stopped at the sight of it and the thought of what the instrument could possibly be used for.

"Yes, well, they will need as much sunlight as possible to see—"

A coughing fit seized me. Not a real one, per se, but the kind born out of mortification. I rushed to a nearby pitcher and poured a glass of water. Not stopping to think whether the water had been purified for drinking or was merely there for washing, I slurped the cool liquid down and then poured another glass. I had to stop myself from drinking more by reminding myself that consuming too much water would lead to another embarrassing situation altogether.

"Are you all right, Lady Frances?" Forman drew up beside me, slipping a hand under my elbow.

I sputtered some more until Mistress Turner came to my rescue. "She has not been feeling well, Doctor. She's had a tickle in her throat for several days, then woke up this morning with her voice completely gone."

"Oh dear," the doctor said. "Perhaps I should take a look."

I shook my head violently, then shrunk away from him. "No," I hissed in the loudest whisper possible.

Mistress Turner spoke up again. "Doctor, my lady is nervous about this examination and just wants to get it over with. Will Doctor Mayerne be here soon?"

Forman ran a hand over his thick beard. "Doctor Mayerne will not be performing the examination."

Mistress Turner and I exchanged glances. With an almost horrified expression on her face Mistress Turner asked, "Are *you* to perform the examination?"

The doctor chuckled. "No. Archbishop Abbot has demanded a panel of women do the examination."

Mistress Turner nodded sagely, and I felt something in my belly ease a little. I would much prefer a woman do the exam. But a panel?

"And who, pray tell, will be on this panel? You know my mistress has enemies. Are there any women who might be biased?" she asked with a scathing tone.

Forman gaped, his eyes wide in innocence. "I am not privy to the names of the ladies. All I can tell you is it is a panel of six, four gentlewomen and two midwives."

By God and Saint George! How many people did it take to determine whether a woman was a virgin? And how exactly were they supposed to determine that anyway? A sweat broke out on my forehead and my hands became clammy as I thought about the execution of this examination. Under normal circumstances, I would have wanted my mother with me during such an ordeal. What would the Countess of

Stratford think if she could see me now or knew what I had gotten myself into?

Doctor Forman adjusted the piece of linen that had been laid across the bed and held out a hand to assist me as I climbed upon the four-poster bed. My heart was pounding now, and I wondered if it was too late to ask for a chamber pot to relieve myself one more time. I really had not thought this through. I tried to focus on the bed coverings. Thick, golden curtains that hung like festoons were draped from post to post. Small, burgundy tassels had been sewn along the hem and one of them hung askew, as if someone had pulled on it too hard. To distract myself, I counted fifty tassels on the right side alone, noting two more had gone missing, having been pulled completely off. I squirmed on my spot upon the bed and adjusted myself once more. It felt like I was lying on a carpet of ants the way my skin was crawling from nerves. I tried to settle in, preparing to begin my count of tassels on the other side of the bed curtains, when Forman leaned toward me and whispered in my ear.

"Franklin said to tell you he has a good quantity of ruby sulfur on hand, but the corrosive sublimate will need to be sent for. The cantharides can be obtained from Mistress Woods."

My mind was so preoccupied with my imminent ordeal his words almost didn't compute. He spoke of rubies or something. I opened my mouth to ask him to repeat himself but luckily remembered I wasn't who he thought I was. I stared at him blankly and he must have thought I had forgotten a previous conversation with him for he said, "James Franklin, the apothecary from Yorkshire. Shall I have him prepare the correct doses?"

I nodded dumbly. I had no idea what I was agreeing to but granted permission, nonetheless. At least he had given me something to put my mind upon other than the uncomfortable physical examination. A useful tool to wield as I watched the women who would be overseeing the examination file quietly into the room.

Mistress Turner's eyes caught on Doctor Forman. She watched us with a suspicious eye, until Forman stepped away and she pounced.

"What did he say to you?"

I was still processing his words. I couldn't remember the first two items, but I caught *cantharides* and now I remembered where I had heard the word. The ground Spanish fly, the scintillating green, *poisonous* powder Mother had shown me.

I shook my head. "Nothing of importance," I stammered out in a whisper. "He's just trying to calm my nerves." I was not about to share any information with her that I might use against Frances. Excitement twittered in my belly like butterflies. This was exactly the kind of information I had hoped to happen upon during this ordeal. One of the only reasons I had agreed to this ridiculous farce. That, and to get my satchel back.

Mistress Turner watched me with curious eyes. I wasn't sure she believed the lie I told her, but I didn't care. Once this ordeal was over, I would have no more dealings with her or her mistress.

"Shall we begin?" A woman, whom I judged to be one of the midwives, based on her state of dress, peered down at me, awaiting my answer.

I nodded my head without speaking, then squeezed my eyes shut, bracing myself for my most mortifying experience yet.

Chapter 35

Chadwyck House, London
September 1613
Isobel

"Thomas Overbury is dead."

The announcement came from a missive sent to my father as our family sat at supper at Chadwyck House. We were celebrating my mother's birthday, and Father had just returned from an extended trip to Edinburgh on business.

"That man set his star too high. He was not careful, and now he has burned out before he had a chance to shine his brightest." It was my grandfather, Thomas, who spoke. At seventy-seven years of age, my grandfather was a wise man that had insight into many things. He had not lived at court since the days of Queen Mary in Scotland, but he was well-versed in courtly intrigue, having worked so closely to the Scottish queen.

The bite of pheasant I was chewing seemed to lodge in my throat and I worked to get it down. "How did he die, Father?" I dared to ask, as memories of my last conversation with Overbury came flooding back.

My father continued to read the missive, skimming the contents for information. "It seems the suspected cause is poisoning."

I felt the bottom fall out of my stomach. The combination of ingredients that Doctor Forman had spoken to me about, that I had given approval for when he thought I was Frances. Had those poisons been meant for Overbury? I set my spoon down, unable to take another bite. Ever since Frances had approached me about getting more poison for her, I had been confident that she had been planning on poisoning someone else. My first thought was always Essex. She hated him. And even though I knew it would be very dangerous for her to attempt it, I was almost sure that it was her husband she had her eye on. But Overbury was her enemy as well, and he had been so worried about his own safety.

"I heard he had a falling out with his good friend, the Viscount Rochester," Tom said with his mouth full of food.

"Don't talk with your mouth full," I snapped at Tom. His words confirmed my growing suspicions which magnified my unease. I might have felt more guilty for the lecture, if our mother hadn't nodded her agreement at my scolding.

"Yes, Mother Isobel," he said, then shoveled another bite of food into his mouth and showed it to me.

"How old are we?" I shot back, pinning him with my most hateful glare.

"My children, who are children no longer," my mother said in her familiar warning tone. "Let's not bicker at the table. Isobel, be nice. Tom, chew with your mouth closed." I stuck my tongue out at my brother, and he flashed another bite of food at me before swallowing it with a laugh. This was the best part of being at home, not having to worry about courtly table manners and arguing with my siblings.

"I'm not sure if it was his falling out with Rochester, or the ire of the king that led to his arrest," I said, finally spooning a bite of mushroom into my mouth. I hoped it was the latter.

Tom's eyes danced as he leaned over the table. "What have you heard, Issy? You probably know all the court gossip."

"He told me at Princess Elizabeth's wedding feast he had made the king angry by not accepting a position as ambassador to Russia the king had offered him." Everyone became eerily quiet. I flitted a look around the table, trying to gauge the source of silence. "What?" I asked before swallowing the mushroom and shooting a glance at Tom to see if he noticed me talking with my mouth full.

My father spoke up. "Are you insinuating the king had Overbury arrested for simply refusing to go to Russia as ambassador?"

"I'm not insinuating anything. I'm simply telling you what Overbury told me at the feast." I pushed a carrot around on my plate. "He wanted me to speak with you, Father. He said he needed some legal advice. But you were away in Edinburgh for so long it slipped my mind." My food churned in my stomach. I hoped my forgetfulness had not caused the death of Overbury. As much as I didn't like the man, I wished him no ill will.

Father frowned. "It is illegal for the king to force someone into exile who has not broken the law." He set his utensil down and wiped his mouth.

"It wasn't exile, William," Mother pointed out. "It was a job offer."

"It might as well be exile," Will said dryly. "Who would want to live *there?*"

"I'd live there!" chimed in my little brother. "I want to be a Tsar!" he shouted, holding up his spoon like a sword and pointing it at Mary. She giggled before grabbing her own spoon and knocking it against Harry's in a mock sword fight.

"Children!" Mother said again, running a hand across her forehead. "Not at the table." Turning to my father, she asked, "Do you think the king had Overbury arrested with the intent to kill him? He was in the Tower for quite a long while."

"Arrests like Overbury's usually only last a few days. A week or two at the most. Just enough to scare the victim into obedience." Father mused. "It is suspicious that he was kept in the Tower for so long and has now died. He was a young, healthy man from all appearances."

"I wouldn't put it past the king to use some sinister means, if he didn't have a legal case against the man," Grandfather put in. He never liked King James. It had something to do with James's lack of effort to save his own mother when the English queen had ordered her execution.

I wanted to share what I knew about the countess and the poison she had obtained. I was almost positive Frances had something to do with Overbury's murder. Mother and Father would know what to do with that information. But if I told them, I would be forced to confess my own involvement with Frances and the poisoning of the maids. However, Father might be able to obtain justice for Overbury with the knowledge I held.

And what if Overbury had misconstrued my warning about spreading gossip? What if he thought I was threatening him, and he told someone? What if someone overheard our conversation and thought I was threatening him? I was torn.

While I vacillated about what to do, a footman entered with a message for Father, and bent low to whisper in his ear. "Direct him to a guest room, Wells, and invite him to take a bite to eat with us if he would like."

The footman bowed and departed. "Who is here, Father?" Tom inquired.

"Robert Stewart," he answered. "I requested his expertise on horses. I want to breed Honeycomb again."

"Father!" I cried. "Leave her be, it has only been a few months since she gave birth to Sticks." My concern for Honeycomb was only a partial perturbation. It was born more from a desire to cover my growing anticipation at seeing Robert again.

"His name is not *Sticks*," Tom said with disgust. "Just because his legs are as skinny as twigs, doesn't mean you can change his name, Issy. He is the progeny of a great steed," he gloated.

"But which steed, that is the question," Will said cleverly.

Tom guffawed. "Honeycomb is a loose mare."

"A common doxy," Will tossed in. Both of my older brothers laughed.

"Boys," Mother groaned. "Little ears at the table." She motioned with her chin at Harry and Mary who sat wide-eyed, listening to the conversation, food and spoon swords forgotten.

When Robert entered the dining room a few minutes later, I couldn't help but watch him as he crossed the room and bowed to my father, then took my mother's hand and planted a soft kiss atop it. "Yer Grace."

He looked stunning. His russet hair seemed to beam in the sunlight that shone through the windows. It fell in waves and brushed his broad shoulders in a soft sweep. A black leather jerkin stretched tightly across his expanse of chest and a tunic left unbuttoned at the neck where a scatter of freckles peeped out. The look was completed with the red and black plaid wrapped around his waist that I had seen him wear on many occasions. It brushed the top of his knees, hanging slightly lower in the back and his black leather boots practically met the hemline of his kilt. The look was not new to him. I had seen it many times on him. The difference was today it didn't irritate me. I rather enjoyed the image he struck.

"You're gawking," Will whispered, leaning into me. I snapped my mouth closed and gave him a look that said *mind your own business.*

Mother motioned for him to have a seat.

"What brings you to Chadwyck, Robert?" Tom asked. "It's good to see you here again after such a lengthy hiatus."

"Yer mother and I had a bet that yer father would form a sudden interest in horse breeding after he saw the fine foal Honeycomb birthed. I tried to give His Grace the benefit of the doubt, but yer mother was sure he would take up the pursuit. He was so aggravated about the news when I first told him the mare was increasing that I thought that was my surety. Now I owe yer mother two crowns."

"Two crowns!" Tom exclaimed. "Never bet against my mother, Robert. She rarely loses."

"I have learned my lesson," he said, taking a seat near me at the end of the table.

"It is nice to know I can still provide my wife such amusing enter-tainments," Father said wryly.

"Oh, my love, ye have no idea," Mother cooed, laying her hand atop his. His eyes flew toward hers, a smile kicking up the corners of his mouth.

"God's teeth," Tom cursed, pouring himself some more wine. "Not at the table, please." Tom loved it when he could turn the tables on Mother's chastisements.

"Language, Tom," Father chided.

Tom's eyes shifted to our younger siblings across the table, then he said, "Sorry, sir." Turning to Robert who was dishing some meat onto his plate, he said, "Our parents are too amorous."

"Is there such a thing?" Robert quipped, flicking me an undis-cernible glance.

"It is when it is our parents. Ack," Tom said, visibly shivering.

"On that note," Grandfather said, scooting his chair away from the table. "I think I shall retire." He stood shakily to protests from all around the table.

"Not before the birthday cake, Grandpoppy!" Mary squealed.

"What? Why didn't you say so?" Grandfather teased. "You should have served that first. I am an old man. You never know when I won't live long enough to have dessert."

"Grandpoppy!" Mary cried again. "Don't say such things!" He winked at me, then made to sit again, but couldn't get his legs to cooperate.

Robert stood quickly. "Allow me, sir," he said, taking my grandfa-ther's arm and pushing the chair a little more to easily buckle his knees.

"Thank you, young man," Grandfather's labored breathing forced out. "I don't care what Issy says, you are a good man."

My face burned under the course of his teasing. "I have never said an ill word against you."

"Not to our grandfather, at least," Tom tossed at him, teasing.

"I havenae a doubt," Robert said, his voice coming out with the husky sound of a grizzly bear. I thought he was irritated until he looked at me once again and winked. My heart skipped a beat, and I bit my bottom lip to keep a smile at bay. Since when did Robert's smoldering eyes make my insides turn to jelly?

After Grandfather left the table, each member of the supper party went their separate ways. I lingered around the table, hoping Robert felt the pull to be as near to me and I was to him. I realized I should be more concerned over the death of Overbury. I should be concerned that it appeared Lady Frances had eliminated another enemy. And I should be worried I could be her next victim, especially if the divorce she so desperately wanted from Essex never gets granted. She could easily blame me for her plan going awry. But I was distracted by Robert's presence throughout supper, and I wanted to speak to him of all these concerns. Also, if I was completely honest, I wanted to kiss him again.

As he spoke with Father about horses, I watched his every move. The way he brought his spoon to his lips. The way he tore the meat of the pheasant apart with his teeth. The way he wiped the corner of his mouth with this thumb. It was pathetic how I lusted after him, after his body, his lips, his hands. My face burned as I thought about the times we had kissed and the times he had put his hands on me. I had loved the prince, but I had never felt the desire between us like I felt with Robert. The Scot was like a magnet, and I was his polar opposite. We were as different as night and day and he should have repelled me, but instead I felt the pull of his attraction and I couldn't seem to resist.

"I have something for ye," he said reaching into his pocket after everyone was gone. My pulse raced. If he had something for me, that meant he had been thinking of me while we were apart.

I watched as he pulled out a small damask bag. He untied the string and dumped the contents into his hand. I sucked in a breath, covering my mouth with my hands.

"My necklace," I said with awe, reaching to remove the necklace I currently wore.

He unfastened the clasp on the chain and moved behind me. A shiver went through me as his fingers brushed lightly against the back of my neck. It wasn't until he stepped away that I could breathe again. I reached up and clasped the necklace, wrapping my fingers around the silver thistle. It seemed like so long ago that he had pulled it from my neck. It felt comforting to hold it in my hand again.

"I'm sorry it took so long to get it back to ye. I repaired the chain, then gave it to Prince Henry and asked him to make sure ye got it back. But then—"

He broke off his sentence, unable to finish. *But then Henry died.* I reached out a hand and laid it atop his. I wanted to comfort him. I understood the hurt all too well.

He swiped the back of his wrist across his eyes. The sight of this man, being moved to tears by his love for his prince, done funny things to my insides. It was the most attractive thing I had ever seen.

He drew in a deep breath. "The necklace, along with all the prince's other effects, has been under strict watch since Henry's passing. I had to leap through fire to prove it didnae belong to the prince or the crown."

"How did you prove that?" I asked, tugging softly on the amethyst, and drawing it gently along the chain. It made a rigid noise as it moved along the silver rope.

"I had to write to Elizabeth and ask her to confirm the necklace belonged to ye. As ye can imagine, it took months."

"Thank you," I said softly. "It means a lot to me."

I picked at a piece of cake, and he nursed a glass of fine port. "Ye never wrote to tell me how the physical examination went," he said, changing the subject. Twisting the stem of his cup between his fingers, he watched me as I plucked a cake crumb from my plate and dabbed it on the tip of my tongue.

"It was horrendous," I said, too embarrassed to talk about the intimate details. "But I did get some useful information from it."

"So, it was worth it?" His eyes seemed to darken as he followed each movement of my hand to my mouth. I licked a smudge of cream from my thumb soliciting a choking sound from his direction.

I lowered my voice, though there wasn't anyone in Chadwyck House whom I did not trust, my family and staff alike. "Frances is getting poison now from an apothecary from Yorkshire named James Franklin. I'm not sure what the poison is for, but she ordered more for some special use. Or, I should say, I ordered more. Doctor Forman asked me if he should have this Franklin fellow prepare the doses. He thought I was Frances, of course, for that was the plan. I was to pose as her, and it went off without a hitch."

"Ye gave the order for more poison?" His right brow lifted, and I felt a twinge of guilt.

"It couldn't be helped," I said defensively. "I couldn't very well speak aloud and tell him no." I stabbed the air with my spoon. "She has also obtained poison from a woman named Mistress Woods. I think this is Mary Woods, the woman Thomas Overbury spoke to me about. I'm thinking she is the person who might have helped Frances bewitch the Earl of Essex, for the woman is known for such trickery. Overbury told me Frances's family would not tolerate her associating with a woman of such ill repute. Their family's reputation would be in grave danger."

"Aye," he said, watching my mouth as I took another bite of cake. "And did she give ye the satchel back?"

I frowned at the thought. "No. And I have written to her several times about it. I haven't heard from her since the exam. Her divorce has still not been granted. I wondered if she was holding me responsible for the delay."

"Perhaps," Robert said as he shifted in his seat.

I dipped the utensil into my cake once more and stuck the spoon in my mouth, licking the sticky cake and cream topping from the edges. Robert watched me like a starving man in prison. "Would you like a bite?" I teased, offering a spoonful of cake, but he pressed his lips together and swallowed hard, his Adam's apple bobbing in tandem.

"God's teeth, Isobel, just eat the damnable cake and be done with it."

I scowled. "I'm getting full. Help me." I pushed my bottom lip out in a pout as I stuck the spoon in front of his lips, urging him to open his mouth. He shook his head, and I continued to taunt him, touching the tip of the spoon to the bow of his lip. He tried to move his head, but I just kept at it, laughing as he tried to avoid the spoon. When he finally parted his lips to speak, I shoved the utensil in and practically choked him. Cream was smeared across his lip and onto his chin.

"I'm so sorry!" I said, unable to control my laughter. "You shouldn't have moved. Let me help clean it up."

I swiped my thumb across his chin first, clearing away the cream. When I licked the tip of my thumb, Robert's eyes flared, watching my every move. I reached to wipe the remaining cream from his lip, and he suddenly seized my wrist, guiding my thumb into his mouth and licking the cream clean off.

I felt my insides turn to molten lava. Heat suffused my cheeks and neck, sending a tingling sensation to my core. When I choked on my words, Robert offered his own instead.

"Ye are playing a dangerous game, Isobel."

"I ken," I whispered, using his Scottish word and brogue to answer him.

He tugged harder on my wrist, pulling me out of my chair and onto his lap. I straddled him with a knee on each side of his hips and felt the delicious danger of being discovered at any moment. He slammed his lips against mine and the fervency of his tongue swept across my lips.

He released my wrist and laid his hands on my hips. I pushed my hands into his hair, scraping my nails across his scalp and pulling gently on his locks. We kissed, barely able to breathe and when we finally gasped for air, he dragged in a rugged breath. "Issy," he breathed, and I could feel him trembling beneath me. "Ye dinnae ken what ye do to me."

"I imagine it is a little like what you do to me," I said, leaning my forehead against his.

"I think about ye all the time. I think about yer hands on me and my lips on ye. I drive myself crazy with want for ye."

My breath caught on a gasp, and I tilted my head back to take in more air. With my neck exposed, he laid siege to my throat, planting hot kisses down the column of my neck. His teeth grazed my skin and when he nipped at me, I inhaled sharply.

"Don't leave a mark," I said breathily.

"I willnae," he promised as he bit softly on my earlobe. He then trailed his lips across my cheek until his mouth took mine once more.

The warm glow of sunlight in the dining room was quickly fading as the sun sunk below the horizon beyond the knolls. A lavender and honey-kissed sky was transforming, and a blue, serene gloaming was slowly engulfing us.

Robert tucked his hands beneath my legs and lifted me, not breaking our kiss. He deposited me on the table, sweeping aside dishes and cups before pulling away from me. Grabbing a candelabra and finding steel and flint on the mantlepiece, he struck a fire and lit the candles, spilling golden light across the table.

The soft light reflected in his hazy green eyes, and for the first time since I met him, he looked at peace.

"You are happy," I said, not taking my eyes from his.

"Aye. I thought ye hated me."

"I do," I smirked. "I hate the way you look in that ridiculous kilt."

He took a step closer, parting my knees so he could draw closer again. "I love the way yer skirts swish under the sway of yer hips."

I ran my hands up his chest. "And I hate the color of your eyes. They are green."

He chuckled before threading his left hand into my hair and bringing it to rest at the back of my neck. With his right hand he cupped my cheek and his eyes fell to my lips once more. "I love the silvery coils of yer hair that feel like gossamer between my fingertips."

His light touch sent a shiver through me. I continued our little game, trading barb for adulation.

"I hate the coppery freckles on your body that turn your skin to bronze when the sun hits it just right." I fisted his jerkin with both hands and pulled him to me.

"I love the scent of yer skin and the satiny smoothness of it against my palm." He ran a thumb over my bottom lip, pushing the skin against my teeth.

"I hate the way the maids and the ladies-in-waiting look at you like they could eat you alive." I let my own eyes rove over his form, devouring him in one sweep.

The emotion in his eyes intensified and a humorless smile quirked his lips. "Finally, something we can agree on. For I hate the way every courtier within the realm of King James ogles ye and takes their fill of ye anytime ye are in the room. It makes me want to gouge their eyes out."

We stared at each other for a long moment, our chests heaving. When Robert ran his tongue over his bottom lip, a flame ignited beneath my belly spreading an ache through my body that needed quenching. I wiggled closer to the edge of the table and pressed myself against him.

I sighed, and he slowed his touch. "Have ye changed yer mind about me lass?"

I looked up at him from beneath heavy lids. "No," I said, more than a little breathless. "Don't take your hands from me."

"'Tis not what I mean. Every time I touch ye, I lose another wee piece of myself. Ye kiss me, then draw away, putting up a wall and telling yerself that ye dinnae like me. I didnae ken what I ever did to earn yer hatred of me, although I was sure it was well deserved. But I cannae bear it any longer. If ye want me, I will give ye all of me, nothing held back. My heart, my mind, my body, and my soul. But if ye cannae give me the same in return, I will be forced to draw the line here."

"I want you," I said, a little too desperately. Frustration was building inside me the longer he hesitated. When he didn't speak, I softened my voice. "You know all my faults. You've never judged me, never tried to change me, and certainly never betrayed me. You know the real me. Every broken, ugly, messed up part of me."

He tucked a strand of hair behind my ear. "And I love every part of ye. The beautiful and the broken."

His touch sent an exquisite shimmer across my skin. "I want you," I said again in a whisper.

"And I want ye. More than the air I breathe," he whispered back.

He leaned toward me and brushed a chaste kiss across my lips. "But nay here. Nay on yer parents' table where anyone can see."

"I don't care—" I whimpered, but he cut me off with his languorous words.

"When I take ye—and I will take ye, lass—it will be on a bed of down, surrounded by soft candlelight, or in a field of heather with the Scottish breeze blowing yer silvery blonde locks across my skin. Not on some wooden chair or hard table." His desire was still evident in his taut muscles and stiff movements, but he began adjusting his clothing as he took a step back from me. "When we are married, I will never stop worshipping ye."

"Married?" I squeaked, righting my bodice, and putting myself in order as well. On more than one occasion I had allowed myself to imagine a life with Robert. But now that he broached the subject, panic seemed to rear its head. "I wasn't thinking of marriage at the moment." I couldn't hide the astonishment in my voice.

He ran a hand over his face as if trying to get control. "I wisnae thinking of anything but yer body beneath me." He turned away from me and dragged both of his hands through his hair, gripping handfuls of coppery tufts in his fists. "Give me a minute." I watched a vein in his neck pulse in frustration as his back rose and fell under his labored breaths. Several moments passed before he finally turned back to me. "Ye are in grave danger." The burr of his voice sent a ripple of waves across my skin once more. Everything this man did affected me.

"In danger of you?" I teased, but I couldn't ignore the sensation of my nerves suddenly on edge.

He took a swig of wine that he had left on the table, emptying his cup. "Ye have heard what has happened to Overbury?"

My brows drew together in confusion. "Yes, we have just learned of it this evening. Father received a missive about it before you arrived."

"How much do ye ken?"

Now I was a little irritated. I didn't want to talk of Overbury. There were other things I wanted to talk about. I let out a sigh. "Overbury has died, and it is rumored he was poisoned. I suspect Frances had something to do with it." Robert's face was as pale as marble which sent concern coursing through me. "What is it?"

"A young man, an apothecary's apprentice named William Reeve, confessed to having administered a poisonous enema to Overbury. The boy is sick unto death and wanted to clear his conscience. This is what I came here to tell ye. Not to...accost ye like this." He motioned toward me still sitting on the table then dropped his hand to his side, resigned.

I hopped down from the table, anger coursing through me now. "Don't you dare become all high and mighty now, Robert Stewart." My voice grew louder than I intended. "You didn't accost me. I *let* you kiss me, touch me. I have finally opened to you completely, and now you push me away?"

A garbled sound choked from his mouth. "It isnae that." He spat out. "Ye have finally opened yerself to me completely, and now ye are in more danger than ever before. I have already lost two of the most important people in my life. I willnae lose another. Nay when I can do something about it."

I stared at him, my heart breaking. I knew he spoke of his father. And of Henry. The prince who had swept into everybody's lives and made them feel like they were the most important person in the world, then left us all floundering at his death. It almost made me angry all over again. For in the phases of grief I had worked myself through over the course of the last ten months, anger had certainly been a part of my repertoire. It was silly to blame the prince for something he had no control over, of course. But that knowledge didn't keep me from being angry, nonetheless. And now, I had finally reached a point in my grief where just the memories of him, and just the mention of his name, did not bring me to tears. I was ready to move on with my life. Perhaps even think of a life possibly with Robert, though I wasn't sure what that would look like. But I hadn't for a moment thought about how Henry's death might have affected him.

"An apothecary's apprentice," I said, trying to focus on what Robert was saying. I swept a hand across my coiffure to put my hair back in place. "I wonder if he worked for the apothecary that Forman spoke of, James Franklin."

"Perhaps."

I took a deep breath and tried to calm my nerves. "Well, I don't see how anyone can tie this to me." I ran my hands down my waist and smoothed my bodice, then shook out my blue taffeta skirts that had become wrinkled from sitting all evening and—other things.

Robert ran a hand through his hair. "Isobel, there are letters."

"What do you mean?" My voice shook even as I tried to convince myself I was not in any danger.

He reached into his pocket and pulled out a folded piece of parchment that had been sealed with wax at some point. "Hester snuck this out of Mistress Turner's personal effects." He handed it to me, and I unfolded it hastily and began reading.

A sickening coil began to tighten my stomach. I licked my lips, feeling as though my mouth was suddenly as dry as the parchment I held in my hands. "This is addressed to Doctor Forman," I observed. "Frances speaks of *obtaining a form of poison from a supplier who refuses to cooperate any longer.*" I looked at Robert. "That's me, isn't it?"

"Keep reading."

I skimmed the letter and felt my hands become clammy as I read further. "*My supplier, a learned healer from which I obtained my first poison, is a powerful member of the nobility. I do not wish to reveal my source just yet, for fear of burning my bridges, but may find the need to do so if I need to force the healer's hand in the future.*" I read aloud. I looked up at Robert, confusion pulling my brows together. "I don't understand. I'm not a powerful member of the nobility. To whom does she refer?"

He cleared his throat. "I believe she speaks of yer mother."

"Oh, dear God." I said, choking down a cry. I stared at Robert. My hands began to shake insomuch that I couldn't even refold the letter properly. "But my mother knows nothing of what the countess has done. She is innocent!"

"Of course, she is," Robert soothed. "But have ye not told her about taking the poison from her apothecary?"

I shook my head then paced across the room to the window at the far end of the supper hall. I chewed on my thumbnail as I looked out across the expanse of Chadwyck Park. How had things gotten so out of hand? It seemed at every turn I was making poor choices that put myself and others in danger.

"Perhaps it is time ye tell her." Robert had drawn up behind me and I felt the brush of his breath against the back of my neck when he spoke. I wanted very much to just throw my arms around him and sob into his chest.

"I cannot. I could not bear the look in her eyes when she saw my betrayal. It would tear her apart. And Father—" I choked, unable to finish.

"They might be able to help ye. Yer father and mother *are* powerful nobles. I think they should be told."

"No!" I said firmly, turning to look at him. "This is my mess. I made it, and I need to figure out how to fix it."

He stared at me for several minutes, his eyes darkened into a brackish green. "So, what are we going to do?"

"We?" I repeated, laughing without humor. "This isn't your problem, Robert. I don't expect you to involve yourself." I swiped at my cheek where a tear had already escaped and was running down my face.

He took a step closer and cupped my face with both hands. "Havenae I made it clear, whatever happens we will face it together?"

I laughed again, but this time there was amusement in my voice. "And if I was a coldblooded murderess? Would you help me even then?" I sniffed before pulling away to retrieve a piece of cloth from my sleeve to wipe my nose.

"Aye." The word rumbled from his throat like a growl, and the intensity with which he answered sent a whisper across my skin, creating gooseflesh on my arms and the back of my neck. I already knew his answer to my question, but it felt good to hear his reassurance.

I hurried toward the door. "I must go to Forman's house. I must see what other letters he might have."

Robert grabbed me by the arm before I reached the door. "Dinnae be a fool, Isobel. Do ye even ken where the man lives?"

Hopelessness overwhelmed me, and I let out a stifled cry. "I'll send a servant to find him." I pulled on my arm, trying to free myself from his grasp.

"Isobel." My name on his tongue rumbled through me, sending a chill down my spine.

"You must let go of me, Robert." I was truly beginning to panic. The thought of my mother being implicated in crimes she did not commit all because of my foolishness was more than I could bear. I tugged once more, trying to free myself from his hold.

"Send a servant to find out Forman's location. Then ye and I will go speak with him together."

Chapter 36

The Forman residence, London
September 1613
Robert

Simon Forman's study looked more like a cabinet of curiosities than a physician's home. His shelves were stuffed to the brim with books bearing esoteric titles and strange subjects. Tomes bound in leathers of browns and blacks and reds, organized by various sizes and colors, filled the spaces along every wall. A large mahogany desk sat at the far end, covered with scrolls of parchment. Astrological charts on crisp paper and hand-drawn maps of celestial bodies inked in colorful motifs were stacked carefully atop the desk. Several neatly trimmed pens in tidy rows lined the black tabletop, along with an inkwell wiped clean of any stain. A magnifying glass with an ebony handle lay to the right of the desk, ready for use. Body parts of various animals occupied the remaining space. The pelt of a sea otter, the skull of some rodent, the sharp teeth of an unknown creature, a jar with a gelatinous substance containing a bizarre beastie floating inside. Mysterious and exotic alike clashed in the doctor's study.

There was one other thing, the likes of which sent a cold chill down my spine.

A small figurine, a doll of sorts that looked to be formed from a waxy substance. Nay unlike the ones my brothers had molded from mud so many years ago. Verra much like the one my brother Francis had seen my father using.

The doctor's wife seated us next to the hearth. The woman, who looked to be 30 years the doctor's junior, was scurrying about, getting refreshments in order, and poking at the dying fire to rekindle its flame.

"I should have already had all this in order," she was saying, as she set a tray of biscuits on the table between us. "It isn't like I wasn't expecting you."

Isobel and I looked at each other. Isobel cleared her throat before addressing the woman. "Forgive me, Mistress Forman, but how could you be expecting us?"

The woman hurried into the kitchen and returned momentarily with a set of lace napkins she set beside the tray. When she didnae answer Isobel's question, she tried a different tack.

"I see Doctor Forman is not here at the moment. Will he be returning shortly? There is really no need to go through all this trouble, if he shan't be here soon."

The petite woman stopped short, a lock of raven-black hair getting caught on her equally dark eyelashes. She swept the hair away with the back of her hand and looked at Isobel with a queer expression.

"Doctor Forman is no longer with us," she said, continuing her ministrations.

Isobel looked at me again, shock shaping her expression. "What do you mean?"

The woman glanced at her, a look of tranquility contradicting her troubling words. "My husband passed away last week."

Isobel opened her mouth, but nay a sound came out. I spoke up instead. "Ye sound quite calm for a woman who has just lost her husband."

"Robert," Isobel gasped. "Be gentle."

Mistress Forman's lips quirked upward slightly. "If you are insinuating I am not upset, you are mistaken. But it was not unexpected, and therefore I have had time to prepare. I am at peace with his death."

Isobel tilted her head slightly. "Had he been sick? He seemed healthy when I last spoke with him."

The woman poked the fire once more before turning toward us. "My husband predicted his own death. He told me the week before, and he left his affairs in order. We will be well-cared for. We are comfortable and happy. Albeit Clemmy is young and talks of his father constantly, I will certainly not miss all the foot traffic coming to the house all the time."

"Foot traffic?" I repeated.

She turned her head toward me. "Yes. My husband entertained guests at all hours of the day and night. Many of his patients could only come under the cover of darkness, so there were frequent disturbances, even at night."

"Why must they come at night? What was there to hide?" Isobel took a sip of the nettle tea Mistress Forman had offered us and stared at the woman innocently.

She sat down across from us, taking her own tea in her hands. An amused expression lit up her face. "My dear, my husband read people's stars." She took a sip of her tea, but when she lowered her cup, her smile was gone. "My husband had many female clients. He was extremely popular with the ladies and not just because of his ability to read their stars." She looked at us with one raised eyebrow as if to make herself clear.

Isobel's mouth hung open. "Oh," she said, left speechless by the widow's confession.

"In fact, I have stopped receiving his grieving female callers altogether. Especially after that rude Mistress Turner came calling, demanding letters her mistress had written to my husband. If it hadn't been for the fact my husband had told me you would come, I would not have opened the door to you at all."

"Mistress Turner came to see ye?" I said, sitting up straighter.

"Yes, she is very bossy. I gave her most of the letters." Mistress Forman took a small bite of biscuit and wiped her mouth with her napkin. "But I kept back two of the most incriminating ones. The Countess of Essex is cunning. I wouldn't put it past her to try to drag my husband's name through the mud in an effort to absolve herself. So, I only gave her lady the most innocent of her letters."

I chewed the dry, flavorless biscuit and tried to swallow. Isobel beat me to the next question before I could wash the biscuit down.

"You said your husband told you I was coming. How did he know? How did you know it was me he spoke of?"

"He said a beautiful, young nobleman's daughter would come calling. He said you needed help." She set her cup down and folded her hands in her lap.

"But how do you know I am the woman of whom he spoke?"

The doctor's wife gave Isobel an impatient look. "Do you mean other than the fact you are the most beautiful woman I have ever laid eyes upon? Certainly, the most beautiful to ever grace our doors, even more than the countess herself." Then she nodded toward Isobel's necklace. "Simon said I would know you by the lavender thistle."

Isobel's hand immediately shot to her necklace. She wrapped her hand around the small amethyst and sucked in a breath. "He has never seen me wearing this. It has just come into my possession after a long many months of it missing."

"My husband had a sense of such things," the widow said. She then rose to her feet and went to the desk. Pulling out a drawer, she removed a mustard colored, leather bound book. She pulled on the ribbon marker, opening it to a marked page and scanning the contents momentarily with her finger. "Ah, here it is." She handed the book to Isobel and stepped back to watch her.

Isobel took the book and read the page. Her eyes flicked to me, and her face flushed with a pretty pink blush. She snapped the book shut. "That's the most ridiculous thing I have ever read."

Mistress Forman's brows rose in what appeared to be part amusement and part aggravation. "Make no mistake, dear. My husband was very good at what he did. Although, if you have never come to visit him and answered his plethora of questions that he always asked his patients, I must admit I'm not sure how he read your stars."

Read her stars? Now I was truly intrigued. "What does it say?" I inquired.

"Nothing," Isobel retorted sharply.

Mistress Forman chuckled. "I would think you would be pleased. He is a handsome one." She let her eyes rake over me, and I felt the tips of my ears burn.

"What does it say?" I demanded, taking the book from her hands. Isobel squeaked out a protest as I opened to the marked page and read quickly. I fought to hide my pleasure upon reading the doctor's penned words concerning Isobel's future.

"You can wipe that smile off your face, Robert Stewart. He certainly could not have meant us."

I held the book up and read. "*Upon the tapestry of life, woven by the loom of fate, lies a destiny bound in the placement of stars. In the heavens' grand design, the daughter of noble birth, born in England but not of English blood will find her purpose entwined with a son of the northern lands, noble in birth, slighted by fate. Where the thistle blooms there shall they make their home.*" I closed the book. "It sounds like us, if ye ask me."

"Well, I didn't," Isobel sniped in her usual way, snatching the book from my hands.

"Rest assured, my husband most certainly was speaking of you, my lady." Mistress Forman walked to the desk again and with a small key that hung from a chatelaine tied about her waist, opened a locked drawer in the desk. This time she pulled out another book, bound in black leather and of an ample size. She carried it with both hands and handed it to Isobel as well.

Isobel watched the woman with curiosity. "What is this?" she asked, taking the book from the widow's hands.

"That is the book my husband instructed me to give to you," Mistress Forman said. "I am hesitant to part with it, for it contains a great many secrets belonging to my husband. But I fear if I do not heed his instructions, he may just as easily haunt my quarters." Isobel stared at her with mouth agape, then looked at me. I shrugged. I didnae understand the woman's statement either.

"Was yer husband a necromancer?" I asked, feeling a twinge of sympathy if for nothing more than the sake of my father's memory. I looked again at the wax doll lying on the doctor's desk. It was in the shape of a man with anatomically accurate body parts. Such dolls could be used to wreak quite a bit of havoc on a man, should a disgruntled wife wish to do so.

Her black eyes shot toward me, then at the wax figure before drawing back to me. "It has been said," she replied. "But I am not at liberty to confirm nor deny the fact."

Isobel set the thick book on her lap and opened it. She read silently for a moment until an odd expression overtook her face. She glanced at Mistress Forman before chewing on her bottom lip and resuming her study. She turned the page, running a delicate finger down the length of the book as she read. After several more minutes, she gathered the remaining pages in her hands and leafed through them, stopping occasionally to read an entry.

Finally, she closed the book and swallowed hard, before handing it to me. "Why are you showing this to me?" she asked the widow.

I opened the book to a random page. It was a list of entries, written like a diary or journal, with explicit details of the doctor's clients. The men and women with whom he met, the ailments treated and with what physics. But tucked away amongst the mundane physic details, were other entries. Names of women with whom he had liaisons, along with the dates and times of their trysts, and all the sordid details of their affairs.

"I am not merely showing it to you. My husband instructed me to give it to you."

"But why?" Isobel quizzed.

"It seems a dangerous piece of information to have," I threw in.

She eyed me thoughtfully. "Be that as it may, Doctor Forman asked me to give it to my lady, and I did as he asked. I can rest easier knowing I have followed his instructions."

Isobel coughed lightly. "There is a lot of personal information contained within these pages. Aren't you afraid the information might besmudge your husband's name?"

A crease appeared between the woman's brow as she stared at Isobel momentarily. She took another sip of tea then set the cup on the table. "I was ten and seven when I met and married Simon Forman. He was forty-seven. I was young and inexperienced and erroneously believed I would be a cherished wife and he would give up his rakish ways once we wed. Instead, I was just part of his façade. A means of making him look prestigious and successful. And while I fulfilled my duties as homemaker and mother of his children, he did not change his ways. I suffered the humiliation of opening the door time and time again to every woman, whether married or single, who sought my husband's services. I am free from that humiliation now. Free to live with the comfortable living that Doctor Forman left for Clemmy and me, and as long as my son is protected, the book makes no difference to me. Besides, it was my husband's dying wish you have it, for whatever reason. What kind of wife would I be if I denied my dead husband his final request?"

A pause hung over us after Mistress Forman finished her soliloquy. Isobel took another sip of her tea then asked the burning question we both wanted to know. "Is Lady Essex one of your husband's liaisons?"

Just then, a door opened across from us and a small boy of about six years of age came barging through with his nursemaid behind him. A mop of red curls flew wildly about his head as he ran toward his mother.

"Mama!" he cried and clambered onto her lap. "I'm hungry!"

"I bet you are, moppet," she said, smoothing his hair away from his eyes then cupping his cheeks. "Napping does tend to make one hungry." She kissed the top of his head then looked toward us. "Clemmonte, say hello to Lady Isobel and Sir Robert."

"Hello," the lad said shyly. "Shall I read to you?"

"No love, that won't be necessary," Mistress Forman said, setting the boy on his feet then standing. "My husband used to like to show his clients how smart our boy is. He used to have him read to his patients to show off his intelligence. He's known his letters for over a year now and can read short passages."

"Already?" said Isobel, smiling. "And so young."

Mistress Forman beamed. "He is six years old. He will surely follow in his father's footsteps."

Hopefully nay in everything, I thought to myself.

"Now, if you will excuse us. It is time for Clemmy to resume his lessons. I usually prepare a refreshment for him, and we chat while he eats before finishing his tasks."

"Of course," Isobel cooed, picking up the black book and holding it to her chest. Mistress Forman led us to the door but before we said our goodbyes, Isobel had one last request. "Mistress Forman, would it be too much to ask for the two letters that you refused to give to Mistress Turner?" Isobel's eyes danced with mirth, and she flashed her irresistible smile at the widow. "I can assure you; I am not a friend of the countess. In fact, I might be able to make good use of them."

The woman paused at the threshold, a determined line flattening her lips. "If ye can help me get a place for Clemmy with one of the prince's private tutors, I would be willing to work with you."

Isobel eagerly opened the letters as soon as we climbed into the coach.

"How likely are ye to get one of Prince Charles's tutors to take on Clemmonte?" I asked, as I settled into the seat next to her.

Isobel waved off my concern. "Father can arrange that. I'll just tell him I owe her a favor."

My brows shot up. "He willnae ask questions?"

"I'll think of something to tell him. Oh," she said in awe, as we pulled away from the Forman's home and headed back toward Chadwyck House. "And I thought Mary Woods was the person who helped

Frances bewitch Essex." She kept her eyes trained on the pages of the letter and didnae look up until she had reached the end.

"Was Forman providing her with charms?" I asked, leaning in to get a look at the letter she held in her hands. "I saw a wax doll lying on the doctor's desk. The kind I believe my father used to employ, when wanting to bring harm upon people."

Isobel looked up at me, her blue eyes softening into pools of summer sky. "I wasn't aware your father did things like that," she said, her voice barely above a whisper.

I nodded. "I dinnae ken a lot about it. I have a few memories from my childhood, and the stories my mother and your father have told me. I never witnessed anything for myself since I never met the man."

She looked at me with such intensity before cupping my cheek with her hand. "I am sorry things didn't work out for you and him to meet. I would have liked to have met him as well."

"Why? So ye could give him a piece of yer mind?" I laughed sardonically. But instead of answering me, she leaned in and kissed me, a soft, slow kiss that ended with her gently biting my bottom lip. "Careful," I growled, "ye might find yerself flat on yer back before we reach Chadwyck House."

She scooted back to her spot on the bench. "No, I just want to see what you will look like in thirty more years." She patted my cheek then looked at the letter again. "I do believe you are correct. I think Forman was the one helping Frances bewitch the earl." She continued reading before sitting back against the seat, astonished.

"What does it say?" I inquired, noting her stunned silence.

"Apparently, the countess has been poisoning Overbury for months."

"What took so long for him to die? He must have had a strong constitution."

"This letter is dated 18 June. She says here they obtained the recommended aqua fortis from Franklin. They tried testing it on a cat, but it took two days for the poor thing to die." She stopped reading and looked at me. "How awful!"

"Then what happened?" I prompted.

She turned back to the letter. "So, she took Forman's advice and requested realgar. They administered that to a cat as well and it died quickly." She looked at me again. "I think I'm going to be sick."

I brushed a hand across her back to sooth her. "How does this pertain to Overbury?"

My question grounded her and caused her to focus on the letter. "Overbury was allowed a servant to assist him while in prison. A man was selected to serve, named Richard Weston. But he was under Mistress Turner's employ. The phial of realgar was given to him, and he stirred it into Overbury's soup."

She stopped and looked out the window. A soft rain had begun to fall since leaving the house this morning, and the raindrops glistened off the fading green and emerging yellow leaves of the oak trees along the way. "I still cannot believe the woman I thought was my friend was such a cold-blooded murderess," she murmured. Tears had pooled in her blue eyes, and she brushed her palm over her face to erase a tear that had escaped.

"The realgar evidently didnae have the same effect on Overbury. What happened next?"

Isobel turned back to the letter. "That is all this letter contains." She handed the letter to me to read and opened the second.

"Ah, here," she started, but fell silent as she continued to read. I watched as her lips moved wordlessly, skimming the page. Finally, she spoke again. "Evidently, Overbury fell seriously ill and wrote to the viscount asking for an emetic powder he could take to cure his sickness. Frances sent white arsenic to Weston, and he mixed it with the powder Rochester sent and administered it as an enema." I winced, thinking of the residual effects such an enema would bring. Isobel paused, then said, "My mother showed me what white arsenic looks like. She has some in her apothecary."

"That isnae helping yer cause," I warned.

"That's true," she admitted, before turning back to the letter.

"That didn't kill him either," she continued. "Next, she tried corrosive sublimate. Gah! The amount of poison this woman has gotten her hands on is astonishing. Forman must have advised her of all of this, for she didn't get these poisons from me."

"That is probably the reason why Mistress Forman didnae want to turn over the letters. Surely, she kent her husband had a hand in some of this."

"She must not have been too worried about it, if she used the letters to get what she wanted in return." Isobel continued reading. "They mixed the poison in some tarts and jellies and sent them to Overbury."

"'Tis diabolical to mess with a man's food. Is that what killed him?"

She turned the letter over and looked at the back, then turned it back over. "I don't know. That is all it says. This letter is dated 12 September."

"According to his wife, that is the day Forman died. He probably didnae see this letter."

"Which means Mistress Forman would have opened it," she countered.

We sat in silence for a moment, pondering all we had learned from Frances's letters. I stared out the window, watching the timber buildings amble by as the coach rumbled along. After several minutes, I turned and looked at Isobel and she was staring at me. She said, "These letters are interesting, but there is nothing contained therein to help my cause."

I scooted closer to her on the seat. "Let's have another look at the black book."

Isobel picked up the book and set it on her lap. "Did you see the Earl of Shrewsbury's name listed in here?"

"Aye. Did ye see Lady Coke's name?"

"No!" she said, conspiratorially. "Sir Edward Coke, the judge's wife?"

"Aye. And it wisnae for an ailment that she visited Forman."

Isobel's eyes went as round as saucers. "Lady Coke and Forman had a tryst?" Her eyes showed shock, but her lips quirked in amusement.

I leaned closer so I could see the pages. The faint fragrance of lemongrass teased my nose and my hands itched to touch her. I wanted to run my fingers over her soft skin, brush my nose across the underside of her jaw and drink in the aroma of her. Taste her essence and claim her. It took all my restraint not to fist her glossy tresses in my hand and pull until I heard her cry out with my name upon her lips.

She kept reading, but the book had lost my attention long ago. Occasionally she would point out another name, another duke's wife or earl's daughter who had formed a liaison with the doctor. In all, Isobel had uncovered more than twenty people who stood to lose a fair piece, should she decide to share the information she had been given.

I stole glances at her as she studied Forman's book. I thought about her determination to go after the things she wanted, and her perseverance when things didnae go as planned. She wisnae perfect. She had made many poor choices since I had met her, but her drive to accomplish her goals, mixed with her sincerity and penitence when faced with her wrongdoing, made me love her all the more. Her outward beauty made her desirable. From the delicate white brows over cerulean blue eyes to the pale pink of her cheeks against milk-white skin. And those pouty, red lips that begged to be kissed. My body wanted hers and would never be sated.

But it was her heart that made me determined to have her. Her sense of justice and concern for those whose stations were beneath her own. And her love for those she held dear, whether sibling or servant.

I swallowed my heart that seemed to lodge in my throat. I didnae ken Isobel's true feelings for me. It was clear she felt the same attraction I did. But when she was confronted with Forman's prediction, her reaction wisnae what I would have wanted. Was she truly appalled at the thought of sharing a life with me? Or was she embarrassed someone had made plain her feelings after she had tried so hard to deny them?

I couldnae hide my intentions any longer. Reaching over, I picked the book up from her lap and laid it on the seat next to me. Isobel's eyes followed my movement then her mouth fell open when I knelt before her on the hard floor of the carriage.

"Isobel," I began, suddenly feeling like my mouth was stuffed with sow thistle. But before I could say anything further, she laid a finger to my lips.

"Don't say it, Robert." Her finger felt cold against my lips, and I longed to enfold her hands in mine and warm them. But I didnae move. Instead, I watched her, knowing my heart was in my eyes.

"Issy." I breathed, feeling the desperation clawing at my chest.

"Robert, I know what you are going to say." She looked away from me, then ran her tongue over her lips as if she would speak again, but no words came.

"I havenae hid my feelings. In fact, I have made them more than plain, time and time again. I have told ye I would do anything for ye, say anything for ye." I took her hands in mine and held the back of her fingers to my lips. I pressed a kiss to them, then released her to cup her face in my hands. "Do ye want to see me beg, lass, is that it? For I'll crawl on my hands and knees if I have to."

"Robert, no—"

"Command me as ye please. Discipline me as ye must. But whatever ye do, let me love ye and protect ye for ye willnae find anyone as loyal as I."

Her lips trembled but she dinnae speak. Her eyes had turned a watery blue, but something kept her from accepting my proposal. My power of persuasion was slipping from my hands, and so I did the one thing that would reveal her true feelings. I pulled her to me and kissed her like my lungs were void and she, my last breath of air.

She kissed me back, clinging to me as if I were her salvation. I brushed my lips across her cheek and down her neck, burying my nose in the spot between her neck and shoulder and savoring her sweet scent. In a fumble of hands and clothing, Isobel reached up to untied my collar and made quick work of opening my shirt. I watched her with hooded eyes, anticipating the scorch of her touch, yet determining how much I would allow her to get away with. When she finished, she laid her hands upon my chest and branded me with her searing touch. She stared at me momentarily with desperate need before setting her lips to my skin. A moment later, I felt the soft nip of her teeth against my flesh. Her rough kisses were like poppy tears, and I was an addict. The sensation was energizing, but when I pulled back to look at her, there were tears running down her porcelain cheeks. I hid nae changed her mind, and the conflict was written all over her face.

I grabbed her wrists, staying her movement. "I meant what I said last night, Isobel. I will give ye all of me, but I want yer whole heart in return." She opened her mouth, but the silence that followed was loud and clear. "What are ye afraid of, lass?"

"I-I—" she choked on her words then buried her face in her hands.

"Ye what, lass? Talk to me!"

"The prince—" she started, then pressed her lips together and shook her head.

"The prince is dead!" I reminded her. "How long will ye mourn the man who is only a ghost now, when there is a real, living, breathing, flesh and blood man in front of ye that adores ye?"

Pain filled her eyes, then she turned her head from me and looked out the window of the coach. Perhaps I had been too harsh. I shouldnae have spoken of the prince in such a manner. But I was drowning in a sea of emotion, and she was holding my head underwater.

She sniffled then wiped her nose with a piece of cloth. Taking a ragged breath, she said, "You're right. I need to move on. And I thought I was ready, but—" She trailed off. After another lengthy pause, she said, "I just need more time." I didnae move, didnae speak. I merely let her work out her emotions and prayed they would lead her back to me. I watched as she twisted the pink material of her skirts in her hands. After another moment of contemplation she said, "I'm not sure I would fit into your world."

A beat of silence hung between us as I thought about her words. That was the true issue. She had rejected her Scottish roots before and she was rejecting the Scotsman before her now.

"Which is it, lass? Ye arnae ready or ye dinnae want it?" I said bitterly.

"Robert, please," she began. But when I looked at her, she couldnae hold my gaze.

I pulled myself off the floor and sat on the edge of the seat across from her. Rejection wisnae a new feeling for me, but for the first time in my life, I felt utter humiliation and a complete sense of failure.

I ran a hand through my hair, shoving the russet locks away from my face. In a last-ditch effort to make her see reason, I spat the words at her. "Never forget, I am written in yer stars. Ye may hate me, and ye may not want me, but ye will never be rid of me." I banged on the roof of the carriage with my fist, signaling to the driver I wanted out. "I'll walk the rest of the way." Before the carriage came to a complete stop, I hopped out of the wagon, slamming the door behind me.

"Robert, wait—" I heard Isobel call, but it was too late. I had closed the door on her excuses and possibly any future we may have had together.

By the time I reached Chadwyck House later that day, Isobel was already in the king's custody.

Chapter 37

Chadwyck House, London
September 1613
Isobel

W hat had I done?

After Robert slammed the door of the carriage, regret immediately started to eat away at me. All the things I wanted to say to him were ready to spill out. Defend myself, defend my love for Henry. And defend my love for him, regardless of the guilt.

When I read the words Doctor Forman had written about me, I was aghast. I had spent almost two years fighting the growing feelings I had for Robert. Even before Henry's death, I felt myself wanting to be near Robert. Wanting to hear his voice and feel his touch, taste his kiss. Guilt had plagued me for months and while Henry lay on his deathbed, I found myself thinking about Robert. I loved Henry. There is no one who could convince me otherwise. So, why did I dream about Robert? And when Henry died, I truly was heartbroken. There will never be another prince as noble as he. But if I were completely honest, in my heart of hearts, I recognized a path of escape. A means for easing my conscience and fleeing my duplicity. Which in turn made me even more of a terrible person.

And since Henry's death, I have wanted Robert even more. So, why did I stop him from proposing?

The answer was simple, really. I was scared.

And perhaps I felt a little guilty. I loved Robert Stewart. I had loved him for a while now. Which meant I hadn't been completely honest with myself, nor Robert. And I especially had not been honest with Henry. I had been so blinded by my own expectations of love, the idea of love that I thought I had with the prince. And that blindness had not only led me to unrealistic expectations of Henry, but it caused me to hurt Robert, and lie to myself.

And I had to admit that the thought of leaving England and making a life in Scotland was mortifying to me. I had spent my whole life trying to fit into my station. To shun my roots and make myself into the English lady I thought everyone wanted and expected me to be. All those lessons in civility and instruction in social graces, all the experience at court. Was it all for naught?

But when Robert climbed from our carriage, it was like a veil was torn from my eyes. And the thought of him walking out of my life forever, scared me even more than the thought of all that I was giving up. I realized that none of it mattered. The nobility, the court. None of it. I was always going to be the daughter of the rebellious Scottish inquisitor and his fiery, Scottish wife. And I was always going to love Robert Stewart, the son of an exiled Scottish earl. And every time our bodies touched, there was no denying it. We were destined to be together. I didn't need Doctor Forman to read my stars to tell me that.

As the carriage pulled up to Chadwyck House, I dried my eyes and tried to make myself look presentable. My epiphany during the ride home made me almost giddy with excitement. It would take a while for Robert to make it back, since he was coming on foot. But I had made a decision, and I could barely wait to seek him out. I was ready to let him know that he could have all of me as well, just as he had promised himself to me. However, when I entered the house, an eerie quiet met me there and I was immediately set on edge.

The visit with Mistress Forman took longer than I anticipated. I fully expected to be greeted with questions as to where I had been. But there was no one about upon my entry, until I came upon Edith who rushed toward me when she saw me.

"My lady!" she cried; her face flushed a splotchy red. "They are waiting for you in your father's study."

"They who?" I inquired, but she turned me about, straightening my skirts and pinching my cheeks to add color.

"The king's guard and a very important looking man," she explained as she ushered me toward the door to the study. I dug my heels in, not allowing her to push me any further until I knew what, or rather, who I was facing.

"What is this about, Edith?" I barely choked out the words before we were standing right in front of the door.

"I do not know," she whispered. "They have been here for an hour, but they won't tell Lord Stratford what it is concerning."

"How do you know that?"

"I listened at the door, of course." She offered me a weak smile in sympathy. "His Grace said to send you straightway when you got home." She reached to knock on the door.

"Wait," I said, and she paused, her hand in mid-air. "Take these to my chamber. Hide them safely away in my trunk, beneath the other contents and be sure to lock it afterward." I handed her Doctor Forman's black book with the two letters tucked safely inside. "Do you remember where I keep the key?"

She nodded and took the book from my hands. She then knocked on the door and waited. When my father's gruff voice called for her to enter, she opened the door.

"Lady Isobel, Your Grace." She pushed me gently through the doorway and quietly closed the door behind me.

An awkward silence riddled the study. A floorboard creaked under my slippers as I stepped into the room, and it might as well have been a sounding gong. I shuffled forward, trying not to look frightened, and looked about me to assess the situation. Mother, Father, and Grandfather were all there, with a handful of guards and a man that looked vaguely familiar, but I couldn't place where I knew him.

Mother was the first to speak. She rushed toward me and blurted, "Isobel! Where have ye been? Nay, don't answer that," she corrected, before brushing a gentle hand over my face and smoothing a few stray strands of hair away. "Are ye all right?" She looked closely at my face, apparently ascertaining I had been crying.

"I went for a carriage ride," I said, only telling half the truth.

Father cleared his throat. "Issy, this is Sir Francis Bacon. He is an advocate here on behalf of the king's legal council. He wishes to ask you a few questions."

"Concerning what?" I said, trying to sound uninterested. "Will this take long? I promised Mary I would take her walnut gathering when I returned home." I blinked innocently at Sir Francis, hoping he couldn't see right through my façade.

The advocate stepped forward and with calculating eyes that seemed to see everything, said, "That all depends on you, Lady Isobel. Perhaps we could talk somewhere privately."

I liked that idea, for I knew exactly why he was here, and I was not prepared to see my mother's disappointed face when she found out what I had done. I nodded, but Father spoke up.

"What you have to say could not be so very private my daughter need not speak of it in front of her parents. You will stay here, and we will stay here, and I will determine if your line of questioning is appropriate."

The advocate chewed on something, and the long whiskers that hung above his top lip shook back and forth. He turned his bleak eyes on my father and sighed. "Yes, how could I forget you are an advocate yourself, Lord Stratford?" Father stared hard at him but said nothing further.

"Lady Isobel, as you have probably heard, Sir Thomas Overbury has recently died in prison after a rather lengthy bout of sickness. It was originally believed this sickness to be of natural causes, but information has recently come to light that leads us to believe otherwise. Are you familiar with Sir Thomas Overbury?"

I swallowed hard then chose my words carefully. "I am acquainted with Sir Thomas and met him on several occasions during my time at the queen's court."

Bacon circled around me, eyeing me as he posed his next question. "And do you know of any reason to believe he may have been poisoned?"

He was cutting right to the chase. I took a long, slow breath, trying not to let on his question troubled me.

"Overbury shared with me he thought he had made some enemies at court, and he felt his life was possibly in danger."

Bacon's eyebrow shot up. "He told *you* that information?"

"Yes," I said, looking straight at Bacon.

He frowned and pulled something out of his pocket. Holding up a small black velvet bag he said, "Does this look familiar to you?" From behind me I heard my mother's quick intake of breath.

I squeezed my eyes shut. So, she had done it. Frances had implicated me in her crimes by playing the one card she held against me, my satchel embroidered with my initials. I bit down on the inside of my lip. "That is a satchel that was given to me by my grandfather on my sixteenth birthday."

He held the bag up for everyone to see. "Aren't you the least bit curious as to how it came to be in my possession?"

I lifted my chin. "I know how. I gave it to Lady Essex, and she gave it to you."

Bacon studied me. "You are a clever girl. You have probably already deduced we have reason to believe you had a hand in obtaining the poison used to kill him."

Mother gasped and Father voiced his protest, both expressing their belief in my innocence. Father gritted his teeth. "Now wait just a minute, Bacon."

At this moment it occurred to me I had a decision to make. I could be completely honest about my relationship with Lady Frances and tell him what I knew. Or I could lie and pretend I knew nothing of the countess's plan. Neither option looked attractive to me, and both probably led to ruination. I was hurt how Frances used me for her sinister gains. I had been more than a little naïve and was embarrassed at how foolish I had been when I agreed to help her. Had I really thought the poison was for rats? I'd like to think I did, but didn't Mother's warning give me reason to doubt?

I had no qualms about telling him what I knew of Frances. I had letters and Forman's black book to back me up. But what of all the other innocent women whose names were listed in the doctor's book? And even Mistress Turner's name, mentioned in the letters. Would I be willing to sacrifice their reputations to save myself?

I deserved everything I had coming to me. I had stolen from my mother and provided poison used to kill innocent people. I killed George Preston and covered up his disappearance. And I posed as the countess to help her evade the law. My sins were many. Perhaps losing Henry was my punishment for all the terrible things I had done. And if that was the case, I certainly couldn't sacrifice someone else's life to save my own.

"I gave Lady Frances poison once to help her take care of what she said was a rat problem. I later had reason to believe she used that poison on a couple of her maids, and when she came to me to obtain more, I refused her."

Mother released a choked cry. "Isobel," she gasped. "What have ye done?"

I looked at my mother. The hurt I now saw in her amber eyes did not surprise me. It is what I had feared for too long. Robert was right. Perhaps if I had told my mother and father what I had done, they might have been able to help me. But this is the path I chose, and now I must face the consequences.

"I'm sorry, Mother," I said, not looking away from her anguished face. I did not mention I had stolen the poison from her apothecary, for fear the advocate might question her next. But she would realize the truth.

Bacon cleared his throat and stepped closer. "I'm afraid I must insist you come with me, Lady Isobel. Lord Stratford, I'm sure you understand the need for her apprehension."

My father looked as if he himself could kill someone. A dark mien had enveloped his face and for the first time, the wrinkles at the corners of his eyes showed as he narrowed his eyes at Sir Francis Bacon.

"And I'm sure you understand the need for discretion in this matter," he gritted out. "We are not finished here. I will be gathering my daughter's defense and will speak with the king by this evening."

Sir Francis looked as though he truly did pity me and my father. "You know the king will not allow you to defend your own daughter. You are too close to this case. Another advocate will be chosen for her."

"I will speak with the king regarding it," Father said, a note of irritation ringing in his voice.

"So be it," Bacon said. "Guards." He motioned toward me, and three guards stepped forward.

Mother yelped. "Is that necessary? Do not treat our daughter as a common criminal. She will go willingly to be questioned. There is no need for shackles."

The advocate regarded my mother beneath his bushy brows. Then he motioned with two fingers for two of the guards to step back. "Go quietly and calmly, and we will not restrain you, Lady Isobel."

I stood there motionless as the guard, a young man with scruffy brown hair and eyes the color of whisky, stepped up beside me and gently took my arm. "Forgive me," he said quietly as he led me out the door of the study and into the waiting carriage.

Chapter 38

Tower of London
September 1613
Isobel

My room in the Tower of London was humble to say the least. Large stone walls and floors the color of dried mud and a window with lead-lined lattice panes and a quatrefoil at the top that let in plenty of sunlight was the extent of my view within. Luckily, I had a nice view of the Tower Green, and I could even see the ravens that made the Tower their home. With their glossy black feathers and shiny, obsidian eyes, they would scavenge for food on the lawn, scaring the robins and other smaller birds away. It was my only form of amusement for the first several days.

I was told I had several visitors while in the Tower, but few were allowed entrance. Edith and Hester both attempted to visit me on different occasions but were denied. My brothers, Tom and Will came together, but were also not permitted. They were, however, allowed to leave some tarts and a large piece of strawberry cake that our cook had baked. I ate the cake but could not bring myself to eat the tarts, given what I knew about Overbury's poisoning. Not that I thought my brothers would poison me, but I left them untouched, nonetheless.

My advocate, Sir Jerome Morrison, was the first permitted entrance. He was a kindly old man with snowy-white hair and a long, flowing beard that reached halfway down his chest. He listened intently to my confession, nodding and musing at the appropriate times, but gave little in the way of helpful advice. He told me he would return on the morrow but didn't come again for three or four days. It was just as well. He remained useless at helping me see a way of acquittal.

Surprisingly, Mother and Father were also allowed to visit. Mother came in like a whirlwind, changing the bed linens and emptying the chamber pot before assisting me with a change of clothing she had brought.

"Mother, these tasks are beneath you," I said, unable to look her in the eye now. I had had plenty of time to think about the pain and shame I had caused not only to her but my father. I had a hard time looking at either of them due to the guilt I felt.

"Oh, pish," she said, waving off my comment. "These hands have seen plenty of labor in my lifetime. Besides, this place is filthy. I will not have one of my children living in such squalor."

I appreciated the clean room and clothes. But I wanted her to yell at me, or at least, lecture me. Tell me how she tried to warn me or point out how my actions had done me little good since the prince was no longer with us. But she did none of those things. Her love and kindness were punishment in a different form, for they made me feel even more ashamed.

"I have petitioned the king to replace your advocate," Father said to me quietly, while Mother busied herself cleaning.

My brows lifted. "Morrison is a kind man," I said, "but he has not been helpful."

"Which is why I am trying to get him replaced. He has shunned all the legal advice I have given him concerning your case. And the king rejected my petition to represent you myself." My heart sank. Father was the only advocate I trusted to have my best interest at heart. "Is there any other information you can share with me that might help your case? Anything at all?"

I swallowed the guilt that clawed at me. I believed my father would love me regardless of whatever I told him. But I couldn't bring myself to tell him about George Preston. Not that his death had anything to do with Overbury's murder. I couldn't bear the thought of how the knowledge would probably crush him. It was bad enough watching my mother shrivel under the knowledge that I had stolen from her. Who knew how he would react to the news that his daughter had stabbed someone to death?

I wanted to tell him about Forman's black book but was afraid of what might come of it for the other women mentioned within. I had not had a chance to read through it thoroughly to see if any other gems could be found within its pages. I wanted to find Forman's entry concerning Frances's visit. Perhaps there was information contained there about the countess she didn't mention in her letters.

I decided to tell him about how I posed as Frances for her physical examination. I wasn't sure if it would hurt my case more for my fraudulent behavior, but Father would know what information could be used and what should be tucked away.

"What a web of lies and deceit that woman has woven," Mother said from behind me. "I never liked that woman." She continued cleaning without another word. I guessed that was the closest thing to an *I told you so* I was going to get from her.

Father stood by the door, waiting for Mother to gather all her things. I was sure he had aged in just the short amount of time I had been in the Tower, the stress and worry taking their toll on him. I wished I could tell him everything, but it was for this reason I felt I couldn't share all my secrets. But as they prepared to go, I felt an overwhelming need to speak to my mother one more time.

"Mother, may I have a moment alone with you?" I asked as they were about to leave. She flicked a glance at Father, and he nodded before calling for the gaoler to open the door. When he had gone, she turned to me, her amber eyes softening on me.

"What is it, love?" She took my hands in hers and squeezed gently.

I wrestled with all the things I wanted to say to her, but I began with the most important thing.

"I want to apologize. I am sorry for taking the poison from your apothecary and disregarding your sound advice concerning Frances." I felt my voice warble and I swallowed down the tears that threatened to overwhelm me.

Mother wrapped her arms around me and hugged me tightly. "I have already forgiven ye," she said softly. I cried into her shoulder, feeling all the guilt and sorrow leak into the ornately embroidered shawl she had wrapped around herself.

"I have often wondered, if Henry had lived and my plan had worked to catch his attention and secure a marriage, if I would feel differently," I said, wiping my nose. "I have thought about this many times since his death. It is hard to know for sure, given the circumstances now. Yet, I regret any part I have played in the death of the maids, no matter how ignorant I was of Frances's intentions."

Mother didn't try to comfort me with shallow words. She just held me close and let me spill all my confessions upon her bosom as she soothingly rubbed her hands across my back.

"I also killed a man."

I felt my mother stiffen, and her hands paused briefly before resuming their task. "Do ye wish to tell me about it?"

I nodded, feeling the softness of her silk shawl rub against my cheek. I then poured out my heart to her, telling her about the countess's threats, George Preston's attack, and how Robert had saved my life.

"It sounds to me as if ye saved *his* life." I could hear the mirth in her voice before I even lifted my head and looked at her serene face.

"We saved each other, I suppose."

The corner of Mother's lips ticked up slightly. "Aye." She brushed a stray lock of hair off my forehead.

My stomach was a bundle of nerves. "Please don't tell Father what I've done. I don't know what that would do to him."

"Never," Mother promised. "He is a man of principle. He rarely understands the need to break the rules."

My brows shot up. "You have broken the rules from time to time?"

"That's a story for another time," she said, patting my hand. "As for ye, I imagine the taking of this man's life has been a heavy load to bear. But ye cannot hold onto that. He would have killed ye or Robert, if ye had not stepped in. Ye were only protecting the man ye love."

My mouth fell open. "H-how do you know how I feel about Robert Stewart?"

"Isn't it obvious, my dear?" she asked, running her hands down my arms, and taking my hands once more. "Ye would have never soiled your hands or your frock for anything less than love." I started to protest, but she chuckled. "I'm only teasing. I have seen the way ye look at him, and how your demeanor around him has changed. That cannot be anything but love."

I should have known my mother would notice everything. I blinked back tears and swallowed the lump in my throat. "We did not part on good terms. I was cruel and felt such guilt about Henry, I would not allow him to propose. Now," I swallowed again, feeling like my mouth was full of wool. "I may never see him again. I'll never be able to tell him how I really feel about him." The tears began to flow all over again, and mother handed me a piece of cloth to dry my eyes.

"We cannot give up hope," she said, wiping her own eyes as well.

Before I could say anything more, my mother's time was up. I nearly revealed what I knew about the other women in Forman's book. The information might be useful in some way, if for nothing more than to put pressure on some very important men, but I could not bring myself to do it. I had already done so much damage.

I realized there was only one person I could trust, with whom I would feel comfortable sharing my darkest secrets. I certainly could not have shared my secrets with Henry. But Robert never judged me. He never lectured me about my decisions. He offered advice but stood by me and supported me regardless of the consequences. I had no doubt I could ask anything of him, and he would do it. That thought sent a thrill through me I couldn't explain.

Unless he had forsaken me because of my rejection.

I wanted to write to Robert to see if he would find the book I had hidden away and see what he could discover. But Father had told me Robert had left Chadwyck House the very day I had been arrested, and he had not told anyone where he was going. I would have sent him a letter at Richmond, for he was finishing up some things there before returning to Scotland. But I couldn't trust that the missive would not end up in the wrong hands.

I paced the length and breadth of my small room every day, reliving the last few moments Robert and I had spent together in the carriage. I thought of the words that were spoken and the touches that were exchanged. "*I am written in yer stars,*" he had said. "*Ye may hate me, and ye may not want me, but ye will never be rid of me.*" And he was right. I had not been rid of him since coming to the Tower. He was always in my waking thoughts and invading my nightly dreams. I didn't hate him. On the contrary, I wanted him more than anything—would give more than anything—to have those green eyes locked on mine and feel his arms around me once more.

I had been in the Tower for about three weeks when the missive arrived. Sir Jerome delivered the message, for the king had refused to replace my advocate. The old man shuffled up behind me as I sat feeding the ravens on the Tower Green. It was a small freedom I had been allowed thrice a week if the weather held.

He held the missive out to me, and I took it with shaking hands. I broke the seal and unrolled the scroll, taking a wobbly breath as I read over the formal charges.

I was being tried as an accomplice to murder. I tamped down the hysterical laugh that bubbled in my throat. I knew this day would come; I had only hoped I would be able to fight the charges with proof of my innocence. But there was little of that to go around.

When the guard indicated my free time on the lawn was finished, I gathered my little bag of crumbs that I fed the ravens. I followed obediently behind him, watching my steps on the stones beneath my feet. I had twisted my ankle earlier on the way down and didn't want a repeat of the injury.

"Franklin and Weston were executed this morning," the gaoler mumbled as he led me back to my room. He barely spoke ten words to me the whole time we've interacted. I wondered why he felt the need to share that horrid news with me now.

So, the apothecary and the gaoler that helped kill Overbury were dead. Dear God! Would I be next? Fear clenched my heart, and my legs turned to willow branches beneath me. I reached out a hand to the gaoler's arm to steady myself as we walked. My lungs felt tight, I couldn't drag enough air into them.

We had just reached my corridor, when an overly friendly voice rang out, striking my ears like a stone scraping metal. I jerked my head up to behold Lady Frances coming out of a room just three doors down from mine. But she was not a prisoner. I reached that conclusion by the lovely flush to her cheeks and the beautiful gown she wore. Jealousy curled inside my chest, and I resisted the urge to lash out at her.

"Lady Isobel," she began, as if surprised to see me here. "I had no idea you were being kept so close to where Anne is being held."

Anne? She meant Mistress Turner. I had no idea we had been placed so close together either. An oversight, I would think, if we were co-conspirators. But I had not even heard she had been arrested. They were closing in on the guilty ones, and yet Frances still walked free.

"Your Grace," I said, the words tasting bitter on my tongue. I curtseyed low, but kept my eyes trained on the ground. I stared at her shoes and thought about how lovely they were. How unfairly lovely.

She took a step closer to me. "You must know it was Anne's idea to hand over your black velvet purse. She insisted an apothecary would be able to tell what kind of poison had been stored within. She said it would prove it wasn't the same kind of poison the doctors say was used on poor Thomas Overbury. We both thought it would surely clear your name."

Lies. All lies. Her voice was so honey-sweet it practically made my teeth ache. Fear of my own fate since hearing the news of the executed men was consuming me, twisting my stomach into knots. But at last, I lifted my eyes to hers and felt indignation unfurling within me.

"You must think me the same naïve girl that you deceived two years ago. You can't honestly expect me to believe that you thought you were helping me. You knew exactly what you were doing. I've no doubt you handed over my purse to throw the scent off your own trail." Her eyes narrowed on me, and she opened her mouth to speak, but I cut her off. "I trusted you. I was young and credulous and believed you truly wanted to be my friend and help me. I should have listened to my mother. She always said you couldn't be trusted."

"Excuse me?" She looked truly appalled. Then she sniffed, "Well, I was going to help you, as I am doing for Anne Turner. My family connections will practically guarantee she will walk free. I could have done the same for you."

I laughed bitterly. "I do not want any more of your assistance. Besides, with the proof I have, I can almost guarantee she will not walk free, and neither will you."

The countess's nose flared in anger. "To what do you refer, you silly girl?"

I ignored the irritation I felt at her insult, for I held the upper hand. Feeling strengthened by this new realization, I said, "Just a couple of letters written by you to Doctor Forman. Your details are fascinating."

Her smile shone like the sun. "Now I know you are lying. Anne retrieved my letters from Mistress Forman after the doctor's death. You have proof of nothing."

"Don't I? Let's see, whose poor cat did you poison with aqua fortis?" The color drained from her face, replaced with distress. "The poor thing suffered for days. At least the realgar worked faster. I guess that cat was lucky."

"Who told you that?" she asked vehemently.

"As I said, I have the letters. Oh, and Doctor Forman's black book." She stared at me blankly, and I let satisfaction spread across my face. "You don't know about the black book? The one where Forman recorded all his patients' treatments and all their trysts." Frances's face drained of color, and I felt a surge of triumph shooting through my veins.

"All right, enough chit chat," the gaoler said, goading me in the back to keep me moving. I began walking, feeling a little lighter than I had just five minutes before.

"We are not through speaking, Isobel," Frances called, a note of desperation in her voice.

"Actually, I think I've said all I want to say to you," I retorted, then walked into my room and closed the door.

I was shaking, and my mind was racing. I had to find Robert one way or another and solicit his help one more time.

Chapter 39

London
October 1613
Robert

I counted out the last of my coin and dropped it into a leather pouch. Swallowing the last of the Friar Cor whisky, a bottle of the finest malt whisky to be had this side of Hadrian's Wall, I dropped my cup onto the table and wiped my mouth with the back of my hand. Darkness had fallen a half hour earlier. My bags were packed, my business at Richmond Palace was settled, and I was going home.

But not for good. And not until I had spoken to Isobel and tried one last time to convince her to use Forman's black book to obtain her release.

I had promised Isobel I widnae leave her. I intended to keep that promise, although my track record for keeping promises wisnae stellar. And although she had rejected my offer of a life spent together, I widnae abandon her. At least not altogether.

I had some business to tend to in Scotland. Henry had wanted to expand the riding school he had started in London to Stirling Castle, in Scotland, where he was born. He had asked me long ago if I would oversee it. I had agreed, nay realizing at the time how hard it would be to leave London when the time came. Plans had already been set in motion, and I couldnae put it off any longer. But I would be back as soon as I could, and hopefully one day, I could convince Isobel to marry me.

I dropped the coin into my saddlebag and swept one more look around the room. I had made a good life for myself here. Earned a lot of money I had stashed away until the day came I could return to Scotland and build my own home. But I was going to use that money now to bribe the Tower guard into allowing me to see Isobel. I'd earn it back eventually with Henry's school. But even if I didnae, it would be worth the cost just to see her again.

~

"Martin told me ye might be in need of some coin."

I had been watching the grounds at the Tower for more than two hours now, waiting for the changing of the guard and for the brother of the Richmond Palace hostler to appear.

The man, whom his brother had called Gerald, grunted, not looking me in the eye.

"I've got a hundred pounds sterling here, if ye can get me in to see Lady Isobel."

The man stopped walking and glared at me. "I ain't for sale. And if my brother would get off his palatial high horse and come around more, he might have known that." He started walking again, dismissing me with the upturning of his nose.

"A hundred pounds is enough to buy 24 horses, man. Surely ye willnae turn yer nose up at such an offer."

With a quick flick of his wrist, Gerald had me pinned to the stone wall. I could have had my sgian dubh in him in half that time, but I needed to get to Isobel, and I wisnae about to ruin my chances with a wee blood squabble.

"Twenty-four horses won't save my skin when it's discovered I got you in to see one of the suspects in the century's most talked about murder trial." He gritted out. His black eyes bore into me, and he stood so close I could smell what the man had eaten for dinner.

"With one hundred pounds, ye widnae even have to stay in London. Ye could see the world on that kind of coin. Take yer lady on an extended tour. Ye would never have to be seen again."

The man studied me for a moment. Then he grunted again and released me, shoving me away forcefully. "Go on with you," he said, then turned his back on me.

Well, at least he didnae arrest me on the spot.

I skulked about for a while, and it wisnae long before another man stepped out of the shadows. Painfully thin and with wisps of graying hair spread sparsely across his forehead, he eyed me greedily. I clutched my purse closer to me, for I didnae ken his intent.

"I'll get you in to see the Lady," he said with a raspy scrape to his voice. His eyes shifted to and fro. "But you will have to pay up front."

My eyes roved over him skeptically. He wore the uniform of a gaoler but looked like he hid nae eaten in days. Probably drank his earnings down instead of feeding his family. But who was I to judge?

"You will get half the bag up front and the rest when I'm standing in her room," I said, not trusting him.

He spit at my feet. "Deal," he said, then held out his hand for the coin.

He led me up two flights of stairs and down a long corridor before stopping outside of an unmanned door. I lifted by brow in question. "No guard?" I whispered, not sure we widnae be caught any minute.

"She isn't a danger." He chuckled. "At least not in escaping." He shuffled a set of keys that hung from his hip then unlocked the door quickly. He pushed the door open, then said, "But she is a beauty." He whistled and I resisted the urge to knock his teeth down his throat. When I growled at his ogling her, he said, "You have twenty minutes." He held out his grubby hand for the rest of his coin.

"I'm not paying fifty pounds for twenty minutes," I hissed. "Make it three-quarters of an hour." Of course, I would have paid more for even less time, just to see her again.

"Thirty minutes, and that is all I can risk. There is another guard that patrols this corridor every half hour. You need to be gone by then."

"Fine," I said, shoving the coin into his hand and turning to Isobel.

She stood wide-eyed in front of me, with her mouth agape. "Robert?" she said softly as if she thought she were dreaming.

I stood staring at her with my hands empty at my sides. I fisted my hands, itching to touch her, but after our last conversation, I wisnae sure of my reception. But she ran to me and threw her arms around my neck.

"Robert," she said again, this time her voice warbling. "I thought I'd never see you again."

"I told ye. Ye willnae be rid of me so easily."

She laughed—the sweetest melodic sound my ears had ever heard—and buried her face into my chest. I ran a hand down the back of her head, following the blonde strands that hung in curls all the way to her waist. It was a rare thing to see her hair down, and I gloried at the feel of her satiny tresses running across my fingertips.

"Robert," she said for the third time, and then the tears began to flow. "I tried to write to you. They have executed James Franklin and Richard Weston."

"Aye. And Sir Gervase Helwys, the Lieutenant of the Tower, is scheduled for tomorrow." When she began to cry harder, I considered whether I should have shared that information with her. I soothed her with a hush then wiped her tears from her cheeks with my thumbs. "I didnae receive yer letters."

She squeezed me tighter. "I thought you hated me, when you didn't answer."

"Never." It tore my guts out to imagine her thinking I could hate her. "Isobel, listen to me, we havenae much time." She sniffled, wiped her nose, and looked up at me with those big, blue eyes. "I must leave for Scotland. I will only be gone for a couple of weeks. I must take care of some business regarding Henry's riding school. But

I will come back, then we can talk about anything you want to talk about."

Her brows crinkled into wee crestfallen mounds. She swallowed so hard; I could hear the working of her throat. "I will most likely be gone by then."

I moved my hands from her cheeks and grasped her upper arms. "Dinnae say such things. Yer father is the best advocate England has ever seen. He will make sure yer defense is sound."

A second round of tears began to fall. "My father's hands are tied. The king will not allow him to defend me. It is not looking good for me."

A sense of panic clawed at my chest. "Ye must tell the judge about Forman's black book."

A sad expression twisted her lips. "You'll never believe what judge was assigned to this case." When I stared at her blankly, she said, "Coke."

My heart sank. The man whose wife's name we had seen in one of Forman's entries. She had a tryst with Forman, and he recorded it.

I pulled her back to me, and we stood like that for the remaining minutes. I kissed her forehead, then her temples and finally her lips. They were as sweet as plum wine and doubly intoxicating.

Isobel broke the kiss first. "Robert, can you do something for me?"

"Anything," I choked. I would do anything for this woman.

"I want you to go to Chadwyck House. The letters Mistress Forman gave me are tucked inside Forman's book and buried in the bottom of a chest in my chamber. Edith can show you where the key is. Take the letters and give them to Sir Francis Bacon. I want to make sure they have all the evidence they can get to convict Lady Frances." The heat was unmistakable in her voice. "The evidence may not free me, but I want that woman to pay for all the harm she has brought to everyone."

I looked into her clear, blue eyes. She almost looked at peace. "And the black book? Will ye use that too?"

"So many women would be affected," she said, wiping her nose.

Shaking her head she continued. "Besides, with Coke as the judge, we might as well admit he won't permit it as evidence. Not with his wife's name inscribed within."

"Isobel, I dinnae mean to sound heartless, but I dinnae care about all those other women." Emotion choked me. "We must do whatever is necessary to see ye acquitted. At least let me try."

She turned her palms upward in surrender. "There is nothing in the black book that will clear my name. But if you feel there is a chance that something written therein could bring about my freedom, then by all means, do with it as you must."

I shook my head. "This isnae like ye. The Isobel I ken would use any means necessary to gain her freedom." I searched her face, trying to understand where all her fight had gone.

"It is as it should be, Robert. All my sins have caught up with me. It's time to pay the piper."

I wanted to argue, but just then the gaoler pounded on the door in warning. "He's coming," he whispered loudly.

Isobel tightened her grip on me. "Robert, there is one more thing I must say to you." Her lips trembled and I watched as she fought back more tears. "I would have married you. If our circumstances were different, I would have been honored to be your wife and make a home with you. I'm only sorry it took me so long to realize that—" she choked on her words. "To realize that I love you. I-I just had to tell you that before you go." She released her hold on me and wiped her eyes.

I held her face in my hands. "Ye would have made me the happiest man on earth. But since I am written in yer stars, I will just have to settle for the heavens instead. Maybe in the next life I'll be able to show ye how much I love ye. For it's more than life itself."

Isobel may have had qualms about revealing the secrets of noble women, but I didnae. I rode to Chadwyck House as she asked, and instructed Edith to retrieve the letters and the black book. There must have been a reason Forman wanted Isobel to have that book. I didnae understand it, but I believed it, nonetheless.

And somewhere between my conversation with Isobel and arriving at Chadwyck, something had dawned on me. If the judge in Isobel's case was Sir Edward Coke, then perhaps he could be brought to reason with a little persuasion. If I kent men who had worked their way up into the lofty positions of English society, and I did, then this judge widnae want his business aired for the whole courtroom to hear.

But it wisnae the judge I was worried about. I was sure he would see things my way. The person I worried about the most was His Majesty. And it was he with whom I was on my way to speak. His Majesty had summoned me just a day prior to discuss some last-minute details of the riding school opening in Stirling. This would be the perfect opportunity to speak of Isobel.

The king dinnae look in my direction when I stepped into his antechamber where a game of Primero was in full swing. I was surprised to see Robert Carr, the Viscount Rochester, seated next to him, given the fact his fiancé was under suspicion for Overbury's murder. Rochester looked up at me standing in the doorway, but he acted as if he had no cause for concern, as he had no idea the woman I loved was about to incriminate the woman he loved.

When the king finally noticed me, he waved me over. "Robert, come, sit." He leaned back in his chair as a young page arranged James's cards for him on a rack in front of him. The king didnae hold his own cards, and usually depended on someone else to play the cards for him when it was his turn.

"Forgive me, Yer Majesty, but I am departing for Scotland this night. Ye requested to speak with me before I left."

His brow furrowed. "By the beard! Leaving tonight? That is a bit dangerous, is it not? Travelling at night."

I ran a hand over my face. "I had some business I needed to see to first. It couldnae be helped."

He sighed heavily then overturned the rack that held his cards. "Gentlemen, we shall have to continue this game tomorrow night. I must speak with my cousin." It was the first time he addressed me as such.

Groans and objections came from all corners, especially from Rochester who apparently had a good hand. He threw his cards down on the table and laid a hand on my shoulder. "I do hope you will have returned by December. Frances and I would be honored to have you at our wedding celebrations." He squeezed my shoulder, and I fought the urge to knock that annoying smile off his face.

"Aye, I heard her divorce from Essex was finally granted." That was all I could muster. I couldnae bring myself to speak words of congratulations. He eyed me wearily, as if he half expected me to voice my objections to the marriage.

James motioned for me to follow him into his private chamber. A guard closed the door behind us then stood as sentinel nearby. The king shuffled some papers around on his desk, then tossed an unsealed missive at me and said, "I believe this may be of interest to you."

I picked up the letter and unfolded it. I went still when I recognized the familiar flourish of Henry's handwriting. I glanced at James, but he busied himself with something at his desk, not giving me a second look.

When I finished, I looked at him again. "I dinnae understand."

The king cleared his throat. "Apparently you made quite the impression on my firstborn son," he said, scratching the side of his nose with a long, narrow finger. "Before he died, I requested of him what he wanted for his birthday. Unfortunately, he passed before we could celebrate his birth and before I could give him his gift."

This still didnae fully explain the letter I held in my hand. "And this?" I asked, holding the letter up in front of him. "What does this have to do with anything?"

"For his birthday, Henry asked that I lift your father's exile and return the Bothwell title."

I stared at him blankly. "That was verra kind of him."

"Yes, well, seeing how your father is dead, I guess it makes no difference now." He waved his hand in the air as if dismissing the idea. Leave it to James to say the blunt thing. "My son also wanted to sign the deed of his hunting lodge over to you," he continued. "It is a small house located near Stirling Castle. It was given to Henry as a birthday present when he turned five years old, purchased as a gift from his mother with funds she brought with her from Denmark."

I was vaguely familiar with the "small" house he spoke of. It was known as Bellkirk and sat on a parcel of land that measured about forty hectares. It also contained about one hundred rooms if I remembered correctly. Hunting lodge indeed!

I blinked at him, stupefied. "Henry wanted to give me a house?" I asked, still not believing what I was hearing.

"Yes. Although I don't think his mother would be happy to know he gave away her gift so carelessly." The king moved around his desk and came to the front of it, leaning heavily upon it.

"Are ye—are ye going to grant the prince's request?"

"I am. I will even restore the Bothwell title to your oldest brother, Francis, in lieu of your father's death." He leveled his watery blue gaze on me and waited for my reply.

"I am speechless, Yer Grace. Thank ye, on behalf of my mother, and my family," I said, feeling stunned.

He went to a nearby shelf and perused the books. Without turning around, he said, "You have become quite attached to Lady Isobel Broune. But she is on trial for murder, and I think it best if you return home and forget the Broune family. Henry would not want you to be tangled up in such affairs."

Fury rippled through my body at his words. How could he presume to ken what Henry would have wanted? Especially when it came to Isobel. But I wisnae about to argue this gift. I would take the house, and one day the lass, and we would live happily in Scotland—I hoped.

"About Lady Isobel," I began, thinking this the perfect opening for what I wanted to talk to the king about. "I have something with which I need to speak with ye. It is regarding the Lady's innocence."

James turned suddenly. "Oh? You presume her to be innocent?"

I licked my lips, preparing my words. "We are in possession of some letters that indicate the true mastermind behind the Overbury murder."

The king held out his hand. "Let me see them," he demanded, and I pulled them from my pocket. He opened the first one and read quickly. His face darkened, and I couldnae read his expression. The guilt of the woman to whom his favorite was affianced, didnae bode well for him. He folded the first letter and opened the second. He read it just as quickly, then returned it to its original form.

"Who knows about these?" he asked, tucking them into his desk drawer and locking it with a small key.

"Isobel and me. And Mistress Forman, for it was her who gave the letters to Isobel. I suspect Mistress Turner, as well, for Lady Frances sent the woman to retrieve them from Forman but was denied access."

The king ran a finger over his chin. "It is as I suspected," he said, then sat down at his desk. "Thank you. I will be sure Sir Francis Bacon gets these," he said practically dismissing me.

"There is one more thing," I said, pulling the black book from my pocket. James looked at me again, a tired expression haunting his eyes. I opened the book to the desired page and handed it to him. Pointing to the entry I wanted him to read, I released it to his hands and stepped back, waiting.

His face remained expressionless for a moment, then I could tell when realization hit him. He looked up at me through heavy-lidded eyes then back at the book. When he was finished, he rubbed his forehead in frustration and snapped the book closed.

"This is damning information; I am sure you are aware." He pinned me with an assessing look and waited for me to reply.

I cocked my head sideways, hearing the little bones in my neck crackle as it released the tension building there. "I am aware," I said simply, waiting for further comment.

"If this information were to come to light, the damage would be irreparable." He stabbed the top of the book with his finger. "Not only to Sir Edward Coke's wife but to Coke as well."

I leveled my gaze at him. If he was expecting sympathy, he widnae get it from me. "I'm curious, was Coke aware of how long Overbury spent in the Tower?"

The king squinted as if not understanding my question. "What are you insinuating?"

I stepped up to the desk that stood in the middle of the chamber. Picking up Forman's book, I said, "I thought it strange that Overbury was thrown into prison for not accepting the post in Russia. Then, the length of time he was kept at the Tower seemed extremely excessive. But what do I ken? I'm an outsider."

"Are you questioning me for having Overbury arrested? He refused his king and his duty to country. It is within my sovereign right to see that he obeys." The king's face was turning a funny shade of purple. "You have overstepped, Robert."

"My apologies," I offered. "Lord Stratford pointed out it was against the law for the king to force someone into exile for such a minor offense. But I'm not an expert in law."

"Lord Stratford." The king spat. "My former inquisitor enjoys being a constant thorn in my side." King James pressed his lips together then stepped back to his desk.

He was getting angry, but I had one more card up my sleeve. There was no need to weigh the consequences. The house and title he had granted, I would risk it all for the woman in the Tower.

"How is Rochester handling his responsibilities now that Overbury is gone?"

He narrowed his eyes at me. "Rochester fulfills his duties well enough."

"Truly? 'Tis nice that employing Rochester over the clearly more qualified Overbury, his nae been a stain on yer judgement."

"Speak plainly," the king demanded.

"I noticed every time I played cards with Rochester that the man cannae count to save his life," I chuckled, shaking my head as if it were all just a joke. "With Overbury doing all of Rochester's work and threatening the viscount with all the state secrets he kent, 'tis no wonder the man ended up dead. He had the king's favorite, and some might even say the king, right in the palm of his hand."

"What do you want?" the king said dangerously low.

"Excuse me?" I asked, feigning ignorance.

"You seem to have a lot of knowledge about me and my dealings with Overbury and Rochester. You hold dangerous information concerning my appointed judge, Coke. And you are flinging churlish accusations at me from all sides. Is it money you want? For I warn you, extortion may not be punishable by death, but it can carry a hefty fine and imprisonment."

I stiffened my back "I have no need for yer money, Yer Grace. But if ye dismissed the charges against Isobel Broune, we could forget all of this. She was an innocent pawn in Lady Frances's dangerous game. I believe there has been a grave misunderstanding." I smiled at the king but underneath my easy façade a devil lurked, and I would stop at nothing to save the woman I loved.

The king stared hard at me. "There is evidence to implicate Lady Isobel."

"Do ye mean her innocently providing poison for what she was told was a rat problem, or the fact she posed as the virgin countess in order for Lady Frances to obtain her divorce?" I haphazardly spun the large globe that sat beside his desk, watching the painted colors twirl by. "From what I understand, ye approved of that divorce, did ye nay? How would that look if yer subjects found out that Lady Frances's divorce had been granted under false pretenses?"

All the color drained from the king's face. Then, without another word, he opened his desk drawer and drew out a piece of foolscap. He dipped his pen into an inkwell and began to write. "I hereby decree that you are to take complete ownership of Bellkirk in the city of Fife. You shall be responsible for the upkeep and staffing of the residence from this moment on. You shall settle your affairs here in London, and you are not to set foot in this city again. If I see your face here again, you shall be exiled from the British Isles completely. The apple doesn't fall far from the tree, does it?"

"Nay, Yer Grace." He spoke of my father and his exile from Scotland.

"Furthermore, Lady Isobel shall be acquitted of all charges regarding the murder of Sir Thomas Overbury. I'm sure Coke will support this in light of—this new information. She too shall not show her face here at court in London again. That is the price you both shall pay for presuming to blackmail the king of England." He finished by scribbling his name at the bottom. He held a stick of wax to a nearby candle and dripped wax beneath the writing and sealed it with his ring. He handed me the scroll and held out his other hand for Forman's book. I placed it in his hand, bowing slightly. "If I see either of you again, my gifts shall be null and void." He then stood to his feet. "Did William Broune tutor you on what to say? For this reeks of the inquisitor's antics."

"Nay, Yer Grace," I said, tamping down my gratification. "I figured this out all on my own."

The king glared at me momentarily, then left his privy chamber without another look back or another word.

As for me, I said not a word about desiring to marry William Broune's daughter. I was heading home to Scotland and my new duties there. But first, a short stop at the Tower of London to retrieve my bonny bride.

Epilogue

Bellkirk, Stirling, Scotland
April 1625
Robert

I stood on the steps of Bellkirk, observing the expanse of ground surrounding me. The knoll was filled with pink and purple crocuses, yellow daffodils, and the smell of fresh green grass. I took a deep breath, drinking in the mild spring air and considering the building plans to annex the stables on the north side of the estate.

A door slammed, and squeals of laughter pealed behind me as two rapscallions scuffled by. They were the same age but looked as different from each other as night and day. Lizbet got her looks from me with copper-colored hair that hung in ringlets to her waist and eyes the color of a misty, Scottish morning. Her brother, Henry looked more like his mother, a towhead with wide, blue eyes. It was hard to believe they had shared the same space for nine months, for if they wurnae wreaking havoc together, they were fighting like cats and dogs.

"You better have shoes on those feet when you come home," Isobel called to the twins as they scurried off on another adventure. She stood behind me, rocking the newest member of our family, another blonde bairn so aptly named Grace.

A smile pulled at my lips. "I never wore shoes when I was their age," I said, as I watched Lizbet stoop to pick a sprig of purple heather that grew at the edge of the moor just beyond the knoll.

"That's because you were a heathen," she quipped.

I turned to look at her with my mouth agape. "Not everyone born and raised in Scotland are godless scoundrels," I explained, trying to sound highly offended. She pretended to kiss the top of the baby's head, but what she was really doing was hiding her self-satisfied smile. "I'll have ye ken I was a good lad who never caused my mother any trouble. It was all my older siblings who turned her hair gray."

"That is not what your mother told me." Her eyes glinted with mirth. "I was told you wreaked your fair share of havoc. Does rolling yourself up in the carpet to hide spark a recollection?"

"Aye," I said, grinning at her. Then I remembered the missive I held in my hand. "Speaking of mothers, would ye like to go home to see yer parents? Charles's coronation would be a good time to visit."

"Is it safe? King James made it quite clear we weren't to show our faces there again." She shifted Grace in her arms, leaning the babe against her other shoulder, and continuing to pat her back.

"I dinnae see why not. I highly doubt the king bothered to share our offenses with this son. Besides, Charlie always liked ye. In fact, it may have bordered on love."

Isobel scoffed. "That was years ago. He was just a child."

I chuckled, remembering how the prince had always pined after Isobel whenever she was in his presence.

We stood in silence for a spell, both lost in our own thoughts. But when Isobel spoke, she proved her thoughts were one with mine. "It should have been Henry," she said quietly, brushing her lips across the top of Grace's feathery wisps of baby-fine hair.

"Aye," I said. "He would have made a spectacular king."

"Do you think he would have pardoned Lady Frances and

Viscount Rochester, as his father did?" Isobel searched my face with her big, blue eyes.

"Do ye mean the Earl and Countess of Somerset? Dinnae forget Rochester was given the earldom less than two months after Frances's divorce from Essex. By the time Frances married Rochester, he was already an earl."

Isobel drew up beside me. I wrapped an arm around her waist and planted a kiss atop Grace's soft head.

"I am sure that helped their cause since he had been elevated to the Earl of Somerset before his involvement in Overbury's murder had come to light," Isobel mused. "I mean, they were both convicted and kept under house arrest for years, but I wasn't surprised when they were eventually pardoned and released." Here Grace let out a tiny shriek as if to contest the wrongness of it all, and Isobel rocked her faster in response. "There was no justice for Overbury, and it doesn't seem fair to all her accomplices that were executed either. I think Henry would have handled it differently."

"I dinnae ken, love. Henry was a just prince. I'd like to think he would have made a fair king as well."

Isobel leaned her head against my shoulder, and we stood there, silently watching the children romp across the moor, squealing and laughing until Lizbet shoved her brother, and he went airborne, taking a nosedive to the ground.

"Best go tell them to come home, before someone loses an eye," Isobel said with a sigh, shifting Grace in her arms again.

"Home," I repeated under my breath as I went to retrieve the children. "And what a wonderful home it is."

Historical Notes

The Earl and Countess of Essex and Viscount Rochester

Lady Frances was known by several names throughout the course of the events in this story. To keep it as simple as possible, I used the name that she would have been known by at the time of the events in this book: the Countess of Essex. She was born Frances Howard. She married the 3rd Earl of Essex, Robert Devereux at the age of 15. She is most famously known as the Countess of Somerset, for this was the title she held at the time of the Overbury murder trial as her second husband Robert Carr (known in this book as Viscount Rochester) had been made the Earl of Somerset by that time.

Frances enlisted the help of several people in her efforts to obtain her divorce from the Earl of Essex and secure the love of Viscount Rochester. Rumors at the time said that she tried to bewitch Essex, making him incapable of consummating their marriage. According to Essex's testimony during the divorce trial, it is likely that her dislike of him and tendency to call her husband every deplorable name she could think of when they were in the bedchamber contributed the most to his inability to do the deed. It would certainly kill the mood. It is believed

Frances used the help of Doctor Forman and "Cunning Mary" Woods, along with their jellies and charms, to get what she wanted.

Thomas Overbury is the only person known to have suffered poisoning at the hands of the countess. The maids killed in this book by her are fictional.

Viscount Rochester's Dyscalculia (Number Dyslexia) is made up. However, he was known to have benefitted from his good friend, Thomas Overbury's skill, and he succeeded in his task as the king's secretary due to Overbury's assistance. In fact, Overbury's talent with the pen must have been amazing, as he was known to have written several love letters for Rochester to give to Frances in his efforts to woo her. A decision that obviously backfired on him and he surely came to regret.

Frances's Physical Examination to Determine Her Virginity

Did it really happen? Yes. Did she really recruit a maiden to take her place? Possibly. Contemporary rumors claim that she did.

Frances was required to submit to a physical examination to determine whether she was telling the truth about her and the earl's inability to consummate their marriage. But by the spring of 1612, it was believed that she and Rochester were already lovers. Her reputation was such that no one believed if she submitted to an examination, that it would truly prove her to be a virgin.

King James ordered the examination, and six women were appointed to conduct the exam. Are you wondering how they were able to determine her virginity enough to get her divorce granted? Yep, me too.

Simon Forman's involvement with the Overbury Murder

Doctor Forman was a real physician and astrologer that had close contact with the Countess of Essex. She referred to him as "Father" in her letters to him, and he was known to have given Frances help with keeping Viscount Rochester's interest. He also provided "jellies" for her to use. Whether these jellies were meant to encourage amorous feelings from Rochester or prevent the Earl of Essex from performing his marital duty, it is not certain.

Doctor Forman gained recognition for his ability to predict the future and read patrons' stars. He could predict whether a woman's husband would return safely from a journey or recommend the best time to have a medical procedure performed. According to his wife, he also predicted his own death one week before it happened. Doctor Forman kept meticulous records of all his patients and their medical treatments. He was known as a real lady's man, having dozens of affairs with women, and recording all the details such as names and dates and times the trysts took place. Many of these liaisons were with his patients, but not all.

Doctor Forman's book was brought forth as evidence at the murder trial of Thomas Overbury. Although there is no evidence that Forman aided Frances with any poisons to rid herself of Overbury (he was long dead before that happened), it might have been used as a testament to her character. However, the presiding judge, Sir Edward Coke would not permit the book to be used as evidence. Presumably because his wife's name and her tryst with Forman did indeed appear within the pages of Forman's book.

Prince Henry Frederick Stuart

Henry was given his own court by this father in 1610 when he became the Prince of Wales at the age of 16. King James took a great interest in his firstborn son, even writing his famous work, Basilikon Doron, as an instruction guide on how to conduct oneself as a king. Henry had many pursuits and was known for his military prowess and intelligence. He loved art and innovation and exploration, even to the point that he longed to sail to the newly founded settlement named Jamestown. The first map drawn of the Chesapeake Bay area by Robert

Tyndall was given to the prince for him to name. Henrico County in Virginia and Cape Henry on Virginia Beach in the United States still bear the name of this most loved prince.

Henry's funeral was one of the most heavily attended funerals in the history of England up till that time. Over two thousand people gathered on that December day to honor the young prince and to mourn the loss of a man in whom they had instilled so much hope. Though the king and queen did not attend the funeral, the throng of people crying, shouting, wailing, and wringing their hands signified the deep anguish the kingdom felt over the loss of the prince. An effigy made of a wooden frame and covered in wax was created in the likeness of the prince. It was dressed in the clothing Henry wore at his creation as Prince of Wales, along with his armor and was placed on top of his casket for the funeral procession. Eventually the effigy would be picked clean of every scrap of cloth and likeness of Henry. Over the centuries it has suffered admirers snatching pieces of it. Today only the torso and legs remain. A sad, yet accurate display of Henry's descent into obscurity.

The young men at Henry's court fully expected to be absorbed into the king's court, or maybe even a new court set up for Prince Charles. However, James did not give Charles his own court for many years. Some speculate this stemmed from a fear of the popularity that Henry had enjoyed. Instead, Henry's courtiers were turned out, expected to find their own living.

Within fifteen months of Henry's death, John Harington died of smallpox. He was 22 years old. The Earl of Essex, Robert Devereux would eventually play a role in the uprising that saw Henry's brother, King Charles I beheaded 37 years later.

Acknowledgments

I want to give a thank you to a few people who have been a tremendous help with the creation of this book. To Gemma Lynn, podcaster at *If It Ain't Baroque*, for your undying patience with me and all my "Scottish related" questions. You have been a fountain of information, particularly when it came to writing Robert's dialect, and other questions about the Scottish culture as the series has taken a turn into the 17th century.

Thank you to Dr. Joanna Strong for sharing your historical knowledge with me. Your input was extremely helpful, and I appreciate it. Thank you to author Heather Carter for sharing your understanding of British culture and historic clothing and for letting me bounce plot ideas off you when I got stuck. You have been a huge help, and I am truly grateful. A thank you to author Tonya Mitchell for keeping me on the straight and narrow with my period-appropriate language. After writing two novels taking place in 16th century Scotland, you would think that I would have this period language down pat, but you can always spot my modern-day flubs. Thanks for keeping me in line!

Thank you to Laura Loney, Misty Wyatt, Kelsey Belcher, Brandy Ashley, Debbie Gillem, Rhonda Keslar, Maria Myers, and Maddy McGlynn for your time reading the unpolished manuscript and your input that makes this book all it could be. I appreciate your help.

And finally, a huge shout out to my editor, Janice Broyles, for your infinite wisdom and guidance without which this book would not be possible.

Thank you for purchasing
The Prince's Darling
by Tonya Ulynn Brown

Please visit the Late November Literary website for more compelling books!
www.latenovemberliterary.com